With a  slapped Aunt Pol sharply across the face. "You really must control your tongue, Polgara," Asharak said.

Garion's brain seemed to explode. He felt a terrible force building in him, and the image of Asharak wrapped in seething flame stood before him.

"Now!" commanded the dry voice within his mind. "Do it!"

Garion swung his right arm. As his palm struck the Grolim's scarred left cheek, he felt the force surge out from the silvery mark on his palm. "Burn!" he commanded.

For an instant, Asharak stared at Garion in horror, and then his face contorted in agony. His cheek began to smoke and seethe where Garion's hand had touched it. Wisps of smoke drifted from his black robe. Then he shrieked and clutched at his face. His fingers burst into flame.

"Master," he croaked. "Have mercy!"

THE BELGARIAD

Published by Ballantine Books

*Forthcoming

Book Two of The Belgariad

QUEEN OF SORCERY

DAVID EDDINGS

A Del Rey Book

BALLANTINE BOOKS · NEW YORK

A Del Rey Book
Published by Ballantine Books

Library of Congress Catalog Card Number: 82-90440

ISBN 0-345-30079-3

Manufactured in the United States of America

First Edition: November 1982
Fourth Printing: May 1983

Cover art by Laurence Schwinger

For Helen,
    who gave me the most precious thing in
    my life,
and for Mike,
    who taught me how to play.

Prologue

Being an Account of the Battle of the Kingdoms of the West against the most heinous Invasion and Evil of Kal Torak.
—based upon *The Battle of Vo Mimbre*

In the youth of the world, the evil God Torak stole the Orb of Aldur and fled, seeking dominion. The Orb resisted, and its fire maimed him with a dreadful burning. But he would not give it up, for it was precious to him.

Then Belgarath, a sorcerer and disciple of the God Aldur, led forth the king of the Alorns and his three sons, and they reclaimed the Orb from the iron tower of Torak. Torak sought to pursue, but the wrath of the Orb repelled him and drove him back.

Belgarath set Cherek and his sons to be kings over four great kingdoms in eternal guard against Torak. The Orb he gave to Riva to keep, saying that so long as a descendant of Riva held the Orb the West would be safe.

Century followed century with no menace from Torak, until the spring of 4865, when Drasnia was invaded by a vast horde of Nadraks, Thulls, and Murgos. In the center of this sea of Angaraks was borne the huge iron pavilion of one called Kal Torak, which means King and God. Cities and villages were razed and burned, for Kal Torak came to destroy, not to conquer. Those of the people who lived were given to the steel-masked Grolim priests for sacrifice in the unspeakable rites of the Angaraks. None survived save those who fled to Algaria or were taken from the mouth of the Aldur River by Cherek warships.

Next the horde struck south at Algaria. But there they found no cities. The nomadic Algarian horsemen fell back

before them, then struck in vicious hit-and-run attacks.
The traditional seat of the Algarian kings was the Stronghold, a man-made mountain with stone walls thirty feet
thick. Against this, the Angaraks hurled themselves in vain
before settling down to besiege the place. The siege lasted
for eight futile years.

This gave the West time to mobilize and prepare. The
generals gathered at the Imperial War College in Tol
Honeth and planned their strategy. National differences
were set aside, and Brand, the Warder of Riva, was chosen
to have full command. With him came two strange advisers:
an ancient but vigorous man who claimed knowledge even
of the Angarak kingdoms; and a strikingly handsome
woman with a silver lock at her brow and an imperious
manner. To these Brand listened, and to them he paid almost deferential respect.

In the late spring of 4875, Kal Torak abandoned his
siege and turned west toward the sea, pursued still by Algar horsemen. In the mountains, the Ulgos came forth
from their caverns by night and wreaked fearful slaughter
on the sleeping Angaraks. But still were the forces of Kal
Torak beyond counting. After a pause to regroup, the host
proceeded down the valley of the River Arend toward the
city of Vo Mimbre, destroying all in its path. Early in the
summer, the Angaraks deployed for the assault upon the
city.

On the third day of the battle, a horn was heard to blow
three times. Then the gates of Vo Mimbre opened, and the
Mimbrate knights charged out to fall upon the front of the
Angarak horde, the iron-shod hoofs of their chargers trampling living and dead. From the left came Algar cavalry,
Drasnian pikemen, and veiled Ulgo irregulars. And from
the right came the Cherek berserks and the legions of Tolnedra.

Attacked on three sides, Kal Torak committed his re-
serves. It was then that the gray-clad Rivans, the Sendars,
and the Asturian archers came upon his forces from the
rear. The Angaraks began to fall like mown wheat and
were overcome by confusion.

Then the Apostate, Zedar the Sorcerer, went in haste to
the black iron pavilion from which Kal Torak had not yet

emerged. And to the Accursed One he said, "Lord, thine enemies have thee surrounded in great numbers. Yea, even the gray Rivans have come in their numbers to cast defiance at thy might."

Kal Torak arose in anger and declared, "I will come forth, that the false keepers of Cthrag Yaska, the jewel which was mine, shall see me and know fear of me. Send to me my kings."

"Great Lord," Zedar told him, "thy kings are no more. The battle hath claimed their lives and those of a multitude of thy Grolim priests as well."

Kal Torak's wrath grew great at these words, and fire spat from his right eye and from the eye that was not. He ordered his servants to bind his shield to the arm on which he had no hand and he took up his dread black sword. With this, he went forth to do battle.

Then came a voice from the midst of the Rivans, saying, "In the name of Belar I defy thee, Torak. In the name of Aldur I cast my despite in thy teeth. Let the bloodshed be abated, and I will meet thee to decide the battle. I am Brand, Warden of Riva. Meet me or take thy stinking host away and come no more against the kingdoms of the West."

Kal Torak strode apart from the host and cried, "Where is he who dares pit his mortal flesh against the King of the World? Behold, I am Torak, King of Kings and Lord of Lords. I will destroy this loud-voiced Rivan. Mine enemies shall perish, and Cthrag Yaska shall again be mine."

Brand stood forth. He bore a mighty sword and a shield muffled with cloth. A grizzled wolf marched at his side, and a snowy owl hovered over his head. Brand said, "I am Brand and I will contend with thee, foul and misshapen Torak."

When Torak saw the wolf, he said, "Begone, Belgarath. Flee if thou wouldst save thy life." And to the owl he said, "Abjure thy father, Polgara, and worship me. I will wed thee and make thee Queen of the World."

But the wolf howled defiance, and the owl screeched her scorn.

Torak raised his sword and smote down upon the shield of Brand. Long they fought, and many and grievous were the blows they struck. Those who stood near to see them were amazed. The fury of Torak grew great, and his sword battered the shield of Brand until the Warder fell back before the onslaught of the Accursed One. Then the wolf howled and the owl shrieked in one voice together, and the strength of Brand was renewed.

With a single motion, the Rivan Warder unveiled his shield, in the center of which stood a round jewel, in size like the heart of a child. As Torak gazed upon it, the stone began to glow and flame. The Accursed One drew back from it. He dropped his shield and sword and raised his arms before his face to ward away the dread fire of the stone.

Brand struck, and his sword pierced Torak's visor to strike into the eye that was not and plunge into the Accursed One's head. Torak fell back and gave a great cry. He plucked out the sword and threw off his helmet. Those who watched recoiled in terror, for his face was seared by some great fire and was horrible to behold. Weeping blood, Torak cried out again as he beheld the jewel which he had named Cthrag Yaska and for which he had brought his war into the West. Then he collapsed, and the earth resounded with his fall.

A great cry went up from the host of the Angaraks when they saw what had befallen Kal Torak, and they sought to flee in their panic. But the armies of the West pursued them and slew them, so that when the smoky dawn broke on the fourth day, the host was no more.

Brand asked that the body of the Accursed One be brought to him, that he might behold him who would be king of all the world. But the body was not to be found. In the night, Zedar the Sorcerer had cast an enchantment and passed unseen through the armies of the West, bearing away the one he had chosen as master.

Then Brand took counsel with his advisers. And Belgarath said to him, "Torak is not dead. He only sleeps. For he is a God and cannot be slain by any mortal weapon."

"When will he awaken?" Brand asked. "I must prepare the West against his return."

Polgara answered, "When once again a King of Riva's

line sits on his northern throne, the Dark God will waken to do war with him."

Brand frowned, saying, "But that is never!" For all knew that the last Rivan King had been slain with his family in 4002 by Nyissan assassins.

Again the woman spoke. "In the fullness of time the Rivan King will rise to claim his own, as the ancient Prophecy foretells. More cannot be said."

Brand was content and set his armies to cleaning the battlefield of the wreckage of Angaraks. And when that was finished, the kings of the West gathered before the city of Vo Mimbre and held council. Many were the voices raised in praise of Brand.

Soon men began crying that Brand should henceforth be chosen as ruler of all the West. Only Mergon, ambassador of Imperial Tolnedra, protested in the name of his Emperor, Ran Borune IV. Brand refused the honor, and the proposal was dropped, so that there was again peace among those assembled in council. But in return for peace, a demand was made of Tolnedra.

The Gorim of the Ulgos spoke first in a loud voice. "In fulfillment of the Prophecy, there must be promised a princess of Tolnedra to be wife unto the Rivan King who will come to save the world. This the Gods require of us."

Again Mergon protested. "The Hall of the Rivan King is empty and desolate. No king sits upon the Rivan throne. How may a princess of Imperial Tolnedra be wed with a phantom?"

Then the woman who was Polgara replied. "The Rivan King will return to assume his throne and claim his bride. From this day forward, therefore, each princess of Imperial Tolnedra shall present herself in the Hall of the Rivan King upon her sixteenth birthday. She shall be clad in her wedding gown and shall abide there for three days against the coming of the King. If he comes not to claim her, then she shall be free to return to her father for whatever he may decree for her."

Mergon cried out. "All Tolnedra shall rise against this indignity. No! It shall not be!"

The wise Gorim of the Ulgos spoke again. "Tell your

Emperor that this is the will of the Gods. Tell him also that in the day Tolnedra fails in this, the West shall rise against him and scatter the sons of Nedra to the winds and pull down the might of the Empire, until Imperial Tolnedra is no more."

At that, seeing the might of the armies before him, the ambassador submitted to the matter. All then agreed and were bound to it.

When that was done, the nobles of strife-torn Arendia came to Brand, saying, "The king of the Mimbrates is dead and the duke of the Asturians also. Who now shall rule us? For two thousand years has war between Mimbre and Asturia rent fair Arendia. How may we become one people again?"

Brand considered. "Who is heir to the Mimbrate throne?"

"Korodullin is crown prince of the Mimbrates," the nobles replied.

"And to whom descends the Asturian line?"

"Mayaserana is the daughter of the Asturian duke," they told him.

Brand said, "Bring them to me." And when they were brought before Brand, he said to them, "The bloodshed between Mimbre and Asturia must end. Therefore, it is my will that you be wed to each other and that the houses which so long have warred shall thus be joined."

The two cried against the judgment, for they were filled with ancient enmity and with the pride of their separate lines. But Belgarath took Korodullin aside and spoke in private with him. And Polgara withdrew Mayaserana to a separate place and was long in converse with her. No man learned then or later what was said to the two young people. But when they returned to where Brand waited, Mayaserana and Korodullin were content that they should be wed. And this was the final act of the council that met after the battle of Vo Mimbre.

Brand spoke to all the kings and nobles one final time before departing for the north.

"Much has been wrought here that is good and shall endure. Behold, we have met together against the Angaraks and they have been overthrown. Evil Torak is quelled. And the covenant we have made here among us prepares the

West for the day of the Prophecy when the Rivan King shall return and Torak shall wake from his long sleep to contend again for empire and dominion. All that may be done in this day to prepare for the great and final war has been done. We can do no more. And here, perchance, the wounds of Arendia have been healed, and the strife of more than two thousand years may see its end. So far as may be, I am content with it all.

"Hail, then, and farewell!"

He turned from them and rode north with the grizzled man who was Belgarath and the queenly woman who was Polgara by his side. They took ship at Camaar in Sendaria and set sail for Riva. And Brand returned no more to the kingdoms of the West.

But of his companions are many tales told. And of that telling, what may be true and what false few men may know.

Part One

ARENDIA

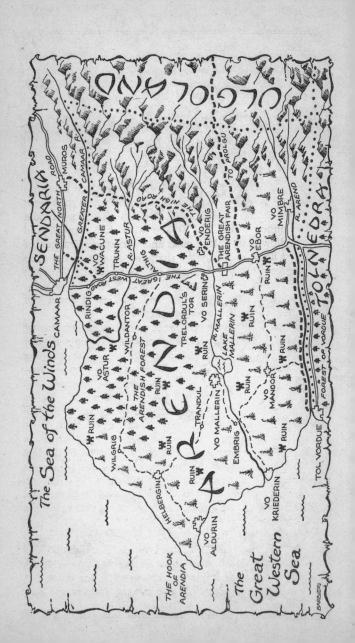

Chapter One

VO WACUNE WAS NO MORE. Twenty-four centuries had passed since the city of the Wacite Arends had been laid waste, and the dark, endless forests of northern Arendia had reclaimed the ruins. Broken walls had toppled and been swallowed up in the moss and wet brown bracken of the forest floor, and only the shattered stumps of the once proud towers moldered among the trees and fog to mark the place where Vo Wacune had stood. Sodden snow blanketed the mist-shrouded ruins, and trickles of water ran down the faces of ancient stones like tears.

Garion wandered alone down the tree-choked avenues of the dead city, his stout gray wool cloak drawn tight against the chill, and his thoughts as mournful as the weeping stones around him. Faldor's farm with its green, sun-drenched fields was so far behind him that it seemed lost in a kind of receding haze, and he was desperately homesick. No matter how hard he tried to hold onto them, details kept escaping him. The rich smells of Aunt Pol's kitchen were only a faint memory; the ring of Durnik's hammer in the smithy faded like the dying echo of the last note of a bell, and the sharp, clear faces of his playmates wavered in his remembrance of them until he could no longer be sure that he would even recognize them. His childhood was slipping away, and try though he might he could not hold on to it.

Everything was changing; that was the whole problem. The core of his life, the rock upon which his childhood had been built, had always been Aunt Pol. In the simple world of Faldor's farm she had been Mistress Pol, the cook, but in the world beyond Faldor's gate she was Polgara the Sor-

11

ceress, who had watched the passage of four millennia with a purpose beyond mortal comprehension.

And Mister Wolf, the old vagabond storyteller, had also changed. Garion knew now that this old friend was in fact his great-great grandfather—with an infinite number of additional "greats" added on for good measure—but that behind that roguish old face there had always been the steady gaze of Belgarath the Sorcerer, who had watched and waited as he had looked upon the folly of men and Gods for seven thousand years. Garion sighed and trudged on through the fog.

Their very names were unsettling. Garion had never wanted to believe in sorcery or magic or witchcraft. Such things were unnatural, and they violated his notion of solid, sensible reality. But too many things had happened to allow him to hold on to his comfortable skepticism any longer. In a single, shattering instant the last vestiges of his doubt had been swept away. As he had watched with stunned disbelief, Aunt Pol had erased the milky stains from the eyes of Martje the witch with a gesture and a single word, restoring the madwoman's sight and removing her power to see into the future with a brutal evenhandedness. Garion shuddered at the memory of Martje's despairing wail. That cry somehow marked the point at which the world had become less solid, less sensible, and infinitely less safe.

Uprooted from the only place he had ever known, unsure of the identities of the two people closest to him, and with his whole conception of the difference between the possible and the impossible destroyed, Garion found himself committed to a strange pilgrimage. He had no idea what they were doing in this shattered city swallowed up in trees, and not the faintest idea where they would go when they left. The only certainty that remained to him was the single grim thought to which he now clung: somewhere in the world there was a man who had crept through the predawn darkness to a small house in a forgotten village and had murdered Garion's parents; if it took him the rest of his life, Garion was going to find that man, and when he found him, he was going to kill him. There was something strangely comforting in that one solid fact.

He carefully climbed over the rubble of a house that had fallen outward into the street and continued his gloomy exploration of the ruined city. There was really nothing to see. The patient centuries had erased nearly all of what the war had left behind, and slushy snow and thick fog hid even those last remaining traces. Garion sighed again and began to retrace his steps toward the moldering stump of the tower where they had all spent the previous night.

As he approached, he saw Mister Wolf and Aunt Pol standing together some distance from the ruined tower, talking quietly. The old man's rust-colored hood was turned up, and Aunt Pol's blue cloak was drawn about her. There was a look of timeless regret on her face as she looked out at the foggy ruins. Her long, dark hair spilled down her back, and the single white lock at her brow seemed paler than the snow at her feet.

"There he is now," Mister Wolf said to her as Garion approached them.

She nodded and looked gravely at Garion. "Where have you been?" she asked.

"No place," Garion replied. "I was thinking, that's all."

"I see you've managed to soak your feet."

Garion lifted one of his sodden brown boots and looked down at the muddy slush clinging to it. "The snow's wetter than I thought," he apologized.

"Does wearing that thing really make you feel better?" Mister Wolf asked, pointing at the sword Garion always wore now.

"Everybody keeps saying how dangerous Arendia is," Garion explained. "Besides, I need to get used to it." He shifted the creaking new leather sword belt around until the wirebound hilt was not so obvious. The sword had been an Erastide present from Barak, one of several gifts he had received when the holiday had passed while they were at sea.

"It doesn't really suit you, you know," the old man told him somewhat disapprovingly.

"Leave him alone, father," Aunt Pol said almost absently. "It's his, after all, and he can wear it if he likes."

"Shouldn't Hettar be here by now?" Garion asked, wanting to change the subject.

"He may have run into deep snow in the mountains of Sendaria," Wolf replied. "He'll be here. Hettar's very dependable."

"I don't see why we just didn't buy horses in Camaar."

"They wouldn't have been as good," Mister Wolf answered, scratching at his short, white beard. "We've got a long way to go, and I don't want to have to worry about a horse foundering under me somewhere along the way. It's a lot better to take a little time now than to lose more time later."

Garion reached back and rubbed at his neck where the chain of the curiously carved silver amulet Wolf and Aunt Pol had given him for Erastide had chafed his skin.

"Don't worry at it, dear," Aunt Pol told him.

"I wish you'd let me wear it outside my clothes," he complained. "Nobody can see it under my tunic."

"It has to be next to your skin."

"It's not very comfortable. It looks nice enough, I suppose, but sometimes it seems cold, and other times it's hot, and once in a while it seems to be awfully heavy. The chain keeps rubbing at my neck. I guess I'm not used to ornaments."

"It's not entirely an ornament, dear," she told him. "You'll get used to it in time."

Wolf laughed. "Maybe it will make you feel better to know that it took your Aunt ten years to get used to hers. I was forever telling her to put it back on."

"I don't know that we need to go into that just now, father," Aunt Pol answered coolly.

"Do you have one, too?" Garion asked the old man, suddenly curious about it.

"Of course."

"Does it mean something that we all wear them?"

"It's a family custom, Garion," Aunt Pol told him in a tone that ended the discussion. The fog eddied around them as a chill, damp breeze briefly swirled through the ruins.

Garion sighed. "I wish Hettar would get here. I'd like to get away from this place. It's like a graveyard."

"It wasn't always this way," Aunt Pol said very quietly.

"What was it like?"

"I was happy here. The walls were high, and the towers soared. We all thought it would last forever." She pointed toward a rank patch of winter-browned brambles creeping over the broken stones. "Over there was a flower-filled garden where ladies in pale yellow dresses used to sit while young men sang to them from beyond the garden wall. The voices of the young men were very sweet, and the ladies would sigh and throw bright red roses over the wall to them. And down that avenue was a marble-paved square where the old men met to talk of forgotten wars and long-gone companions. Beyond that there was a house with a terrace where I used to sit with friends in the evening to watch the stars come out while a boy brought us chilled fruit and the nightingales sang af if there hearts were breaking." Her voice drifted off into silence. "But then the Asturians came," she went on, and there was a different note then. "You'd be surprised at how little time it takes to tear down something that took a thousand years to build."

"Don't worry at it, Pol," Wolf told her. "These things happen from time to time. There's not a great deal we can do about it."

"I *could* have done something, father," she replied, looking off into the ruins. "But you wouldn't let me, remember?"

"Do we have to go over that again, Pol?" Wolf asked in a pained voice. "You have to learn to accept your losses. The Wacite Arends were doomed anyway. At best, you'd have only been able to stall off the inevitable for a few months. We're not who we are and what we are in order to get mixed up in things that don't have any meaning."

"So you said before." She looked around at the filmy trees marching away in the fog down the empty streets. "I didn't think the trees would come back so fast," she said with a strange little catch in her voice. "I thought they might have waited a little longer."

"It's been almost twenty-five centuries, Pol."

"Really? It seems like only last year."

"Don't brood about it. It'll only make you melancholy. Why don't we go inside? The fog's beginning to make us all a bit moody."

Unaccountably, Aunt Pol put her arm about Garion's

shoulders as they turned toward the tower. Her fragrance and the sense of her closeness brought a lump to his throat. The distance that had grown between them in the past few months seemed to vanish at her touch.

The chamber in the base of the tower had been built of such massive stones that neither the passage of centuries nor the silent, probing tendrils of tree roots had been able to dislodge them. Great, shallow arches supported the low stone ceiling, making the room seem almost like a cave. At the end of the room opposite the narrow doorway a wide crack between two of the rough-hewn blocks provided a natural chimney. Durnik had soberly considered the crack the previous evening when they had arrived, cold and wet, and then had quickly constructed a crude but efficient fireplace out of rubble. "It will serve," the smith had said. "Not very elegant perhaps, but good enough for a few days."

As Wolf, Garion and Aunt Pol entered the low, cavelike chamber, a good fire crackled in the fireplace, casting looming shadows among the low arches and radiating a welcome warmth. Durnik in his brown leather tunic was stacking firewood along the wall. Barak, huge, red-bearded, and mail-shirted, was polishing his sword. Silk, in an unbleached linen shirt and black leather vest, lounged idly on one of the packs, toying with a pair of dice.

"Any sign of Hettar yet?" Barak asked, looking up.

"It's a day or so early," Mister Wolf replied, going to the fireplace to warm himself.

"Why don't you change your boots, Garion?" Aunt Pol suggested, hanging her blue cloak on one of the pegs Durnik had hammered into a crack in the wall.

Garion lifted his pack down from another peg and began rummaging through it.

"Your stockings, too," she added.

"Is the fog lifting at all?" Silk asked Mister Wolf.

"Not a chance."

"If I can persuade you all to move out from in front of the fire, I'll see about supper," Aunt Pol told them, suddenly very businesslike. She began setting out a ham, a few loaves of dark, peasant bread, a sack of dried peas and a dozen or so leathery-looking carrots, humming softly to herself as she always did when she was cooking.

The next morning after breakfast, Garion pulled on a fleece-lined overvest, belted on his sword, and went back out into the fog-muffled ruins to watch for Hettar. It was a task to which he had appointed himself, and he was grateful that none of his friends had seen fit to tell him that it wasn't really necessary. As he trudged through the slush-covered streets toward the broken west gate of the city, he made a conscious effort to avoid the melancholy brooding that had blackened the previous day. Since there was absolutely nothing he could do about his circumstances, chewing on them would only leave a sour taste in his mouth. He was not exactly cheerful when he reached the low piece of wall by the west gate, but he was not precisely gloomy either.

The wall offered some protection, but the damp chill still crept through his clothes, and his feet were already cold. He shivered and settled down to wait. There was no point in trying to see any distance in the fog, so he concentrated on listening. His ears began to sort out the sounds in the forest beyond the wall, the drip of water from the trees, the occasional sodden thump of snow sliding from the limbs, and the tapping of a woodpecker working on a dead snag several hundred yards away.

"That's my cow," a voice said suddenly from somewhere off in the fog.

Garion froze and stood silently, listening.

"Keep her in your own pasture, then," another voice replied shortly.

"Is that you, Lammer?" the first voice asked.

"Right. You're Detton, aren't you?"

"I didn't recognize you. How long's it been?"

"Four or five years, I suppose," Lammer judged.

"How are things going in your village?" Detton asked.

"We're hungry. The taxes took all our food."

"Ours too. We've been eating boiled tree roots."

"We haven't tried that yet. We're eating our shoes."

"How's your wife?" Detton asked politely.

"She died last year," Lammer answered in a flat, unemotional voice. "My lord took our son for a soldier, and he was killed in a battle somewhere. They poured boiling pitch on him. After that my wife stopped eating. It didn't take her long to die."

"I'm sorry," Detton sympathized. "She was very beautiful."

"They're both better off," Lammer declared. "They aren't cold or hungry anymore. Which kind of tree roots have you been eating?"

"Birch is the best," Detton told him. "Spruce has too much pitch, and oak's too tough. You boil some grass with the roots to give them a bit of flavor."

"I'll have to try it."

"I've got to get back," Detton said. "My lord's got me clearing trees, and he'll have me flogged if I stay away too long."

"Maybe I'll see you again sometime."

"If we both live."

"Good-bye, Detton."

"Good-bye, Lammer."

The two voices drifted away. Garion stood quite still for a long time after they were gone, his mind numb with shock and with tears of sympathy standing in his eyes. The worst part of it was the matter-of-fact way in which the two had accepted it all. A terrible anger began to burn in his throat. He wanted suddenly to hit somebody.

Then there was another sound off in the fog. Somewhere in the forest nearby someone was singing. The voice was a light, clear tenor, and Garion could hear it quite plainly as it drew closer. The song was filled with ancient wrongs, and the refrain was a call to battle. Irrationally, Garion's anger focused on the unknown singer. His vapid bawling about abstract injustices seemed somehow obscene in the face of the quiet despair of Lammer and Detton. Without thinking, Garion drew his sword and crouched slightly behind the shattered wall.

The song came yet nearer, and Garion could hear the step of a horse's hooves in the wet snow. Carefully he poked his head out from behind the wall as the singer appeared out of the fog no more than twenty paces away. He was a young man dressed in yellow hose and a bright red jerkin. His fur-lined cloak was tossed back, and he had a long, curved bow slung over one shoulder and a well-sheathed sword at his opposite hip. His reddish-gold hair fell smoothly down his back from beneath a pointed cap with a feather rising from it. Although his song was grim and he sang it in a voice throbbing with passion, there was about his youthful face a kind of friendly openness that no amount of scowling could erase. Garion glared at this empty-headed young nobleman, quite certain that the singing fool had never made a meal of tree roots or mourned the passing of a wife who had starved herself to death out of grief. The stranger turned his horse and, still singing, rode directly toward the broken arch of the gateway beside which Garion lurked in ambush.

Garion was not normally a belligerent boy, and under other circumstances he might have approached the situation differently. The gaudy young stranger, however, had presented himself at precisely the wrong time. Garion's quickly devised plan had the advantage of simplicity. Since there was nothing to complicate it, it worked admirably—up to a point. No sooner had the lyric young man passed through the gate than Garion stepped from his hiding place, grasped the back of the rider's cloak and yanked him bodily out of the saddle. With a startled outcry and a wet splat, the stranger landed unceremoniously on his back in the slush at Garion's feet. The second part of Garion's plan, however, fell completely apart. Even as he moved in to take the fallen rider prisoner at sword point, the young man rolled, came to his feet, and drew his own sword, seemingly all in one motion. His eyes were snapping with anger, and his sword weaved threateningly.

Garion was not a fencer, but his reflexes were good and the chores he had performed at Faldor's farm had hardened his muscles. Despite the anger which had moved him to attack in the first place, he had no real desire to hurt this young man. His opponent seemed to be holding his sword lightly, almost negligently, and Garion thought that a smart blow on the blade might very well knock it out of his hand. He swung quickly, but the blade flicked out of the path of his heavy swipe and clashed with a steely ring down on his own sword. Garion jumped back and made another clumsy swing. The swords rang again. Then the air was filled with clash and scrape and bell-like rattle as the two of them banged and parried and feinted with their blades. It took Garion only a moment to realize that his opponent was much better at this than he was but that the young man had ignored several opportunities to strike at him. In spite of himself he began to grin in the excitement of their noisy contest. The stranger's answering grin was open, even friendly.

"All right, that's enough of that!" It was Mister Wolf. The old man was striding toward them with Barak and Silk close on his heels. "Just exactly what do you two think you're doing?"

Garion's opponent, after one startled glance, lowered his sword. "Belgarath—" he began.

"Lelldorin," Wolf's tone was scathing, "have you lost what little sense you had to begin with?"

Several things clicked into place in Garion's mind simultaneously as Wolf turned on him coldly. "Well, Garion, would you like to explain this?"

Garion instantly decided to try guile. "Grandfather," he said, stressing the word and giving the younger stranger a quick warning look, "you didn't think we were *really* fighting, did you? Lelldorin here was just showing me how you block somebody's sword when he attacks, that's all."

"Really?" Wolf replied skeptically.

"Of course," Garion said, all innocence now. "What possible reason could there be for us to be trying to hurt each other?"

Lelldorin opened his mouth to speak, but Garion deliberately stepped on his foot.

"Lelldorin's really very good," he rushed on, putting his hand in a friendly fashion on the young man's shoulder. "He taught me a lot in just a few minutes."

—*Let it stand*—Silk's fingers flickered at him in the minute gestures of the Drasnian secret language. —*Always keep a lie simple*—

"The lad is an apt pupil, Belgarath," Lelldorin said lamely, finally understanding.

"He's agile, if nothing else," Mister Wolf replied dryly. "What's the idea behind all the frippery?" He indicated Lelldorin's gaudy clothes. "You look like a maypole."

"The Mimbrates had started detaining honest Asturians for questioning," the young Arend explained, "and I had to pass several of their strongholds. I thought that if I dressed like one of their toadies I wouldn't be bothered."

"Maybe you've got better sense than I thought," Wolf conceded grudgingly. He turned to Silk and Barak. "This is Lelldorin, son of the Baron of Wildantor. He'll be joining us."

I wanted to talk to you about that, Belgarath," Lelldorin put in quickly. "My father commanded me to come here and I can't disobey him, but I'm pledged in a matter of extremest urgency."

"Every young nobleman in Asturia's pledged in at least two or three such matters of urgency," Wolf replied. "I'm sorry, Lelldorin, but the matter *we're* involved in is much too important to be postponed while you go out to ambush a couple of Mimbrate tax collectors."

Aunt Pol approached them out of the fog then, with Durnik striding protectively at her side. "What are they doing with the swords, father?" she demanded, her eyes flashing.

"Playing," Mister Wolf replied shortly. "Or so they say. This is Lelldorin. I think I've mentioned him to you."

Aunt Pol looked Lelldorin up and down with one raised eyebrow. "A very colorful young man."

"The clothes are a disguise," Wolf explained. "He's not as frivolous as all that—not quite, anyway. He's the best bowman in Asturia, and we might need his skill before we're done with all this."

"I see," she said, somewhat unconvinced.

"There's another reason, of course," Wolf continued, "but I don't think we need to get into that just now, do we?"

"Are you still worried about that passage, father?" she asked with exasperation. "The Mrin Codex is very obscure, and none of the other versions say anything at all about the people it mentions. It could be pure allegory, you know."

"I've seen a few too many allegories turn out to be plain fact to start gambling at this point. Why don't we all go back to the tower?" he suggested. "It's a bit cold and wet out here for lengthy debates on textual variations."

Garion glanced at Silk, baffled by this exchange, but the little man returned his look with blank incomprehension.

"Will you help me catch my horse, Garion?" Lelldorin asked politely, sheathing his sword.

"Of course," Garion replied, also putting away his weapon. "I think he went that way."

Lelldorin picked up his bow, and the two of them followed the horse's tracks off into the ruins.

"I'm sorry I pulled you off your horse," Garion apologized when they were out of sight of the others.

"No matter." Lelldorin laughed easily. "I should have been paying more attention." He looked quizzically at Garion. "Why did you lie to Belgarath?"

"It wasn't *exactly* a lie," Garion replied. "We weren't really trying to hurt each other, and sometimes it takes hours trying to explain something like that."

Lelldorin laughed again, an infectious sort of laugh. In spite of himself, Garion could not help joining in.

Both laughing, they continued together down an overgrown street between the low mounds of slush-covered rubble.

Chapter Two

LELLDORIN OF WILDANTOR was eighteen years old, although his ingenuous nature made him seem more boyish. No emotion touched him that did not instantly register in his expression, and sincerity shone in his face like a beacon. He was impulsive, extravagant in his declarations, and probably, Garion reluctantly concluded, not overly bright. It was impossible not to like him, however.

The following morning when Garion pulled on his cloak to go out and continue his watch for Hettar, Lelldorin immediately joined him. The young Arend had changed out of his garish clothing and now wore brown hose, a green tunic, and a dark brown wool cape. He carried his bow and wore a quiver of arrows at his belt; as they walked through the snow toward the broken west wall he amused himself by loosing arrows at targets only half-visible ahead of him.

"You're awfully good," Garion said admiringly after one particularly fine shot.

"I'm an Asturian," Lelldorin replied modestly. "We've been bowmen for thousands of years. My father had the limbs of this bow cut on the day I was born, and I could draw it by the time I was eight."

"I imagine you hunt a great deal," Garion said, thinking of the dense forest all around them and the tracks of game he had seen in the snow.

"It's our most common pastime." Lelldorin stopped to pull the arrow he had just shot from a tree trunk. "My father prides himself on the fact that beef or mutton are never served at his table."

"I went hunting once, in Cherek."

"Deer?" Lelldorin asked.

"No. Wild boars. We didn't use bows though. The Chereks hunt with spears."

"Spears? How can you get close enough to kill anything with a spear?"

Garion laughed a bit ruefully, remembering his bruised ribs and aching head. "Getting close isn't the problem. It's getting away after you've speared him that's the difficult part."

Lelldorin didn't seem to grasp that.

"The huntsmen form a line," Garion explained, "and they crash through the woods, making as much noise as they can. You take your spear and wait where the boars are likely to pass when they try to get away from the noise. Being chased makes them bad-tempered, and when they see you, they charge. That's when you spear them."

"Isn't that dangerous?" Lelldorin's eyes were wide.

Garion nodded. "I almost got all my ribs broken." He was not exactly boasting, but he admitted to himself that he was pleased by Lelldorin's reaction to his story.

"We don't have many dangerous animals in Asturia," Lelldorin said almost wistfully. "A few bears and once in a while a pack of wolves." He seemed to hesitate for a moment, looking closely at Garion. "*Some* men, though, find more interesting things to shoot at than wild stags." He said it with a kind of secretive sidelong glance.

"Oh?" Garion was not quite sure what he meant.

"Hardly a day goes by that some Mimbrate's horse doesn't come home riderless."

Garion was shocked at that.

"*Some* men think that there are too many Mimbrates in Asturia," Lelldorin explained with heavy emphasis.

"I thought that the Arendish civil war was over."

"There are many who don't believe that. There are many who believe that the war will continue until Asturia is free of the Mimbrate crown." Lelldorin's tone left no question as to where he stood in the matter.

"Wasn't the country unified after the Battle of Vo Mimbre?" Garion objected.

"Unified? How could anybody believe that? Asturia is treated like a subject province. The king's court is at Vo Mimbre; every governor, every tax collector, every bailiff, every high sheriff in the kingdom is a Mimbrate. There's not a single Asturian in a position of authority anywhere in Arendia. The Mimbrates even refuse to recognize our titles. My father, whose line extends back a thousand years, is called *landowner*. A Mimbrate would sooner bite out his tongue than call him Baron." Lelldorin's face had gone white with suppressed indignation.

"I didn't know that," Garion said carefully, not sure how to handle the young man's feelings.

"Asturia's humiliation is almost at an end, however," Lelldorin declared fervently. "There are some men in Asturia for whom patriotism is not dead, and the time is not far off when these men will hunt *royal* game." He emphasized his statement by snapping an arrow at a distant tree.

That confirmed the worst of Garion's fears. Lelldorin was a bit too familiar with the details not to be involved in this plot.

As if he had realized himself that he had gone too far, Lelldorin stared at Garion with consternation. "I'm a fool," he blurted with a guilty look around him. "I've never learned to control my tongue. Please forget what I just said, Garion. I know you're my friend, and I know you won't betray what I said in a moment of heat."

That was the one thing Garion had feared. With that single statement, Lelldorin had effectively sealed his lips. He knew that Mister Wolf should be warned that some wild scheme was afoot, but Lelldorin's declaration of friendship and trust had made it impossible for him to speak. He wanted to grind his teeth with frustration as he stared full in the face of a major moral dilemma.

They walked on, neither of them speaking and both a little embarrassed, until they reached the bit of wall where Garion had waited in ambush the day before. For a time they stared out into the fog, their strained silence growing more uncomfortable by the moment.

"What's it like in Sendaria?" Lelldorin asked suddenly. "I've never been there."

"There aren't so many trees," Garion answered, looking over the wall at the dark trunks marching off in the fog. "It's an orderly kind of place."

"Where did you live there?"

"At Faldor's farm. It's near Lake Erat."

"Is this Faldor a nobleman?"

"Faldor?" Garion laughed. "No, Faldor's as common as old shoes. He's just a farmer—decent, honest, good-hearted. I miss him."

"A commoner, then," Lelldorin said, seeming ready to dismiss Faldor as a man of no consequence.

"Rank doesn't mean very much in Sendaria," Garion told him rather pointedly. "What a man does is more important than what he is." He made a wry face. "I was a scullery boy. It's not very pleasant, but somebody's got to do it, I suppose."

"Not a serf, certainly?" Lelldorin sounded shocked.

"There aren't any serfs in Sendaria."

"No serfs?" The young Arend stared at him uncomprehendingly.

"No," Garion said firmly. "We've never found it necessary to have serfs."

Lelldorin's expression clearly showed that he was baffled by the notion. Garion remembered the voices that had come to him out of the fog the day before, but he resisted the urge to say something about serfdom. Lelldorin would never understand, and the two of them were very close to friendship. Garion felt that he needed a friend just now and he didn't want to spoil things by saying something that would offend this likeable young man.

"What sort of work does your father do?" Lelldorin asked politely.

"He's dead. So's my mother." Garion found that if he said it quickly, it didn't hurt so much.

Lelldorin's eyes filled in sudden, impulsive sympathy. He put his hand consolingly on Garion's shoulder. "I'm sorry," he said, his voice almost breaking. "It must have been a terrible loss."

"I was a baby." Garion shrugged, trying to sound offhand about it. "I don't even remember them." It was still too personal to talk about.

"Some pestilence?" Lelldorin asked gently.

"No," Garion answered in the same flat tone. "They were murdered."

Lelldorin gasped and his eyes went wide.

"A man crept into their village at night and set fire to their house," Garion continued unemotionally. "My grandfather tried to catch him, but he got away. From what I understand, the man is a very old enemy of my family."

"Surely you're not going to let it stand like that?" Lelldorin demanded.

"No," Garion replied, still looking out into the fog. "As soon as I'm old enough, I'm going to find him and kill him."

"Good lad!" Lelldorin exclaimed, suddenly catching Garion in a rough embrace. "We'll find him and cut him to pieces."

"We?"

"I'll be going with you, of course," Lelldorin declared. "No true friend could do any less." He was obviously speaking on impulse, but just as obviously he was totally sincere. He gripped Garion's hand firmly. "I swear to you, Garion, I won't rest until the murderer of your parents lies dead at your feet."

The sudden declaration was so totally predictable that Garion silently berated himself for not keeping his mouth shut. His feelings in the matter were very personal, and he was not really sure he wanted company in his search for his faceless enemy. Another part of his mind, however, rejoiced in Lelldorin's impulsive but unquestioning support. He decided to let the subject drop. He knew Lelldorin well enough by now to realize that the young man undoubtedly made a dozen devout promises a day, quickly offered in absolute sincerity, and just as quickly forgotten.

They talked then of other things, standing close together beside the shattered wall with their dark cloaks drawn tightly about them.

Shortly before noon Garion heard the muffled sound of horses' hooves somewhere out in the forest. A few minutes later, Hettar materialized out of the fog with a dozen wild-looking horses trailing after him. The tall Algar wore a short, fleece-lined leather cape. His boots were mud-spattered and his clothes travel-stained, but otherwise he seemed unaffected by his two weeks in the saddle.

"Garion," he said gravely by way of greeting and Garion and Lelldorin stepped out to meet him.

"We've been waiting for you," Garion told him and introduced Lelldorin. "We'll show you where the others are."

Hettar nodded and followed the two young men through the ruins to the tower where Mister Wolf and the others were waiting. "Snow in the mountains," the Algar remarked laconically by way of explanation as he swung down from his horse. "It delayed me a bit." He pulled his hood back from his shaved head and shook out his long, black scalp lock.

"No harm's been done," Mister Wolf replied. "Come inside to the fire and have something to eat. We've got a lot to talk about."

Hettar looked at the horses, his tan, weathered face growing strangely blank as if he were concentrating. The horses all looked back at him, their eyes alert and their ears pointed sharply forward. Then they turned and picked their way off among the trees.

"Won't they stray?" Durnik wanted to know.

"No," Hettar answered. "I asked them not to."

Durnik looked puzzled, but he let it pass.

They all went into the tower and sat near the fireplace.

Aunt Pol cut dark bread and pale, yellow cheese for them while Durnik put more wood on the fire.

"Cho-Hag sent word to the Clan-Chiefs," Hettar reported, pulling off his cape. He wore a black, long-sleeved horsehide jacket with steel discs riveted to it to form a kind of flexible armor. "They're gathering at the Stronghold for council." He unbelted the curved sabre he wore, laid it to one side and sat near the fire to eat.

Wolf nodded. "Is anyone trying to get through to Prolgu?"

"I sent a troop of my own men to the Gorim before I left," Hettar responded. "They'll get through if anyone can."

"I hope so," Wolf stated. "The Gorim's an old friend of mine, and I'll need his help before all this is finished."

"Aren't your people afraid of the land of the Ulgos?" Lelldorin inquired politely. "I've heard that there are monsters there that feed on the flesh of men."

Hettar shrugged. "They stay in their lairs in the wintertime. Besides, they're seldom brave enough to attack a full troop of mounted men." He looked over at Mister Wolf. "Southern Sendaria's crawling with Murgos. Or did you know that?"

"I could have guessed," Wolf replied. "Did they seem to be looking for anything in particular?"

"I don't talk with Murgos," Hettar said shortly. His hooked nose and fierce eyes made him look at that moment like a hawk about to swoop down to the kill.

"I'm surprised you weren't delayed even more," Silk bantered. "The whole world knows how you feel about Murgos."

"I indulged myself once," Hettar admitted. "I met two of them alone on the highway. It didn't take very long."

"Two less to worry about, then," Barak grunted with approval.

"I think it's time for some plain talk," Mister Wolf said, brushing crumbs off the front of his tunic. "Most of you have some notion of what we're doing, but I don't want anybody blundering into something by accident. We're after a man named Zedar. He used to be one of my Master's disciples—then he went over to Torak. Early last fall he somehow slipped into the throne room at Riva and stole the Orb of Aldur. We're going to chase him down and get it back."

"Isn't he a sorcerer too?" Barak asked, tugging absently at a thick red braid.

"That's not the term we use," Wolf replied, "but yes, he does have a certain amount of that kind of power. We all did—me, Beltira and Belkira, Belzedar—all the rest of us. That's one of the things I wanted to warn you about."

"You all seem to have the same sort of names," Silk noticed.

"Our Master changed our names when he took us as disciples. It was a simple change, but it meant a great deal to us."

"Wouldn't that mean that your original name was Garath?" Silk asked, his ferret eyes narrowing shrewdly.

Mister Wolf looked startled and then laughed. "I haven't heard *that* name for thousands of years. I've been Belgarath for so long that I'd almost completely forgotten Garath. It's probably just as well. Garath was a troublesome boy—a thief and a liar among other things."

"Some things never change," Aunt Pol observed.

"Nobody's perfect," Wolf admitted blandly.

"Why did Zedar steal the Orb?" Hettar asked, setting aside his plate.

"He's always wanted it for himself," the old man replied. "That could be it—but more likely he's trying to take it to Torak. The one who delivers the Orb to One-Eye is going to be his favorite."

"But Torak's dead," Lelldorin objected. "The Rivan Warder killed him at Vo Mimbre."

"No," Wolf said. "Torak isn't dead; only asleep. Brand's sword wasn't the one destined to kill him. Zedar carried him off after the battle and hid him someplace. Someday he'll awaken—probably someday fairly soon, if I'm reading the signs right. We've got to get the Orb back before that happens."

"This Zedar's caused a lot of trouble," Barak rumbled. "You should have dealt with him a long time ago."

"Possibly," Wolf admitted.

"Why don't you just wave your hand and make him disappear?" Barak suggested, making a sort of gesture with his thick fingers.

Wolf shook his head. "I can't. Not even the Gods can do that."

"We've got some big problems, then," Silk said with a frown. "Every Murgo from here to Rak Goska's going to try to stop us from catching Zedar."

"Not necessarily," Wolf disagreed. "Zedar's got the Orb, but Ctuchik commands the Grolims."

"Ctuchik?" Lelldorin asked.

"The Grolim High Priest. He and Zedar hate each other. I thing we can count on him to try to keep Zedar from getting to Torak with the Orb."

Barak shrugged. "What difference does it make? You and Polgara can use magic if we run into anything difficult, can't you?"

"There are limitations on that sort of thing," Wolf said a bit evasively.

"'I don't understand," Barak said, frowning.

Mister Wolf took a deep breath. "All right. As long as it's come up, let's go into that too. Sorcery—if that's what you want to call it—is a disruption of the natural order of things. Sometimes it has certain unexpected effects. so you have to be very careful about what you do with it. Not only that, it makes—" He frowned. "—Let's call it a sort of noise. That's not exactly what it is, but it serves well enough to explain. Others with the same abilities can hear that noise. Once Polgara and I start changing things, every Grolim in the West is going to know exactly where we are and what we're doing. They'll keep piling things in front of us until we're exhausted."

"It takes almost as much energy to do things that way as it does to do them with your arms and back," Aunt Pol explained. "It's very tiring." She sat beside the fire, carefully mending a small tear in one of Garion's tunics.

"I didn't know that," Barak admitted.

"Not many people do."

"If we have to, Pol and I can take certain steps," Wolf went on, "but we can't keep it up forever and we can't simply make things vanish. I'm sure you can see why."

"Oh, of course," Silk professed, though his tone indicated that he did not.

"Everything that exists depends on everything else," Aunt Pol explained quietly. "If you were to unmake one thing, it's altogether possible that everything would vanish."

The fire popped, and Garion jumped slightly. The vaulted chamber seemed suddenly dark, and shadows lurked in the corners.

"That can't happen, of course," Wolf told them. "When you try to unmake something, your will simply recoils on you. If you say, 'Be not,' then *you* are the one who vanishes. That's why we're very careful about what we say."

"I can understand why," Silk said, his eyes widening slightly.

"Most of the things we'll encounter can be dealt with by ordinary means," Wolf continued. "That's the reason we've brought you together—at least that's one of the reasons. Among you, you'll be able to handle most of the things that get in our way. The important thing to remember is that Polgara and I have to get to Zedar before he can reach Torak with the Orb. Zedar's found some way to touch the Orb—I don't know how. If he can show Torak how it's done, no power on earth will be able to stop One-Eye from becoming King and God over the whole world."

They all sat in the ruddy, flickering light of the fire, their faces serious as they considered that possibility.

"I think that pretty well covers everything, don't you, Pol?"

"I believe so, father," she replied, smoothing the front of her gray, homespun gown.

Later, outside the tower as gray evening crept in among the foggy ruins of Vo Wacune and the smell of the thick stew Aunt Pol was cooking for supper drifted out to them, Garion turned to Silk. "Is it all really true?" he asked.

The small man looked out into the fog. "Let's act as if we believed that it is," he suggested. "Under the circumstances, I think it would be a bad idea to make a mistake."

"Are you afraid too, Silk?" Garion asked.

Silk sighed. "Yes," he admitted, "but we can behave as if we believed that we aren't, can't we?"

"I guess we can try," Garion said, and the two of them turned to go back into the chamber at the foot of the tower where the firelight danced on the low stone arches, holding the fog and chill at bay.

Chapter Three

THE NEXT MORNING Silk came out of the tower wearing a rich maroon doublet and a baglike black velvet cap cocked jauntily over one ear.

"What's all that about?" Aunt Pol asked him.

"I chanced across an old friend in one of the packs," Silk replied airily. "Radek of Boktor by name."

"What happened to Ambar of Kotu?"

"Ambar's a good enough fellow, I suppose," Silk said a bit deprecatingly, "but a Murgo named Asharak knows about him and may have dropped his name in certain quarters. Let's not look for trouble if we don't have to."

"Not a bad disguise," Mister Wolf agreed. "One more Drasnian merchant on the Great West Road won't attract any attention—whatever his name."

"Please," Silk objected in an injured tone. "The name's very important. You hang the whole disguise on the name."

"I don't see any difference," Barak asserted bluntly.

"There's all the difference in the world. Surely you can see that Ambar's a vagabond with very little regard for ethics, while Radek's a man of substance whose word is good in all the commercial centers of the West. Besides, Radek's always accompanied by servants."

"Servants?" One of Aunt Pol's eyebrows shot up.

"Just for the sake of the disguise," Silk assured her quickly. "You, of course, could never be a servant, Lady Polgara."

"Thank you."

"No one would ever believe it. You'll be my sister instead, traveling with me to see the splendors of Tol Honeth."

"*Your* sister?"

"You could be my mother instead, if you prefer," Silk suggested blandly, "making a religious pilgrimage to Mar Terrin to atone for a colorful past."

Aunt Pol gazed steadily at the small man for a moment while he grinned impudently at her. "Someday your sense of humor's going to get you into a great deal of trouble, Prince Kheldar."

"I'm always in trouble, Lady Polgara. I wouldn't know how to act if I weren't."

"Do you two suppose we could get started?" Mister Wolf asked.

"Just a moment more," Silk replied. "If we meet anyone and have to explain things, you, Lelldorin, and Garion are Polgara's servants. Hettar, Barak, and Durnik are mine."

"Anything you say," Wolf agreed wearily.

"There are reasons."

"All right."

"Don't you want to hear them?"

"Not particularly."

Silk looked a bit hurt.

"Are we ready?" Wolf asked.

"Everything's out of the tower," Durnik told him. "Oh—just a moment. I forgot to put out the fire." He went back inside.

Wolf glanced after the smith in exasperation. "What difference does it make?" he muttered. "This place is a ruin anyway."

"Leave him alone, father," Aunt Pol said placidly. "It's the way he is."

As they prepared to mount, Barak's horse, a large, sturdy gray, sighed and threw a reproachful look at Hettar, and the Algar chuckled.

"What's so funny?" Barak demanded suspiciously.

"The horse said something," Hettar replied. "Never mind."

Then they swung into their saddles and threaded their

way out of the foggy ruins and along the narrow, muddy track that wound into the forest. Sodden snow lay under wet trees, and water dripped continually from the branches overhead. They all drew their cloaks about them to ward off the chill and dampness. Once they were under the trees, Lelldorin pulled his horse in beside Garion's, and they rode together. "Is Prince Kheldar always so—well—extremely complicated?" he asked.

"Silk? Oh yes. He's very devious. You see, he's a spy, and disguises and clever lies are second nature to him."

"A spy? Really?" Lelldorin's eyes brightened as his imagination caught hold of the idea.

"He works for his uncle, the King of Drasnia," Garion explained. "From what I understand, the Drasnians have been at this sort of thing for centuries."

"We've got to stop and pick up the rest of the packs," Silk was reminding Mister Wolf.

"I haven't forgotten," the old man replied.

"Packs?" Lelldorin asked.

"Silk picked up some wool cloth in Camaar," Garion told him. "He said it would give us a legitimate reason to be on the highway. We hid them in a cave when we left the road to come to Vo Wacune."

"He thinks of everything, doesn't he?"

"He tries. We're lucky to have him with us."

"Maybe we could have him show us a few things about disguises," Lelldorin suggested brightly. "It might be very useful when we go looking for your enemy."

Garion had thought that Lelldorin had forgotten his impulsive pledge. The young Arend's mind seemed too flighty to keep hold of one idea for very long, but he saw now that Lelldorin only seemed to forget things. The prospect of a serious search for his parents' murderer with this young enthusiast adding embellishments and improvisations at every turn began to present itself alarmingly.

By midmorning, after they had picked up Silk's packs and lashed them to the backs of the spare horses, they were back out on the Great West Road, the Tolnedran highway running through the heart of the forest. They rode south at a loping canter that ate up the miles.

They passed a heavily burdened serf clothed in scraps

and pieces of sackcloth tied on with bits of string. The serf's face was gaunt, and he was very thin under his dirty rags. He stepped off the road and stared at them with apprehension until they had passed. Garion felt a sudden stab of compassion. He briefly remembered Lammer and Detton, and he wondered what would finally happen to them. It seemed important for some reason. "Is it really necessary to keep them so poor?" he demanded of Lelldorin, unable to hold it in any longer.

"Who?" Lelldorin asked, looking around.

"That serf."

Lelldorin glanced back over his shoulder at the ragged man.

"You didn't even see him," Garion accused.

Lelldorin shrugged. "There are so many."

"And they all dress in rags and live on the edge of starvation."

"Mimbrate taxes," Lelldorin replied as if that explained everything.

"*You* seem to have always had enough to eat."

"I'm not a serf, Garion," Lelldorin answered patiently. "The poorest people always suffer the most. It's the way the world is."

"It doesn't have to be," Garion retorted.

"You just don't understand."

"No. And I never will."

"Naturally not," Lelldorin said with infuriating complacency. "You're not Arendish."

Garion clenched his teeth to hold back the obvious reply.

By late afternoon they had covered ten leagues, and the snow had largely disappeared from the roadside. "Shouldn't we start to give some thought to where we're going to spend the night, father?" Aunt Pol suggested.

Mister Wolf scratched thoughtfully at his beard as he squinted at the shadows hovering in the trees around them.

"I have an uncle who lives not far from here," Lelldorin offered, "Count Reldegen. I'm sure he'll be glad to give us shelter."

"Thin?" Mister Wolf asked. "Dark hair?"

"It's gray now," Lelldorin replied. "Do you know him?"

"I haven't seen him for twenty years," Wolf told him. "As I recall, he used to be quite a hothead."

"Uncle Reldegen? You must have him confused with somebody else, Belgarath."

"Maybe," Wolf said. "How far is it to his house?"

"No more than a league and a half away."

"Let's go see him," Wolf decided.

Lelldorin shook his reins and moved into the lead to show them the way.

"How are you and your friend getting along?" Silk asked, falling in beside Garion.

"Fine, I suppose," Garion replied, not quite sure how the rat-faced little man intended the question. "It seems to be a little hard to explain things to him though."

"That's only natural," Silk observed. "He's an Arend, after all."

Garion quickly came to Lelldorin's defense. "He's honest and very brave."

"They all are. That's part of the problem."

"I like him," Garion asserted.

"So do I, Garion, but that doesn't keep me from realizing the truth about him."

"If you're trying to say something, why don't you just go ahead and say it?"

"All right, I will. Don't let friendship get the better of your good sense. Arendia's a very dangerous place, and Arends tend to blunder into disasters quite regularly. Don't let your exuberant young companion drag you into something that's none of your business." Silk's look was direct, and Garion realized that the little man was quite serious.

"I'll be careful," he promised.

"I knew I could count on you," Silk said gravely.

"Are you making fun of me?"

"Would I do that, Garion?" Silk asked mockingly. Then he laughed and they rode on together through the gloomy afternoon.

The gray stone house of Count Reldegen was about a mile back in the forest from the highway, and it stood in the center of a clearing that extended beyond bowshot in every direction. Although it had no wall, it had somehow the look of a fort. The windows facing out were narrow and covered with iron gratings. Strong turrets surmounted by battlements stood at each corner, and the gate which opened into the central courtyard of the house was made of whole tree trunks, squared off and strapped together with iron bands. Garion stared at the brooding pile as they approached in the rapidly fading light. There was a kind of haughty ugliness about the house, a grim solidity that seemed to defy the world. "It's not a very pleasant-looking sort of place, is it?" he said to Silk.

"Asturian architecture's a reflection of their society," Silk replied. "A strong house isn't a bad idea in a country where neighborhood disputes sometimes get out of hand."

"Are they all so afraid of each other?"

"Just cautious, Garion. Just cautious."

Lelldorin dismounted before the heavy gate and spoke to someone on the other side through a small grill. There was finally a rattling of chains and the grinding sound of heavy, iron-shod bars sliding back.

"I wouldn't make any quick moves once we're inside," Silk advised quietly. "There'll probably be archers watching us."

Garion looked at him sharply.

"A quaint custom of the region," Silk informed him.

They rode into a cobblestoned courtyard and dismounted.

Count Reldegen, when he appeared, was a tall, thin man with iron-gray hair and beard who walked with the aid of a stout cane. He wore a rich green doublet and black hose; despite the fact that he was in his own house, he carried a sword at his side. He limped heavily down a broad flight of stairs from the house to greet them.

"Uncle," Lelldorin said, bowing respectfully.

"Nephew," the count replied in polite acknowledgment.

"My friends and I found ourselves in the vicinity," Lelldorin stated, "and we thought we might impose on you for the night."

"You're always welcome, nephew," Reldegen answered with a kind of grave formality. "Have you dined yet?"

"No, uncle."

"Then you must all take supper with me. May I know your friends?"

Mister Wolf pushed back his hood and stepped forward. "You and I are already acquainted, Reldegen," he said.

The count's eyes widened. "Belgarath? Is it really you?"

Wolf grinned. "Oh, yes. I'm still wandering about the world, stirring up mischief."

Reldegen laughed then and grasped Wolf's upper arm warmly. "Come inside, all of you. Let's not stand about in the cold." He turned and limped up the steps to the house.

"What happened to your leg?" Wolf asked him.

"An arrow in the knee." The count shrugged. "The result of an old disagreement—long since forgotten."

"As I recall, you used to get involved in quite a few of those. I thought for a while that you intended to go through life with your sword half-drawn."

"I was an excitable youth," the count admitted, opening the broad door at the top of the steps. He led them down a long hallway to a room of imposing size with a large blazing fireplace at each end. Great curving stone arches supported the ceiling. The floor was of polished black stone, scattered with fur rugs, and the walls, arches, and ceiling were whitewashed in gleaming contrast. Heavy, carved chairs of dark brown wood sat here and there, and a great table with an iron candelabra in its center stood near the fireplace at one end. A dozen or so leather-bound books were scattered on its polished surface.

"Books, Reldegen?" Mister Wolf said in amazement as he and the others removed their cloaks and gave them to the servants who immediately appeared. "You *have* mellowed, my friend."

The count smiled at the old man's remark.

"I'm forgetting my manners," Wolf apologized. "My daugher, Polgara. Pol, this is Count Reldegen, an old friend."

"My Lady," the count acknowledged with an exquisite bow, "my house is honored."

Aunt Pol was about to reply when two young men burst into the room, arguing heatedly. "You're an idiot, Berentain!" the first, a dark-haired youth in a scarlet doublet, snapped.

"It may please thee to think so, Torasin," the second, a stout young man with pale, curly hair and wearing a green and yellow striped tunic, replied, "but whether it please thee or not, Asturia's future is in Mimbrate hands. Thy rancorous denouncements and sulfurous rhetoric shall not alter that fact."

"Don't thee me or thou me, Berentain," the dark-haired one sneered. "Your imitation Mimbrate courtesy turns my stomach."

"Gentlemen, that's enough!" Count Reldegen said sharply, rapping his cane on the stone floor. "If you two are going to insist on discussing politics, I'll have you separated—forcibly, if necessary."

The two young men scowled at each other and then stalked off to opposite sides of the room. "My son, Torasin," the count admitted apologetically, indicating the dark-haired youth, "and his cousin Berentain, the son of my late wife's brother. They've been wrangling like this for two weeks now. I had to take their swords away from them the day after Berentain arrived."

"Political discussion is good for the blood, my Lord," Silk observed, "especially in the winter. The heat keeps the veins from clogging up."

The count chuckled at the little man's remark.

"Prince Kheldar of the royal house of Drasnia," Mister Wolf introduced Silk.

"Your Highness," the count responded, bowing.

Silk winced slightly. "Please, my Lord. I've spent a lifetime running from that mode of address, and I'm sure that my connection with the royal family embarrasses my uncle almost as much as it embarrasses me."

The count laughed again with easy good nature. "Why don't we all adjourn to the dining table?" he suggested. "Two fat deer have been turning on spits in my kitchen since daybreak, and I recently obtained a cask of red wine from southern Tolnedra. As I recall, Belgarath has always had a great fondness for good food and fine wines."

"He hasn't changed, my Lord," Aunt Pol told him. "My father's terribly predictable, once you get to know him."

The count smiled and offered her his arm as they all moved toward a door on the far side of the room.

"Tell me, my Lord," Aunt Pol said, "do you by chance have a bathtub in your house?"

"Bathing in winter is dangerous, Lady Polgara," the count warned her.

"My Lord," she stated gravely, "I've been bathing winter or summer for more years than you could possibly imagine."

"Let her bathe, Reldegen," Mister Wolf urged. "Her temper deteriorates quite noticeably when she thinks she's getting dirty."

"A bath wouldn't hurt you either, Old Wolf," Aunt Pol retorted tartly. "You're starting to get a bit strong from the downwind side."

Mister Wolf looked a bit injured.

Much later, after they had eaten their fill of venison, gravy-soaked bread, and rich cherry tarts, Aunt Pol excused herself and went with a maidservant to oversee the preparation of her bath. The men all lingered at the table over their wine cups, their faces washed with the golden light of the many candles in Reldegen's dining hall.

"Let me show you to your rooms," Torasin suggested to Lelldorin and Garion, pushing back his chair and casting a look of veiled contempt across the table at Berentain.

They followed him from the room and up a long flight of stairs toward the upper stories of the house. "I don't want to offend you, Tor," Lelldorin said as they climbed, "but your cousin has some peculiar ideas."

Torasin snorted. "Berentain's a jackass. He thinks he can impress the Mimbrates by imitating their speech and by fawning on them." His dark face was angry in the light of the candle he carried to light their way.

"Why should he want to?" Lelldorin asked.

"He's desperate for some kind of holding he can call his own," Torasin replied. "My mother's brother has very little land to leave him. The fat idiot's all calf-eyed over the daughter of one of the barons in his district, and since the baron won't even consider a landless suitor, Berentain's trying to wheedle an estate from the Mimbrate governor. He'd swear fealty to the ghost of Kal Torak himself, if he thought it would get him land."

"Doesn't he realize that he hasn't got a chance?" Lelldorin inquired. "There are too many land-hungry Mimbrate knights around the governor for him to even think of granting an estate to an Asturian."

"I've told him the same thing myself," Torasin declared with scathing contempt, "but there's no reasoning with him. His behavior degrades our whole family."

Lelldorin shook his head commiseratingly as they reached an upper hall. He looked around quickly then. "I have to talk with you, Tor," he blurted, his voice dropping to a whisper.

Torasin looked at him sharply.

"My father's committed me to Belgarath's service in a matter of great importance," Lelldorin hurried on in that same hushed voice. "I don't know how long we'll be gone, so you and the others will have to kill Korodullin without me."

Torasin's eyes went wide with horror. "We're not alone, Lelldorin!" he said in a strangled voice.

"I'll go down to the other end of the hall," Garion said quickly.

"No," Lelldorin replied firmly, taking hold of Garion's arm. "Garion's my friend, Tor. I have no secrets from him."

"Lelldorin, please," Garion protested. "I'm not an Asturian—I'm not even an Arend. I don't want to know what you're planning."

"But you *will* know, Garion, as proof of my trust in you," Lelldorin declared. "Next summer, when Korodullin journeys to the ruined city of Vo Astur to hold court there for the six weeks that maintain the fiction of Arendish unity, we're going to ambush him on the highway."

"Lelldorin!" Torasin gasped, his face turning white.

But Lelldorin was already plunging on. "It won't be just a simple ambush, Garion. This will be a master stroke at Mimbre's heart. We're going to ambush him in the uniforms of Tolnedran legionnaires and cut him down with Tolnedran swords. Our attack will force Mimbre to declare war on the Tolnedran Empire, and Tolnedra will crush Mimbre like an eggshell. Mimbre will be destroyed, and Asturia will be free!"

"Nachak will have you killed for this, Lelldorin," Torasin cried. "We've all been sworn to secrecy on a blood oath."

"Tell the Murgo that I spit on his oath," Lelldorin said hotly. "What need have Asturian patriots for a Murgo henchman?"

"He's providing us with gold, you blockhead!" Torasin raged, almost beside himself. "We need his good red gold to buy the uniforms, the swords, and to strengthen the backbones of some of our weaker friends."

"I don't need weaklings with me," Lelldorin said intensely. "A patriot does what he does for love of his country—not for Angarak gold."

Garion's mind was moving quickly now. His moment of stunned amazement had passed. "There was a man in Cherek," he recalled. "The Earl of Jarvik. He also took Murgo gold and plotted to kill a king."

The two stared at him blankly.

"Something happens to a country when you kill its king," Garion explained. "No matter how bad the king is or how good the people are who kill him, the country falls apart for a while. Everything is confused, and there's nobody to point the country in any one direction. Then, if you start a war between that country and another one at the same time, you add just that much more confusion. I think that if I were a Murgo, that's exactly the kind of confusion I'd want to see in all the kingdoms of the West."

Garion listened to his own voice almost in amazement. There was a dry, dispassionate quality in it that he instantly recognized. From the time of his earliest memories that voice had always been there—inside his mind—occupying some quiet, hidden corner, telling him when he was wrong or foolish. But the voice had never actively interfered before in his dealings with other people. Now, however, it spoke directly to these two young men, patiently explaining.

"Angarak gold isn't what it seems to be," he went on. "There's a kind of power in it that corrupts you. Maybe that's why it's the color of blood. I'd think about that before I accepted any more red gold from this Murgo Nachak. Why do you suppose he's giving you gold and helping you with this plan of yours? He's not an Asturian, so patriotism couldn't have anything to do with it, could it? I'd think about that, too."

Lelldorin and his cousin looked suddenly troubled.

"I'm not going to say anything about this to anybody," Garion said. "You told me about it in confidence, and I really wasn't supposed to hear about it anyway. But remember that there's a lot more going on in the world right now than what's happening here in Arendia. Now I think I'd like to get some sleep. If you'll show me where my bed is, I'll leave you to talk things over all night, if you'd like."

All in all, Garion thought he'd handled the whole thing rather well. He'd planted a few doubts at the very least. He knew Arends well enough by now to realize that it probably wouldn't be enough to turn these two around, but it was a start.

Chapter Four

THE FOLLOWING MORNING they rode out early while the mist still hung among the trees. Count Reldegen, wrapped in a dark cloak, stood at his gate to bid them farewell; and Torasin, standing beside his father, seemed unable to take his eyes off Garion's face. Garion kept his expression as blank as possible. The fiery young Asturian seemed to be filled with doubts, and those doubts might keep him from plunging headlong into something disastrous. It wasn't much, Garion realized, but it was the best he could manage under the circumstances.

"Come back soon, Belgarath," Reldegen said. "Sometime when you can stay longer. We're very isolated here, and I'd like to know what the rest of the world's doing. We'll sit by the fire and talk away a month or two."

Mister Wolf nodded gravely. "Maybe when this business of mine is over, Reldegen." Then he turned his horse and

led the way across the wide clearing that surrounded Reldegen's house and back once again into the gloomy forest.

"The count's an unusual Arend," Silk said lightly as they
rode along. "I think I actually detected an original thought
or two in him last evening."

"He's changed a great deal," Wolf agreed.

"He sets a good table," Barak said. "I haven't felt this
full since I left Val Alorn."

"You should," Aunt Pol told him. "You ate the biggest
part of one deer by yourself."

"You're exaggerating, Polgara," Barak said.

"But not by very much," Hettar observed in his quiet
voice.

Lelldorin had pulled his horse in beside Garion's, but he
had not spoken. His face was as troubled as his cousin's
had been. It was obvious that he wanted to say something
and just as obvious that he didn't know how to begin.

"Go ahead," Garion said quietly. "We're good enough
friends that I'm not going to be upset if it doesn't come out
exactly right."

Lelldorin looked a little sheepish. "Am I really that obvious?"

"Honest is a better word for it," Garion told him.
"You've just never learned to hide your feelings, that's all."

"Was it really true?" Lelldorin blurted. "I'm not doubt-
ing your word, but was there really a Murgo in Cherek
plotting against King Anheg?"

"Ask Silk," Garion suggested, "or Barak, or Hettar—
any of them. We were all there."

"Nachak isn't like that, though," Lelldorin said quickly,
defensively.

"Can you be sure?" Garion asked him. "The plan was
his in the first place, wasn't it? How did you happen to
meet him?"

"We'd all gone down to the Great Fair, Torasin, me,
several of the others. We bought some things from a Murgo
merchant, and Tor made a few remarks about Mimbrates—you know how Tor is. The merchant said that he
knew somebody we might be interested in meeting and he
introduced us to Nachak. The more we talked with him,

the more sympathetic he seemed to become to the way we felt."

"Naturally."

"He told us what the king is planning. You wouldn't believe it."

"Probably not."

Lelldorin gave him a quick, troubled look. "He's going to break up our estates and give them to landless Mimbrate nobles." He said it accusingly.

"Did you verify that with anybody but Nachak?"

"How could we? The Mimbrates wouldn't admit it if we confronted them with it, but it's the kind of thing Mimbrates *would* do."

"So you've only got Nachak's word for it? How did this plan of yours come up?"

"Nachak said that if he were an Asturian, he wouldn't let anybody take *his* land, but he said that it'd be too late to try to stop them when they came with knights and soldiers. He said that if he were doing it, he'd strike before they were ready and that he'd do it in such a way that the Mimbrates wouldn't know who'd done it. That's when he suggested the Tolnedran uniforms."

"When did he start giving you money?"

"I'm not sure. Tor handled that part of it."

"Did he ever say why he was giving you money?"

"He said it was out of friendship."

"Didn't that seem a little odd?"

"I'd give someone money out of friendship," Lelldorin protested.

"You're an Asturian," Garion told him. "You'd give somebody your life out of friendship. Nachak's a Murgo, though, and I've never heard that they were all that generous. What it comes down to, then, is that a stranger tells you that the king's planning to take your land. Then he gives you a plan to kill the king and start a war with Tolnedra; and to make sure you succeed with his plan, he gives you money. Is that about it?"

Lelldorin nodded mutely, his eyes stricken.

"Weren't any of you just the least bit suspicious?"

Lelldorin seemed almost about to cry. "It's such a *good* plan," he burst out finally. "It couldn't help but succeed."

"That's what makes it so dangerous," Garion replied.

"Garion, what am I going to do?" Lelldorin's voice was anguished.

"I don't think there's anything you can do right now," Garion told him. "Maybe later, after we've had time to think about it, we'll come up with something. If we can't, we can always tell my grandfather about it. He'll think of a way to stop it."

"We can't tell anybody," Lelldorin reminded him. "We're pledged to silence."

"We might have to break that pledge," Garion said somewhat reluctantly. "I don't see that either of us owes that Murgo anything, but it's going to have to be up to you. I won't say anything to anybody without your permission."

"*You* decide," Lelldorin pleaded then. "I can't do it, Garion."

"You're going to have to," Garion told him. "I'm sure that if you think about it, you'll see why."

They reached the Great West Road then, and Barak led them south at a brisk trot, cutting off the possibility of further discussion.

A league or so down the road they passed a muddy village, a dozen or so turf-roofed huts with walls made of wattles plastered over with mud. The fields around the village were dotted with tree stumps, and a few scrawny cows grazed near the edge of the forest. Garion could not control his indignation as he looked at the misery implicit in the crude collection of hovels. "Lelldorin," he said sharply, "look!"

"What? Where?" The blond young man came out of his troubled preoccupation quickly as if expecting some danger.

"The village," Garion told him. "Look at it."

"It's only a serfs' village," Lelldorin said indifferently. "I've seen hundreds like it." He seemed ready to return to his own inner turmoil.

"In Sendaria we wouldn't keep pigs in places like that." Garion's voice rang with fervor. If he could only make his friend *see*!

Two ragged serfs were dispiritedly hacking chunks of firewood from one of the stumps near the road. As the party approached, they dropped their axes and bolted in terror for the forest.

"Does it make you proud, Lelldorin?" Garion demanded. "Does it make you feel good to know that your own countrymen are so afraid of you that they run from the very sight of you?"

Lelldorin looked baffled. "They're *serfs*, Garion," he said as if that explained.

"They're men. They're not animals. Men deserve to be treated better."

"I can't do anything about it. They aren't *my* serfs." And with that Lelldorin's attention turned inward again as he continued to struggle with the dilemma Garion had placed upon him.

By late afternoon they had covered ten leagues and the cloudy sky was gradually darkening as evening approached. "I think we're going to have to spend the night in the forest, Belgarath," Silk said, looking around. "There's no chance of reaching the next Tolnedran hostel."

Mister Wolf had been half-dozing in his saddle. He looked up, blinking a bit. "All right," he replied, "but let's get back from the road a bit. Our fire could attract attention, and too many people know we're in Arendia already."

"There's a woodcutter's track right there." Durnik pointed at a break in the trees just ahead. "It should lead us back into the trees."

"All right," Wolf agreed.

The sound of their horses' hooves was muffled by the sodden leaves on the forest floor as they turned in among the trees to follow the narrow track. They rode silently for the better part of a mile until a clearing opened ahead of them.

"How about here?" Durnik asked. He indicated a brook trickling softly over mossy stones on one side of the clearing.

"It will do," Wolf agreed.

"We're going to need shelter," the smith observed.

"I bought tents in Camaar," Silk told him. "They're in the packs."

"That was foresighted of you," Aunt Pol complimented him.

"I've been in Arendia before, my Lady. I'm familiar with the weather."

"Garion and I'll go get wood for a fire then," Durnik said, climbing down from his horse and untying his axe from his saddle.

"I'll help you," Lelldorin offered, his face still troubled.

Durnik nodded and led the way off into the trees. The woods were soaked, but the smith seemed to know almost instinctively where to find dry fuel. They worked quickly in the lowering twilight and soon had three large bundles of limbs and fagots. They returned to the clearing where Silk and the others were erecting several dun-colored tents. Durnik dropped his wood and cleared a space for the fire with his foot. Then he knelt and began striking sparks with his knife from a piece of flint into a wad of dry tinder he always carried. In a short time he had a small fire going, and Aunt Pol set out her pots beside it, humming softly to herself.

Hettar came back from tending the horses, and they all stood back watching Aunt Pol prepare a supper from the stores Count Reldegen had pressed on them before they had left his house that morning.

After they had eaten, they sat around the fire talking quietly. "How far have we come today?" Durnik asked.

"Twelve leagues," Hettar estimated.

"How much farther do we have to go to get out of the forest?"

"It's eighty leagues from Camaar to the central plain," Lelldorin replied.

Durnik sighed. "A week or more. I'd hoped that it'd be only a few days."

"I know what you mean, Durnik," Barak agreed. "It's gloomy under all these trees."

The horses, picketed near the brook, stirred uneasily. Hettar rose to his feet.

"Something wrong?" Barak asked, also rising.

"They shouldn't be——" Hettar started. Then he stopped. "Back!" he snapped. "Away from the fire. The horses say there are men out there. Many—with weapons." He jumped back from the fire, drawing his sabre.

Lelldorin took one startled look at him and bolted for

one of the tents. Garion's sudden disappointment in his friend was almost like a blow to the stomach.

An arrow buzzed into the light and shattered on Barak's mail shirt. "Arm yourselves!" the big man roared, drawing his sword.

Garion grasped Aunt Pol's sleeve and tried to pull her from the light.

"Stop that!" she snapped, jerking her sleeve free. Another arrow whizzed out of the foggy woods. Aunt Pol flicked her hand as if brushing away a fly and muttered a single word. The arrow bounced back as if it had struck something solid and fell to the ground.

Then with a hoarse shout, a gang of rough, burly men burst from the edge of the trees and splashed across the brook, brandishing swords. As Barak and Hettar leaped forward to meet them, Lelldorin reemerged from the tent with his bow and began loosing arrows so rapidly that his hands seemed to blur as they moved. Garion was instantly ashamed that he had doubted his friend's courage.

With a choked cry, one of the attackers stumbled back, an arrow through his throat. Another doubled over sharply, clutching at his stomach, and fell to the ground, groaning. A third, quite young and with a pale, downy beard on his cheeks, dropped heavily and sat plucking at the feathers on the shaft protruding from his chest with a bewildered expression on his boyish face. Then he sighed and slumped over on his side with a stream of blood coming from his nose.

The ragged-looking men faltered under the rain of Lelldorin's arrows, and then Barak and Hettar were upon them. With a great sweep, Barak's heavy sword shattered an upflung blade and crunched down into the angle between the neck and shoulder of the black-whiskered man who had held it. The man collapsed. Hettar made a quick feint with his sabre, then ran it smoothly through the body of a pockmarked ruffian. The man stiffened, and a gush of bright blood burst from his mouth as Hettar pulled out his blade. Durnik ran forward with his axe, and Silk drew his long dagger from under his vest and ran directly at a man with a shaggy brown beard. At the last moment, he dived forward, rolled and struck the bearded man full in the chest with both feet. Without pausing he came up and ripped his dagger into his enemy's belly. The dagger made a wet, tearing sound as it sliced upward, and the stricken man clutched at his stomach with a scream, trying to hold in the blue-colored loops and coils of his entrails that seemed to come boiling out through his fingers.

Garion dived for the packs to get his own sword, but was suddenly grabbed roughly from behind. He struggled for an instant, then felt a stunning blow on the back of his head, and his eyes filled with a blinding flash of light.

"This is the one we want," a rough voice husked as Garion sank into unconsciousness.

He was being carried—that much was certain. He could feel the strong arms under him. He didn't know how long it had been since he had been struck on the head. His ears still rang, and he was more than a little sick to his stomach. He stayed limp, but carefully opened one eye. His vision was blurred and uncertain, but he could make out Barak's bearded face looming above him in the darkness, and merged with it, as once before in the snowy woods outside Val Alorn, he seemed to see the shaggy face of a great bear. He closed his eyes, shuddered, and started to struggle weakly.

"It's all right, Garion," Barak said, his voice sunk in a kind of despair. "It's me."

Garion opened his eyes again, and the bear seemed to be gone. He wasn't even sure he had ever really seen it.

"Are you all right?" Barak asked, setting him on the ground.

"They hit me on the head," Garion mumbled, his hand going to the swelling behind his ear.

"They won't do it again," Barak muttered, his tone still despairing. Then the huge man sank to the ground and buried his face in his hands. It was dark and difficult to see, but it looked as if Barak's shoulders were shaking with a kind of terrible suppressed grief—a soundless, wrenching series of convulsive sobs.

"Where are we?" Garion asked, looking around into the darkness.

Barak coughed and wiped at his face. "Quite a ways

from the tents. It took me a little while to catch up to the two who were carrying you off."

"What happened?" Garion was still a bit confused.

"They're dead. Can you stand up?"

"I don't know." Garion tried to get up, but a wave of giddiness swept over him, and his stomach churned.

"Never mind. I'll carry you," Barak said in a now-grimly practical voice. An owl screeched from a nearby tree, and its ghostly white shape drifted off through the trees ahead of them. As Barak lifted him, Garion closed his eyes and concentrated on keeping his stomach under control.

Before long they came out into the clearing and its circle of firelight. "Is he all right?" Aunt Pol asked, looking up from bandaging a cut on Durnik's arm.

"A bump on the head is all," Barak replied, setting Garion down. "Did you run them off?" His voice was harsh, even brutal.

"Those that could still run," Silk answered, his voice a bit excited and his ferret eyes bright. "They left a few behind." He pointed at a number of still shapes lying near the edge of the firelight.

Lelldorin came back into the clearing, looking over his shoulder and with his bow half-drawn. He was out of breath, his face was pale, and his hands were shaking. "Are you all right?" he asked as soon as he saw Garion.

Garion nodded, gently fingering the lump behind his ear.

"I tried to find the two who took you," the young man declared, "but they were too quick for me. There's some kind of animal out there. I heard it growling while I was looking for you—awful growls."

"The beast is gone now," Barak told him flatly.

"What's the matter with you?" Silk asked the big man.

"Nothing."

"Who were these men?" Garion asked.

"Robbers, most likely," Silk surmised, putting away his dagger. "It's one of the benefits of a society that holds men in serfdom. They get bored with being serfs and go out into the forest looking for excitement and profit."

"You sound just like Garion," Lelldorin objected. "Can't

you people understand that serfdom's part of the natural order of things here? Our serfs couldn't take care of themselves alone, so those of us in higher station accept the responsibility of caring for them."

"Of course you do," Silk agreed sarcastically. "They're not so well-fed as your pigs nor as well-kenneled as your dogs, but you do care for them, don't you?"

"That'll do, Silk," Aunt Pol said coolly. "Let's not start bickering among ourselves." She tied a last knot on Durnik's bandage and came over to examine Garion's head. She touched her fingers gently to the lump, and he winced. "It doesn't seem too serious," she observed.

"It hurts all the same," he complained.

"Of course it does, dear," she said calmly. She dipped a cloth in a pail of cold water and held it to the lump. "You're going to have to learn to protect your head, Garion. If you keep banging it like this, you're going to soften your brains."

Garion was about to answer that, but Hettar and Mister Wolf came back into the firelight just then. "They're still running," Hettar announced. The steel discs on his horsehide jacket gleamed red in the flickering light, and his sabre was streaked with blood.

"They seemed to be awfully good at that part of it," Wolf said. "Is everyone all right?"

"A few bumps and bruises is about all," Aunt Pol told him. "It could have been much worse."

"Let's not start worrying about what could have been."

"Shall we remove those?" Barak growled, pointing at the bodies littering the ground near the brook.

"Shouldn't they be buried?" Durnik asked. His voice shook a little, and his face was very pale.

"Too much trouble," Barak said bluntly. "Their friends can come back later and take care of it—if they feel like it."

"Isn't that just a little uncivilized?" Durnik objected.

Barak shrugged. "It's customary."

Mister Wolf rolled one of the bodies over and carefully examined the dead man's gray face. "Looks like an ordinary Arendish outlaw," he grunted. "It's hard to say for sure, though."

Lelldorin was retrieving his arrows, carefully pulling them out of the bodies.

"Let's drag them all over there a ways," Barak said to Hettar. "I'm getting tired of looking at them."

Durnik looked away, and Garion saw two great tears standing in his eyes. "Does it hurt, Durnik?" he asked sympathetically, sitting on the log beside his friend.

"I killed one of those men, Garion," the smith replied in a shaking voice. "I hit him in the face with my axe. He screamed, and his blood splashed all over me. Then he fell down and kicked on the ground with his heels until he died."

"You didn't have any choice, Durnik," Garion told him. "They were trying to kill us."

"I've never killed anyone before," Durnik said, the tears now running down his face. "He kicked the ground for such a long time—such a terribly long time."

"Why don't you go to bed, Garion?" Aunt Pol suggested firmly. Her eyes were on Durnik's tear-streaked face.

Garion understood. "Good night, Durnik," he said. He got up and started toward one of the tents. He glanced back once. Aunt Pol had seated herself on the log beside the smith and was speaking quietly to him with one of her arms comfortingly about his shoulders.

Chapter Five

THE FIRE HAD BURNED down to a tiny orange flicker outside the tent, and the forest around the clearing was silent. Garion lay with a throbbing head trying to sleep. Finally, long past midnight, he gave it up. He slid out from under his blanket and went searching for Aunt Pol.

Above the silvery fog a full moon had risen, and its light

made the mist luminous. The air around him seemed almost to glow as he picked his way carefully through the silent camp. He scratched on the outside of her tent flap and whispered, "Aunt Pol?" There was no answer. "Aunt Pol," he whispered a bit louder, "it's me, Garion. May I come in?" There was still no answer, nor even the faintest sound. Carefully he pulled back the flap and peered inside. The tent was empty.

Puzzled, even a bit alarmed, he turned and looked around the clearing. Hettar stood watch not far from the picketed horses, his hawk face turned toward the foggy forest and his cape drawn about him. Garion hesitated a moment and then stepped quietly behind the tents. He angled down through the trees and the filmy, luminous fog toward the brook, thinking that if he bathed his aching head in cold water it might help. He was about fifty yards from the tents when he saw a faint movement among the trees ahead. He stopped.

A huge gray wolf padded out of the fog and stopped in the center of a small open space among the trees. Garion drew in his breath sharply and froze beside a large, twisted oak. The wolf sat down on the damp leaves as if he were waiting for something. The glowing fog illuminated details Garion would not have been able to see on an ordinary night. The wolf's ruff and shoulders were silvery, and his muzzle was shot with gray. He carried his age with enormous dignity, and his yellow eyes seemed calm and very wise somehow.

Garion stood absolutely still. He knew that the slightest sound would instantly reach the sharp ears of the wolf, but it was more than that. The blow behind his ear had made him light-headed, and the strange glow of moon-drenched fog made this encounter seem somehow unreal. He found that he was holding his breath.

A large, snowy white owl swooped over the open space among the trees on ghosting wings, settled on a low branch and perched there, looking down at the wolf with an unblinking stare. The gray wolf looked calmly back at the perched bird. Then, though there was no breath of wind, it seemed somehow that a sudden eddy in the shimmering fog made the figures of the owl and the wolf hazy and indistinct. When it cleared again, Mister Wolf stood in the center of the opening, and Aunt Pol in her gray gown was seated rather sedately on the limb above him.

"It's been a long time since we've hunted together, Polgara," the old man said.

"Yes, it has, father." She raised her arms and pushed her fingers through the long, dark weight of her hair. "I'd almost forgotten what it was like." She seemed to shudder then with a strange kind of pleasure. "It's a very good night for it."

"A little damp," he replied, shaking one foot.

"It's very clear above the treetops, and the stars are particularly bright. It's a splendid night for flying."

"I'm glad you enjoyed yourself. Did you happen to remember what you were supposed to be doing?"

"Don't be sarcastic, father."

"Well?"

"There's no one in the vicinity but Arends, and most of them are asleep."

"You're sure?"

"Of course. There isn't a Grolim for five leagues in any direction. Did you find the ones you were looking for?"

"They weren't hard to follow," Wolf answered. "They're staying in a cave about three leagues deeper into the forest. Another one of them died on their way back there, and a couple more probably won't live until morning. The rest of them seemed a little bitter about the way things turned out."

"I can imagine. Did you get close enough to hear what they were saying?"

He nodded. "There's a man in one of the villages nearby who watches the road and lets them know when somebody passes by who might be worth robbing."

"Then they're just ordinary thieves?"

"Not exactly. They were watching for us in particular. We'd all been described to them in rather complete detail."

"I think I'll go talk to this villager," she said grimly. She flexed her fingers in an unpleasantly suggestive manner.

"It's not worth the time it would take," Wolf told her,

scratching thoughtfully at his beard. "All he'd be able to tell you is that some Murgo offered him gold. Grolims don't bother to explain very much to their hirelings."

"We should attend to him, father," she insisted. "We don't want him lurking behind us, trying to buy up every brigand in Arendia to send after us."

"After tomorrow he won't buy much of anything," Wolf replied with a short laugh. "His friends plan to lure him out into the woods in the morning and cut his throat for him—among other things."

"Good. I'd like to know who the Grolim is, though."

Wolf shrugged. "What difference does it make? There are dozens of them in northern Arendia, all stirring up as much trouble as they can. They know what's coming as well as we do. We can't expect them to just sit back and let us pass."

"Shouldn't we put a stop to it?"

"We don't have the time," he said. "It takes forever to explain things to Arends. If we move fast enough, maybe we can slip by before the Grolims are ready."

"And if we can't?"

"Then we'll do it the other way. I've got to get to Zedar before he crosses into Cthol Murgos. If too many things get in my way, I'll have to be more direct."

"You should have done that from the beginning, father. Sometimes you're too delicate about things."

"Are you going to start that again? That's always your answer to everything, Polgara. You're forever fixing things that would fix themselves if you'd just leave them alone, and changing things when they don't have to be changed."

"Don't be cross, father. Help me down."

"Why not fly down?" he suggested.

"Don't be absurd."

Garion slipped away among the mossy trees, trembling violently as he went.

When Aunt Pol and Mister Wolf returned to the clearing, they roused the others. "I think we'd better move on," Wolf told them. "We're a little vulnerable out here. It's safer on the highway, and I'd like to get past this particular stretch of woods."

The dismantling of their night's encampment took less

than an hour, and they started back along the woodcutter's track toward the Great West Road. Though it was still some hours before dawn, the moon-bathed fog filled the night with misty luminosity, and it seemed almost as if they rode through a shining cloud that had settled among the dark trees. They reached the highway and turned south again.

"I'd like to be a good way from here when the sun comes up," Wolf said quietly, "but we don't want to blunder into anything, so keep your eyes and ears open."

They set off at a canter and had covered a good three leagues by the time the fog had begun to turn a pearly gray with the approach of morning. As they rounded a broad curve, Hettar suddenly raised his arm, signaling for a halt.

"What's wrong?" Barak asked him.

"Horses ahead," Hettar replied. "Coming this way."

"Are you sure? I don't hear anything."

"Forty at least," Hettar answered firmly.

"There," Durnik said, his head cocked to one side. "Hear that?"

Faintly they all heard a jingling clatter some distance off in the fog.

"We could hide in the woods until they've passed," Lelldorin suggested.

"It's better to stay on the road," Wolf replied.

"Let me handle it," Silk said confidently, moving into the lead. "I've done this sort of thing before." They proceeded at a careful walk.

The riders who emerged from the fog were encased in steel. They wore full suits of polished armor and round helmets with pointed visors that made them look strangely like huge insects. They carried long lances with colored pennons at their tips, and their horses were massive beasts, also encased in armor.

"Mimbrate knights," Lelldorin snarled, his eyes going flat.

"Keep your feelings to yourself," Wolf told the young man. "If any of them say anything to you, answer in such a way that they'll think you're a Mimbrate sympathizer— like young Berentain back at your uncle's house."

Lelldorin's face hardened.

"Do as he tells you, Lelldorin," Aunt Pol said. "This isn't the time for heroics."

"Hold!" the leader of the armored column commanded, lowering his lance until the steel point was leveled at them. "Let one come forward so that I may speak with him." The knight's tone was peremptory.

Silk moved toward the steel-cased man, his smile ingratiating. "We're glad to see you, Sir Knight," he lied glibly. "We were set upon by robbers last night, and we've been riding in fear of our lives."

"What is thy name?" the knight demanded, raising his visor, "and who are these who accompany thee?"

"I am Radek of Boktor, my Lord," Silk answered, bowing and pulling off his velvet cap, "a merchant of Drasnia bound for Tol Honeth with Sendarian woolens in hopes of catching the winter market."

The armored man's eyes narrowed suspiciously. "Thy party seems overlarge for so simple an undertaking, worthy merchant."

"The three there are my servants," Silk told him, pointing at Barak, Hettar, and Durnik. "The old man and the boy serve my sister, a widow of independent means who accompanies me so that she might visit Tol Honeth."

"What of the other?" the knight pressed. "The Asturian?"

"A young nobleman traveling to Vo Mimbre to visit friends there. He graciously consented to guide us through this forest."

The knight's suspicion seemed to relax a bit. "Thou madest mention of robbers," he said. "Where did this ambush take place?"

"About three or four leagues back. They set upon us after we had made our night's encampment. We managed to beat them off, but my sister was terrified."

"This province of Asturia seethes with rebellion and brigandage," the knight said sternly. "My men and I are sent to suppress such offenses. Come here, Asturian."

Lelldorin's nostrils flared, but he obediently came forward.

"I will require thy name of thee."

"My name is Lelldorin, Sir Knight. How may I serve thee?"

"These robbers thy friends spoke of—were they commons or men of quality?"

"Serfs, my Lord," Lelldorin replied, "ragged and uncouth. Doubtless fled from lawful submission to their masters to take up outlawry in the forest."

"How may we expect duty and proper submission from serfs when nobles raise detestable rebellion against the crown?" the knight asserted.

"Truly, my Lord," Lelldorin agreed with a show of sadness that was a trifle overdone. "Much have I argued that selfsame point with those who speak endlessly of Mimbrate oppression and o'erweening arrogance. My appeals for reason and dutiful respect for His Majesty, our Lord King, however, are greeted with derision and cold despite." He sighed.

"Thy wisdom becomes thee, young Lelldorin," the knight approved. "Regrettably, I must detain thee and thy companions in order that we may verify certain details."

"Sir Knight!" Silk protested vigorously. "A change in the weather could destroy the value of my merchandise in Tol Honeth. I pray you, don't delay me."

"I regret the necessity, good merchant," the knight replied, "but Asturia is filled with dissemblers and plotters. I can permit none to pass without meticulous examination."

There was a stir at the rear of the Mimbrate column. In single file, resplendent in burnished breastplates, plumed helmets and crimson capes, a half a hundred Tolnedran legionnaires rode slowly along the flank of the armored knights. "What seems to be the problem here?" the legion commander, a lean, leather-faced man of forty or so, asked politely as he stopped not far from Silk's horse.

"We do not require the assistance of the legions in this matter," the knight said coldly. "Our orders are from Vo Mimbre. We are sent to help restore order in Asturia and we were questioning these travelers to that end."

"I have a great respect for order, Sir Knight," the Tolnedran replied, "but the security of the highway is *my* responsibility." He looked inquiringly at Silk.

"I am Radek of Boktor, Captain," Silk told him, "a

Drasnian merchant bound for Tol Honeth. I have documents, if you wish to see them."

"Documents are easily forged," the knight declared.

"So they are," the Tolnedran agreed, "but to save time I
make it a practice to accept all documents at face value. A
Drasnian merchant with goods in his packs has a legitimate
reason to be on an Imperial Highway, Sir Knight. There's
no reason to detain him, is there?"

"We seek to stamp out banditry and rebellion," the
knight asserted hotly.

"Stamp away," the captain said, "but *off* the highway, if
you don't mind. By treaty the Imperial Highway is Tolnedran territory. What you do once you're fifty yards back in
the trees is your affair; what happens on this road is *mine*.
I'm certain that no true Mimbrate knight would want to
humiliate his king by violating a solemn agreement between
the Arendish crown and the Emperor of Tolnedra, would
he?"

The knight looked at him helplessly.

"I think you should proceed, good merchant," the Tolnedran told Silk. "I know that all Tol Honeth awaits your
arrival breathlessly."

Silk grinned at him and bowed floridly in his saddle.
Then he gestured to the others and they all rode slowly
past the fuming Mimbrate knight. After they had passed,
the legionnaires closed ranks across the highway, effectively cutting off any pursuit.

"Good man there," Barak said. "I don't think much of
Tolnedrans ordinarily, but that one's different."

"Let's move right along," Mister Wolf said. "I'd rather
not have those knights doubling back on us after the Tolnedrans leave."

They pushed their horses into a gallop and rode on,
leaving the knights behind, arguing heatedly with the legion commander in the middle of the road.

They stayed that night at a thick-walled Tolnedran hostel, and for perhaps the first time in his life Garion bathed
without the insistence or even the suggestion of his Aunt.
Though he had not had the chance to become directly involved in the fight in the clearing the night before, he
felt somehow as if he were spattered with blood or worse.

He had not before realized how grotesquely men could be mutilated in close fighting. Watching a living man disembowled or brained had filled him with a kind of deep shame that the ultimate inner secrets of the human body could be so grossly exposed. He felt unclean. He removed his clothing in the chilly bathhouse and even, without thinking, the silver amulet Mister Wolf and Aunt Pol had given him, and then he entered the steaming tub where he scrubbed at his skin with a coarse brush and strong soap, much harder than even the most meticulous obsession with personal cleanliness would have required.

For the next several days they moved southward at a steady pace, stopping each night at the evenly spaced Tolnedran hostels where the presence of the hard-faced legionnaires was a continual reminder that all the might of Imperial Tolnedra guaranteed the safety of travelers who sought refuge there.

On the sixth day after the fight in the forest, however, Lelldorin's horse pulled up lame. Durnik and Hettar, under Aunt Pol's supervision, spent several hours brewing poultices over a small fire by the roadside and applying steaming compresses to the animal's leg while Wolf fumed at the delay. By the time the horse was fit to continue, they all realized that there was no chance to reach the next hostel before dark.

"Well, Old Wolf," Aunt Pol said after they had remounted, "what now? Do we ride on at night, or do we try to take shelter in the forest again?"

"I haven't decided," Wolf answered shortly.

"If I remember right, there's a village not far ahead," Lelldorin, now mounted on an Algar horse, stated. "It's a poor place, but I think it has an inn—of sorts."

"That sounds ominous," Silk said. "What exactly do you mean by 'of sorts'?"

"The Lord of this demesne is notoriously greedy," Lelldorin replied. "His taxes are crushing, and his people have little left for themselves. The inn isn't good."

"We'll have to chance it," Wolf decided, and led them off at a brisk trot. As they approached the village, the heavy clouds began to clear off, and the sun broke through wanly.

The village was even worse than Lelldorin's description had led them to believe. A half-dozen ragged beggars stood in the mud on the outskirts, their hands held out imploringly and their voices shrill. The houses were nothing more than rude hovels oozing smoke from the pitiful fires within. Scrawny pigs rooted in the muddy streets, and the stench of the place was awful.

A funeral procession slogged through the mud toward the burial ground on the other side of the village. The corpse, carried on a board, was wrapped in a ragged brown blanket, and the richly robed and cowled priests of Chaldan, the Arendish God, chanted an age-old hymn that had much to do with war and vengeance, but little to do with comfort. The widow, a whimpering infant at her breast, followed the body, her face blank and her eyes dead.

The inn smelled of stale beer and half-rotten food. A fire had destroyed one end of the common room, charring and blackening the low-beamed ceiling. The gaping hole in the burned wall was curtained off with a sheet of rotting canvas. The fire pit in the center of the room smoked, and the hard-faced innkeeper was surly. For supper he offered only bowls of watery gruel—a mixture of barley and turnips.

"Charming," Silk said sardonically, pushing away his untouched bowl. "I'm a bit surprised at you, Lelldorin. Your passion for correcting wrongs seems to have overlooked this place. Might I suggest that your next crusade include a visit to the Lord of this demesne? His hanging seems long overdue."

"I hadn't realized it was so bad," Lelldorin replied in a subdued voice. He looked around as if seeing certain things for the first time. A kind of sick horror began to show itself in his transparent face.

Garion, his stomach churning, stood up. "I think I'll go outside," he declared.

"Not too far," Aunt Pol warned.

The air outside was at least somewhat cleaner, and Garion picked his way carefully toward the edge of the village, trying to avoid the worst of the mud.

"Please, my Lord," a little girl with huge eyes begged, "have you a crust of bread to spare?"

Garion looked at her helplessly. "I'm sorry." He fumbled

through his clothes, looking for something to give her, but the child began to cry and turned away.

In the stump-dotted field beyond the stinking streets, a ragged boy about Garion's own age was playing a wooden flute as he watched a few scrubby cows. The melody he played was heartbreakingly pure, drifting unnoticed among the hovels squatting in the slanting rays of the pale sun. The boy saw him, but did not break off his playing. Their eyes met with a kind of grave recognition, but they did not speak.

At the edge of the forest beyond the field, a dark-robed and hooded man astride a black horse came out of the trees and sat watching the village. There was something ominous about the dark figure, and something vaguely familiar as well. It seemed somehow to Garion that he should know who the rider was, but, though his mind groped for a name, it tantalizingly eluded him. He looked at the figure at the edge of the woods for a long time, noticing without even being aware of it that though the horse and rider stood in the full light of the setting sun, there was no shadow behind them. Deep in his mind something tried to shriek at him, but, all bemused, he merely watched. He would not say anything to Aunt Pol or the others about the figure at the edge of the woods because there was nothing to say; as soon as he turned his back, he would forget.

The light began to fade, and, because he had begun to shiver, he turned to go back to the inn with the aching song of the boy's flute soaring toward the sky above him.

Chapter Six

DESPITE THE PROMISE of the brief sunset, the next day dawned cold and murky with a chill drizzle that wreathed down among the trees and made the entire forest sodden and gloomy. They left the inn early and soon entered a part of the wood that seemed more darkly foreboding than even the ominous stretches through which they had previously passed. The trees here were enormous, and many vast, gnarled oaks lifted their bare limbs among the dark firs and spruces. The forest floor was covered with a kind of gray moss that looked diseased and unwholesome.

Lelldorin had spoken little that morning, and Garion assumed that his friend was still struggling with the problem of Nachak's scheme. The young Asturian rode along, wrapped in his heavy green cloak, his reddish-gold hair damp and dispirited-looking in the steady drizzle. Garion pulled in beside his friend, and they rode silently for a while. "What's troubling you, Lelldorin?" he asked finally.

"I think that all my life I've been blind, Garion," Lelldorin replied.

"Oh? In what way?" Garion said it carefully, hoping that his friend had finally decided to tell Mister Wolf everything.

"I saw only Mimbre's oppression of Asturia. I never saw our own oppression of our own people."

"I've been trying to tell you that," Garion pointed out. "What made you see it finally?"

"That village where we stayed last night," Lelldorin explained. "I've never seen so poor and mean a place—or people crushed into such hopeless misery. How can they bear it?"

"Do they have any choice?"

"My father at least looks after the people on his land," the young man asserted defensively. "No one goes hungry or without shelter—but those people are treated worse than animals. I've always been proud of my station, but now it makes me ashamed." Tears actually stood in his eyes.

Garion was not sure how to deal with his friend's sudden awakening. On the one hand, he was glad that Lelldorin had finally seen what had always been obvious; but on the other, he was more than a little afraid of what this new-found perception might cause his mercurial companion to leap into.

"I'll renounce my rank," Lelldorin declared suddenly, as if he had been listening to Garion's thoughts, "and when I return from this quest, I'll go among the serfs and share their lives—their sorrows."

"What good will that do? How would your suffering in any way make theirs less?"

Lelldorin looked up sharply, a half-dozen emotions chasing each other across his open face. Finally he smiled, but there was a determination in his blue eyes. "You're right, of course," he said. "You always are. It's amazing how you can always see directly to the heart of a problem, Garion."

"Just what have you got in mind?" Garion asked a little apprehensively.

"I'll lead them in revolt. I'll sweep across Arendia with an army of serfs at my back." His voice rang as his imagination fired with the idea.

Garion groaned. "Why is that always your answer to everything, Lelldorin?" he demanded. "In the first place, the serfs don't have any weapons and they don't know how to fight. No matter how hard you talk, you'd never get them to follow you. In the second place, if they did, every nobleman in Arendia would join ranks against you. They'd butcher your army; and afterward, things would be ten times worse. In the third place, you'd just be starting another civil war; and that's exactly what the Murgos want."

Lelldorin blinked several times as Garion's words sank in. His face gradually grew mournful again. "I hadn't thought of that," he confessed.

"I didn't think you had. You're going to keep making these mistakes as long as you keep carrying your brain in the same scabbard with your sword, Lelldorin."

Lelldorin flushed at that, and then he laughed ruefully. "That's a pointed way of putting it, Garion," he said reproachfully.

"I'm sorry," Garion apologized quickly. "Maybe I should have said it another way."

"No," Lelldorin told him. "I'm an Arend. I tend to miss things if they aren't said directly."

"It's not that you're stupid, Lelldorin," Garion protested. "That's a mistake everyone makes. Arends aren't stupid—they're just impulsive."

"All *this* was more than just impulsiveness," Lelldorin

insisted sadly, gesturing out at the damp moss lying under the trees.

"This what?" Garion asked, looking around.

"This is the last stretch of forest before we come out on the plains of central Arendia," Lelldorin explained. "It's the natural boundary between Mimbre and Asturia."

"The woods look the same as all the rest," Garion observed, looking around.

"Not really," Lelldorin said somberly. "This was the favorite ground for ambush. The floor of this forest is carpeted with old bones. Look there." He pointed.

At first it seemed to Garion that what his friend indicated was merely a pair of twisted sticks protruding from the moss with the twigs at their ends entangled in a scrubby bush. Then, with revulsion, he realized that they were the greenish bones of a human arm, the fingers clutched at the bush in a last convulsive agony. Outraged, he demanded, "Why didn't they bury him?"

"It would take a thousand men a thousand years to gather all the bones that lie here and commit them to earth," Lelldorin intoned morbidly. "Whole generations of Arendia rest here—Mimbrate, Wacite, Asturian. All lie where they fell, and the moss blankets their endless slumber."

Garion shuddered and pulled his eyes away from the mute appeal of that lone arm rising from the sea of moss on the floor of the forest. The curious lumps and hummocks of that moss suggested the horror which lay moldering beneath. As he raised his eyes, he realized that the uneven surface extended as far as he could see. "How long until we reach the plain?" he asked in a hushed voice.

"Two days, probably."

"*Two days*? And it's all like *this*?"

Lelldorin nodded.

"*Why*?" Garion's tone was harsher, more accusing than he'd intended.

"At first for pride—and honor," Lelldorin replied. "Later for grief and revenge. Finally it was simply because we didn't know how to stop. As you said before, sometimes we Arends aren't very bright."

"But always brave," Garion answered quickly.

"Oh yes," Lelldorin admitted. "Always brave. It's our national curse."

"Belgarath," Hettar said quietly from behind them, "the horses smell something."

Mister Wolf roused himself from the doze in which he usually rode. "What?"

"The horses," Hettar repeated. "Something out there's frightening them."

Wolf's eyes narrowed and then grew strangely blank. After a moment he drew in a sharp breath with a muttered curse. "Algroths," he swore.

"What's an Algroth?" Durnik asked.

"A non-human—somewhat distantly related to Trolls."

"I saw a Troll once," Barak said. "A big ugly thing with claws and fangs."

"Will they attack us?" Durnik asked.

"Almost certainly." Wolf's voice was tense. "Hettar, you're going to have to keep the horses under control. We don't dare get separated."

"Where did they come from?" Lelldorin asked. "There aren't any monsters in this forest."

"They come down out of the mountains of Ulgo sometimes when they get hungry," Wolf answered. "They don't leave survivors to report their presence."

"You'd better do something, father," Aunt Pol said. "They're all around us."

Lelldorin looked quickly around as if getting his bearings. "We're not far from Elgon's tor," he offered. "We might be able to hold them off if we get there."

"Elgon's tor?" Barak said. He had already drawn his heavy sword.

"It's a high hillock covered with boulders," Lelldorin explained. "It's almost like a fort. Elgon held it for a month against a Mimbrate army."

"Sounds promising," Silk said. "It would get us out of the trees at least." He looked nervously around at the forest looming about them in the drizzling rain.

"Let's try for it," Wolf decided. "They haven't worked themselves up to the point of attacking yet, and the rain's confusing their sense of smell."

A strange barking sound came from back in the forest.

"Is that them?" Garion asked, his voice sounding shrill in his own ears.

"They're calling to each other," Wolf told him. "Some of them have seen us. Let's pick up the pace a bit, but don't start running until we see the tor."

They nudged their nervous horses into a trot and moved steadily along the muddy road as it began to climb toward the top of a low ridge. "Half a league," Lelldorin said tensely. "Half a league and we should see the tor."

The horses were difficult to hold in, and their eyes rolled wildly at the surrounding woods. Garion felt his heart pounding, and his mouth was suddenly dry. It started to rain a bit harder. He caught a movement out of the corner of his eye and looked quickly. A manlike figure was loping along parallel to the road about a hundred paces back in the forest. It ran half-crouched, its hands touching the ground. It seemed to be a loathsome gray color. "Over there!" Garion cried.

"I saw him," Barak growled. "Not quite as big as a Troll."

Silk grimaced. "Big enough."

"If they attack, be careful of their claws," Wolf warned. "They're venomous."

"That's exciting," Silk said.

"There's the tor," Aunt Pol announced quite calmly.

"Let's run!" Wolf barked.

The frightened horses, suddenly released, leaped forward and fled up the road, their hoofs churning. An enraged howl came from the woods behind them, and the barking sound grew louder all around them.

"We're going to make it!" Durnik shouted in encouragement. But suddenly a half-dozen snarling Algroths were in the road in front of them, their arms spread wide and their mouths gaping hideously. They were huge, with apelike arms and claws instead of fingers. Their faces were goatish, surmounted by short, sharp-pointed horns, and they had long, yellow fangs. Their gray skin was scaly, reptilian.

The horses screamed and reared, trying to bolt. Garion clung to his saddle with one hand and fought the reins with the other.

Barak beat at his horse's rump with the flat of his sword and kicked savagely at the animal's flanks until the horse, finally more afraid of him than the Algroths, charged. With two great sweeps, one to either side, Barak killed two of the beasts as he plunged through. A third, claws outstretched, tried to leap on his back, but stiffened and collapsed facedown in the mud with one of Lelldorin's arrows between its shoulders. Barak wheeled his horse and chopped at the three remaining creatures. "Let's go!" he bellowed.

Garion heard Lelldorin gasp and turned quickly. With sick horror he saw that a lone Algroth had crept out of the woods beside the road and was clawing at his friend, trying to hook him out of the saddle. Weakly, Lelldorin beat at the goat face with his bow. Garion desperately drew his sword, but Hettar, coming from behind, was already there. His curved sabre ran through the beast's body, and the Algroth shrieked and fell writhing to the ground beneath the pounding hoofs of the pack animals.

The horses, running now in sheer panic, scrambled toward the slope of the boulder-strewn tor. Garion glanced back over his shoulder and saw Lelldorin swaying dangerously in his saddle, his hand pressed to his bleeding side. Garion pulled in savagely on his reins and turned his horse.

"Save yourself, Garion!" Lelldorin shouted, his face deadly pale.

"No!" Garion sheathed his sword, pulled in beside his friend and took his arm, steadying him in the saddle. Together they galloped toward the tor with Garion straining to hold the injured young man.

The tor was a great jumble of earth and stone thrusting up above the tallest trees around it. Their horses scrambled and clattered up the side among the wet boulders. When they reached the small flat area at the top of the tor where the pack animals huddled together, trembling in the rain, Garion slid out of his saddle in time to catch Lelldorin, who toppled slowly to one side.

"Over here," Aunt Pol called sharply. She was pulling her small bundle of herbs and bandages out of one of the packs. "Durnik, I'll need a fire—at once."

Durnik looked around helplessly at the few scraps of
wood lying in the rain at the top of the tor. "I'll try," he
said doubtfully.

Lelldorin's breathing was shallow and very fast. His face
was still a deadly white, and his legs would not hold him.
Garion held him up, a sick fear in the pit of his stomach.
Hettar took the wounded man's other arm, and between
them they half-carried him to where Aunt Pol knelt, opening her bundle. "I have to get the poison out immediately,"
she told them. "Garion, give me your knife."

Garion drew his dagger and handed it it her. Swiftly she
ripped open Lelldorin's brown tunic along his side, revealing the savage wounds the Algroth's claws had made. "This
will hurt," she said. "Hold him."

Garion and Hettar took hold of Lelldorin's arms and
legs, holding him down.

Aunt Pol took a deep breath and then deftly sliced open
each of the puffy wounds. Blood spurted and Lelldorin
screamed once. Then he fainted.

"Hettar!" Barak shouted from atop a boulder near the
edge of the slope. "We need you!"

"Go!" Aunt Pol told the hawk-faced Algar. "We can
handle this now. Garion, you stay here." She was crushing
some dried leaves and sprinkling the fragments into the
bleeding wounds. "The fire, Durnik," she ordered.

"It won't start, Mistress Pol," Durnik replied helplessly.
"It's too wet."

She looked quickly at the pile of sodden wood the smith
had gathered. Her eyes narrowed, and she made a quick
gesture. Garion's ears rang strangely and there was a sudden hissing. A cloud of steam burst from the wood, and
then crackling flames curled up from the sticks. Durnik
jumped back, startled.

"The small pot, Garion," Aunt Pol instructed, "and water. Quickly." She pulled off her blue cloak and covered
Lelldorin with it.

Silk, Barak and Hettar stood at the edge of the slope,
heaving large rocks over the edge. Garion could hear the
clatter and clash of the rocks striking the boulders below
and the barking of the Algroths, punctuated by an occasional howl of pain.

He cradled his friend's head in his lap, terribly afraid. "Is he going to be all right?" he appealed to Aunt Pol.

"It's too early to tell," she answered. "Don't bother me with questions just now."

"They're running!" Barak shouted.

"They're still hungry," Wolf replied grimly. "They'll be back."

From far off in the forest there came the sound of a brassy horn.

"What's that?" Silk asked, still puffing from the effort of heaving the heavy stones over the edge.

"Someone I've been expecting," Wolf answered with a strange smile. He raised his hands to his lips and whistled shrilly.

"I can manage now, Garion," Aunt Pol said, mashing a thick paste into a steaming pad of wet linen bandage. "You and Durnik go help the others."

Reluctantly Garion lowered Lelldorin's head to the wet turf and ran over to where Wolf stood. The slope below was littered with dead and dying Algroths, crushed by the rocks Barak and the others had hurled down on them.

"They're going to try again," Barak said, hefting another rock. "Can they get at us from behind?"

Silk shook his head. "No. I checked. The back of the hill's a sheer face."

The Algroths came out of the woods below, barking and snarling as they loped forward with their half-crouched gait. The first of them had already crossed the road when the horn blew again, very close this time.

And then a huge horse bearing a man in full armor burst out of the trees and thundered down upon the attacking creatures. The armored man crouched over his lance and plunged directly into the midst of the startled Algroths. The great horse screamed as he charged, and his iron-shod hoofs churned up big clots of mud. The lance crashed through the chest of one of the largest Algroths and splintered from the force of the blow. The splintered end took another full in the face. The knight discarded the shattered lance and drew his broadsword with a single sweep of his arm. With wide swings to the right and left he chopped his way through the pack, his warhorse trampling the living and the dead alike into the mud of the road. At the end of his charge he whirled and plunged back again, once more opening a path with his sword. The Algroths turned and fled howling into the woods.

"Mandorallen!" Wolf shouted. "Up here!"

The armored knight raised his blood-spattered visor and looked up the hill. "Permit me to disperse this rabble first, my ancient friend," he answered gaily, clanged down his visor, and plunged into the rainy woods after the Algroths.

"Hettar!" Barak shouted, already moving.

Hettar nodded tersely, and the two of them ran to their horses. They swung into their saddles and plunged down the wet slope to the aid of the stranger.

"Your friend shows a remarkable lack of good sense," Silk observed to Mister Wolf, wiping the rain from his face. "Those things will turn on him any second now."

"It probably hasn't occurred to him that he's in any danger," Wolf replied. "He's a Mimbrate, and they tend to think they're invincible."

The fight in the woods seemed to last for a long time. There were shouts and ringing blows and shrieks of terror from the Algroths. Then Hettar, Barak, and the strange knight rode out of the trees and trotted up the tor. At the top, the armored man clanged down from his horse. "Well met, my old friend," he boomed to Mister Wolf. "Thy friends below were most frolicsome." His armor gleamed wetly in the rain.

"I'm glad we found something to entertain you," Wolf said dryly.

"I can still hear them," Durnik reported. "I think they're still running."

"Their cowardice hath deprived us of an amusing afternoon," the knight observed, regretfully sheathing his sword and removing his helmet.

"We must all make sacrifices," Silk drawled.

The knight sighed. "All too true. Thou art a man of philosophy, I see." He shook the water out of the white plume on his helmet.

"Forgive me," Mister Wolf said. "This is Mandorallen, Baron of Vo Mandor. He'll be going with us. Mandorallen, this is Prince Kheldar of Drasnia and Barak, Earl of Trellheim and cousin to King Anheg of Cherek. Over there is Hettar, son of Cho-Hag, chief of the Clan-Chiefs of Algaria. The practical one is Goodman Durnik of Sendaria, and this boy is Garion, my grandson—several times removed."

Mandorallen bowed deeply to each of them. "I greet you, comrades all," he declaimed in his booming voice. "Our adventure hath seen a fortuitous beginning. And pray tell, who is this lady, whose beauty doth bedazzle mine eye?"

"A pretty speech, Sir Knight," Aunt Pol replied with a rich laugh, her hand going almost unconsciously to her damp hair. "I'm going to like this one, father."

"The legendary Lady Polgara?" Mandorallen asked. "My life hath now seen its crown." His courtly bow was somewhat marred by the creaking of his armor.

"Our injured friend is Lelldorin, son of the Baron of Wildantor," Wolf continued. "You may have heard of him."

Mandorallen's face darkened slightly. "Indeed. Rumor, which sometimes doth run before us like a barking dog, hath suggested that Lelldorin of Wildantor hath raised on occasion foul rebellion against the crown."

"That's of no matter now," Wolf stressed. "The business which has brought us together is much more serious than all that. You'll have to put it aside."

"It shall be as you say, noble Belgarath," Mandorallen declared immediately, though his eyes still lingered on the unconscious Lelldorin.

"Grandfather!" Garion called, pointing at a mounted figure that had suddenly appeared on the side of the stony hilltop. The figure was robed in black and sat a black horse. He pushed back his hood to reveal a polished steel mask cast in the form of a face that was at once beautiful and strangely repelling. A voice deep in Garion's mind told him that there was something important about the strange rider—something he should remember—but whatever it was eluded him.

"Abandon this quest, Belgarath." The voice was hollow behind the mask.

"You know me better than that, Chamdar," Mister Wolf

said calmly, quite obviously recognizing the rider. "Was this childishness with the Algroths your idea?"

"And you should know *me* better than that," the figure retorted derisively. "When I come against you, you can expect things to be a bit more serious. For now, there are enough underlings about to delay you. That's all we really need. Once Zedar has carried Cthrag Yaska to my Master, you can try your power against the might and will of Torak, if you'd like."

"Are you running errands for Zedar, then?" Wolf asked.

"I run no man's errands," the figure replied with heavy contempt. The rider seemed solid, as real as any of them standing on the hilltop, but Garion could see the filmy drizzle striking the rocks directly beneath horse and man. Whatever the figure was, the rain was falling right through it.

"Why are you here then, Chamdar?" Wolf demanded.

"Let's call it curiosity, Belgarath. I wanted to see for myself how you'd managed to translate the Prophecy into everyday terms." The figure looked around at the others on the hilltop. "Clever," it said with a certain grudging admiration. "Where did you find them all?"

"I didn't have to find them, Chamdar," Wolf answered. "They've been there all along. If any part of the Prophecy is valid, then it all has to be valid, doesn't it? There's no contrivance involved at all. Each one has come down to me through more generations than you can imagine."

The figure seemed to hiss with a sharp intake of its breath. "It isn't complete yet, old man."

"It will be, Chamdar," Wolf replied confidently. "I've already seen to that."

"Which is the one who will live twice?" the figure asked suddenly.

Wolf smiled coldly, but did not answer.

"Hail, my Queen," the figure said mockingly then to Aunt Pol.

"Grolim courtesy always leaves me quite cold," she returned with a frosty look. "I'm not your queen, Chamdar."

"You will be, Polgara. My Master said that you are to become his wife when he comes into his kingdom. You'll be queen of all the world."

"That puts you at a bit of a disadvantage, doesn't it, Chamdar? If I'm to become your queen, you can't really cross me, can you?"

"I can work around you, Polgara, and once you've become the bride of Torak, his will becomes your will. I'm sure you won't hold any old grudges at that point."

"I think we've had about enough of this, Chamdar," Mister Wolf said. "Your conversation's beginning to bore me. You can have your shadow back now." He waved his hand negligently as if brushing away a troublesome fly. "Go," he commanded.

Once again Garion felt that strange surge and that hollow roaring in his mind. The horseman vanished.

"You didn't destroy him, did you?" Silk gasped in a shocked voice.

"No," Mister Wolf told him. "It was all just an illusion. It's a childish trick the Grolims find impressive. A shadow can be projected over quite some distance if you want to take the trouble. All I did was send his shadow back to him." He grinned suddenly with a sly twist to his lips. "Of course I selected a somewhat indirect route. It may take a few days to make the trip. It won't actually hurt him, but it's going to make him a bit uncomfortable—and extremely conspicuous."

"A most unseemly specter," Mandorallen observed. "Who was this rude shade?"

"It was Chamdar," Aunt Pol said, returning her attention to the injured Lelldorin, "one of the chief priests of the Grolims. Father and I have met him before."

"I think we'd getter get off this hilltop," Wolf stated. "How soon will Lelldorin be able to ride?"

"A week at least," Aunt Pol replied, "if then."

"That's out of the question. We can't stay here."

"He can't ride," she told him firmly.

"Couldn't we make a litter of some sort?" Durnik suggested. "I'm sure I can make something we can sling between two horses so we can move him without hurting him."

"Well, Pol?" Wolf asked.

"I suppose it will be all right," she said a little dubiously.

"Let's do it then. We're much too exposed up here, and we've got to move on."

Durnik nodded and went to the packs for rope to use in building the litter.

Chapter Seven

SIR MANDORALLEN, BARON OF VO MANDOR, was a man of slightly more than medium height. His hair was black and curly, his eyes were deep blue, and he had a resonant voice in which he expressed firmly held opinions. Garion did not like him. The knight's towering self-confidence, an egotism so pure that there was a kind of innocence about it, seemed to confirm the worst of Lelldorin's dark pronouncements about Mimbrates; and Mandorallen's extravagant courtesy to Aunt Pol struck Garion as beyond the bounds of proper civility. To make matters even worse, Aunt Pol seemed quite willing to accept the knight's flatteries at face value.

As they rode through the continuing drizzle along the Great West Road, Garion noted with some satisfaction that his companions appeared to share his opinion. Barak's expression spoke louder than words; Silk's eyebrows lifted sardonically at each of the knight's pronouncements; and Durnik scowled.

Garion, however, had little time to sort out his feelings about the Mimbrate. He rode close beside the litter upon which Lelldorin tossed painfully as the Algroth poison seared in his wounds. He offered his friend what comfort he could and exchanged frequent worried looks with Aunt Pol, who rode nearby. During the worst of Lelldorin's paroxysms, Garion helplessly held the young man's hand, unable to think of anything else to do to ease his pain.

"Bear thine infirmity with fortitude, good youth," Mandorallen cheerfully advised the injured Asturian after a particularly bad bout that left Lelldorin gasping and moaning. "This discomfort of thine is but an illusion. Thy mind can put it to rest if thou wouldst have it so."

"That's exactly the kind of comfort I'd expect from a Mimbrate," Lelldorin retorted from between clenched teeth. "I think I'd rather you didn't ride so close. Your opinions smell almost as bad as your armor."

Mandorallen's face flushed slightly. "The venom which doth rage through the body of our injured friend hath, it would seem, bereft him of civility as well as sense," he observed coldly.

Lelldorin half-raised himself in the litter as if to respond hotly, but the sudden movement seemed to aggravate his injury, and he lapsed into unconsciousness.

"His wounds are grave," Mandorallen stated. "Thy poultice, Lady Polgara, may not suffice to save his life."

"He needs rest," she told him. "Try not to agitate him so much."

"I will place myself beyond the reach of his eye," Mandorallen replied. "Through no fault of mine own, my visage is hateful to him and doth stir him to unhealthful choler." He moved his warhorse ahead at a canter until he was some distance in front of the rest of them.

"Do they all talk like that?" Garion asked with a certain rancor. "Thee's and thou's and doth's?"

"Mimbrates tend to be very formal," Aunt Pol explained. "You'll get used to it."

"I think it sounds stupid," Garion muttered darkly, glaring after the knight.

"An example of good manners won't hurt you all that much, Garion."

They rode on through the dripping forest as evening settled among the trees. "Aunt Pol?" Garion asked finally.

"Yes, dear?"

"What was that Grolim talking about when he said that about you and Torak?"

"It's something Torak said once when he was raving. The Grolims took it seriously, that's all." She pulled her blue cloak tighter about her.

"Doesn't it worry you?"

"Not particularly."

"What was that Prophecy the Grolim was talking about? I didn't understand any of that." The word "Prophecy" for some reason stirred something very deep in him.

"The Mrin Codex," she answered. "It's a very old version, and the writing's almost illegible. It mentions companions—the bear, the rat, and the man who will live twice. It's the only version that says anything about them. Nobody knows for certain that it really means anything."

"Grandfather thinks it does, doesn't he?"

"Your grandfather has a number of curious notions. Old things impress him—probably because he's so old himself."

Garion was going to ask her about this Prophecy that seemed to exist in more than one version, but Lelldorin moaned then and they both immediately turned to him.

They arrived shortly thereafter at a Tolnedran hostel with thick, whitewashed walls and a red tile roof. Aunt Pol saw to it that Lelldorin was placed in a warm room, and she spent the night sitting by his bed caring for him. Garion padded worriedly down the dark hallway in his stocking feet a half-dozen times before morning to check on his friend, but there seemed to be no change.

By daybreak the rain had let up. They started out in the grayish dawn with Mandorallen still riding some distance ahead until they reached at last the edge of the dark forest and saw before them the vast, open expanse of the Arendish central plain, dun-colored and sere in the last few weeks of winter. The knight stopped there and waited for them to join him, his face somber.

"What's the trouble?" Silk asked him.

Mandorallen pointed gravely at a column of black smoke rising from a few miles out on the plain.

"What is it?" Silk inquired, his rat face puzzled.

"Smoke in Arendia can mean but one thing," the knight replied, pulling on his plumed helmet. "Abide here, dear friends. I will investigate, but I fear the worst." He set his spurs to the flanks of his charger and leaped forward at a thunderous gallop.

"Wait!" Barak roared after him, but Mandorallen rode on obliviously. "That idiot," the big Cherek fumed. "I'd better go with him in case there's trouble."

"It isn't necessary," Lelldorin advised weakly from his litter. "Not even an army would dare to interfere with him."

"I thought you didn't like him," Barak said, a little surprised.

"I don't," Lelldorin admitted, "but he's the most feared man in Arendia. Even in Asturia we've heard of Sir Mandorallen. No sane man would stand in his way."

They drew back into the shelter of the forest and waited for the knight to come back. When he returned, his face was angry. "It is as I feared," he announced. "A war doth rage in our path—a senseless war, since the two barons involved are kinsmen and the best of friends."

"Can we go around it?" Silk asked.

"Nay, Prince Kheldar," Mandorallen replied. "Their conflict is so widespread that we would be waylaid ere we had gone three leagues. I must, it would appear, buy us passage."

"Do you think they'll take money to let us pass?" Durnik asked dubiously.

"In Arendia there is another way to make such purchase, Goodman," Mandorallen responded. "May I prevail upon thee to obtain six or eight stout poles perhaps twenty feet in length and about as thick as my wrist at the butt?"

"Of course." Durnik took up his axe.

"What have you got in mind?" Barak rumbled.

"I will challenge them," Mandorallen announced calmly, "one or all. No true knight could refuse me without being called craven. Wilt thou be my second and deliver my challenge, my Lord?"

"What if you lose?" Silk suggested.

"*Lose?*" Mandorallen seemed shocked. "*I?* Lose?"

"Let it pass," Silk said.

By the time Durnik had returned with the poles, Mandorallen had finished tightening various straps beneath his armor. Taking one of the poles, he vaulted into his saddle and started at a rolling trot toward the column of smoke, with Barak at his side.

"Is this really necessary, father?" Aunt Pol asked.

"We have to get through, Pol," Mister Wolf replied. "Don't worry. Mandorallen knows what he's doing."

After a couple of miles they reached the top of a hill and looked down at the battle below. Two grim, black castles faced each other across a broad valley, and several villages dotted the plain on either side of the road. The nearest village was in flames, with a great pillar of greasy smoke rising from it to the lead-gray sky overhead, and serfs armed with scythes and pitchforks were attacking each other with a sort of mindless ferocity on the road itself. Some distance off, pikemen were gathering for a charge, and the air was thick with arrows. On two opposing hills parties of armored knights with bright-colored pennons on their lances watched the battle. Great siege engines lofted boulders into the air to crash down on the struggling men, killing, so far as Garion could tell, friend and foe indiscriminately. The valley was littered with the dead and the dying.

"Stupid," Wolf muttered darkly.

"No one I know of has ever accused Arends of brilliance," Silk observed.

Mandorallen set his horn to his lips and blew a shattering blast. The battle paused as the soldiers and serfs all stopped to stare up at him. He sounded his horn again, and then again, each brassy note a challenge in itself. As the two opposing bodies of knights galloped through the knee-high, winter-yellowed grass to investigate, Mandorallen turned to Barak. "If it please thee, my Lord," he requested politely, "deliver my challenge as soon as they approach us."

Barak shrugged. "It's your skin," he noted. He eyed the advancing knights and then lifted his voice in a great roar. "Sir Mandorallen, Baron of Vo Mandor, desires entertainment," he declaimed. "It would amuse him if each of your parties would select a champion to joust with him. If, however, you are all such cowardly dogs that you have no stomach for such a contest, cease this brawling and stand aside so that your betters may pass."

"Splendidly spoken, my Lord Barak," Mandorallen said with admiration.

"I've always had a way with words," Barak replied modestly.

The two parties of knights warily rode closer.

"For shame, my Lords," Mandorallen chided them. "Ye will gain no honor in this sorry war. Sir Derigen, what hath caused this contention?"

"An insult, Sir Mandorallen," the noble replied. He was a large man, and his polished steel helmet had a golden circlet riveted above the visor. "An insult so vile that it may not go unpunished."

"It was *I* who was insulted," a noble on the other side contended hotly.

"What was the nature of this insult, Sir Oltorain?" Mandorallen inquired.

Both men looked away uneasily, and neither spoke.

"Ye have gone to war over an insult which cannot even be recalled?" Mandorallen said incredulously. "I had thought, my Lords, that ye were serious men, but I now perceive my error."

"Don't the nobles of Arendia have anything better to do?" Barak asked in a voice heavy with contempt.

"Of Sir Mandorallen the bastard we have all heard," a swarthy knight in black enamelled armor sneered, "but who is this red-bearded ape who so maligns his betters?"

"You're going to take that?" Barak asked Mandorallen.

"It's more or less true," Mandorallen admitted with a pained look, "since there was some temporary irregularity about my birth which still raises questions about my legitimacy. This knight is Sir Haldorin, my third cousin—twice removed. Since it's considered unseemly in Arendia to spill the blood of kinsmen, he thus cheaply gains reputation for boldness by casting the matter in my teeth."

"Stupid custom," Barak grunted. "In Cherek kinsmen kill each other with more enthusiasm than they kill strangers."

"Alas." Mandorallen sighed. "This is not Cherek."

"Would you be offended if I dealt with this?" Barak asked politely.

"Not at all."

Barak moved closer to the swarthy knight. "I am Barak, Earl of Trellheim," he announced in a loud voice, "kinsman to King Anheg of Cherek, and I see that certain nobles in Arendia have even fewer manners than they have brains."

"The Lords of Arendia are not impressed by the self-bestowed titles of the pig-sty kingdoms of the north," Sir Haldorin retorted coldly.

"I find your words offensive, friend," Barak said ominously.

"And I find thy ape face and scraggly beard amusing," Sir Haldorin replied.

Barak did not even bother to draw his sword. He swung his huge arm in a wide circle and crashed his fist with stunning force against the side of the swarthy knight's helmet. Sir Haldorin's eyes glazed as he was swept from his saddle, and he made a vast clatter when he struck the ground.

"Would anyone else like to comment about my beard?" Barak demanded.

"Gently, my Lord," Mandorallen advised. He glanced down with a certain satisfaction at the unconscious form of his senseless kinsman twitching in the tall grass.

"Will we docilely accept this attack on our brave companion?" one of the knights in Baron Derigen's party demanded in a harshly accented voice. "Kill them all!" He reached for his sword.

"In the instant thy sword leaves its sheath thou art a dead man, Sir Knight," Mandorallen coolly advised him.

The knight's hand froze on his sword hilt.

"For shame, my Lords," Mandorallen continued accusingly. "Surely ye know that by courtesy and common usage my challenge, until it is answered, guarantees my safety and that of my companions. Choose your champions or withdraw. I tire of all this and presently will become irritable."

The two parties of knights pulled back some distance to confer, and several men-at-arms came to the hilltop to pick up Sir Haldorin.

"That one who was going to draw his sword was a Murgo," Garion said quietly.

"I noticed that," Hettar murmured, his dark eyes glittering.

"They're coming back," Durnik warned.

"I will joust with thee, Sir Mandorallen," Baron Derigen

announced as he approached. "I doubt not that thy reputation is well-deserved, but I also have taken the prize in no small number of tourneys. I would be honored to try a lance with thee."

"And I too will try my skill against thine, Sir Knight," Baron Oltorain declared. "My arm is also feared in some parts of Arendia."

"Very well," Mandorallen replied. "Let us seek level ground and proceed. The day wears on, and my companions and I have business to the south."

They all rode down the hill to the field below where the two groups of knights drew up on either side of a course which had been quickly trampled out in the high, yellow grass. Derigen galloped to the far end, turned and sat waiting, his blunted lance resting in his stirrup.

"Thy courage becomes thee, my Lord," Mandorallen called, taking up one of the poles Durnik had cut. "I shall try not to injure thee too greatly. Art thou prepared to meet my charge?"

"I am," the baron replied, lowering his visor.

Mandorallen clapped down his visor, lowered his lance, and set his spurs to his warhorse.

"It's probably inappropriate under the circumstances," Silk murmured, "but I can't help wishing that our overbearing friend could suffer some humiliating defeat."

Mister Wolf gave him a withering look. "Forget it!"

"Is he *that* good?" Silk asked wistfully.

"Watch," Wolf told him.

The two knights met in the center of the course with a resounding crash, and their lances both shattered at the stunning impact, littering the trampled grass with splinters. They thundered past each other, turned and rode back, each to his original starting place. Derigen, Garion noticed, swayed somewhat in the saddle as he rode.

The knights charged again, and their fresh lances also shattered.

"I should have cut more poles," Durnik said thoughtfully.

But Baron Derigen swayed even more as he rode back this time, and on the third charge his faltering lance glanced off Mandorallen's shield. Mandorallen's lance, however, struck true, and the baron was hurled from his saddle by the force of their meeting.

Mandorallen reined in his charger and looked down at him. "Art thou able to continue, my Lord?" he asked politely.

Derigen staggered to his feet. "I do not yield," he gasped, drawing his sword.

"Splendid," Mandorallen replied. "I feared that I might have done thee harm." He slid out of his saddle, drew his sword and swung directly at Derigen's head. The blow glanced off the baron's hastily raised shield, and Mandorallen swung again without pause. Derigen managed one or two feeble swings before Mandorallen's broadsword caught him full on the side of the helmet. He spun once and collapsed facedown on the earth.

"My Lord?" Mandorallen inquired solicitously. He reached down, rolled over his fallen opponent and opened the dented visor of the baron's helmet. "Art thou unwell, my Lord?" he asked. "Dost thou wish to continue?"

Derigen did not reply. Blood ran freely from his nose, and his eyes were rolled back in his head. His face was blue, and the right side of his body quivered spasmodically.

"Since this brave knight is unable to speak for himself," Mandorallen announced, "I declare him vanquished." He looked around, his broadsword still in his hand. "Would any here gainsay my words?"

There was a vast silence.

"Will some few then remove him from the field?" Mandorallen suggested. "His injuries do not appear grave. A few months in bed should make him whole again." He turned to Baron Oltorain, whose face had grown visibly pale. "Well, my Lord," he said cheerfully, "shall we proceed? My companions and I are impatient to continue our journey."

Sir Oltorain was thrown to the ground on the first charge and broke his leg as he fell.

"Ill luck, my Lord," Mandorallen observed, approaching on foot with drawn sword. "Dost thou yield?"

"I cannot stand," Oltorain said from between clenched teeth. "I have no choice but to yield."

"And I and my companions may continue our journey?"

"Ye may freely depart," the man on the ground replied painfully.

"Not just yet," a harsh voice interrupted. The armored Murgo pushed his horse through the crowd of other mounted knights until he was directly in front of Mandorallen.

"I thought he might decide to interfere," Aunt Pol said quietly. She dismounted and stepped out onto the hoof-churned course. "Move out of the way, Mandorallen," she told the knight.

"Nay, my Lady," Mandorallen protested.

Wolf barked sharply. "Move, Mandorallen!"

Mandorallen looked startled and stepped aside.

"Well, Grolim?" Aunt Pol challenged, pushing back her hood.

The mounted man's eyes widened as he saw the white lock in her hair, and then he raised his hand almost despairingly, muttering rapidly under his breath.

Once again Garion felt that strange surge, and the hollow roaring filled his mind.

For an instant Aunt Pol's figure seemed surrounded by a kind of greenish light. She waved her hand indifferently, and the light disappeared. "You must be out of practice," she told him. "Would you like to try again?"

The Grolim raised both hands this time, but got no further. Maneuvering his horse carefully behind the armored man, Durnik had closed on him. With both hands he raised his axe and smashed it down directly on top of the Grolim's helmet.

"Durnik!" Aunt Pol shouted. "Get away!"

But the smith, his face set grimly, swung again, and the Grolim slid senseless from his saddle with a crash.

"You fool!" Aunt Pol raged. "What do you think you're doing?"

"He was attacking you, Mistress Pol," Durnik explained, his eyes still hot.

"Get down off that horse."

He slid down.

"Do you have any idea how dangerous that was?" she demanded. "He could have killed you."

"I *will* protect you, Mistress Pol," Durnik replied stubbornly. "I'm not a warrior or a magician, but I won't let anybody try to hurt you."

Her eyes widened in surprise for an instant, then narrowed, then softened. Garion who had known her from childhood, recognized her rapid changes of emotion. Without warning she suddenly embraced the startled Durnik. "You great, clumsy, dear fool," she said. "*Never* do that again—never! You almost made my heart stop."

Garion looked away with a strange lump in his throat and saw the brief, sly smile that flickered across Mister Wolf's face.

A peculiar change had come over the knights lining the sides of the course. Several of them were looking around with the amazed expressions of men who had just been roused from some terrible dream. Others seemed suddenly lost in thought. Sir Oltorain struggled to rise.

"Nay, my Lord," Mandorallen told him, pressing him gently back down. "Thou wilt do thyself injury."

"What have we done?" the baron groaned, his face anguished.

Mister Wolf dismounted and knelt beside the injured man. "It wasn't your fault," he informed the baron. "Your war was the Murgo's doing. He twisted your minds and set you on each other."

"Sorcery?" Oltorain gasped, his face growing pale.

Wolf nodded. "He's not really a Murgo, but a Grolim priest."

"And the spell is now broken?"

Wolf nodded again, glancing at the unconscious Grolim.

"Chain the Murgo," the baron ordered the assembled knights. He looked back at Wolf. "We have ways of dealing with sorcerers," he said grimly. "We will use the occasion to celebrate the end of our unnatural war. This Grolim sorcerer hath cast his last enchantment."

"Good," Wolf replied with a bleak smile.

"Sir Mandorallen," Baron Oltorain said, wincing as he shifted his broken leg, "in what way may we repay thee and thy companions for bringing us to our senses?"

"That peace hath been restored is reward enough," Mandorallen replied somewhat pompously, "for, as all the world knows, I am the most peace-loving man in the kingdom." He glanced once at Lelldorin lying nearby on the ground in his litter, and a thought seemed to occur to him. "I would, however, ask a boon of thee. We have in our company a brave Asturian youth of noble family who hath suffered grievous injury. We would leave him, if we might, in thy care."

"His presence shall honor me, Sir Mandorallen," Oltorain assented immediately. "The women of my household will care for him most tenderly." He spoke briefly to one of his retainers, and the man mounted and rode quickly toward one of the nearby castles.

"You're not going to leave me behind," Lelldorin protested weakly. "I'll be able to ride in a day or so." He began to cough rackingly.

"I think not," Mandorallen disagreed with a cool expression. "The results of thy wounding have not yet run their natural course."

"I won't stay with Mimbrates," Lelldorin insisted. "I'd rather take my chances on the road."

"Young Lelldorin," Mandorallen replied bluntly, even harshly, "I know thy distaste for the men of Mimbre. Thy wound, however, will soon begin to abscess and then suppurate, and raging fever and delirium will afflict thee, making thy presence a burden upon us. We have not the time to care for thee, and thy sore need would delay us in our quest."

Garion gasped at the brutal directness of the knight's words. He glared at Mandorallen with something very close to hatred.

Lelldorin's face meanwhile had gone white. "Thank you for pointing that out to me, Sir Mandorallen," he said stiffly. "I should have considered it myself. If you'll help me to my horse, I'll leave immediately."

"You'll stay right where you are," Aunt Pol told him flatly.

Baron Oltorain's retainer returned with a group of household servants and a blonde girl of about seventeen wearing a rose-colored gown of stiff brocade and a velvet cloak of teal.

"My younger sister, Lady Ariana," Oltorain introduced

her. "She's a spirited girl, and though she is young she is already well-versed in the care of the sick."

"I won't trouble her for long, my Lord," Lelldorin declared. "I'll be returning to Asturia within a week."

Lady Ariana laid a professional hand to his forehead. "Nay, good youth," she disagreed. "Thy visit, I think, will be protracted."

"I'll leave within the week," Lelldorin repeated stubbornly.

She shrugged. "As it please thee. I expect that my brother will be able to spare some few servants to follow after thee to provide thee that decent burial which, if I misjudge not, thou wilt require before thou hast gone ten leagues."

Lelldorin blinked.

Aunt Pol took Lady Ariana to one side and spoke with her at some length, giving her a small packet of herbs and certain instructions. Lelldorin motioned to Garion, and Garion went to him immediately and knelt beside the litter.

"So it ends," the young man murmured. "I wish I could go on with you."

"You'll be well in no time at all," Garion assured him, knowing that it wasn't true. "Maybe you can catch up with us later."

Lelldorin shook his head. "No," he disagreed, "I'm afraid not." He began to cough again, the spasms seeming to tear at his lungs. "We don't have much time, my friend," he gasped weakly, "so listen carefully."

Garion, near tears, took his friend's hand.

"You remember what we were talking about that morning after we left my uncle's house?"

Garion nodded.

"You said that *I* was the one who'd have to decide if we were to break our pledge to Torasin and the others to keep silent."

"I remember," Garion told him.

"All right," Lelldorin said. "I've decided. I release you from your pledge. Do what you have to do."

"It would be better if you told my grandfather about it yourself, Lelldorin," Garion protested.

"I can't, Garion," Lelldorin groaned. "The words would stick in my throat. I'm sorry, but it's the way I am. I know that Nachak's only using us, but I gave the others my word. I'm an Arend, Garion. I'll keep my word even though I know it's wrong, so it's up to you. You're going to have to keep Nachak from destroying my country. I want you to go straight to the king himself."

"To the king? He'd never believe me."

"*Make* him believe you. Tell him everything."

Garion shook his head firmly. "I won't tell him your name," he declared, "or Torasin's. You know what he'd do to you if I did."

"We don't matter," Lelldorin insisted, coughing again.

"I'll tell him about Nachak," Garion said stubbornly, "but not about you. Where do I tell him to find the Murgo?"

"He'll know," Lelldorin replied, his voice very weak now. "Nachak's the ambassador to the court at Vo Mimbre. He's the personal representative of Taur Urggs, King of the Murgos."

Garion was stunned at the implications of that.

"He's got all the gold from the bottomless mines of Cthol Murgos at his command," Lelldorin continued. "The plot he gave my friends and me could be just one of a dozen or more all aimed at destroying Arendia. You've got to stop him, Garion. Promise me." The pale young man's eyes were feverish, and his grip on Garion's hand tightened.

"I'll stop him, Lelldorin," Garion vowed. "I don't know how yet, but one way or another, I'll stop him."

Lelldorin sank weakly back on the litter, his strength seeming to run out as if the necessity for extracting that promise had been the only thing sustaining him.

"Good-bye, Lelldorin," Garion said softly, his eyes filling with tears.

"Good-bye, my friend," Lelldorin barely more than whispered, and then his eyes closed, and the hand gripping Garion's went limp. Garion stared at him with a dreadful fear until he saw the faint flutter of his pulse in the hollow of his throat. Lelldorin was still alive—if only barely. Garion tenderly put down his friend's hand and pulled the rough gray blanket up around his shoulders. Then he stood up and walked quickly away with tears running down his cheeks.

The rest of the farewells were brief, and they remounted and rode at a trot toward the Great West Road. There were a few cheers from the serfs and pikemen as they passed, but in the distance there was another sound. The women from the villages had come out to search for their men among the bodies littering the field, and their wails and shrieks mocked the cheers.

With deliberate purpose, Garion pushed his horse forward until he drew in beside Mandorallen. "I have something to say to you," he said hotly. "You aren't going to like it, but I don't really care."

"Oh?" the knight replied mildly.

"I think the way you talked to Lelldorin back there was cruel and disgusting," Garion told him. "You might think you're the greatest knight in the world, but I think you're a loud-mouthed braggart with no more compassion than a block of stone, and if you don't like it, what do you plan to do about it?"

"Ah," Mandorallen said. "That! I think that thou hast misunderstood, my young friend. It was necessary in order to save his life. The Asturian youth is very brave and so gives no thought to himself. Had I not spoken so to him, he would surely have insisted upon continuing with us and would soon have died."

"Died?" Garion scoffed. "Aunt Pol could have cured him."

"It was the Lady Polgara herself who informed me that his life was in danger," Mandorallen replied. "His honor would not permit him to seek proper care, but that same honor prevailed upon him to remain behind lest he delay us." The knight smiled wryly. "He will, I think, be no fonder of me for my words than thou art, but he will be alive, and that's what matters, is it not?"

Garion stared at the arrogant-seeming Mimbrate, his anger suddenly robbed of its target. With painful clarity he realized that he had just made a fool of himself. "I'm sorry," he apologized grudgingly. "I didn't realize what you were doing."

Mandorallen shrugged. "It's not important. I'm frequently misunderstood. As long as *I* know that my motives are good, however, I'm seldom very concerned with the opinions of others. I'm glad, though, that I had the opportunity to explain this to thee. Thou art to be my companion, and it ill-behooves companions to have misapprehensions about each other."

They rode on in silence as Garion struggled to readjust his thinking. There was, it seemed, much more to Mandorallen than he had suspected.

They reached the highway then and turned south again under a threatening sky.

Chapter Eight

THE ARENDISH PLAIN WAS A VAST, rolling grassland only sparsely settled. The wind sweeping across the dried grass was raw and chill, and dirty-looking clouds scudded overhead as they rode. The necessity for leaving the injured Lelldorin behind had put them all into a melancholy mood, and for the most part they traveled in silence for the next several days. Garion rode at the rear with Hettar and the packhorses, doing his best to stay away from Mandorallen.

Hettar was a silent man who seemed undisturbed by hours of riding without conversation; but after two days of this, Garion made a deliberate effort to draw the hawk-faced Algar out. "Why is it that you hate Murgos so much, Hettar?" he asked for want of something better to say.

"All Alorns hate Murgos," Hettar answered quietly.

"Yes," Garion admitted, "but it seems to be something personal with you. Why is that?"

Hettar shifted in his saddle, his leather clothing creaking. "They killed my parents," he replied.

Garion felt a sudden shock as the Algar's words struck a responsive note. "How did it happen?" he asked before he realized that Hettar might prefer not to talk about it.

"I was seven," Hettar told him in an unemotional voice. "We were going to visit my mother's family—she was from a different clan. We had to pass near the eastern escarpment, and a Murgo raiding-party caught us. My mother's horse stumbled, and she was thrown. The Murgos were on us before my father and I could get her back on her horse. They took a long time to kill my parents. I remember that my mother screamed once, near the end." The Algar's face was as bleak as rock, and his flat, quiet voice made his story seem that much more dreadful.

"After my parents were dead, the Murgos tied a rope around my feet and dragged me behind one of their horses," he continued. "When the rope finally broke, they thought I was dead, and they all rode off. They were laughing about it as I recall. Cho-Hag found me a couple of days later."

As clearly as if he had been there, Garion had a momentary picture of a child, dreadfully injured and alone, wandering in the emptiness of eastern Algaria with only grief and a terrible hatred keeping him alive.

"I killed my first Murgo when I was ten," Hettar went on in the same flat voice. "He was trying to escape from us, and I rode him down and put a javelin between his shoulders. He screamed when the javelin went through him. That made me feel better. Cho-Hag thought that if he made me watch the Murgo die, it might cure me of the hatred. He was wrong about that, though." The tall Algar's face was expressionless, and his wind-whipped scalp lock tossed and flowed out behind him. There was a kind of emptiness about him as if he were devoid of any feeling but that one driving compulsion.

For an instant Garion dimly understood what Mister Wolf had been driving at when he had warned about the danger of becoming obsessed with a desire for revenge, but he pushed the notion out of his mind. If Hettar could live with it, so could he. He felt a sudden fierce admiration for this lonely hunter in black leather.

Mister Wolf was deep in conversation with Mandorallen,

and the two of them loitered until Hettar and Garion caught up with them. For a time they rode along together.

"It is our nature," the knight in his gleaming armor was saying in a melancholy voice. "We are over-proud, and it is our pride that dooms our poor Arendia to internecine war."

"That can be cured," Mister Wolf said.

"How?" Mandorallen asked. "It is in our blood. I myself am the most peaceful of men, but even I am subject to our national disease. Moreover, our divisions are too great, too buried in our history and our souls to be purged away. The peace will not last, my friend. Even now Asturian arrows sing in the forests, seeking Mimbrate targets, and Mimbre in reprisal burns Asturian houses and butchers hostages. War is inevitable, I fear."

"No," Wolf disagreed, "it's not."

"How may it be prevented?" Mandorallen demanded. "Who can cure our insanity?"

"I will, if I have to," Wolf told him quietly, pushing back his gray hood.

Mandorallen smiled wanly. "I appreciate thy good intentions, Belgarath, but that is impossible, even for thee."

"Nothing is actually impossible, Mandorallen," Wolf answered in a matter-of-fact voice. "Most of the time I prefer not to interfere with other people's amusements, but I can't afford to have Arendia going up in flames just now. If I have to, I'll step in and put a stop to any more foolishness."

"Hast thou in truth such power?" Mandorallen asked somewhat wistfully as if he could not quite bring himself to believe it.

"Yes," Wolf replied prosaically, scratching at his short white beard, "as a matter of fact, I do."

Mandorallen's face grew troubled, even a bit awed at the old man's quiet statement, and Garion found his grandfather's declaration profoundly disturbing. If Wolf could actually stop a war single-handedly, he'd have no difficulty at all thwarting Garion's own plans for revenge. It was something else to worry about.

Then Silk rode back toward them. "The Great Fair's just ahead," the rat-faced man announced. "Do we want to stop, or should we go around it?"

"We might as well stop," Wolf decided. "It's almost evening, and we need some supplies."

"The horses could use some rest, too," Hettar said. "They're starting to complain."

"You should have told me," Wolf said, glancing back at the pack train.

"They're not really in bad shape yet," Hettar informed him, "but they're starting to feel sorry for themselves. They're exaggerating of course, but a little rest wouldn't hurt them."

"Exaggerating?" Silk sounded shocked. "You don't mean to say that horses can actually lie, do you?"

Hettar shrugged. "Of course. They lie all the time. They're very good at it."

For a moment Silk looked outraged at the thought, and then he suddenly laughed. "Somehow that restores my faith in the order of the universe," he declared.

Wolf looked pained. "Silk," he said pointedly, "you're a very evil man. Did you know that?"

"One does one's best," Silk replied mockingly.

The Arendish Fair lay at the intersection of the Great West Road and the mountain track leading down out of Ulgoland. It was a vast collection of blue, red and yellow tents and broad-striped pavilions stretching for a league or more in every direction. It appeared like a brightly hued city in the midst of the dun-colored plain, and its brilliant pennons snapped bravely in the endless wind under a lowering sky.

"I hope I'll have time to do some business," Silk said as they rode down a long hill toward the Fair. The little man's sharp nose was twitching. "I'm starting to get out of practice."

A half-dozen mud-smeared beggars crouched miserably beside the road, their hands outstretched. Mandorallen paused and scattered some coins among them.

"You shouldn't encourage them," Barak growled.

"Charity is both a duty and a privilege, my Lord Barak," Mandorallen replied.

"Why don't they build houses here?" Garion asked Silk as they approached the central part of the Fair.

"Nobody stays here that long," Silk explained. "The

Fair's always here, but the population's very fluid. Besides, buildings are taxed; tents aren't."

Many of the merchants who came out of their tents to watch the party pass seemed to know Silk, and some of them greeted him warily, suspicion plainly written on their faces.

"I see that your reputation's preceded you, Silk," Barak observed dryly.

Silk shrugged. "The price of fame."

"Isn't there some danger that somebody'll recognize you as that other merchant?" Durnik asked. "The one the Murgos are looking for?"

"You mean Ambar? It's not very likely. Ambar doesn't come to Arendia very often, and he and Radek don't look a bit alike."

"But they're the same man," Durnik objected. "They're both you."

"Ah," Silk said, raising one finger, "you and I both know that, but *they* don't. To you I always look like myself, but to others I look quite different."

Durnik looked profoundly skeptical.

"Radek, old friend," a bald Drasnian merchant called from a nearby tent.

"Delvor," Silk replied delightedly. "I haven't seen you in years."

"You look prosperous," the bald man observed.

"Getting by," Silk responded modestly. "What are you dealing in now?"

"I've got a few Mallorean carpets," Delvor told him. "Some of the local nobles are interested, but they don't like the price." His hands, however, were already speaking of other matters. —*Your uncle sent out word that we were to help you if necessary. Do you need anything?*— "What are you carrying in your packs?" he asked aloud.

"Sendarian woolens," Silk answered, "and a few other odds and ends." —*Have you seen any Murgos here at the Fair?*—

—*One, but he left for Vo Mimbre a week ago. There are some Nadraks on the far side of the Fair, though*—

—*They're a long way from home*— Silk gestured. —*Are they really in business?*—

It's hard to say— Delvor answered.

—Can you put us up for a day or so?—

—I'm sure we can work something out— Delvor replied with a sly twinkle in his eyes.

Silk's fingers betrayed his shock at the suggestion.

—Business is business, after all— Delvor gestured. "You must come inside," he said aloud. "Take a cup of wine, have some supper. We have years of catching up to do."

"We'd be delighted," Silk returned somewhat sourly.

"Could it be that you've met your match, Prince Kheldar?" Aunt Pol inquired softly with a faint smile as the little man helped her down from her horse in front of Delvor's brightly striped pavilion.

"Delvor? Hardly. He's been trying to get even with me for years—ever since a ploy of mine in Yar Gorak cost him a fortune. I'll let him think he's got me for a while though. It will make him feel good, and I'll enjoy it that much more when I pull the rug out from under him."

She laughed. "You're incorrigible."

He winked at her.

The interior of Delvor's main pavilion was ruddy in the light of several glowing braziers that put out a welcome warmth. The floor was covered with a deep blue carpet, and large red cushions were scattered here and there to sit upon. Once they were inside, Silk quickly made the introductions.

"I'm honored, Ancient One," Delvor murmured, bowing deeply to Mister Wolf and then to Aunt Pol. "What can I do to help?"

"Right now we need information more than anything," Wolf replied, pulling off his heavy cloak. "We ran into a Grolin stirring up trouble a few days north of here. Can you nose about and find out what's happening between here and Vo Mimbre? I'd like to avoid any more neighborhood squabbles if possible."

"I'll make inquiries," Delvor promised.

"I'll be moving around too," Silk said. "Between us, Delvor and I should be able to sift out most of the loose information in the Fair."

Wolf looked at him inquiringly.

"Radek of Boktor never passes up a chance to do business," the little man explained just a bit too quickly. "It would look very strange if he stayed in Delvor's tent."

"I see," Wolf said.

"We wouldn't want anything to spoil our disguise, would we?" Silk asked innocently. His long nose, however, was twitching even more violently.

Wolf surrendered. "All right. But don't get exotic. I don't want a crowd of outraged customers outside the tent in the morning howling for your head."

Delvor's porters took the packs from the spare horses, and one of them showed Hettar the way to the horse pens on the outskirts of the Fair. Silk began rummaging through the packs. A myriad of small, expensive items began to pile up on Delvor's carpet as Silk's quick hands dipped into the corners and folds of the wool cloth.

"I wondered why you needed so much money in Camaar," Wolf commented dryly.

"Just part of the diguise," Silk replied. "Radek always has a few curios with him for trade along the way."

"That's a very convenient explanation," Barak observed, "but I wouldn't run it into the ground if I were you."

"If I can't double our old friend's money in the next hour, I'll retire permanently," Silk promised. "Oh, I almost forgot. I'll need Garion to act as a porter for me. Radek always has at least one porter."

"Try not to corrupt him too much," Aunt Pol said.

Silk bowed extravagantly and set his black velvet cap at a jaunty angle; with Garion at his heels, carrying a stout sack of his treasures, he swaggered out into the Great Arendish Fair like a man going into battle.

A fat Tolnedran three tents down the way proved troublesome and succeeded in getting a jeweled dagger away from Silk for only three times what it was worth, but two Arendish merchants in a row bought identical silver goblets at prices which, though widely different, more than made up for that setback. "I love to deal with Arends," Silk gloated as they moved on down the muddy streets between the pavilions.

The sly little Drasnian moved through the Fair, wreaking havoc as he went. When he could not sell, he bought; when he could not buy, he traded; and when he could not trade, he dredged for gossip and information. Some of the merchants, wiser than their fellows, saw him coming and promptly hid from him. Garion, swept along by the little man's enthusiasm, began to understand his friend's fascination with this game where profit was secondary to the satisfaction of besting an opponent.

Silk's predations were broadly ecumenical. He was willing to deal with anyone. He met them all on their own ground. Tolnedrans, Arends, Chereks, fellow Drasnians, Sendars—all fell before him. By midafternoon he had disposed of all of what he had bought in Camaar. His full purse jingled, and the sack on Garion's shoulder was still as heavy, but now it contained entirely new merchandise.

Silk, however, was frowning. He walked along bouncing a small, exquisitely blown glass bottle on the palm of his hand. He had traded two ivory-bound books of Wacite verse to a Rivan for the little bottle of perfume. "What's the trouble?" Garion asked him as they walked back toward Delvor's pavilions.

"I'm not sure who won," Silk told him shortly.

"What?"

"I don't have any idea what this is worth."

"Why did you take it, then?"

"I didn't want him to know that I didn't know its value."

"Sell it to somebody else."

"How can I sell it if I don't know what to ask for it? If I ask too much, nobody'll talk to me; and if I ask too little, I'll be laughed out of the Fair."

Garion started to chuckle.

"I don't see that it's all that funny, Garion," Silk said sensitively. He remained moody and irritable as they entered the pavilion. "Here's the profit I promised you," he told Mister Wolf somewhat ungraciously as he poured coins into the old man's hand.

"What's bothering you?" Wolf asked, eyeing the little man's grumpy face.

"Nothing," Silk replied shortly. Then he glanced over at Aunt Pol, and a broad smile suddenly appeared on his face. He crossed to her and bowed. "My dear Lady Polgara, please accept this trifling momento of my regard for you." With a flourish he presented the perfume bottle to her.

Aunt Pol's look was a peculiar mixture of pleasure and suspicion. She took the small bottle and carefully worked out the tightly fitting stopper. Then with a delicate gesture she touched the stopper to the inside of her wrist and raised the wrist to her face to catch the fragrance. "Why, Kheldar," she exclaimed with delight, "this is a princely gift."

Silk's smile turned a bit sickly, and he peered sharply at her, trying to determine if she was serious or not. Then he sighed and went outside, muttering darkly to himself about the duplicity of Rivans.

Delvor returned not long afterward, dropped his striped cloak in one corner and held out his hands to one of the glowing braziers. "As near as I was able to find out, things are quiet between here and Vo Mimbre," he reported to Mister Wolf, "but five Murgos just rode into the Fair with two dozen Thulls behind them."

Hettar looked up quickly, his hawk face alert.

Wolf frowned. "Did they come from the north or the south?"

"They claim to have come from Vo Mimbre, but there's red clay on the Thulls' boots. I don't think there's any clay between here and Vo Mimbre, is there?"

"None," Mandorallen declared firmly. "The only clay in the region is to the north."

Wolf nodded. "Get Silk back inside," he told Barak.

Barak went to the tent flap.

"Couldn't it just be a coincidence?" Durnik wondered.

"I don't think we want to take that chance," Wolf answered. "We'll wait until the Fair settles down for the night and then slip away."

Silk came back inside, and he and Delvor spoke together briefly.

"It won't take the Murgos long to find out we've been here," Barak rumbled, tugging thoughtfully at his red beard. "Then we'll have them dogging our heels every step of the way from here to Vo Mimbre. Wouldn't it simplify things if Hettar, Mandorallen, and I go pick a fight with them? Five dead Murgos aren't going to follow anybody."

Hettar nodded with a certain dreadful eagerness.

"I don't know if that would set too well with the Tolne-dran legionnaires who police the Fair," Silk drawled. "Po-licemen seem to worry about unexplained bodies. It upsets their sense of neatness."

Barak shrugged. "It was a thought."

"I think I've got an idea," Delvor said, pulling on his cloak again. "They set up their tents near the pavilions of the Nadraks. I'll go do some business with them." He started toward the tent flap, then paused. "I don't know if it means anything," he told them, "but I found out that the leader is a Murgo named Asharak."

Garion felt a sudden chill at the mention of the name.

Barak whistled and looked suddenly very grim. "We're going to have to attend to that one sooner or later, Belgar-ath," he declared.

"You know him?" Delvor did not seem very surprised.

"We've met a time or two," Silk replied in an offhand way.

"He's starting to make a nuisance of himself," Aunt Pol agreed.

"I'll get started," Delvor said.

Garion lifted the tent flap to allow Delvor to leave; but as he glanced outside, he let out a startled gasp and jerked the flap shut again.

"What's the matter?" Silk asked him.

"I think I just saw Brill out there in the street."

"Let me see," Durnik said. His fingers parted the flap slightly, and he and Garion both peered out. A slovenly figure loitered in the muddy street outside. Brill had not changed much since they'd left Faldor's farm. His tunic and hose were still patched and stained; his face was still unshaven, and his cast eye still gleamed with a kind of unwholesome whiteness.

"It's Brill, all right," Durnik confirmed. "He's close enough for me to smell him."

Delvor looked at the smith inquiringly.

"Brill bathes irregularly," Durnik explained. "He's a fra-grant sort of a fellow."

"May I?" Delvor asked politely. He glanced out over

Durnik's shoulder. "Ah," he said, "that one. He works for the Nadraks. I thought that was a little strange, but he didn't seem important, so I didn't bother to investigate."

"Durnik," Wolf said quickly, "step outside for a moment. Make sure he sees you, but don't let him know that you know he's there. After he sees you, come back inside. Hurry. We don't want to let him get away."

Durnik looked baffled, but he lifted the tent flap and stepped out.

"What are you up to, father?" Aunt Pol asked rather sharply. "Don't just stand there smirking, old man. That's very irritating."

"It's perfect," Wolf chortled, rubbing his hands together.

Durnik came back in, his face worried. "He saw me," he reported. "Are you sure this is a good idea?"

"Of course," Wolf replied. "Asharak's obviously here because of us, and he's going to be looking all over the Fair for us."

"Why make it easy for him?" Aunt Pol asked.

"We won't," Wolf replied. "Asharak's used Brill before—in Murgos, remember? He brought Brill down here because Brill would recognize you or me or Durnik or Garion—probably Barak too, and maybe Silk. Is he still out there?"

Garion peered out through the narrow opening. After a moment he saw the unkempt Brill half-hidden between two tents across the street. "He's still there," he answered.

"We'll want to keep him there," Wolf said. "We'll have to be sure that he doesn't get bored and go back to report to Asharak that he's found us."

Silk looked at Delvor, and they both began to laugh.

"What's funny?" Barak demanded suspiciously.

"You almost have to be a Drasnian to appreciate it," Silk replied. He looked at Wolf admiringly. "Sometimes you amaze me, old friend."

Mister Wolf winked at him.

"Thy plan still escapes me," Mandorallen confessed.

"May I?" Silk asked Wolf. He turned back to the knight. "It goes like this, Mandorallen. Asharak's counting on Brill to find us for him, but as long as we keep Brill interested enough, he'll delay going back to tell Asharak where we are. We've captured Asharak's eyes, and that puts him at quite a disadvantage."

"But will this curious Sendar not follow us as soon as we leave the tent?" Mandorallen asked. "When we ride from the Fair, the Murgos will be immediately behind us."

"The back wall of the tent is only canvas, Mandorallen," Silk pointed out gently. "With a sharp knife you can make as many doors in it as you like."

Delvor winced slightly, then sighed. "I'll go see the Murgos," he said. "I think I can delay them even more."

"Durnik and I'll go out with you," Silk told his bald friend. "You go one way, and we'll go another. Brill will follow us, and we can lead him back here."

Delvor nodded, and the three of them went out.

"Isn't all this unnecessarily complicated?" Barak asked sourly. "Brill doesn't know Hettar. Why not just have Hettar slip out the back, circle around behind him, and stick a knife between his ribs? Then we could stuff him in a sack and drop him in a ditch somewhere after we leave the Fair."

Wolf shook his head. "Asharak would miss him," he replied. "I want him to tell the Murgos that we're in this tent. With any luck, they'll sit outside for a day or so before they realize that we're gone."

For the next several hours various members of the party went out into the street in front of the tent on short and wholly imaginary errands to hold the attention of the lurking Brill. When Garion stepped out into the gathering darkness, he put on a show of unconcern, although his skin prickled as he felt Brill's eyes on him. He went into Delvor's supply tent and waited for several minutes. The noise from a tavern pavilion several rows of tents over seemed very loud in the growing stillness of the Fair as Garion waited nervously in the dark supply tent. Finally he drew a deep breath and went out again, one arm tucked up as if he were carrying something. "I found it, Durnik," he announced as he reentered the main pavilion.

"There's no need to improvise, dear," Aunt Pol remarked.

"I just wanted to sound natural," he replied innocently.

Delvor returned soon after that, and they all waited in the warm tent as it grew darker outside and the streets emptied. Once it was fully dark, Delvor's porters pulled the packs out through a slit in the back of the tent. Silk, Delvor, and Hettar went with them to the horse pens on the outskirts of the Fair while the rest remained long enough to keep Brill from losing interest. In a final attempt at misdirection, Mister Wolf and Barak went outside to discuss the probable conditions of the road to Prolgu in Ulgoland.

"It might not work," Wolf admitted as he and the big red-bearded man came back inside. "Asharak's sure to know that we're following Zedar south, but if Brill tells him that we're going to Prolgu, it might make him divide his forces to cover both roads." He looked around the inside of the tent. "All right," he said. "Let's go."

One by one they squeezed out through the slit in the back of the tent and crept into the next street. Then, walking at a normal pace like serious people on honest business, they proceeded toward the horse pens. They passed the tavern pavilion where several men were singing. The streets were mostly empty by now, and the night breeze brushed the city of tents, fluttering the pennons and banners.

Then they reached the edge of the Fair where Silk, Delvor and Hettar waited with their mounts. "Good luck," Delvor said as they prepared to mount. "I'll delay the Murgos for as long as I can."

Silk shook his friend's hand. "I'd still like to know where you got those lead coins."

Delvor winked at him.

"What's this?" Wolf asked.

"Delvor's got some Tolnedran crowns stamped out of lead and gilded over," Silk told him. "He hid some of them in the Murgos' tent, and tomorrow morning he's going to go to the legionnaires with a few of them and accuse the Murgos of passing them. When the legionnaires search the Murgos' tent, they're sure to find the others."

"Money's awfully important to Tolnedrans," Barak observed. "If the legionnaires get excited enough about those coins, they might start hanging people."

Delvor smirked. "Wouldn't that be a terrible shame?"

They mounted then and rode away from the horse pens

toward the highway. It was a cloudy night, and once they were out in the open the breeze was noticeably brisk. Behind them the Fair gleamed and twinkled under the night sky like some vast city. Garion drew his cloak about him. It was a lonely feeling to be on a dark road on a windy night when everyone else in the world had a fire and a bed and walls around him. Then they reached the Great West Road stretching pale and empty across the dark, rolling Arendish plain and turned south again.

Chapter Nine

THE WIND PICKED UP AGAIN shortly before dawn and was blowing briskly by the time the sky over the low foothills to the east began to lighten. Garion was numb with exhaustion by then, and his mind had drifted into an almost dreamlike trance. The faces of his companions all seemed strange to him as the pale light began to grow stronger. At times he even forgot why they rode. He seemed caught in a company of grim-faced strangers pounding along a road to nowhere through a bleak, featureless landscape with their wind-whipped cloaks flying dark behind them like the clouds scudding low and dirty overhead. A peculiar idea began to take hold of him. The strangers were somehow his captors, and they were taking him away from his real friends. The idea seemed to grow stronger the farther they rode, and he began to be afraid.

Suddenly, without knowing why, he wheeled his horse and broke away, plunging off the side of the road and across the open field beside it.

"Garion!" a woman's voice called sharply from behind, but he set his heels to his horse's flanks and sped even faster across the rough field.

One of them was chasing him, a frightening man in

black leather with a shaved head and a dark lock at his crown flowing behind him in the wind. In a panic Garion kicked at his horse, trying to make the beast run even faster, but the fearsome rider behind him closed the gap quickly and seized the reins from his hands. "What are you doing?" he demanded harshly.

Garion stared at him, unable to answer.

Then the woman in the blue cloak was there, and the others not far behind her. She dismounted quickly and stood looking at him with a stern face. She was tall for a woman, and her face was cold and imperious. Her hair was very dark, and there was a single white lock at her brow.

Garion trembled. The woman made him terribly afraid.

"Get down off that horse," she commanded.

"Gently, Pol," a silvery-haired old man with an evil face said.

A huge red-bearded giant rode closer, threatening, and Garion, almost sobbing with fright, slid down from his horse.

"Come here," he woman ordered. Falteringly, Garion approached her.

"Give me your hand," she said.

Hesitantly, he lifted his hand and she took his wrist firmly. She opened his fingers to reveal the ugly mark on his palm that he seemed to always have hated and then put his hand against the white lock in her hair.

"Aunt Pol," he gasped, the nightmare suddenly dropping away. She put her arms about him tightly and held him for some time. Strangely, he was not even embarrassed by that display of affection in front of the others.

"This is serious, father," she told Mister Wolf.

"What happened, Garion?" Wolf asked, his voice calm.

"I don't know," Garion replied. "I was as if I didn't know any of you, and you were my enemies, and all I wanted to do was run away to try to get back to my real friends."

"Are you still wearing the amulet I gave you?"

"Yes."

"Have you had it off at any time since I gave it to you?"

"Just once," Garion admitted. "When I took a bath in the Tolnedran hostel."

Wolf sighed. "You can't take it off," he said, "not ever—not for any reason. Take it out from under your tunic."

Garion drew out the silver pendant with the strange design on it.

The old man took a medallion out from under his own tunic. It was very bright and there was upon it the figure of a standing wolf so lifelike that it looked almost ready to lope away.

Aunt Pol, her one arm still about Garion's shoulders, drew a similar amulet out of her bodice. Upon the disc of her medallion was the figure of an owl. "Hold it in your right hand, dear," she instructed, firmly closing Garion's fingers over the pendant. Then, holding her amulet in her own right hand, she placed her left hand over his closed fist. Wolf, also holding his talisman, put his hand on theirs.

Garion's palm began to tingle as if the pendant were suddenly alive.

Mister Wolf and Aunt Pol looked at each other for a long moment, and the tingling in Garion's hand suddenly became very strong. His mind seemed to open, and strange things flickered before his eyes. He saw a round room very high up somewhere. A fire burned, but there was no wood in it. At a table there was seated an old man who looked somewhat like Mister Wolf but obviously was someone else. He seemed to be looking directly at Garion, and his eyes were kindly, even affectionate. Garion was suddenly overwhelmed with a consuming love for the old man.

"That should be enough," Wolf judged, releasing Garion's hand.

"Who was the old man?" Garion asked.

"My Master," Wolf replied.

"What happened?" Durnik asked, his face concerned.

"It's probably better not to talk about it," Aunt Pol said. "Do you think you could build a fire? It's time for breakfast."

"There are some trees over there where we can get out of the wind," Durnik suggested.

They all remounted and rode toward the trees.

After they had eaten, they sat by the small fire for a while. They were tired, and none of them felt quite up to facing the blustery morning again. Garion felt particularly exhausted, and he wished that he were young enough to sit close beside Aunt Pol and perhaps to put his head in her lap and sleep as he had done when he was very young. The strange thing that had happened made him feel very much alone and more than a little frightened. "Durnik," he said, more to drive the mood away than out of any real curiosity. "What sort of bird is that?" He pointed.

"A raven, I think," Durnik answered, looking at the bird circling above them.

"I thought so too," Garion said, "but they don't usually circle, do they?"

Durnik frowned. "Maybe it's watching something on the ground."

"How long has it been up there?" Wolf asked, squinting up at the large bird.

"I think I first saw it when we were crossing the field." Garion told him.

Mister Wolf glanced over at Aunt Pol. "What do you think?"

She looked up from one of Garion's stockings she had been mending. "I'll see." Her face took on a strange, probing expression.

Garion felt a peculiar tingling again. On an impulse he tried to push his own mind out toward the bird.

"Garion," Aunt Pol said without looking at him, "stop that."

"I'm sorry," he apologized quickly and pulled his mind back where it belonged.

Mister Wolf looked at him with a strange expression, then winked at him.

"It's Chamdar," Aunt Pol announced calmly. She carefully pushed her needle into the stocking and set it aside. Then she stood up and shook off her blue cloak.

"What have you got in mind?" Wolf asked.

"I think I'll go have a little chat with him," she replied, flexing her fingers like talons.

"You'd never catch him," Wolf told her. "Your feathers are too soft for this kind of wind. There's an easier way." The old man swept the windy sky with a searching gaze. "Over there." He pointed at a barely visible speck above the hills to the west. "You'd better do it, Pol. I don't get along with birds."

"Of course, father," she agreed. She looked intently at the speck, and Garion felt the tingle as she sent her mind out again. The speck began to circle, rising higher and higher until it disappeared.

The raven did not see the plummeting eagle until the last instant, just before the larger bird's talons struck. There was a sudden puff of black feathers, and the raven, screeching with fright, flapped wildly away with the eagle in pursuit.

"Nicely done, Pol," Wolf approved.

"It will give him something to think about." She smiled. "Don't stare, Durnik."

Durnik was gaping at her, his mouth open. "How did you do that?"

"Do you really want to know?" she asked.

Durnik shuddered and looked away quickly.

"I think that just about settles it," Wolf said. "Disguises are probably useless now. I'm not sure what Chamdar's up to, but he's going to be watching us every step of the way. We might as well arm ourselves and ride straight on to Vo Mimbre."

"Aren't we going to follow the trail anymore?" Barak asked.

"The trail goes south," Wolf replied. "I can pick it up again once we cross over into Tolnedra. But first I want to stop by and have a word with King Korodullin. There are some things he needs to know."

"Korodullin?" Durnik looked puzzled. "Wasn't that the name of the first Arendish king? It seems to me somebody told me that once."

"All Arendish kings are named Korodullin," Silk told him. "And the queens are all named Mayaserana. It's part of the fiction the royal family here maintains to keep the kingdom from flying apart. They have to marry as closely within the bloodline as possible to maintain the illusion of the unification of the houses of Mimbre and Asturia. It makes them all a bit sickly, but there's no help for it— considering the peculiar nature of Arendish politics."

"All right, Silk," Aunt Pol said reprovingly.

Mandorallen looked thoughtful. "Could it be that this Chamdar who so dogs our steps is one of great substance in the dark society of the Grolims?" he asked.

"He'd like to be," Wolf answered. "Zedar and Ctuchik's are Torak's disciples, and Chamdar wants to be one as well. He's always been Ctuchik's agent, but he may believe that this is his chance to move up in the Grolim hierarchy. Ctuchik's very old, and he spends all his time in the temple of Torak at Rak Cthol. Maybe Chamdar thinks it's time that someone else became High Priest."

"Is Torak's body at Rak Cthol?" Silk asked quickly.

Mister Wolf shrugged. "Nobody knows for sure, but I doubt it. After Zedar carried him away from the battlefield at Vo Mimbre, I don't think he'd have just handed him over to Ctuchik. He could be in Mallorea or somewhere in the southern reaches of Cthol Murgos. It's hard to say."

"But at the moment, Chamdar's the one we have to worry about," Silk concluded.

"Not if we keep moving," Wolf told him.

"We'd better get moving then," Barak said, standing up.

By midmorning the heavy clouds had begun to break up, and patches of blue sky showed here and there. Enormous pillars of sunlight stalked ponderously across the rolling fields that waited, damp and expectant, for the first touches of spring. With Mandorallen in the lead they had ridden hard and had covered a good six leagues. Finally they slowed to a walk to allow their steaming horses to rest.

"How much farther is it to Bo Mimbre, grandfather?" Garion asked, pulling his horse in beside Mister Wolf.

"Sixty leagues at least," Wolf answered. "Probably closer to eighty."

"That's a long way." Garion winced as he shifted in his saddle.

"Yes."

"I'm sorry I ran away like that back there," Garion apologized.

"It wasn't your fault. Chamdar was playing games."

"Why did he pick me? Couldn't he have done the same thing to Durnik—or Barak?"

Mister Wolf looked at him. "You're younger, more susceptible."

"That's not really it, is it?" Garion accused.

"No," Wolf admitted, "not really, but it's an answer, of sorts."

"This is another one of those things you aren't going to tell me, isn't it?"

"I suppose you could say that," Wolf answered blandly.

Garion sulked about that for a while, but Mister Wolf rode on, seemingly unconcerned by the boy's reproachful silence.

They stopped that night at a Tolnedran hostel, which, like all of them, was plain, adequate, and expensive. The next morning the sky had cleared except for billowy patches of white cloud scampering before the brisk wind. The sight of the sun made them all feel better, and there was even some bantering between Silk and Barak as they rode along—something Garion hadn't heard in all the weeks they'd spent traveling under the gloomy skies of northern Arendia.

Mandorallen, however, scarcely spoke that morning, and his face grew more somber with each passing mile. He was not wearing his armor, but instead a mail suit and a deep blue surcoat. His head was bare, and the wind tugged at his curly hair.

On a nearby hilltop a bleak-looking castle brooded down at them as they passed, its grim walls high and haughty-looking. Mandorallen seemed to avoid looking at it, and his face became even more melancholy.

Garion found it difficult to make up his mind about Mandorallen. He was honest enough with himself to admit that much of his thinking was still clouded by Lelldorin's prejudices. He didn't really want to like Mandorallen; but aside from the habitual gloominess which seemed characteristic of all Arends and the studied and involuted archaism of the man's speech and his towering self-confidence, there seemed little actually to dislike.

A half-league along the road from the castle, a ruin sat at the top of a long rise. It was not much more than a single wall with a high archway in the center and broken columns on either side. Near the ruin a woman sat on horseback, her dark red cape flowing in the wind.

Without a word, almost without seeming to think about

it, Mandorallen turned his warhorse from the road and cantered up the rise toward the woman, who watched his approach without any seeming surprise, but also with no particular pleasure.

"Where's he going?" Barak asked.

"She's an acquaintance of his," Mister Wolf said dryly.

"Are we supposed to wait for him?"

"He can catch up with us," Wolf replied.

Mandorallen had stopped his horse near the woman and dismounted. He bowed to her and held out his hands to help her down from her horse. They walked together toward the ruin, not touching, but walking very close to each other. They stopped beneath the archway and talked. Behind the ruin, clouds raced in the windy sky, and their enormous shadows swept uncaring across the mournful fields of Arendia.

"We should have taken a different route," Wolf said. "I wasn't thinking, I guess."

"Is there some problem?" Durnik asked.

"Nothing unusual—in Arendia," Wolf answered. "I suppose it's my fault. Sometimes I forget the kind of things that can happen to young people."

"Don't be cryptic, father," Aunt Pol told him. "It's very irritating. Is this something we should know about?"

Wolf shrugged. "It isn't any secret," he replied. "Half of Arendia knows about it. A whole generation of Arendish virgins cry themselves to sleep every night over it."

"Father," Aunt Pol snapped exasperatedly.

"All right," Wolf said. "When Mandorallen was about Garion's age, he showed a great deal of promise—strong, courageous, not too bright—the qualities that make a good knight. His father asked me for advice, and I made arrangements for the young man to live for a while with the Baron of Vo Ebor—that's his castle back there. The baron had an enormous reputation, and he provided Mandorallen with the kind of instruction he needed. Mandorallen and the baron became almost like father and son, since the baron was quite a bit older. Everything was going along fine until the baron got married. His bride, however, was much younger—about Mandorallen's age."

"I think I see where this is going," Durnik remarked disapprovingly.

"Not exactly," Wolf disagreed. "After the honeymoon, the baron returned to his customary knightly pursuits and left a very bored young lady wandering around his castle. It's a situation with all kinds of interesting possibilities. Anyway, Mandorallen and the lady exchanged glances—then words—the usual sort of thing."

"It happens in Sendaria too," Durnik observed, "but I'm sure the name we have for it is different from the one they use here." His tone was critical, even offended.

"You're jumping to conclusions, Durnik," Wolf told him. "Things never went any further. It might have been better if they had. Adultery isn't really all that serious, and in time they'd have gotten bored with it. But, since they both loved and respected the baron too much to dishonor him, Mandorallen left the castle before things could get out of hand. Now they both suffer in silence. It's all very touching, but it seems like a waste of time to me. Of course I'm older."

"You're older than everyone, father," Aunt Pol said.

"You didn't have to say that, Pol."

Silk laughed sardonically. "I'm glad to see that our stupendous friend at least has the bad taste to fall in love with another man's wife. His nobility was beginning to get rather cloying." The little man's expression had that bitter, self-mocking cast to it Garion had first seen in Val Alorn when they had spoken with Queen Porenn.

"Does the baron know about it?" Durnik asked.

"Naturally," Wolf replied. "That's the part that makes the Arends get all mushy inside about it. There was a knight once, stupider than most Arends, who made a bad joke about it. The baron promptly challenged him and ran a lance through him during the duel. Since then very few people have found the situation humorous."

"It's still disgraceful," Durnik said.

"Their behavior's above reproach, Durnik," Aunt Pol maintained firmly. "There's no shame in it as long as it doesn't go any further."

"Decent people don't allow it to happen in the first place," Durnik asserted.

"You'll never convince her, Durnik," Mister Wolf told the smith. "Polgara spent too many years associating with the Wacite Arends. They were as bad or worse than the Mimbrates. You can't wallow in that kind of sentimentality for that long without some of it rubbing off. Fortunately it hasn't *totally* blotted out her good sense. She's only occasionally girlish and gushy. If you can avoid her during those seizures, it's almost as if there was nothing wrong with her."

"My time was spent a little more usefully than yours, father," Aunt Pol observed acidly. "As I remember, *you* spent those years carousing in the waterfront dives in Camaar. And then there was that uplifting period you spent amusing the depraved women of Maragor. I'm certain those experiences broadened your concept of morality enormously."

Mister Wolf coughed uncomfortably and looked away.

Behind them, Mandorallen had remounted and begun to gallop back down the hill. The lady stood in the archway with her red cloak billowing in the wind, watching him as he rode away.

They were five days on the road before they reached the River Arend, the boundary between Arendia and Tolnedra. The weather improved as they moved farther south, and by the morning when they reached the hill overlooking the river, it was almost warm. The sun was very bright, and a few fleecy clouds raced overhead in the fresh breeze.

"The high road to Vo Mimbre branches to the left just there," Mandorallen remarked.

"Yes," Wolf said. "Let's go down into that grove near the river and make ourselves a bit more presentable. Appearances are very important in Vo Mimbre, and we don't want to arrive looking like vagabonds."

Three brown-robed and hooded figures stood humbly at the crossroads, their faces down and their hands held out in supplication. Mister Wolf reined in his horse and approached them. He spoke with them briefly, then gave each a coin.

"Who are they?" Garion asked.

"Monks from Mar Terin," Silk replied.

"Where's that?"

"It's a monastery in southeastern Tolnedra where Maragor used to be," Silk told him. "The monks try to comfort
the spirits of the Marags."

Mister Wolf motioned to them, and they rode on past the
three humble figures at the roadside. "They say that no
Murgos have passed here in the last two weeks."

"Are you sure you can believe them?" Hettar asked.

"Probably. The monks won't lie to anybody."

"Then they'll tell anybody who comes by that we've
passed here?" Barak asked.

Wolf nodded. "They'll answer any question anybody puts
to them."

"That's an unsavory habit," Barak grunted darkly.

Mister Wolf shrugged and led the way among the trees
beside the river. "This ought to do," he decided, dismounting in a grassy glade. He waited while the others climbed
down from their horses. "All right," he told them, "we're
going to Vo Mimbre. I want you all to be careful about
what you say there. Mimbrates are very touchy, and the
slightest word can be taken as an insult."

"I think you should wear the white robe Fulrach gave
you, father," Aunt Pol interrupted, pulling open one of the
packs.

"Please, Pol," Wolf said, "I'm trying to explain something."

"They heard you, father. You tend to belabor things too
much." She held up the white robe and looked at it critically. "You should have folded it more carefully. You've
wrinkled it."

"I'm not going to wear that thing," he declared flatly.

"Yes, you are, father," she told him sweetly. "We might
have to argue about it for an hour or two, but you'll wind
up wearing it in the end anyway. Why not just save yourself all the time and aggravation?"

"It's silly," he complained.

"Lots of things are silly, father. I know the Arends better
than you do. You'll get more respect if you look the part.
Mandorallen and Hettar and Barak will wear their armor;
Durnik and Silk and Garion can wear the doublets Fulrach

gave them in Sendar; I'll wear my blue gown, and you'll wear the white robe. I insist, father."

"You *what*? Now listen here, Polgara—"

"Be still, father," she said absently, examining Garion's blue doublet.

Wolf's face darkened, and his eyes bulged dangerously.

"Was there something else?" she asked with a level gaze.

Mister Wolf let it drop.

"He's as wise as they say he is," Silk observed.

An hour later they were on the high road to Vo Mimbre under a sunny sky. Mandorallen, once again in full armor and with a blue and silver pennon streaming from the tip of his lance, led the way with Barak in his gleaming mail shirt and black bearskin cape riding immediately behind him. At Aunt Pol's insistence, the big Cherek had combed the tangles out of his red beard and even rebraided his hair. Mister Wolf in his white robe rode sourly, muttering to himself, and Aunt Pol sat her horse demurely at his side in a short, fur-lined cape and with a blue satin headdress surmounting the heavy mass of her dark hair. Garion and Durnik were ill at ease in their finery, but Silk wore his doublet and black velvet cap with a kind of exuberant flair. Hettar's sole concession to formality had been the replacement of a ring of beaten silver for the leather thong which usually caught in his scalp lock.

The serfs and even the occasional knight they encountered along the way stood aside and saluted respectfully. The day was warm, the road was good, and their horses were strong. By midafternoon they crested a high hill overlooking the plain which sloped down to the gates of Vo Mimbre.

Chapter Ten

THE CITY OF THE MIMBRATE ARENDS reared almost like a mountain beside the sparkling river. Its thick, high walls were surmounted by massive battlements, and great towers and slender spires with bright banners at their tips rose within the walls, gleaming golden in the afternoon sun.

"Behold Vo Mimbre," Mandorallen proclaimed with pride, "queen of cities. Upon that rock the tide of Angarak crashed and recoiled and crashed again. Upon this field met they their ruin. The soul and pride of Arendia doth reside within that fortress, and the power of the Dark One may not prevail against it."

"We've been here before, Mandorallen," Mister Wolf said sourly.

"Don't be impolite, father," Aunt Pol told the old man. Then she turned to Mandorallen and to Garion's amazement she spoke in an idiom he had never heard from her lips before. "Wilt thou, Sir Knight, convey us presently into the palace of thy king? We must needs take council with him in matters of gravest urgency." She delivered this without the least trace of self-consciousness as if the archaic formality came quite naturally to her. "Forasmuch as thou art the mightiest knight on life, we place ourselves under the protection of thy arm."

Mandorallen, after a startled instant, slid with a crash from his warhorse and sank to his knees before her. "My Lady Polgara," he replied in a voice throbbing with respect—with reverence even, "I accept thy charge and will convey thee safely unto King Korodullin. Should any man question thy paramount right to the king's attention, I shall prove his folly upon his body."

Aunt Pol smiled at him encouragingly, and he vaulted into his saddle with a clang and led the way at a rolling trot, his whole bearing seething with a willingness to do battle.

"What was that all about?" Wolf asked.

"Mandorallen needed something to take his mind off his troubles," she replied. "He's been out of sorts for the last few days."

As they drew closer to the city, Garion could see the scars on the great walls where heavy stones from the An-garak catapults had struck the unyielding rock. The battle-ments high above were chipped and pitted from the impact of showers of steel-tipped arrows. The stone archway that led into the city revealed the incredible thickness of the walls, and the ironbound gate was massive. They clattered through the archway and into the narrow, crooked streets. The people they passed seemed for the most part to be commoners, who quickly moved aside. The faces of the men in dun-colored tunics and the women in patched dresses were dull and uncurious.

"They don't seem very interested in us," Garion com-mented quietly to Durnik.

"I don't think the ordinary people and the gentry pay much attention to each other here," Durnik replied. "They live side by side, but they don't know anything about each other. Maybe that's what's wrong with Arendia."

Garion nodded soberly.

Although the commoners were indifferent, the nobles at the palace seemed afire with curiosity. Word of the party's entrance into the city apparently had raced ahead of them through the narrow streets, and the windows and parapets of the palace were alive with people in brightly colored clothes.

"Abate thy pace, Sir Knight," a tall man with dark hair and beard, wearing a black velvet surcoat over his polished mail, called down from the parapet to Mandorallen as they clattered into the broad plaza before the palace. "Lift thy visor so that I may know thee."

Mandorallen stopped in amazement before the closed gate and raised his visor. "What discourtesy is this?" he demanded. "I am, as all the world knows, Mandorallen,

Baron of Vo Mandor. Surely thou canst see my crest upon the face of my shield."

"Any man may wear another's crest," the man above declared disdainfully.

Mandorallen's face darkened. "Art thou not mindful that no man on life would dare to counterfeit my semblance?" he asked in a dangerous tone.

"Sir Andorig," another knight on the parapet told the dark-haired man, "this is indeed Sir Mandorallen. I met him on the field of the great tourney last year, and our meeting cost me a broken shoulder and put a ringing in my ears which hath not yet subsided."

"Ah," Sir Andorig replied, "since thou wilt vouch for him, Sir Helbergin, I will admit that this is indeed the bastard of Vo Mandor."

"You're going to have to do something about that one of these days," Barak said quietly to Mandorallen.

"It would seem so," Mandorallen replied.

"Who, however, are these others with thee who seek admittance, Sir Knight?" Andorig demanded. "I will not cause the gates to open for foreign strangers."

Mandorallen straightened in his saddle. "Behold!" he announced in a voice that could probably be heard all over the city. "I bring you honor beyond measure. Fling wide the palace gate and prepare one and all to make obeisance. You look upon the holy face of Belgarath the Sorcerer, the Eternal Man, and upon the divine countenance of his daughter, the Lady Polgara, who have come to Vo Mimbre to consult with the King of Arendia on diverse matters."

"Isn't that a little overdone?" Garion whispered to Aunt Pol.

"It's customary, dear," she replied placidly. "When you're dealing with Arends, you have to be a little extravagant to get their attention."

"And who hath told thee that this is the Lord Belgarath?" Andorig asked with the faintest hint of a sneer. "I will bend no knee before an unproved vagabond."

"Dost thou question my word, Sir Knight?" Mandorallen returned in an ominously quiet voice. "And wilt thou then come down and put thy doubt to the test? Or is it perhaps that thou wouldst prefer to cringe doglike behind thy parapet and yap at thy betters?"

"Oh, that was *very* good," Barak said admiringly.

Mandorallen grinned tightly at the big man.

"I don't think we're getting anywhere with this," Mister Wolf muttered. "It looks like I'll have to prove something to this skeptic if we're ever going to get in to see Korodullin." He slid down from his saddle and thoughtfully removed a twig from his horse's tail, picked up somewhere during their journey. Then he strode to the center of the plaza and stood there in his gleaming white robe. "Sir Knight," he called up mildly to Andorig, "you're a cautious man, I see. That's a good quality, but it can be carried too far."

"I am hardly a child, old man," the dark-haired knight replied in a tone hovering on the verge of insult, "and I believe only what mine own eye hath confirmed."

"It must be a sad thing to believe so little," Wolf observed. He bent then and inserted the twig he'd been holding between two of the broad granite flagstones at his feet. He stepped back a pace and stretched his hand out above the twig, his face curiously gentle. "I'm going to do you a favor, Sir Andorig," he announced. "I'm going to restore your faith. Watch closely." And then he spoke a single soft word that Garion couldn't quite hear, but which set off the now-familiar surge and a faint roaring sound.

At first nothing seemed to be happening. Then the two flagstones began to buckle upward with a grinding sound as the twig grew visibly thicker and began to reach up toward Mister Wolf's outstretched hand. There were gasps from the palace walls as branches began to sprout from the twig as it grew. Wolf raised his hand higher, and the twig obediently grew at his gesture, its branches broadening. By now it was a young tree and still growing. One of the flagstones cracked with a sharp report.

There was absolute silence as every eye fixed in awed fascination on the tree. Mister Wolf held out both hands and turned them until the palms were up. He spoke again, and the tips of the branches swelled and began to bud. Then the tree burst into flower, its blossoms a delicate pink and white.

"Apple, wouldn't you say, Pol?" Wolf asked over his shoulder.

"It appears to be, father," she replied.

He patted the tree fondly and then turned back to the dark-haired knight who had sunk, white-faced and trembling, to his knees. "Well, Sir Andorig," he inquired, "what do you believe now?"

"Please forgive me, Holy Belgarath," Andorig begged in a strangled voice.

Mister Wolf drew himself up and spoke sternly, his words slipping into the measured cadences of the Mimbrate idiom as easily as Aunt Pol's had earlier. "I charge thee, Sir Knight, to care for this tree. It hath grown here to renew thy faith and trust. Thy debt to it must be paid with tender and loving attention to its needs. In time it will bear fruit, and thou wilt gather the fruit and give it freely to any who ask it of thee. For thy soul's sake, thou wilt refuse none, no matter how humble. As the tree gives freely, so shalt thou."

"That's a nice touch," Aunt Pol approved.

Wolf winked at her.

"I will do even as thou hast commanded me, Holy Belgarath," Sir Andorig choked. "I pledge my heart to it."

Mister Wolf returned to his horse. "At least he'll do *one* useful thing in his life," he muttered.

After that there was no further discussion. The palace gate creaked open, and they all rode into the inner courtyard and dismounted. Mandorallen led them past kneeling and even sobbing nobles who reached out to touch Mister Wolf's robe as he passed. At Mandorallen's heels they walked through the broad, tapestried hallways with a growing throng behind them. The door to the throne room opened, and they entered.

The Arendish throne room was a great, vaulted hall with sculptured buttresses soaring upward along the walls. Tall, narrow windows rose between the buttresses, and the light streaming through their stained-glass panels was jeweled. The floor was polished marble, and on the carpeted stone platform at the far end stood the double throne of Arendia, backed by heavy purple drapes. Flanking the draped wall hung the massive antique weapons of twenty generations of

Arendish royalty. Lances, maces, and huge swords, taller than any man, hung among the tattered war banners of forgotten kings.

Korodullin of Arendia was a sickly-looking young man in a gold-embroidered purple robe, and he wore his large gold crown as if it were too heavy for him. Beside him on the double throne sat his pale, beautiful queen. Together they watched somewhat apprehensively as the throng surrounding Mister Wolf approached the wide steps leading up to the throne.

"My King," Mandorallen announced, dropping to one knee, "I bring into thy presence Holy Belgarath, Disciple of Aldur and the staff upon which the kingdoms of the West have leaned since time began."

"He knows who I am, Mandorallen," Mister Wolf said. He stepped forward and bowed briefly. "Hail Korodullin and Mayaserana," he greeted the king and queen. "I'm sorry we haven't had the chance to get acquainted before."

"The honor is ours, noble Belgarath," the young king replied in a voice whose rich timbre belied his frail appearance.

"My father spoke often of thee," the queen said.

"We were good friends," Wolf told her. "Allow me to present my daughter, Polgara."

"Great Lady," the king responded with a respectful inclination of his head. "All the world knows of thy power, but men have forgotten to speak of thy beauty."

"We'll get along well together," Aunt Pol answered warmly, smiling at him.

"My heart trembles at the sight of the flower of all womanhood," the queen declared.

Aunt Pol looked at the queen thoughtfully. "We must talk, Mayaserana," she said in a serious tone, "in private and very soon."

The queen looked startled.

Mister Wolf introduced the rest of them, and each bowed in turn to the young king.

"Welcome, gentles all," Korodullin said. "My poor court is overwhelmed by so noble a company."

"We don't have much time, Korodullin," Mister Wolf told him. "The courtesy of the Arendish throne is the marvel of the world. I don't want to offend you and your lovely queen by cutting short those stately observances which so ornament your court, but I have certain news which I have to present to you in private. The matter is of extreme urgency."

"Then I am at thy immediate disposal," the king replied, rising from his throne. "Forgive us, dear friends," he said to the assembled nobles, "but this ancient friend of our kingly line hath information which must be imparted to our ears alone with utmost urgency. I pray thee, let us go apart for a little space of time to receive this instruction. We shall return presently."

"Polgara," Mister Wolf said.

"Go ahead, father," she replied. "Just now I have to speak with Mayaserana about something that's very important to her."

"Can't it wait?"

"No, father, it can't." And with that she took the queen's arm, and the two left. Mister Wolf stared after her for a moment; then he shrugged, and he and Korodullin also left the throne room. An almost shocked silence followed their departure.

"Most unseemly," an old courtier with wispy white hair disapproved.

"A necessary haste, my Lord," Mandorallen informed him. "As the revered Belgarath hath intimated, our mission is the hinge-pin of the survival of all the kingdoms of the west. Our Ancient Foe may soon be abroad again. It will not be long, I fear, ere Mimbrate knights will again stand the brunt of titanic war."

"Blessed then be the tongue which brings the news," the white-haired old man declared. "I had feared that I had seen my last battle and would die abed in my dotage. I thank great Chaldan that I still have my vigor, and that my prowess is undiminished by the passage of a mere four-score years."

Garion drew off by himself to one side of the room to wrestle with a problem. Events had swept him into King Korodullin's court before he had had the time to prepare himself for an unpleasant duty. He had given his word to Lelldorin to bring certain things to the king's attention, but he did not have the faintest idea how to begin. The exaggerated formality of the Arendish court intimidated him. This was not at all like the rough, good-natured court of King Anheg in Val Alorn or the almost homey court of King Fulrach in Sendar. This was Vo Mimbre, and the prospect of blurting out news of the wild scheme of a group of Asturian firebrands as he had blurted out the news of the Earl of Jarvik in Cherek now seemed utterly out of the question.

Suddenly the thought of that previous event struck him forcibly. The situation then was so similar to this one that it seemed all at once like some elaborate game. The moves on the board were almost identical, and in each case he had been placed in the uncomfortable position of being required to block that last crucial move where a king would die and a kingdom would collapse. He felt oddly powerless, as if his entire life were in the fingers of two faceless players maneuvering pieces in the same patterns on some vast board in a game that, for all he knew, had lasted for eternity. There was no question about what had to be done. The players, however, seemed content to leave it up to him to come up with a way to do it.

King Korodullin appeared shaken when he returned to the throne room with Mister Wolf a half hour later, and he controlled his expression with obvious difficulty. "Forgive me, gentles all," he apologized, "but I have had disturbing news. For the present time, however, let us put aside our cares and celebrate this historic visit. Summon musicians and command that a banquet be made ready."

There was a stir near the door, and a black-robed man entered with a half-dozen Mimbrate knights in full armor following him closely, their eyes narrow with suspicion and their hands on their sword hilts as if daring anyone to bar their leader's path. As the robed man strode nearer, Garion saw his angular eyes and scarred cheeks. The man was a Murgo.

Barak put a firm hand on Hettar's arm.

The Murgo had obviously dressed in haste and he seemed slightly breathless from his hurried trip to the throne room. "Your Majesty," he rasped, bowing deeply to Korodullin, "I have just been advised that visitors have arrived at thy court and have made haste here to greet them in the name of my king, Taur Urgas."

Korodullin's face grew cold. "I do not recall summoning thee, Nachak," he said.

"It is, then, as I had feared," the Murgo replied. "These messengers have spoken ill of my race, seeking to dissever the friendship which doth exist between the thrones of Arendia and of Cthol Murgos. I am chagrined to find that thou hast given ear to slanders without offering me opportunity to reply. Is this just, august Majesty?"

"Who is this?" Mister Wolf asked Korodullin.

"Nachak," the king replied, "the ambassador of Cthol Murgos. Shall I introduce thee to him, Ancient One?"

"That won't be necessary," Mister Wolf answered bleakly. "Every Murgo alive knows who I am. Mothers in Cthol Murgos frighten their children into obedience by mentioning my name."

"But I am not a child, old man," Nachak sneered. "I'm not afraid of you."

"That could be a serious failing," Silk observed.

The Murgo's name had struck Garion almost like a blow. As he looked at the scarred face of the man who had so misled Lelldorin and his friends, he realized that the players had once again moved their pieces into that last crucial position, and that who would win and who would lose once again depended entirely on him.

"What lies have you told the king?" Nachak was demanding of Mister Wolf.

"No lies, Nachak," Wolf told him. "Just the truth. That should be enough."

"I protest, your Majesty," Nachak appealed to the king. "I protest in the strongest manner possible. All the world knows of his hatred for my people. How can you allow him to poison your mind against us?"

"He forgot the thees and thous that time," Silk commented slyly.

"He's excited," Barak replied. "Murgos get clumsy when they're excited. It's one of their shortcomings."

"Alorns!" Nachak spat.

"That's right, Murgo," Barak said coldly. He was still holding Hettar's arm.

Nachak looked at them, and then his eyes widened as he seemed to see Hettar for the first time. He recoiled from the Algar's hate-filled stare, and his half-dozen knights closed protectively around him. "Your Majesty," he rasped, "I know that man to be Hettar of Algaria, a known murderer. I demand that you arrest him."

"*Demand*, Nachak?" the king asked with a dangerous glint in his eyes. "Thou wilt present demands to me in my own court?"

"Forgive me, your Majesty," Nachak apologized quickly. "The sight of that animal so disturbed me that I forgot myself."

"You'd be wise to leave now, Nachak," Mister Wolf recommended. "It's not really a good idea for a Murgo to be alone in the presence of so many Alorns. Accidents have a way of happening under such conditions."

"Grandfather," Garion said urgently. Without knowing exactly why, he knew that it was time to speak. Nachak must not be allowed to leave the throne room. The faceless players had made their final moves, and the game must end here. "Grandfather," he repeated, "there's something I have to tell you."

"Not now, Garion." Wolf was still looking with hard eyes at the Murgo.

"It's important, grandfather. *Very* important."

Mister Wolf turned as if to reply sharply, but then he seemed to see something—something that no one else in the throne room could see—and his eyes widened in momentary amazement. "All right, Garion," he said in a strangely quiet voice. "Go ahead."

"Some men are planning to kill the king of Arendia. Nachak's one of them." Garion had said it louder than he'd intended, and a sudden silence fell over the throne room at his words.

Nachak's face went pale, and his hand moved involuntarily toward his sword hilt, then froze. Garion was suddenly keenly aware of Barak hulking just behind him and Hettar, grim as death in black leather towering beside him. Nachak stepped back and made a quick gesture to his steel-clad knights. Quickly they formed a protective ring around him, their hands on their weapons. "I won't stay and listen to such slander," the Murgo declared.

"I have not yet given thee my permission to withdraw, Nachak," Korodullin informed him coolly. "I require thy presence yet a while." The young king's face was stern, and his eyes bored into the Murgo's. Then he turned to Garion. "I would hear more of this. Speak truthfully, lad, and fear not reprisal from any man for thy words."

Garion drew a deep breath and spoke carefully. "I don't really know all the details, your Majesty," he explained. "I found out about it by accident."

"Say what thou canst," the king told him.

"As nearly as I can tell, your Majesty, next summer when you travel to Vo Astur, a group of men are going to try to kill you somewhere on the highway."

"Asturian traitors, doubtless," a gray-haired courtier suggested.

"They call themselves patriots," Garion answered.

"Inevitably," the courtier sneered.

"Such attempts are not uncommon," the king stated. "We will take steps to guard against them. I thank thee for this information."

"There's more, your Majesty," Garion added. "When they attack, they're going to be wearing the uniforms of Tolnedran legionnaires."

Silk whistled sharply.

"The whole idea is to make your nobles believe that you've been killed by the Tolnedrans," Garion continued. "These men are sure that Mimbre will immediately declare war on the Empire, and that as soon as that happens the legions will march in. Then, when everybody here is involved in the war, they're going to announce that Asturia's no longer subject to the Arendish throne. They're sure that the rest of Asturia will follow them at that point."

"I see," the king replied thoughtfully. " 'Tis a well-conceived plan, but with a subtlety uncharacteristic of our wild-eyed Asturian brothers. But I have yet heard nothing linking the emissary of Taur Urgas with this treason."

"The whole plan was his, your Majesty. He gave them all the details and the gold to buy the Tolnedran uniforms and to encourage other people to join them."

"He lies!" Nachak burst out.

"Thou shalt have opportunity to reply, Nachak," the king advised him. He turned back to Garion. "Let us pursue this matter further. How camest thou by this knowledge?"

"I can't say, your Majesty," Garion replied painfully. "I gave my word not to. One of the men told me about it to prove that he was my friend. He put his life in my hands to show how much he trusted me. I can't betray him."

"Thy loyalty speaks well of thee, young Garion," the king commended him, "but thy accusation against the Murgo ambassador is most grave. Without violating thy trust, canst thou provide corroboration?"

Helplessly, Garion shook his head.

"This is a serious matter, your Majesty," Nachak declared. "I am the personal representative of Taur Urgas. This lying urchin is Belgarath's creature, and his wild, unsubstantiated story is an obvious attempt to discredit me and to drive a wedge between the thrones of Arendia and Cthol Murgos. This accusation must not be allowed to stand. The boy must be forced to identify these imaginary plotters or to admit that he lies."

"He hath given his pledge, Nachak," the king pointed out.

"He *says* so, your Majesty," Nachak replied with a sneer. "Let us put him to the test. An hour on the rack may persuade him to speak freely."

"I've seldom had much faith in confessions obtained by torment," Korodullin said.

"If it please your Majesty," Mandorallen interjected, "it may be that I can help to resolve this matter."

Garion threw a stricken look at the knight. Mandorallen knew Lelldorin, and it would be a simple thing for him to guess the truth. Mandorallen, moreover, was a Mimbrate, and Korodullin was his king. Not only was he under no compulsion to remain silent, but his duty almost obliged him to speak.

"Sir Mandorallen," the king responded gravely, "thy devotion to truth and duty are legendary. Canst thou perchance identify these plotters?"

The question hung there.

"Nay, Sire," Mandorallen replied firmly, "but I know Garion to be a truthful and honest boy. I will vouch for him."

"That's scanty corroboration," Nachak asserted. "I declare that he lies, so where does that leave us?"

"The lad is my companion," Mandorallen said. "I will not be the instrument of breaking his pledge, since his honor is as dear to me as mine own. By our law, however, a cause incapable of proof may be decided by trial at arms. I will champion this boy. I declare before this company that this Nachak is a foul villain who hath joined with diverse others to slay my king." He pulled off his steel gauntlet and tossed it to the floor. The crash as it struck the polished stone seemed thunderous. "Take up my gage, Murgo," Mandorallen said coldly, "or let one of thy sycophant knights take it up for thee. I will prove thy villainy upon thy body or upon the body of thy champion."

Nachak stared first at the mailed gauntlet and then at the great knight standing accusingly before him. He licked his lips nervously and looked around the throne room. Except for Mandorallen, none of the Mimbrate nobles present were under arms. The Murgo's eyes narrowed with a sudden desperation. "Kill him!" he snarled at the six men in armor surrounding him.

The knights looked shocked, doubtful.

"Kill him!" Nachak commanded them. "A thousand gold pieces to the man who spills out his life!"

The faces of the six knights went flat at his words. As one man they drew their swords and spread out, moving with raised shields toward Mandorallen. There were gasps and cries of alarm as the nobles and their ladies scrambled out of the way.

"What treason is this?" Mandorallen demanded of them. "Are ye so enamored of this Murgo and his gold that ye will draw weapons in the king's presence in open defiance of the law's prohibitions? Put up your swords."

But they ignored his words and continued their grim advance.

"Defend thyself, Sir Mandorallen," Korodullin urged, half-rising from his throne. "I free thee of the law's constraint."

Barak, however, had already begun to move. Noting that Mandorallen had not carried his shield into the throne room, the red-bearded man jerked an enormous two-handed broadsword down from the array of banners and weapons at one side of the dais. "Mandorallen!" he shouted and with a great heave he slid the huge blade skittering and bouncing across the stone floor toward the knight's feet. Mandorallen stopped the sliding weapon with one mailed foot, stooped, and picked it up.

The approaching knights looked a bit less confident as Mandorallen lifted the six-foot blade with both hands.

Barak, grinning hugely, drew his sword from one hip and his war axe from the other. Hettar, his drawn sabre held low, was circling the clumsy knights on catlike feet. Without thinking, Garion reached for his own sword, but Mister Wolf's hand closed on his wrist. "You stay out of it," the old man told him and pulled him clear of the impending fight.

Mandorallen's first blow crashed against a quickly raised shield, shattering the arm of a knight with a crimson surcoat over his armor and hurling him into a clattering heap ten feet away. Barak parried a sword stroke from a burly knight with his axe and battered at the man's raised shield with his own heavy sword. Hettar toyed expertly with a knight in green-enameled armor, easily avoiding his opponent's awkward strokes and flicking the point of his sabre at the man's visored face.

The steely ring of sword on sword echoed through Korodullin's throne room, and showers of sparks cascaded from the clash of edge against edge. With huge blows, Mandorallen smashed at a second man. A vast sweep of his two-handed sword went under the knight's shield, and the man shrieked as the great blade bit through his armor and into his side. Then he fell with blood spouting from the sheared-in gash that reached halfway through his body.

Barak, with a deft backswing of his war axe, caved in the side of the burly knight's helmet, and the knight half-spun and fell to the floor. Hettar feinted a quick move, then drove his sabre point through a slot in the green-armored knight's visor. The stricken knight stiffened as the sabre ran into his brain.

As the mêlée surged across the polished floor, the nobles and ladies scurried this way and that to avoid being overrun by the struggling men. Nachak watched with dismay as his knights were systematically destroyed before his eyes. Then, quite suddenly he turned and fled.

"He's getting away!" Garion shouted, but Hettar was already in pursuit, his dreadful face and blood-smeared sabre melting the courtiers and their screaming ladies out of his path as he ran to cut off Nachak's flight. The Murgo had almost reached the far end of the hall before Hettar's long strides carried him through the crowd to block the doorway. With a cry of despair, the ambassador yanked his sword from its scabbard, and Garion felt a strange, momentary pity for him.

As the Murgo raised his sword, Hettar flicked his sabre almost like a whip, lashing him once on each shoulder. Nachak desperately tried to raise his numbed arms to protect his head, but Hettar's blade dropped low instead. Then, with a peculiar fluid grace, the grim-faced Algar quite deliberately ran the Murgo through. Garion saw the sabre blade come out between Nachak's shoulders, angling sharply upward. The ambassador gasped, dropped his sword and gripped Hettar's wrist with both hands, but the hawk-faced man inexorably turned his hand, twisting the sharp, curved blade inside the Murgo's body. Nachak groaned and shuddered horribly. Then his hands slipped off Hettar's wrist and his legs buckled under him. With a gurgling sigh, he toppled backward, sliding limply off Hettar's blade.

Chapter Eleven

A MOMENT OF DREADFUL SILENCE filled the throne room following the death of Nachak. Then the two members of his bodyguard who were still on their feet threw their weapons down on the blood-spattered floor with a sudden clatter. Mandorallen raised his visor and turned toward the throne. "Sire," he said respectfully, "the treachery of Nachak stands proved by reason of this trial at arms."

"Truly," the king agreed. "My only regret is that thy enthusiasm in pursuing this cause hath deprived us of the opportunity to probe more deeply into the full extent of Nachak's duplicity."

"I expect that the plots he hatched will dry up once word of what happened here gets around," Mister Wolf observed.

"Perhaps so," the king acknowledged. "I would have pursued the matter further, however. I would know if this villainy was Nachak's own or if I must look beyond him to Taur Urgas himself." He frowned thoughtfully, then shook his head as if to put certain dark speculations aside. "Arendia stands in thy debt, Ancient Belgarath. This brave company of thine hath forestalled the renewal of a war best forgotten." He looked sadly at the blood-smeared floor and the bodies littering it. "My throne room hath become as a battlefield. The curse of Arendia extends even here." He sighed. "Have it cleansed," he ordered shortly and turned his head so that he would not have to watch the grim business of cleaning up.

The nobles and ladies began to buzz as the dead were removed and the polished stone floor was quickly mopped to remove the pools of sticky blood.

"Good fight," Barak commented as he carefully wiped his axe blade.

"I am in thy debt, Lord Barak," Mandorallen said gravely. "Thy aid was fortuitous."

Barak shrugged. "It seemed appropriate."

Hettar rejoined them, his expression one of grim satisfaction.

"You did a nice job on Nachak," Barak complimented him.

"I've had a lot of practice," Hettar answered. "Murgos always seem to make that same mistake when they get into a fight. I think there's a gap in their training somewhere."

"That's a shame, isn't it?" Barak suggested with vast insincerity.

Garion moved away from them. Although he knew it was irrational, he nevertheless felt a keen sense of personal responsibility for the carnage he had just witnessed. The blood and violent death had come about as the result of his words. Had he not spoken, men who were now dead would still be alive. No matter how justified—how necessary—his speaking out had been, he still suffered the pangs of guilt. He did not at the moment trust himself to speak with his friends. More than anything he wished that he could talk with Aunt Pol, but she had not yet returned to the throne room, and so he was left to wrestle alone with his wounded conscience.

He reached one of the embrasures formed by the buttresses along the south wall of the throne room and stood alone in somber reflection until a girl, perhaps two years older than he, glided across the floor toward him, her stiff, crimson brocade gown rustling. The girl's hair was dark, even black, and her skin was creamy. Her bodice was cut quite low, and Garion found some difficulty in finding a safe place for his eyes as she bore down on him.

"I would add my thanks to the thanks of all Arendia, Lord Garion," she breathed at him. Her voice was vibrant with all kinds of emotions, none of which Garion understood. "Thy timely revelation of the Murgo's plotting hath in truth saved the life of our sovereign."

Garion felt a certain warmth at that. "I didn't do all that

much, my lady," he replied with a somewhat insincere attempt at modesty. "My friends did all the fighting."

"But it was *thy* brave denunciation which uncovered the foul plot," she persisted, "and virgins will sing of the nobility with which thou protected the identity of thy nameless and misguided friend."

Virgin was not a word with which Garion was prepared to deal. He blushed and floundered helplessly.

"Art thou in truth, noble Garion, the grandson of Eternal Belgarath?"

"The relationship is a bit more distant. We simplify it for the sake of convenience."

"But thou art in his direct line?" she persisted, her violet eyes glowing.

"He tells me I am."

"Is the Lady Polgara perchance thy mother?"

"My aunt."

"A close kinship nonetheless," she approved warmly, her hand coming to rest lightly on his wrist. "Thy blood, Lord Garion, is the noblest in the world. Tell me, art thou perchance as yet unbetrothed?"

Garion blinked at her, his ears growing suddenly redder.

"Ah, Garion," Mandorallen boomed in his hearty voice, striding into the awkward moment, "I had been seeking thee. Wilt thou excuse us, Countess?"

The young lady shot Mandorallen a look filled with sheer venom, but the knight's firm hand was already drawing Garion away.

"We will speak again, Lord Garion," she called after him.

"I hope so, my Lady," Garion replied back over his shoulder. Then he and Mandorallen merged with the crowd of courtiers near the center of the throne room.

"I wanted to thank you, Mandorallen," Garion said finally, struggling with it a little.

"For what, lad?"

"You knew whom I was protecting when I told the King about Nachak, didn't you?"

"Naturally," the knight replied in a rather offhand way.

"You could have told the king—actually it was your duty to tell him, wasn't it?"

"But thou hadst given thy pledge."

"You hadn't, though."

"Thou art my companion, lad. Thy pledge is as binding upon me as it is upon thee. Didst thou not know that?"

Garion was startled by Mandorallen's words. The exquisite involvement of Arendish ethics were beyond his grasp. "So you fought for me instead."

Mandorallen laughed easily. "Of course," he answered, "though I must confess to thee in all honesty, Garion, that my eagerness to stand as thy champion grew not entirely out of friendship. In truth I found the Murgo Nachak offensive and liked not the cold arrogance of his hirelings. I was inclined toward battle before thy need of championing presented itself. Perhaps it is I who should thank thee for providing the opportunity."

"I don't understand you at all, Mandorallen," Garion admitted. "Sometimes I think you're the most complicated man I've ever met."

"I?" Mandorallen seemed amazed. "I am the simplest of men." He looked around then and leaned slightly toward Garion. "I must advise thee to have a care in thy speech with the Countess Vasrana," he warned. "It was that which impelled me to draw thee aside."

"Who?"

"The comely young lady with whom thou wert speaking. She considers herself the greatest beauty in the kingdom and is seeking a husband worthy of her."

"Husband?" Garion responded in a faltering voice.

"Thou art fair game, lad. Thy blood is noble beyond measure by reason of thy kinship to Belgarath. Thou wouldst be a great prize for the countess."

"Husband?" Garion quavered again, his knees beginning to tremble. "Me?"

"I know not how things stand in misty Sendaria," Mandorallen declared, "but in Arendia thou art of marriageable age. Guard well thy speech, lad. The most innocent remark can be viewed as a promise, should a noble choose to take it so."

Garion swallowed hard and looked around apprehensively. After that he did his best to hide. His nerves, he felt, were not up to any more shocks.

The Countess Vasrana, however, proved to be a skilled huntress. With appalling determination she tracked him down and pinned him in another embrasure with smoldering eyes and heaving bosom. "Now perchance we may continue our most interesting discussion, Lord Garion," she purred at him.

Garion was considering flight when Aunt Pol, accompanied by a now-radiant Queen Mayaserana, reentered the throne room. Mandorallen spoke briefly to her, and she immediately crossed to the spot where the violet-eyed countess held Garion captive. "Garion, dear," she said as she approached. "It's time for your medicine."

"Medicine?" he replied, confused.

"A most forgetful boy," she told the countess. "Probably it was all the excitement, but he knows that if he doesn't take the potion every three hours, the madness will return."

"Madness?" the Countess Vasrana repeated sharply.

"The curse of his family," Aunt Pol sighed. "They all have it—all the male children. The potion works for a while, but of course it's only temporary. We'll have to find some patient and self-sacrificing lady soon, so that he can marry and father children before his brains begin to soften. After that his poor wife will be doomed to spend the rest of her days caring for him." She looked critically at the young countess. "I wonder," she said. "Could it be possible that *you* are as yet unbetrothed? You appear to be of a suitable age." She reached out and briefly took hold of Vasrana's rounded arm. "Nice and strong," she said approvingly. "I'll speak to my father, Lord Belgarath, about this immediately."

The countess began to back away, her eyes wide.

"Come back," Aunt Pol told her. "His fits won't start for several minutes yet."

The girl fled.

"Can't you ever stay out of trouble?" Aunt Pol demanded of Garion, leading him firmly away.

"But I didn't say anything," he objected.

Mandorallen joined them, grinning broadly. "I perceive that thou hast routed our predatory countess, my Lady. I should have thought she would prove more persistent."

"I gave her something to worry about. It dampened her enthusiasm for matrimony."

"What matter didst thou discuss with our queen?" he asked. "I have not seen her smile so in years."

"Mayaserana's had a problem of a female nature. I don't think you'd understand."

"Her inability to carry a child to term?"

"Don't Arends have anything better to do than gossip about things that don't concern them? Why don't you go find another fight instead of asking intimate questions?"

"The matter is of great concern to us all, my Lady," Mandorallen apologized. "If our queen does not produce an heir to the throne, we stand in danger of dynastic war. All Arendia could go up in flames."

"There aren't going to be any flames, Mandorallen. Fortunately I arrived in time—though it was very close. You'll have a crown prince before winter."

"Is it possible?"

"Would you like all the details?" she asked pointedly. "I've noticed that men usually prefer not to know about the exact mechanics involved in childbearing."

Mandorallen's face slowly flushed. "I will accept thy assurances, Lady Polgara," he replied quickly.

"I'm *so* glad."

"I must inform the king," he declared.

"You must mind your own business, Sir Mandorallen. The queen will tell Korodullin what he needs to know. Why don't you go clean off your armor? You look as if you just walked through a slaughterhouse."

He bowed, still blushing, and moved away.

"Men!" she said to his retreating back. Then she turned back to Garion. "I hear that you've been busy."

"I had to warn the king," he replied.

"You seem to have an absolute genius for getting mixed up in this sort of thing. Why didn't you tell me—or your grandfather."

"I promised that I wouldn't say anything."

"Garion," she said firmly, "under our present circumstances, secrets are very dangerous. You knew that what Lelldorin told you was important, didn't you?"

"I didn't say it was Lelldorin."

She gave him a withering look. "Garion, dear," she told him bluntly, "don't ever make the mistake of thinking that I'm stupid."

"I didn't," he floundered. "I wasn't. I—Aunt Pol, I gave them my word that I wouldn't tell anybody."

She sighed. "We've got to get you out of Arendia," she declared. "The place seems to be affecting your good sense. The next time you feel the urge to make one of these startling public announcements, talk it over with me first, all right?"

"Yes, ma'am," he mumbled, embarrassed.

"Oh, Garion, what am I ever going to do with you?" Then she laughed fondly and put her arm about his shoulder and everything was all right again.

The evening passed uneventfully after that. The banquet was tedious, and the toasts afterward interminable as each Arendish noble arose in turn to salute Mister Wolf and Aunt Pol with flowery and formal speeches. They went to bed late, and Garion slept fitfully, troubled by nightmares of the hot-eyed countess pursuing him through endless, flower-strewn corridors.

They were up early the next morning, and after breakfast Aunt Pol and Mister Wolf spoke privately with the king and queen again. Garion, still nervous about his encounter with the Countess Vasrana, stayed close to Mandorallen. The Mimbrate knight seemed best equipped to help him avoid any more such adventures. They waited in an antechamber to the throne room, and Mandorallen in his blue surcoat explained at length an intricate tapestry which covered one entire wall.

About midmorning Sir Andorig, the dark-haired knight Mister Wolf had ordered to spend his days caring for the tree in the plaza, came looking for Mandorallen. "Sir Knight," he said respectfully, "the Baron of Vo Ebor hath arrived from the north accompanied by his lady. They have asked after thee and besought me that I should seek thee out for them."

"Thou art most kind, Sir Andorig," Mandorallen replied, rising quickly from the bench where he had been sitting. "Thy courtesy becomes thee greatly."

Andorig sighed. "Alas that it was not always so. I have

this past night stood vigil before that miraculous tree which
Holy Belgarath commended to my care. I thus had leisure
to consider my life in retrospect. I have not been an admir-
able man. Bitterly I repent my faults and will strive ear-
nestly for amendment."

Wordlessly, Mandorallen clasped the knight's hand and
then followed him down a long hallway to a room where
the visitors waited.

It was not until they entered the sunlit room that Garion
remembered that the wife of the Baron of Vo Ebor was the
lady to whom Mandorallen had spoken on that windswept
hill beside the Great West Road some days before.

The baron was a solid-looking man in a green surcoat,
and his hair and beard were touched with white. His eyes
were deep-set, and there seemed to be a great sadness in
them. "Mandorallen," he said, warmly embracing the
younger knight. "Thou art unkind to absent thyself from us
for so long."

"Duty, my Lord," Mandorallen replied in a subdued
voice.

"Come, Nerina," the baron told his wife, "greet our
friend."

The Baroness Nerina was much younger than her husband. Her hair was dark and very long. She wore a rose-
colored gown, and she was beautiful—though, Garion
thought, no more so than any of a half-dozen others he had
seen at the Arendish court.

"Dear Mandorallen," she said, kissing the knight with a
brief, chaste embrace, "we have missed thee at Vo Ebor."

"And the world is desolate for me that I must be absent
from its well-loved halls."

Sir Andorig had bowed and then discreetly departed,
leaving Garion standing awkwardly near the door.

"And who is this likely-appearing lad who accompanies
thee, my son?" the baron asked.

"A Sendarian boy," Mandorallen responded. "His name
is Garion. He and diverse others have joined with me in a
perilous quest."

"Joyfully I greet my son's companion," the baron declared.

Garion bowed, but his mind raced, attempting to find

some legitimate excuse to leave. The situation was terribly embarrassing, and he did not want to stay.

"I must wait upon the king," the baron announced. "Custom and courtesy demand that I present myself to him as soon as possible upon my arrival at his court. Wilt thou, Mandorallen, remain here with my baroness until I return?"

"I will, my Lord."

"I'll take you to where the king is meeting with my aunt and my grandfather, sir," Garion offered quickly.

"Nay, lad," baron demurred. "Thou too must remain. Though I have no cause for anxiety, knowing full well the fidelity of my wife and my dearest friend, idle tongues would make scandal were they left together unattended. Prudent folk leave no possible foundation for false rumor and vile innuendo."

"I'll stay then, sir," Garion replied quickly.

"Good lad," the baron approved. Then, with eyes that seemed somehow haunted, he quietly left the room.

"Wilt thou sit, my Lady?" Mandorallen asked Nerina, pointing to a sculptured bench near a window.

"I will," she said. "Our journey was fatiguing."

"It is a long way from Vo Ebor," Mandorallen agreed, sitting on another bench. "Didst thou and my Lord find the roads passable?"

"Perhaps not yet so dry as to make travel enjoyable," she told him.

They spoke at some length about roads and weather, sitting not far from each other, but not so close that anyone chancing to pass by the open door could have mistaken their conversation for anything less than innocent. Their eyes, however, spoke more intimately. Garion, painfully embarrassed, stood looking out a window, carefully choosing one that kept him in full view of the door.

As the conversation progressed, there were increasingly long pauses, and Garion cringed inwardly at each agonizing silence, afraid that either Mandorallen or the Lady Nerina might in the extremity of their hopeless love cross that unspoken boundary and blurt the one word, phrase, or sentence which would cause restraint and honor to crumble and turn their lives into disaster. And yet a certain part of his mind wished that the word or phrase or sentence might be spoken and that their love could flame, however briefly.

It was there, in that quiet sunlit chamber, that Garion passed a small crossroad. The prejudice against Mandorallen that Lelldorin's unthinking partisanship had instilled in him finally shattered and fell away. He felt a surge of feeling—not pity, for they would not have accepted pity, but compassion rather. More than that, there was the faint beginning of an understanding of the honor and towering pride which, though utterly selfless, was the foundation of that tragedy which had existed in Arendia for uncounted centuries.

For perhaps a half hour more Mandorallen and the Lady Nerina sat, speaking hardly at all now, their eyes lost in each others' faces while Garion, near to tears, stood his enforced watch over them. And then Durnik came to tell them that Aunt Pol and Mister Wolf were getting ready to leave.

Part Two

TOLNEDRA

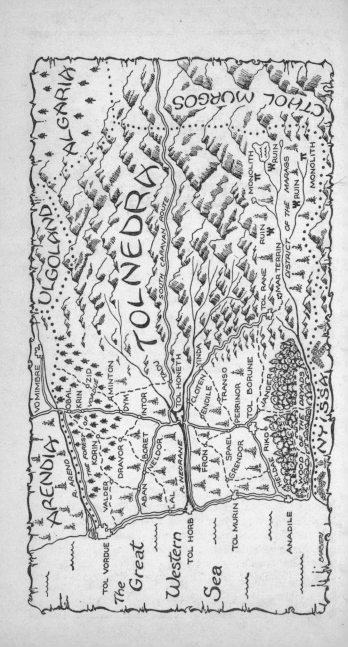

Chapter Twelve

A BRASSY CHORUS OF HORNS saluted them from the battlements of Vo Mimbre as they rode out of the city accompanied by two-score armored knights and by King Korodullin himself. Garion glanced back once and thought he saw the Lady Nerina standing upon the wall above the arched gate, though he could not be sure. The lady did not wave, and Mandorallen did not look back. Garion however, very nearly held his breath until Vo Mimbre was out of sight.

It was midafternoon by the time they reached the ford which crossed the River Arend into Tolnedra, and the bright sun sparkled on the river. The sky was very blue overhead, and the colored pennons on the lances of the escorting knights snapped in the breeze. Garion felt a desperate urgency, an almost unbearable necessity to cross the river and to leave Arendia and the terrible things that had happened there behind.

"Hail and farewell, Holy Belgarath," Korodullin said at the water's edge. "I will, as thou hast advised me, begin my preparations. Arendia will be ready. I pledge my life to it."

"And I'll keep you advised of our progress from time to time," Mister Wolf said.

"I will also examine the activities of the Murgos within my kingdom," Korodullin said. "If what thou hast told me should prove true, as I doubt not that it shall, then I will expell them from Arendia. I will seek them out, one and all, and harry them out of the land. I will make their lives a burden and an affliction to them for sowing discord and contention among my subjects."

Wolf grinned at him. "That's an idea that appeals to me.

143

Murgos are an arrogant people, and a little affliction now and then teaches them humility." He reached out and took the king's hand. "Good-bye, Korodullin. I hope the world's happier next time we meet."

"I will pray that it may be so," the young king said.

Then Mister Wolf led the way down into the rippling water of the shallow ford. Beyond the river Imperial Tolnedra waited, and from the banks behind them the Mimbrate knights saluted with a great fanfare on their horns.

As they emerged on the far side of the river, Garion looked around, trying to see some difference in terrain or foliage which might distinguish Arendia from Tolnedra, but there seemed to be none. The land, indifferent to human boundaries, flowed on unchanged.

About a half-mile from the river they entered the forest of Vordue, an extensive tract of well-kept woodland which extended from the sea to the foothills of the mountains to the east. Once they were under the trees, they stopped and changed back into their traveling clothes. "I think we might as well keep the guise of merchants," Mister Wolf said, settling with obvious comfort back into his patched rust-colored tunic and mismatched shoes. "It won't fool the Grolims, of course, but it will satisfy the Tolnedrans we meet along the way. We can deal with the Grolims in other ways."

"Are there any signs of the Orb about?" Barak rumbled as he stowed his bearskin cloak and helmet in one of the packs.

"A hint or two," Wolf said, looking around. "I'd guess that Zedar went through here a few weeks ago."

"We don't seem to be gaining on him much," Silk said, pulling on his leather vest.

"We're holding our own at least. Shall we go?"

They remounted and continued along the Tolnedran highway, which ran straight through the forest in the afternoon sun. After a league or so, they came to a wide place in the road where a single whitewashed stone building, low and red-roofed, stood solidly at the roadside. Several soldiers lounged indolently about, but their armor and equipment seemed less well-cared-for than that of the legionnaires Garion had seen before.

"Customs station," Silk said. "Tolnedrans like to put them far enough from the border so that they don't interfere with legitimate smuggling."

"Those are very slovenly legionnaires," Durnik said disapprovingly.

"They aren't legionnaires," Silk explained. "They're soldiers of the customs service—local troops. There's a great difference."

"I can see that," Durnik said.

A soldier wearing a rusty breastplate and carrying a short spear stepped into the road and held up his hand. "Customs inspection," he announced in a bored tone. "His excellency will be with you in a moment or two. You can take your horses over there." He pointed to a kind of yard at the side of the building.

"Is trouble likely?" Mandorallen asked. The knight had removed his armor and now wore the mail suit and surcoat in which he customarily traveled.

"No," Silk said. "The customs agent will ask a few questions, and then we'll bribe him and be on our way."

"Bribe?" Durnik asked.

Silk shrugged. "Of course. That's the way things are in Tolnedra. Better let me do the talking. I've been through all this before."

The customs agent, a stout, balding man in a belted gown of a rusty brown color, came out of the stone building, brushing crumbs from the front of his clothes. "Good afternoon," he said in a businesslike manner.

"Good day, your Excellency," Silk replied with a brief bow.

"And what have we here?" the agent asked, looking appraisingly at the packs.

"I'm Radek of Boktor," Silk replied, "a Drasnian merchant. I'm taking Sendarian wool to Tol Honeth." He opened the top of one of the packs and pulled out a corner of woven gray cloth.

"Your prospects are good, worthy merchant," the customs agent said, fingering the cloth. "It's been a chilly winter this year, and wool's bringing a good price."

There was a brief clinking sound as several coins changed hands. The customs agent smiled then, and his manner grew more relaxed. "I don't think we'll need to open all the packs," he said. "You're obviously an honorable man, worthy Radek, and I wouldn't want to delay you."

Silk bowed again. "Is there anything I should know about the road ahead, your Excellency?" he asked, tying up the pack again. "I've learned to rely on the advice of the customs service."

"The road's good," the agent said with a shrug. "The legions see to that."

"Of course. Any unusual conditions anywhere?"

"It might be wise if you kept somewhat to yourselves on your way south," the stout man advised. "There's a certain amount of political turmoil in Tolnedra just now. I'm sure, though, that if you show that you're tending strictly to business, you won't be bothered."

"Turmoil?" Silk asked, sounding a bit concerned. "I hadn't heard about that."

"It's the succession. Things are a bit stirred up at the moment."

"Is Ran Borune ill?" Silk asked with surprise.

"No," the stout man said, "only old. It's a disease no one recovers from. Since he doesn't have a son to succeed him, the Borune Dynasty hangs on his feeblest breath. The great families are already maneuvering for position. It's all terribly expensive of course, and we Tolnedrans get agitated when there's money involved."

Silk laughed briefly. "Don't we all? Perhaps it might be to my advantage to make a few contacts in the right quarters. Which family would you guess is in the best position at the moment?"

"I think we have the edge over the rest of them," the agent said rather smugly.

"We?"

"The Vorduvians. I'm distantly related on my mother's side to the family. The Grand Duke Kador of Tol Vordue's the only logical choice for the throne."

"I don't believe I know him," Silk said.

"An excellent man," the agent said expansively. "A man of force and vigor and foresight. If the selection were based on simple merit, Grand Duke Kador would be given the

throne by general consent. Unfortunately, though, the selection's in the hands of the Council of Advisers."

"Ah!"

"Indeed," the agent agreed bitterly. "You wouldn't believe the size of the bribes some of those men are asking
for their votes, worthy Radek."

"It's an opportunity that comes only once in a lifetime, I
suppose," Silk said.

"I don't begrudge any man the right to a decent, reason-
able bribe," the stout agent complained, "but some of the
men on the council have gone mad with greed. No matter
what position I get in the new government, it's going to
take me years to recoup what I've already been obliged to
contribute. It's the same all over Tolnedra. Decent men are
being driven to the wall by taxes and all these emergency
subscriptions. You don't dare let a list go by that doesn't
have your name on it, and there's a new list out every day.
The expense is making everyone desperate. They're killing
each other in the streets of Tol Honeth."

"That bad?" Silk asked.

"Worse than you can imagine," the customs man said.
"The Horbites don't have the kind of money it takes to
conduct a political campaign, so they've started to poison
off council members. We spend millions to buy a vote, and
the next day our man turns black in the face and falls over
dead. Then we have to raise more millions to buy up his
successor. They're absolutely destroying me. I don't have
the right kind of nerves for politics."

"Terrible," Silk sympathized.

"If Ran Borune would only *die*," the Tolnedran complained desperately. "We're in control now, but the
Honeths are richer than we are. If they unite behind one
candidate, they'll be able to buy the throne right out from
under us. And all the while Ran Borune sits in the palace
doting on that little monster he calls a daughter and with so
many guards around that we can't persuade even the brav-
est assassin to make an attempt on him. Sometimes I think
he intends to live forever."

"Patience, Excellency," Silk advised. "The more we suffer, the greater the rewards in the end."

The Tolnedran sighed. "I'll be very rich someday then. But I've kept you long enough, worthy Radek. I wish you good speed and cold weather in Tol Honeth to bring up the price of your wool."

Silk bowed formally, remounted his horse and led the party at a trot away from the customs station. "It's good to be back in Tolnedra again," the weasel-faced little man said expansively once they were out of earshot. "I love the smell of deceit, corruption, and intrigue."

"You're a bad man, Silk," Barak said. "This place is a cesspool."

"Of course it is." Silk laughed. "But it isn't dull, Barak. Tolnedra's never dull."

They approached a tidy Tolnedran village as evening fell and stopped for the night in a solid, well-kept inn where the food was good and the beds were clean. They were up early the next morning; after breakfast they clattered out of the innyard and onto the cobblestoned street in that curious silver light that comes just before the sun rises.

"A proper sort of place," Durnik said approvingly, looking around at the white stone houses with their red-tiled roofs. "Everything seems neat and orderly."

"It's a reflection of the Tolnedran mind," Mister Wolf explained. They pay great attention to details."

"That's not an unseemly trait," Durnik observed.

Wolf was about to answer that when two brown-robed men ran out of a shadowy side street. "Look out!" the one in the rear yelled. "He's gone mad!"

The man running in front was clutching at his head, his face contorted into an expression of unspeakable horror. Garion's horse shied violently as the madman ran directly at him, and Garion raised his right hand to try to push the bulging-eyed lunatic away. At the instant his hand touched the man's forehead, he felt a surge in his hand and arm, a kind of tingling as if the arm were suddenly enormously strong, and his mind filled with a vast roaring. The madman's eyes went blank, and he collapsed on the cobblestones as if Garion's touch had been some colossal blow.

Then Barak nudged his horse between Garion and the fallen man. "What's this all about?" he demanded of the second robed man who ran up, gasping for breath.

"We're from Mar Terrin," the man answered. "Brother Obor couldn't stand the ghosts anymore, so I was given permission to bring him home until his sanity returned." He knelt over the fallen man. "You didn't have to hit him so hard," he accused.

"I didn't," Garion protested. "I only touched him. I think he fainted."

"You must have hit him," the monk said. "Look at the mark on his face."

An ugly red welt stood on the unconscious man's forehead.

"Garion," Aunt Pol said, "can you do exactly what I tell you to do without asking any questions?"

Garion nodded. "I think so."

"Get down off your horse. Go to the man on the ground and put the palm of your hand on his forehead. Then apologize to him for knocking him down."

"Are you sure it's safe, Polgara?" Barak asked.

"It will be all right. Do as I told you, Garion."

Garion hesitantly approached the stricken man, reached out, and laid his palm on the ugly welt. "I'm sorry," he said, "and I hope you get well soon." There was a surge in his arm again, but quite different from the first one.

The madman's eyes cleared, and he blinked. "Where am I?" he asked. "What happened?" His voice sounded very normal, and the welt on his forehead was gone.

"It's all right now," Garion told him, not knowing exactly why he said it. "You've been sick, but you're better now."

"Come along, Garion," Aunt Pol said. "His friend can care for him now."

Garion went back to his horse, his thoughts churning.

"A miracle!" the second monk exclaimed.

"Hardly that," Aunt Pol said. "The blow restored your friend's mind, that's all. It happens sometimes." But she and Mister Wolf exchanged a long glance that said quite plainly that something else had happened—something unexpected.

They rode on, leaving the two monks in the middle of the street.

"What happened?" Durnik asked, a stunned look on his face.

Mister Wolf shrugged. "Polgara had to use Garion," he said. "There wasn't time to do it any other way."

Durnik looked unconvinced.

"We don't do it often," Wolf explained. "It's a little cumbersome to go through someone else like that, but sometimes we don't have any choice."

"But Garion healed him," Durnik objected.

"It has to come from the same hand as the blow, Durnik," Aunt Pol said. "Please don't ask so many questions."

The dry awareness in Garion's mind, however, refused to accept any of their explanations. It told him that nothing had come from outside. With a troubled face he studied the silvery mark on his palm. It seemed different for some reason.

"Don't think about it, dear," Aunt Pol said quietly as they left the village and rode south along the highway. "It's nothing to worry about. I'll explain it all later." Then, to the caroling of birds that greeted the rising sun, she reached across and firmly closed his hand with her fingers.

Chapter Thirteen

IT TOOK THEM THREE DAYS to pass through the forest of Vordue. Garion, remembering the dangers of the Arendish forest, was apprehensive at first and watched the shadows beneath the trees nervously, but after a day or so with nothing out of the ordinary occurring, he began to relax. Mister Wolf, however, seemed to grow increasingly irritable as they rode south. "They're planning something," he muttered. "I wish they'd get on with it. I hate to ride with one eye over my shoulder ever step of the way."

Garion had little opportunity along the way to speak

with Aunt Pol about what had happened to the crazy monk from Mar Terrin. It seemed almost as if she were deliberately avoiding him; when he finally did manage to ride briefly beside her and question her about the incident, her answers were vague and did little to quiet his unease about the whole affair.

It was the middle of the morning on the third day when they emerged from the trees and rode out into open farmland. Unlike the Arendish plain where vast tracts of land seemed to lie fallow, the ground here was extensively cultivated, and low stone walls surrounded each field. Although it was still far from being warm, the sun was very bright, and the well-turned earth in the fields seemed rich and black as it lay waiting for sowing. The highway was broad and straight, and they encountered frequent travelers along the way. Greetings between the party and these travelers were restrained but polite, and Garion began to feel more at ease. This country appeared to be much too civilized for the kind of dangers they had encountered in Arendia.

About midafternoon they rode into a sizable town where merchants in variously colored mantles called to them from booths and stalls which lined the streets, imploring them to stop and look at merchandise. "They sound almost desperate," Durnik said.

"Tolnedrans hate to see a customer get away," Silk told him. "They're greedy."

Ahead, in a small square, a disturbance suddenly broke out. A half-dozen slovenly, unshaven soldiers had accosted an arrogant-looking man in a green mantle. "Stand aside, I say," the arrogant man protested sharply.

"We just want a word or two with you, Lembor," one of the soldiers said with an evil-looking leer. He was a lean man with a long scar down one side of his face.

"What an idiot," a passer-by observed with a callous laugh. "Lembor's gotten so important that he doesn't think he has to take any precautions."

"Is he being arrested, friend?" Durnik inquired politely.

"Only temporarily," the passer-by said dryly.

"What are they going to do to him?" Durnik asked.

"The usual."

"What's the usual?"

"Watch and see. The fool should have known better than to come out without his bodyguards."

The soldiers had surrounded the man in the green mantle, and two of them took hold of his arms roughly.

"Let me go," Lembor protested. "What do you think you're doing?"

"Just come along quietly, Lembor," the scar-faced soldier ordered. "It will be a lot easier that way." They began pulling him toward a narrow alleyway.

"Help!" Lembor shouted, desperately trying to struggle.

One of the soldiers smashed the captive in the mouth with his fist, and they pulled him into the alley. There was a single, short scream and the sounds of a brief scuffle. There were other sounds as well, a few grunts and the grating sound of steel on bone, then a long, sighing moan. A wide rivulet of bright blood trickled out of the mouth of the alley and ran into the gutter. A minute or so later, the soldiers came back out into the square, grinning and wiping their swords.

"We've got to do something," Garion said, sick with outrage and horror.

"No," Silk said bluntly. "What we have to do is mind our own business. We're not here to get involved in local politics."

"Politics?" Garion objected. "That was deliberate murder. Shouldn't we at least see if he's still alive?"

"Not too likely," Barak said. "Six men with swords can usually do a pretty thorough job."

A dozen other soldiers, as shabby-looking as the first group, ran into the square with drawn swords.

"Too late, Rabbas." The scar-faced soldier laughed harshly to the leader of the newcomers. "Lembor doesn't need you anymore. He just came down with a bad case of dead. It looks like you're out of work."

The one called Rabbas stopped, his expression dark. Then a look of brutal cunning spread across his face. "Maybe you're right, Kragger." His voice was also harsh. "But then again we might be able to create a few vacancies in Elgon's garrison. I'm sure he'd be happy to hire good replacements." He began to move forward again, his short sword swinging in a low, dangerous arc.

Then there came the sound of a jingling trot, and twenty legionnaires in a double column came into the square, their feet striking the cobblestones in unison. They carried short lances, and they stopped between the two groups of soldiers. Each column turned to face one group, their lances leveled. The breastplates of the legionnaires were brightly burnished, and their equipment was spotless.

"All right, Rabbas, Kragger, that's enough," the sergeant in charge said sharply. "I want both of you off the street immediately."

"These swine killed Lembor, Sergeant," Rabbas protested.

"That's too bad," the sergeant said without much sympathy. "Now clear the street. There's not going to be any brawling while I'm on duty."

"Aren't you going to do something?" Rabbas demanded.

"I am," the legionnaire said. "I'm clearing the street. Now get out of here."

Sullenly, Rabbas turned and led his men out of the square.

"That goes for you too, Kragger," the sergeant ordered.

"Of course, Sergeant," Kragger said with an oily smirk. "We were just leaving anyway."

A crowd had gathered, and there were several boos as the legionnaires herded the sloppy-looking soldiers out of the square.

The sergeant looked around, his face dangerous, and the boos died immediately.

Durnik hissed sharply. "Over there on the far side of the square," he said to Wolf in a hoarse whisper. "Isn't that Brill?"

"Again?" Wolf's voice held exasperation. "How does he keep getting ahead of us like this?"

"Let's find out what he's up to," Silk suggested, his eyes bright.

"He'd recognize any of us if we tried to follow him," Barak warned.

"Leave that to me," Silk said, sliding out of his saddle.

"Did he see us?" Garion asked.

"I don't think so," Durnik said. "He's talking to those men over there. He isn't looking this way."

"There's an inn near the south end of town," Silk said quickly, pulling off his vest and tying it to his saddle. "I'll meet you there in an hour or so." Then the little man turned and disappeared into the crowd.

"Get down off your horses," Mister Wolf ordered tersely. "We'll lead them."

They all dismounted and led their mounts slowly around the edge of the square, staying close to the buildings and keeping the animals between them and Brill as much as possible.

Garion glanced once up the narrow alleyway where Kragger and his men had dragged the protesting Lembor. He shuddered and looked away quickly. A green-mantled heap lay in a grimy corner, and there was blood splashed thickly on the walls and the filthy cobblestones in the alley.

After they had moved out of the square, they found the entire town seething with excitement and in some cases consternation. "Lembor, you say?" an ashen-faced merchant in a blue mantle exclaimed to another shaken man. "Impossible."

"My brother just talked to a man who was there," the second merchant said. "Forty of Elgon's soldiers attacked him in the street and cut him down right in front of the crowd."

"What's going to happen to us?" the first man asked in a shaking voice.

"I don't know about you, but I'm going to hide. Now that Lembor's dead, Elgon's soldiers are probably going to try to kill us all."

"They wouldn't dare."

"Who's going to stop them? I'm going home."

"Why did we listen to Lembor?" the first merchant wailed. "We could have stayed out of the whole business."

"It's too late now," the second man said. "I'm going to go home and bar my doors." He turned and scurried away.

The first man stared after him and then he too turned and fled.

"They play for keeps, don't they?" Barak observed.

"Why do the legions allow it?" Mandorallen asked.

"The legions stay neutral in these affairs," Wolf said. "It's part of their oath."

The inn to which Silk had directed them was a neat, square building surrounded by a low wall. They tied their horses in the courtyard and went inside. "We might as well eat, father," Aunt Pol said, seating herself at a table of well-scrubbed oak in the sunny common room.

"I was just—" Wolf looked toward the door which led into the taproom.

"I know," she said, "but I think we should eat first."

Wolf sighed. "All right, Pol."

The serving-man brought them a platter of smoking cutlets and heavy slabs of brown bread soaked in butter. Garion's stomach was still a bit shaky after what he had witnessed in the square, but the smell of the cutlets soon overcame that. They had nearly finished eating when a shabby-looking little man in a linen shirt, leather apron and a ragged hat came in and plunked himself unceremoniously at the end of their table. His face looked vaguely familiar somehow. "Wine!" he bawled at the serving-man, "and food." He squinted around in the golden light streaming through the yellow glass windows of the common room.

"There are other tables, friend," Mandorallen said coldly.

"I like this one," the stranger said. He peered at each of them in turn, and then he suddenly laughed. Garion stared in amazement as the man's face relaxed, the muscles seeming to shift under his skin back into their normal positions. It was Silk.

"How did you do that?" Barak asked, startled.

Silk grinned at him and then reached up to massage his cheeks with his fingertips. "Concentration, Barak. Concentration and lots of practice. It makes my jaws ache a bit, though."

"Useful skill, I'd imagine—under the right circumstances," Hettar said blandly.

"Particularly for a spy," Barak said.

Silk bowed mockingly.

"Where did you get the clothes?" Durnik asked.

"Stole them." Silk shrugged, peeling off the apron.

"What's Brill doing here?" Wolf asked.

"Stirring up trouble, the same as always," Silk replied. "He's telling people that a Murgo named Asharak is offering a reward for any information about us. He describes you quite well, old friend—not very flatteringly, but quite well."

"I expect we'll have to deal with this Asharak before long," Aunt Pol said. "He's beginning to irritate me."

"There's another thing." Silk started on one of the cutlets. "Brill's telling everyone that Garion is Asharak's son—that we've stolen him and that Asharak's offering a huge reward for his return."

"Garion?" Aunt Pol asked sharply.

Silk nodded. "The kind of money he's talking about is bound to make everyone in Tolnedra keep his eyes open." He reached for a piece of bread.

Garion felt a sharp pang of anxiety. "Why me?" he asked.

"It would delay us," Wolf said. "Asharak—whoever he is—knows that Polgara would stop to look for you. So would the rest of us, most likely. That would give Zedar time to get away."

"Just who *is* Asharak?" Hettar asked, his eyes narrowing.

"A Grolim, I expect," Wolf said. "His operations are a little too widespread for him to be an ordinary Murgo."

"How can one tell the difference?" Durnik asked.

"You can't," Wolf answered. "They look very much the same. They're two separate tribes, but they're much more closely related to each other than they are to other Angaraks. Anyone can tell the difference between a Nadrak and a Thull or a Thull and a Mallorean, but Murgos and Grolims are so much alike that you can't tell them apart."

"I've never had any problem," Aunt Pol said. "Their minds are quite different."

"That will make it much easier," Barak commented dryly. "We'll just chop open the head of the next Murgo we meet, and you can point out the differences to us."

"You've been spending too much time with Silk lately," Aunt Pol said acidly. "You're starting to talk like him."

Barak looked over at Silk and winked.

"Let's finish up here and see if we can't get out of town quietly," Wolf said. "Is there a back alley out of this place?" he asked Silk.

"Naturally," Silk said, still eating.

"Are you familiar with it?"

"Please!" Silk looked a little offended. "Of course I'm familiar with it."

"Let it pass," Wolf said.

The alleyway Silk led them through was narrow, deserted, and smelled quite bad, but it brought them to the town's south gate, and they were soon on the highway again.

"A little distance wouldn't hurt at this point," Wolf said. He thumped his heels to his horse's flanks and started off at a gallop. They rode until well after dark. The moon, looking swollen and unhealthy, rose slowly above the horizon and filled the night with a pale light that seemed to leech away all trace of color. Wolf finally pulled to a stop. "There's really no point in riding all night," he said. "Let's move off the road and get a few hours' sleep. We'll start out again early. I'd like to stay ahead of Brill this time if we can."

"Over there?" Durnik suggested, pointing at a small copse of trees looming black in the moonlight not far from the road.

"It will do," Wolf decided. "I don't think we'll need a fire." They led the horses in among the trees and pulled their blankets out of the packs. The moonlight filtered in among the trees and dappled the leaf-strewn ground. Garion found a fairly level place with his feet, rolled up in his blankets and, after squirming around a bit, he fell asleep.

He awoke suddenly, his eyes dazzled by the light of a half-dozen torches. A heavy foot was pushed down on his chest, and the point of a sword was set firmly, uncomfortably against his throat.

"Nobody move!" a harsh voice ordered. "We'll kill anybody who moves."

Garion stiffened in panic, and the sword point at his throat dug in sharply. He rolled his head from side to side and saw that all of his friends were being held down in the same way he was. Durnik, who had been standing guard, was held by two rough-looking soldiers, and a piece of rag was stuffed in his mouth.

"What does this mean?" Silk demanded of the soldiers.

"You'll find out," the one in charge rasped. "Get their weapons." As he gestured, Garion saw that a finger was missing from his right hand.

"There's a mistake here," Silk said. "I'm Radek of Boktor, a merchant, and my friends and I haven't done anything wrong."

"Get on your feet," the three-fingered soldier ordered, ignoring the little man's objections. "If any one of you tries to get away, we'll kill all the rest."

Silk rose and crammed on his cap. "You're going to regret this, Captain," he said. "I've got powerful friends here in Tolnedra."

The soldier shrugged. "That doesn't mean anything to me," he said. "I take my orders from Count Dravor. He told me to bring you in."

"All right," Silk said. "Let's go see this Count Dravor, then. We'll get this cleared up right now, and there's no need for waving your swords around. We'll come along quietly. None of us is going to do anything to get you excited."

The three-fingered soldier's face darkened in the torchlight. "I don't like your tone, merchant."

"You're not being paid to like my tone, friend," Silk said. "You're being paid to escort us to Count Dravor. Now suppose we get moving. The quicker we get there, the quicker I can give him a full report about your behavior."

"Get their horses," the soldier growled.

Garion had edged over to Aunt Pol. "Can't you do anything?" he asked her quietly.

"No talking!" the soldier who had captured him barked.

Garion stood helplessly, staring at the sword leveled at his chest.

Chapter Fourteen

THE HOUSE OF COUNT DRAVOR was a large white building set in the center of a broad lawn with clipped hedges and formal gardens on either side. The moon, fully overhead now, illuminated every detail as they rode slowly up a white-graveled, curving road that led to the house.

The soldiers ordered them to dismount in the courtyard between the house and the garden on the west side of the house, and they were hustled inside and down a long hallway to a heavy, polished door.

Count Dravor was a thin, vague-looking man with deep pouches under his eyes, and he sprawled in a chair in the center of a richly furnished room. He looked up with a pleasant, almost dreamy smile on his face as they entered. His mantle was a pale rose color with silver trim at the hem and around the sleeves to indicate his rank. It was badly wrinkled and none too clean. "And who are these guests?" he asked, his voice slurred and barely audible.

"The prisoners, my Lord," the three-fingered soldier explained. "The ones you ordered arrested."

"Did I order someone arrested?" the count asked, his voice still slurred. "What a remarkable thing for me to do. I hope I haven't inconvenienced you, my friends."

"We were a bit surprised, that's all," Silk said carefully.

"I wonder why I did that." The count pondered. "I must have had a reason—I never do anything without a reason. What have you done wrong?"

"We haven't done anything wrong, my Lord," Silk assured him.

"Then why would I have you arrested? There must be some sort of mistake."

"That's what we thought, my Lord," Silk said.

"Well, I'm glad that's all cleared up," the count said happily. "May I offer you some dinner, perhaps?"

"We've already eaten, my Lord."

"Oh." The count's face fell with disappointment. "I have so few visitors."

"Perhaps your steward Y'diss may remember the reason these people were detained, my Lord," the three-fingered soldier suggested.

"Of course," the count said. "Why didn't I think of that? Y'diss remembers everything. Please send for him at once."

"Yes, my Lord." The soldier bowed and jerked his head curtly at one of his men.

Count Dravor dreamily began playing with one of the folds of his mantle, humming tunelessly as they waited.

After a few moments a door at the end of the room opened, and a man in an iridescent and intricately embroidered robe entered. His face was grossly sensual, and his head was shaved. "You sent for me, my Lord?" His rasping voice was almost a hiss.

"Ah, Y'diss," Count Dravor said happily, "how good of you to join us."

"It's my pleasure to serve you, my Lord," the steward said with a sinuous bow.

"I was wondering why I asked these friends to stop by," the count said. "I seem to have forgotten. Do you by any chance recall?"

"It's just a small matter, my Lord," Ydiss answered. "I can easily handle it for you. You need your rest. You mustn't overtire yourself, you know."

The count passed a hand across his face. "Now that you mention it, I do feel a bit fatigued, Y'diss. Perhaps you could entertain our guests while I rest a bit."

"Of course, my Lord," Y'diss said with another bow.

The count shifted around in his chair and almost immediately fell asleep.

"The count is in delicate health," Y'diss said with an oily smile. "He seldom leaves that chair these days. Let's move away a bit so that we don't disturb him."

"I'm only a Drasnian merchant, your Eminence," Silk said, "and these are my servants—except for my sister there. We're baffled by all of this."

Y'diss laughed. "Why do you persist in this absurb fiction, Prince Kheldar? I know who you are. I know you all, and I know your mission."

"What's your interest in us, Nyissan?" Mister Wolf asked bluntly.

"I serve my mistress, Eternal Salmissra," Y'diss said.

"Has the Snake Woman become the pawn of the Grolims, then?" Aunt Pol asked, "or does she bow to the will of Zedar?"

"My queen bows to no man, Polgara," Y'diss denied scornfully.

"Really?" She raised one eyebrow. "It's curious to find her servant dancing to a Grolim tune, then."

"I have no dealings with the Grolims," Y'diss said. "They're scouring all Tolnedra for you, but I'm the one who found you."

"Finding isn't keeping, Y'diss," Mister Wolf stated quietly. "Suppose you tell us what this is all about."

"I'll tell you only what I feel like telling you, Belgarath."

"I think that's about enough, father," Aunt Pol said. "We really don't have time for Nyissan riddle games, do we?"

"Don't do it, Polgara," Y'diss warned. "I know all about your power. My soldiers will kill your friends if you so much as raise your hand."

Garion felt himself roughly grabbed from behind, and a sword blade was pressed firmly against his throat.

Aunt Pol's eyes blazed suddenly. "You're walking on dangerous ground!"

"I don't think we need to exchange threats," Mister Wolf said. "I gather, then, that you don't intend to turn us over to the Grolims?"

"I'm not interested in the Grolims," Y'diss said. "My queen has instructed me to deliver you to her in Sthiss Tor."

"What's Salmissra's interest in this matter?" Wolf asked. "It doesn't concern her."

"I'll let her explain that to you when you get to Sthiss Tor. In the meantime, there are a few things I'll require you to tell me."

"I think thou wilt have scant success in that," Mandorallen said stiffly. "It is not our practice to discuss private matters with unwholesome strangers."

"And I think you're wrong, my dear Baron," Y'diss replied with a cold smile. "The cellars of this house are deep, and what happens there can be most unpleasant. I have servants highly skilled in applying certain exquisitely persuasive torments."

"I do not fear thy torments, Nyissan," Mandorallen said contemptuously.

"No. I don't imagine you do. Fear requires imagination, and you Arends aren't bright enough to be imaginative. The torments, however, will wear down your will—and provide entertainment for my servants. Good torturers are hard to find, and they grow sullen if they aren't allowed to practice—I'm sure you understand. Later, after you've all had the chance to visit with them a time or two, we'll try something else. Nyissa abounds with roots and leaves and curious little berries with strange properties. Oddly enough, most men prefer the rack or the wheel to my little concoctions." Y'diss laughed then, a brutal sound with no mirth in it. "We'll discuss all this further after I have the count settled in for the night. For right now, the guards will take you downstairs to the places I've prepared for you all."

Count Dravor roused himself and looked around dreamily. "Are our friends departing so soon?" he asked.

"Yes, my Lord," Y'diss told him.

"Well then," the count said with a vague smile, "farewell, dear people. I hope you'll return someday so that we can continue our delightful conversation."

The cell to which Garion was taken was dank and clammy, and it smelled of sewage and rotting food. Worst of all was the darkness. He huddled beside the iron door with the blackness pressing in on him palpably. From one corner of the cell came little scratchings and skittering sounds. He thought of rats and tried to stay as near to the door as possible. Water trickled somewhere, and his throat began to burn with thirst.

It was dark, but it was not silent. Chains clinked in a nearby cell, and someone was moaning. Further off, there was insane laughter, a meaningless cackle repeated over and over again without pause, endlessly rattling in the dark. Someone screamed, a piercing, shocking sound, and then again. Garion cringed back against the slimy stones of the wall, his imagination immediately manufacturing tortures to account for the agony in those screams.

Time in such a place was nonexistent, and so there was no way to know how long he had huddled in his cell, alone and afraid, before he began to hear a faint metallic scraping and clicking that seemed to come from the door itself. He scrambled away, stumbling across the uneven floor of his cell to the far wall. "Go away!" he cried.

"Keep your voice down!" Silk whispered from the far side of the door.

"Is that you, Silk?" Garion almost sobbed with relief.

"Who were you expecting?"

"How did you get loose?"

"Don't talk so much," Silk said from between clenched teeth. "Accursed rust!" he swore. Then he grunted, and there was a grating click from the door. "There!" The cell door creaked open, and the dim light from torches somewhere filtered in. "Come along," Silk whispered. "We have to hurry."

Garion almost ran from the cell. Aunt Pol was waiting a few steps down the gloomy stone corridor. Without a word, Garion went to her. She looked at him gravely for a moment and then put her arms about him. They did not speak.

Silk was working on another door, his face gleaming with perspiration. The lock clicked, and the door creaked open. Hettar stepped out. "What took you so long?" he asked Silk.

"Rust!" Silk snapped in a low voice. "I'd like to flog all the jailers in this place for letting the locks get into this condition."

"Do you suppose we could hurry a bit?" Barak suggested over his shoulder from where he stood guard.

"Do you want to do this?" Silk demanded.

"Just move along as quickly as you can," Aunt Pol said. "We don't have the time for bickering just now." She primly folded her blue cloak over one arm.

Silk grunted sourly and moved on to the next door.

"Is all this oratory actually necessary?" Mister Wolf, the last to be released, asked crisply as he stepped out of his cell. "You've all been babbling like a flock of geese out here."

"Prince Kheldar felt need to make observations about the condition of the locks," Mandorallen said lightly.

Silk scowled at him and led the way toward the end of the corridor where the torches fumed greasy onto the blackened ceiling.

"Have a care," Mandorallen whispered urgently. "There's a guard." A bearded man in a dirty leather jerkin sat on the floor with his back against the wall of the corridor, snoring.

"Can we get past without waking him up?" Durnik breathed.

"He isn't going to wake up for several hours," Barak said grimly. The large purple swelling on the side of the guard's face immediately explained.

"Dost think there might be others?" Mandorallen asked, flexing his hands.

"There were a few," Barak said. "They're sleeping too."

"Let's get out of here, then," Wolf suggested.

"We'll take Y'diss with us, won't we?" Aunt Pol asked.

"What for?"

"I'd like to talk with him." she said. "At great length."

"It would be a waste of time," Wolf said. "Salmissra's involved herself in this affair. That's all we really need to know. Her motives don't really interest me all that much. Let's just get out of here as quietly as we can."

They crept past the snoring guard, turned a corner and moved softly down another corridor.

"Did he die?" a voice, shockingly loud, asked from behind a barred door that emitted a smoky red light.

"No," another voice said, "only fainted. You pulled too hard on the lever. You have to keep the pressure steady. Otherwise they faint, and you have to start over."

"This is a lot harder than I thought," the first voice complained.

"You're doing fine," the second voice said. "The rack's always tricky. Just remember to keep a steady pressure and not to jerk the lever. They usually die if you pull their arms out of the sockets."

Aunt Pol's face went rigid, and her eyes blazed briefly.

She made a small gesture and whispered something. A brief, hushed sound murmured in Garion's mind.

"You know," the first voice said rather faintly, "suddenly I don't feel so good."

"Now that you mention it, I don't either," the second voice agreed. "Did that meat we had for supper taste all right to you?"

"It *seemed* all right." There was a long pause. "I *really* don't feel good at all."

They tiptoed past the barred door, and Garion carefully avoided looking in. At the end of the corridor was a stout oak door bound with iron. Silk ran his fingers around the handle. "It's locked from the outside," he said.

"Someone's coming." Hettar warned.

There was the tramp of heavy feet on the stone stairs beyond the door, the murmur of voices and a harsh laugh.

Wolf turned quickly to the door of a nearby cell. He touched his fingers to the rusty iron lock, and it clicked smoothly. "In here," he whispered. They all crowded into the cell, and Wolf pulled the door shut behind them.

"When we've got some leisure, I'll want to talk to you about that," Silk said.

"You were having such a good time with the locks that I didn't want to interfere." Wolf smiled blandly. "Now listen. We're going to have to deal with these men before they find out that our cells are empty and rouse the whole house."

"We can do that," Barak said confidently.

They waited.

"They're opening the door," Durnik whispered.

"How many are there?" Mandorallen asked.

"I can't tell."

"Eight," Aunt Pol said firmly.

"All right," Barak decided. "We'll let them pass and then jump on them from behind. A scream or two won't matter much in a place like this, but let's put them down quickly."

They waited tensely in the darkness of the cell.

"Y'diss says it doesn't matter if some of them die under the questioning," one of the men outside said. "The only ones we have to keep alive are the old man, the woman, and the boy."

"Let's kill the big one with the red whiskers then," another suggested. "He looks like he might be troublesome, and he's probably too stupid to know anything useful."

"I *want* that one," Barak whispered.

The men in the corridor passed their cell.

"Let's go," Barak said.

It was a short, ugly fight. They swarmed over the startled jailers in a savage rush. Three were down before the others fully realized what was happening. One made a startled outcry, dodged past the fight and ran back toward the stairs. Without thinking, Garion dove in front of the running man. Then he rolled, tangling the man's feet, tripping him up. The guard fell, started to rise, then sagged back down in a limp heap as Silk neatly kicked him just below the ear.

"Are you all right?" Silk asked.

Garion squirmed out from under the unconscious jailer and scrambled to his feet, but the fight was nearly over. Durnik was pounding a stout man's head against the wall, and Barak was driving his fist into another's face. Mandorallen was strangling a third, and Hettar stalked a fourth, his hands out. The wide-eyed man cried out once just as Hettar's hands closed on him. The tall Algar straightened, spun about and slammed the man into the stone wall with terrific force. There was the grating sound of bones breaking, and the man went limp.

"Nice little fight," Barak said, rubbing his knuckles.

"Entertaining," Hettar agreed, letting the limp body slide to the floor.

"Are you about through?" Silk demanded hoarsely from the door by the stairs.

"Almost," Barak said. "Need any help, Durnik?"

Durnik lifted the stout man's chin and examined the vacant eyes critically. Then he prudently banged the jailer's head against the wall once more and let him fall.

"Shall we go?" Hettar suggested.

"Might as well," Barak agreed, surveying the littered corridor.

"The door's unlocked at the top of the stairs," Silk said as they joined him, "and the hallway's empty beyond it. The house seems to be asleep, but let's be quiet."

They followed him silently up the stairs. He paused briefly at the door. "Wait here a moment," he whispered. Then he disappeared, his feet making absolutely no sound. After what seemed a long time, he returned with the weapons the soldiers had taken from them. "I thought we might need these."

Garion felt much better after he had belted on his sword.

"Let's go," Silk said and led them to the end of the hall and around a corner.

"I think I'd like some of the green, Y'diss," Count Dravor's voice came from behind a partially open door.

"Certainly, my Lord," Y'diss said in his sibilant, rasping voice.

"The green tastes bad," Count Dravor said drowsily, "but it gives me such lovely dreams. The red tastes better, but the dreams aren't so nice."

"Soon you'll be ready for the blue, my Lord," Y'diss promised. There was a faint clink and the sound of liquid being poured into a glass. "Then the yellow, and finally the black. The black's best of all."

Silk led them on tiptoe past the half-open door. The lock on the outside door yielded quickly to his skill, and they all slipped out into the cool, moonlit night. The stars twinkled overhead, and the air was sweet. "I'll get the horses," Hettar said.

"Go with him, Mandorallen," Wolf said. "We'll wait over there." He pointed at the shadowy garden. The two men disappeared around the corner, and the rest of them followed Mister Wolf into the looming shadow of the hedge which surrounded Count Dravor's garden.

They waited. The night was chilly, and Garion found himself shivering. Then there was a click of a hoof touching a stone, and Hettar and Mandorallen came back, leading the horses.

"We'd better hurry," Wolf said. "As soon as Dravor drops off to sleep, Y'diss is going to go down to his dungeon and find out that we've left. Lead the horses. Let's get away from the house before we start making any noise."

They went down through the moonlit garden with the horses trailing along after them until they emerged on the open lawn beyond. They mounted carefully.

"We'd better hurry," Aunt Pol suggested, glancing back at the house.

"I bought us a little time before I left," Silk said with a short laugh.

"How'd you manage that?" Barak asked.

"When I went to get our weapons, I also set fire to the kitchen." Silk smirked. "That will keep their attention for a bit."

A tendril of smoke rose from the back of the house.

"Very clever," Aunt Pol said with a certain grudging admiration.

"Why thank you, my Lady." Silk made a mocking little bow.

Mister Wolf chuckled and led them away at an easy trot.

The tendril of smoke at the back of the house became thicker as they rode away, rising black and oily toward the uncaring stars.

Chapter Fifteen

THEY RODE HARD for the next several days, stopping only long enough to rest the horses and catch a few hours' sleep at infrequent intervals. Garion found that he could doze in his saddle whenever they walked the horses. He found, indeed, that if he were tired enough, he could sleep almost anyplace. One afternoon as they rested from the driving pace Wolf set, he heard Silk talking to the old man and Aunt Pol. Curiosity finally won out over exhaustion, and he roused himself enough to listen.

"I'd still like to know more about Salmissra's involvement in this," the little man was saying.

"She's an opportunist," Wolf said. "Any time there's turmoil, she tries to turn it to her own advantage."

"That means we'll have to dodge Nyissans as well as Murgos."

Garion opened his eyes. "Why do they call her Eternal Salmissra?" he asked Aunt Pol. "Is she very old?"

"No," Aunt Pol answered. "The Queens of Nyissa are always named Salmissra, that's all."

"Do you know this particular one?"

"I don't have to," she told him. "They're always exactly the same. They all look alike and act alike. If you know one, you know them all."

"She's going to be terribly disappointed with Y'diss," Silk observed, grinning.

"I imagine that Y'diss has taken some quiet, painless way out by now," Wolf said. "Salmissra grows a bit excessive when she's irritated."

"Is she so cruel then?" Garion asked.

"Not cruel exactly," Wolf explained. "Nyissans admire serpents. If you annoy a snake, he'll bite you. He's a simple creature, but very logical. Once he bites you, he doesn't hold any further grudges."

"Do we have to talk about snakes?" Silk asked in a pained voice.

"I think the horses are rested now," Hettar said from behind them. "We can go now."

They pushed the horses back into a gallop and pounded south toward the broad valley of the Nedrane River and Tol Honeth. The sun turned warm, and the trees along the way were budding in the first days of spring.

The gleaming Imperial City was situated on an island in the middle of the river, and all roads led there. It was clearly visible in the distance as they crested the last ridge and looked down into the fertile valley and it seemed to grow larger with each passing mile as they approached it. It was built entirely of white marble and it dazzled the eye in the midmorning sun. The walls were high and thick, and towers soared above them within the city.

A bridge arched gracefully across the rippled face of the Nedrane to the bronze expanse of the north gate where a glittering detachment of legionnaires marched perpetual guard.

Silk pulled on his conservative cloak and cap and drew

himself up, his face assuming that sober, businesslike expression that meant that he was undergoing a private internal transition that seemed to make him almost believe himself that he was the Drasnian merchant whose identity he assumed.

"Your business in Tol Honeth?" one of the legionnaires asked politely.

"I am Radek of Boktor," Silk said with the preoccupied air of a man whose mind was on business. "I have Sendarian woolens of the finest quality."

"You'll probably want to talk with the Steward of the Central Market, then," the legionnaire suggested.

"Thank you." Silk nodded and led them through the gate into the broad and crowded streets beyond.

"I think I'd better stop by the palace and have a talk with Ran Borune," Mister Wolf said. "The Borunes aren't the easiest emperors to deal with, but they're the most intelligent. I shouldn't have too much trouble convincing him that the situation's serious."

"How are you going to get to see him?" Aunt Pol asked him. "It could take weeks to get an appointment. You know how they are."

Mister Wolf made a sour face. "I suppose I could make a ceremonial visit of it," he said as they pushed their horses through the crowd.

"And announce your presence to the whole city?"

"Do I have any choice? I have to nail down the Tolnedrans. We can't afford to have them neutral."

"Could I make a suggestion?" Barak asked.

"I'll listen to anything at this point."

"Why don't we go see Grinneg?" Barak said. "He's the Cherek Ambassador here in Tol Honeth. He could get us into the palace to see the Emperor without all that much fuss."

"That's not a bad idea, Belgarath," Silk agreed. "Grinneg's got enough connections in the palace to get us inside quickly, and Ran Borune respects him."

"That only leaves the problem of getting in to see the ambassador," Durnik said as they stopped to let a heavy wagon pass into a side street.

"He's my cousin," Barak said. "He and Anheg and I

used to play together when we were children." The big man looked around. "He's supposed to have a house near the garrison of the Third Imperial Legion. I suppose we could ask somebody the way."

"That won't be necessary," Silk said. "I know where it is."

"I should have known." Barak grinned.

"We can go through the north marketplace," Silk said. "The garrison's located near the main wharves on the downstream end of the island."

"Lead the way," Wolf told him. "I don't want to waste too much time here."

The streets of Tol Honeth teemed with people from all over the world. Drasnians and Rivans rubbed elbows with Nyissans and Thulls. There was a sprinkling of Nadraks in the crowd and, to Garion's eye, a disproportionate number of Murgos. Aunt Pol rode close beside Hettar, talking quietly to him and frequently laying her hand lightly on his sword arm. The lean Algar's eyes burned, and his nostrils flared dangerously each time he saw a scarred Murgo face.

The houses along the wide streets were imposing, with white marble facades and heavy doors, quite often guarded by private mercenary soldiers, who glared belligerently at passers-by.

"The Imperial City seems awash with suspicion," Mandorallen observed. "Do they fear their neighbors so?"

"Troubled times," Silk explained. "And the merchant princes of Tol Honeth keep a great deal of the world's wealth in their counting-rooms. There are men along this street who could buy most of Arendia if they wanted to."

"Arendia is not for sale," Mandorallen said stiffly.

"In Tol Honeth, my dear Baron, everything's for sale," Silk told him. "Honor, virtue, friendship, love. It's a wicked city full of wicked people, and money's the only thing that matters."

"I expect you fit right in, then," Barak said.

Silk laughed. "I like Tol Honeth," he admitted. "The people here have no illusions. They're refreshingly corrupt."

"You're a bad man, Silk," Barak stated bluntly.

"So you've said before," the rat-faced little Drasnian said with a mocking grin.

The banner of Cherek, the outline of a white war-boat on an azure background, fluttered from a pole surmounting the gate of the ambassador's house. Barak dismounted a bit stiffly and strode to the iron grill which blocked the gate. "Tell Grinneg that his cousin Barak is here to see him," he announced to the bearded guards inside.

"How do we know you're his cousin?" one of the guards demanded roughly.

Barak reached through the grill almost casually and took hold of the front of the guard's mail shirt. He pulled the man up firmly against the bars. "Would you like to re-phrase that question," he asked, "while you still have your health?"

"Excuse me, Lord Barak," the man apologized quickly. "Now that I'm closer, I do seem to recognize your face."

"I was almost sure you would," Barak said.

"Let me unlock the gate for you," the guard suggested.

"Excellent idea," Barak said, letting go of the man's shirt. The guard opened the gate quickly, and the party rode into a spacious courtyard.

Grinneg, the ambassador of King Anheg to the Imperial Court at Tol Honeth, was a burly man almost as big as Barak. His beard was trimmed very short, and he wore a Tolnedran-style blue mantle. He came down the stairs two at a time and caught Barak in a vast bear hug. "You pirate!" he roared. "What are you doing in Tol Honeth?"

"Anheg's decided to invade the place," Barak joked. "As soon as we've rounded up all the gold and young women, we're going to let you burn the city."

Grinneg's eyes glittered with a momentary hunger. "Wouldn't that infuriate them?" he said with a vicious grin.

"What happened to your beard?" Barak asked.

Grinneg coughed and looked embarrassed. "It's not important," he said quickly.

"We've never had any secrets," Barak accused.

Grinneg spoke quietly to his cousin for a moment, looking very ashamed of himself, and Barak burst out with a great roar of laughter. "Why did you let her do that?" he demanded.

"I was drunk," Grinneg said. "Let's go inside. I've got a keg of good ale in my cellar."

The rest of them followed the two big men into the house, and they went down a broad hallway to a room with Cherek furnishings—heavy chairs and benches covered with skins, a rush-strewn floor and a huge fireplace where the butt end of a large log smoldered. Several pitch-smeared torches smoked in iron rings on the stone wall. "I feel more at home here," Grinneg said.

A servant brought tankards of dark brown ale for them all and then quietly left the room. Garion quickly lifted his tankard and took a large swallow of the bitter drink before Aunt Pol could suggest something more bland. She watched him without comment, her eyes expressionless.

Grinneg sprawled in a large, hand-hewn chair with a bearskin tossed over it. "Why are you really in Tol Honeth, Barak?" he asked.

"Grinneg," Barak said seriously, "this is Belgarath. I'm sure you've heard of him."

The ambassador's eyes widened, and he inclined his head. "My house is yours," he said respectfully.

"Can you get me in to see Ran Borune?" Mister Wolf asked, sitting on a rough bench near the fireplace.

"Without any difficulty."

"Good," Wolf said. "I have to talk to him, and I don't want to stir up any fuss in the process."

Barak introduced the others, and his cousin nodded politely to each of them.

"You've come to Tol Honeth during a turbulent period," he said after the amenities were over. "The nobility of Tolnedra are gathering in the city like ravens on a dead cow."

"We picked up a hint or two of that on our way south," Silk told him. "Is it as bad as we heard?"

"Probably worse," Grinneg said, scratching one ear. "Dynastic succession only happens a few times in each eon. The Borunes have been in power now for over six hundred years, and the other houses are anticipating the changeover with a great deal of enthusiasm."

"Who's the most likely to succeed Ran Borune?" Mister Wolf asked.

"Right at the moment the best would probably be the

Grand Duke Kador of Tol Vordue," Grinneg answered. "He seems to have more money than the rest. The Honeths are richer, of course, but they've got seven candidates, and their wealth is spread out a little too thin. The other families aren't really in the running. The Borunes don't have anyone suitable, and no one takes the Ranites seriously."

Garion carefully set his tankard on the floor beside the stool he sat on. The bitter ale didn't really taste that good, and he felt vaguely cheated somehow. The half-tankard he had drunk made his ears quite warm, though, and the end of his nose seemed a little numb.

"A Vorduvian we met said that the Horbites are using poison," Silk said.

"They all are." Grinneg wore a slightly disgusted look. "The Horbites are just a little more obvious about it, that's all. If Ran Borune dies tomorrow, though, Kador will be the next Emperor."

Mister Wolf frowned. "I've never had much success dealing with the Vorduvians. They don't really have imperial stature."

"The old Emperor's still in pretty fair health," Grinneg said. "If he hangs on for another year or two, the Honeths will probably fall into line behind one candidate—whichever one survives—and then they'll be able to bring all their money to bear on the situation. These things take time, though. The candidates themselves are staying out of town for the most part, and they're all being extremely careful, so the assassins are having a great deal of difficulty reaching them." He laughed, taking a long drink of ale. "They're a funny people."

"Could we go to the palace now?" Mister Wolf asked.

"We'll want to change clothes first," Aunt Pol said firmly.

"Again, Polgara?" Wolf gave her a long-suffering look.

"Just do it, father," she said. "I won't let you embarrass us by wearing rags to the palace."

"I'm not going to wear that robe again." The old man's voice was stubborn.

"No," she said. "It wouldn't be suitable. I'm sure the ambassador can lend you a mantle. You won't be quite so obvious that way."

"Whatever you say, Pol." Wolf sighed, giving up.

After they had changed, Grinneg formed up his honor-guard, a grim-looking group of Cherek warriors, and they were escorted along the broad avenues of Tol Honeth toward the palace. Garion, all bemused by the opulence of the city and feeling just a trifle giddy from the effects of the half-tankard of ale he had drunk, rode quietly beside Silk, trying not to gawk at the huge buildings or the richly dressed Tolnedrans strolling with grave decorum in the noonday sun.

Chapter Sixteen

THE IMPERIAL PALACE sat on a high hill in the center of Tol Honeth. It consisted not of one building, but rather was a complex of many, large and small, all built of marble and surrounded by gardens and lawns where cypress trees cast a pleasing shade. The entire compound was enclosed by a high wall, surmounted by statues spaced at intervals along its top. The legionnaires at the palace gate recognized the Cherek ambassador and sent immediately for one of the Emperor's chamberlains, a gray-haired official in a brown mantle.

"I need to see Ran Borune, Lord Morin," Grinneg told him as they all dismounted in a marble courtyard just inside the palace gate. "It's a matter of urgency."

"Of course, Lord Grinneg," the gray-haired man assented. "His Imperial Highness is always delighted to speak with the personal envoy of King Anheg. Unfortunately, his Highness is resting just now. I should be able to get you in to see him sometime this afternoon—tomorrow morning at the latest."

"This won't wait, Morin," Grinneg said. "We have to see the Emperor immediately. You'd better go wake him up."

Lord Morin looked surprised. "It can't be *that* urgent," he suggested chidingly.

"I'm afraid so," Grinneg said.

Morin pursed his lips thoughtfully as he looked at each member of the party.

"You know me well enough to realize that I wouldn't ask this lightly, Morin," Grinneg said.

Morin sighed. "I'm trusting you a great deal, Grinneg. All right. Come along. Ask your soldiers to wait."

Grinneg made a curt gesture to his guards, and the party followed Lord Morin through a broad courtyard to a columned gallery that ran along one of the buildings.

"How's he been?" Grinneg asked as they walked along the shady gallery.

"His health is still good," Morin answered, "but his temper's been deteriorating lately. The Borunes have been resigning their posts in flocks and returning to Tol Borune."

"That seems prudent under the circumstances," Grinneg said. "I suspect that a certain number of fatalities are likely to accompany the succession."

"Probably so," Morin agreed, "but his Highness finds it a bit distressing to be abandoned by members of his own family." He stopped by an arched marble gate where two legionnaires in gold-embellished breastplates stood stiffly. "Please leave your weapons here. His Highness is sensitive about such things—I'm sure you can understand."

"Of course," Grinneg said, pulling a heavy sword out from under his mantle and leaning it against the wall.

They all followed his example, and Lord Morin's eyes flickered slightly with surprise when Silk removed three different daggers from various places beneath his garments. —*Formidable equipment*— the chamberlain's hands flickered in the gestures of the secret language.

—*Troubled times*— Silk's fingers explained deprecatingly.

Lord Morin smiled faintly and led them through the gate into the garden beyond. The lawn in the garden was neatly manicured. There were softly splashing fountains, and the rosebushes were all well-pruned. Fruit trees that seemed to be very old were budding, almost ready to burst into bloom in the warm sun. Sparrows bickered over nesting sites on the twisted limbs. Grinneg and the others followed Morin along a curving marble walk toward the center of the garden.

Ran Borune XXIII, Emperor of Tolnedra, was a small, elderly man, quite bald and dressed in a gold-colored mantle. He lounged in a heavy chair beneath a budding grape arbor, feeding small seeds to a bright canary perched on the arm of his chair. The Emperor had a little, beaklike nose and bright, inquisitive eyes. "I said I wanted to be left alone, Morin," he said in a testy voice, looking up from the canary.

"A million apologies, your Highness," Lord Morin explained, bowing deeply. "Lord Grinneg, the ambassador of Cherek, wishes to present you a matter of gravest urgency. He convinced me that it simply could not wait."

The Emperor looked sharply at Grinneg. His eyes grew sly, almost malicious. "I see that your beard's beginning to grow back, Grinneg."

Grinneg's face flushed slowly. "I should have known that your Highness would have heard of my little misfortune."

"I know everything that happens in Tol Honeth, Lord Grinneg," the Emperor snapped. "Even if all my cousins and nephews are running like rats out of a burning house, I still have a *few* faithful people around me. Whatever possessed you to take up with that Nadrak woman? I thought you Alorns despised Angaraks."

Grinneg coughed awkwardly and glanced quickly at Aunt Pol. "It was a kind of joke, your Highness," he said. "I thought it might embarrass the Nadrak ambassador— and his wife is, after all, a handsome-looking woman. I didn't know she kept a pair of scissors under her bed."

"She keeps your beard in a little gold box, you know." The emperor smirked. "And she shows it to all her friends."

"She's an evil woman," Grinneg said mournfully.

"Who are these?" the Emperor asked, waving one finger at the members of the party standing on the grass somewhat behind Ambassador Grinneg.

"My cousin Barak and some friends," Grinneg said. "They're the ones who have to talk to you."

"The Earl of Trellheim?" the Emperor asked. "What are you doing in Tol Honeth, my Lord?"

"Passing through, your Highness," Barak replied, bowing.

Ran Borune looked sharply at each of the rest in turn as if actually seeing them for the first time. "And this would be Prince Kheldar of Drasnia," he said, "who left Tol Honeth in a hurry last time he was here—posing as an acrobat in a traveling circus, I believe, and about one jump ahead of the police."

Silk also bowed politely.

"And Hettar of Algaria," the Emperor continued, "the man who's trying to depopulate Cthol Murgos single-handedly."

Hettar inclined his head.

"Morin," the Emperor demanded sharply, "why have you surrounded me with Alorns? I don't like Alorns."

"It's this matter of urgency, your Highness," Morin replied apologetically.

"And an Arend?" the Emperor said, looking at Mandorallen. "A Mimbrate, I should say." His eyes narrowed. "From the descriptions I've heard, he could only be the Baron of Vo Mandor."

Mandorallen's bow was gracefully elaborate. "Thine eye is most keen, your Highness, to have read us each in turn without prompting."

"Not all of you precisely," the Emperor said. "I don't recognize the Sendar or the Rivan lad."

Garion's mind jumped. Barak had once told him that he resembled a Rivan more than anything else, but that thought had been lost in the welter of events which had followed the chance remark. Now the Emperor of Tolnedra, whose eye seemed to have an uncanny ability to penetrate to the true nature of things, had also identified him as a Rivan. He glanced quickly at Aunt Pol, but she seemed absorbed in examining the buds on a rosebush.

"The Sendar is Durnik," Mister Wolf said, "a smith. In Sendaria that useful trade is considered somewhat akin to nobility. The lad is my grandson, Garion."

The Emperor looked at the old man. "It seems that I should know who you are. There's something about you—" He paused thoughtfully.

The canary, which had been perched on the arm of the

Emperor's chair, suddenly burst into song. He launched himself into the air and fluttered directly to Aunt Pol. She held out her finger, and the bright bird landed there, tipped back his head and sang ecstatically as if his tiny heart were breaking with adoration. She listened gravely to his song. She wore a dark blue dress, elaborately laced at the bodice, and a short sable cape.

"What are you doing with my canary?" the Emperor demanded.

"Listening," she said.

"How did you get him to sing? I've been trying to coax him into song for months."

"You didn't take him seriously enough."

"Who is this woman?" the Emperor asked.

"My daughter Polgara," Mister Wolf said. "She has a particularly keen understanding of birds."

The Emperor laughed suddenly, a harshly skeptical laugh. "Oh, come now. You really don't expect me to accept that, do you?"

Wolf looked at him gravely. "Are you really sure you don't know me, Ran Borune?" he asked mildly. The pale green mantle Grinneg had lent him made him look almost like a Tolnedran—almost, but not quite.

"It's a clever ruse," the Emperor said. "You look the part, and so does she, but I'm not a child. I gave up fairy tales a long time ago."

"That's a pity. I'd guess that your life's been a little empty since then." Wolf looked around at the manicured garden with the servants and fountains and the members of the Emperor's personal guard posted unobtrusively here and there among the flowerbeds. "Even with all this, Ran Borune, a life without any wonder left in it is flat and stale." His voice was a little sad. "I think that perhaps you gave up too much."

"Morin," Ran Borune demanded peremptorily, "send for Zereel. We'll settle this immediately."

"At once, your Highness," Morin said and beckoned to one of the servants.

"May I have my canary back?" the Emperor asked Aunt Pol rather plaintively.

"Of course." She moved across the grass toward the

chair, stepping slowly to avoid startling the trilling little bird.

"Sometimes I wonder what they're saying when they sing," Ran Borune said.

"Right now he's telling me about the day he learned to fly," Aunt Pol said. "That's a very important day for a bird." She reached out her hand, and the canary hopped onto the Emperor's finger, still singing and with its bright eye cocked toward Ran Borune's face.

"That's an amusing conceit, I suppose." The little old man smiled, staring out at the sunlight sparkling on the water in one of the fountains. "But I'm afraid I don't have time for that kind of thing. Right now the whole nation is holding its breath in anticipation of my death. They all seem to think that the greatest thing I can do for Tolnedra is to die immediately. Some of them have even gone to the trouble of trying to help me along. We caught four assassins inside the palace grounds just last week. The Borunes, my own family, are deserting me to the point that I scarcely have enough people left to run the palace, much less the Empire. Ah, here comes Zereel."

A lean, bushy-browed man in a red mantle covered with mystic symbols scurried across the lawn and bowed deeply to the emperor. "You sent for me, your Highness?"

"I am informed that this woman is Polgara the Sorceress," the Emperor said, "and that the old man there is Belgarath. Be a good fellow, Zereel, and have a look into their credentials."

"Belgarath and Polgara?" the bushy-browed man scoffed. "Surely your Highness isn't serious. The names are mythological. No such people exist."

"You see," the Emperor said to Aunt Pol. "You don't exist. I have it on the very best authority. Zereel's a wizard himself, you know."

"Really?"

"One of the very best," he assured her. "Of course most of his tricks are just sleight of hand, since sorcery's only a sham, but he amuses me—and he takes himself very seriously. You may proceed, Zereel, but try not to raise an awful stink, as you usually do."

"That won't be necessary, your Highness," Zereel said

flatly. "If they were wizards of any kind, I'd have recognized them immediately. We have special ways of communicating, you know."

Aunt Pol looked at the wizard with one eyebrow slightly raised. "I think that you should look a bit closer, Zereel," she suggested. "Sometimes we miss things." She made an almost imperceptible gesture, and Garion seemed to hear a faint rush of sound.

The wizard stared, his eyes fixed on open air directly in front of him. His eyes began to bulge, and his face turned deathly pale. As if his legs had been cut from under him, he fell onto his face. "Forgive me, Lady Polgara," he croaked, groveling.

"That's supposed to impress me, I assume," the Emperor said. "I've seen men's minds overwhelmed before, however, and Zereel's mind isn't all that strong to begin with."

"This is getting tiresome, Ran Borune," she said tartly.

"You really ought to believe her, you know." The canary spoke in a tiny, piping voice. "I knew who she was immediately—of course we're much more perceptive than you things that creep around on the ground—why do you do that? If you'd just try, I'm sure you'd be able to fly. And I wish you'd stop eating so much garlic—it makes you smell awful."

"Hush, now," Aunt Pol said gently to the bird. "You can tell him all about it later."

The Emperor was trembling violently, and he stared at the bird as if it were a snake.

"Why don't we all just behave as if we believed that Polgara and I are who we say we are?" Mister Wolf suggested. "We could spend the rest of the day trying to convince you, and we really don't have that much time. There are some things I have to tell you, and they're important—no matter who I am."

"I think I can accept that," Ran Borune said, still trembling and staring at the now-silent canary.

Mister Wolf clasped his hands behind his back and stared up at a cluster of bickering sparrows on the limb of a nearby tree. "Early last fall," he began, "Zedar the Apostate crept into the throne room at Riva and stole the Orb of Aldur."

"He did *what*?" Ran Borune demanded, sitting up quickly. "How?"

"We don't know," Wolf answered. "When I catch up with him, maybe I'll ask him. I'm sure, however, that you can see the importance of the event."

"Obviously," the Emperor said.

"The Alorns and the Sendars are quietly preparing for war," Wolf told him.

"War?" Ran Borune asked in a shocked voice. "With whom?"

"The Angaraks, of course."

"What's Zedar got to do with the Angaraks? He could be acting on his own, couldn't he?"

"Surely you're not *that* simple," Aunt Pol remarked.

"You forget yourself, Lady," Ran Borune said stiffly. "Where's Zedar now?"

"He went through Tol Honeth about two weeks ago," Wolf replied. "If he can get across the border into one of the Angarak kingdoms before I can stop him, the Alorns will march."

"And Arendia with them," Mandorallen said firmly. "King Korodullin has also been advised."

"You'll tear the world apart," the Emperor protested.

"Perhaps," Wolf admitted, "but we can't let Zedar get to Torak with the Orb."

"I'll send emissaries at once," Ran Borune said. "This has to be headed off before it gets out of hand."

"It's a little late for that," Barak said grimly. "Anheg and the others aren't in any mood for Tolnedran diplomacy right now."

"Your people have a bad reputation in the north, your Highness," Silk pointed out. "They always seem to have a few trade agreements up their sleeves. Every time Tolnedra mediates a dispute, it seems to cost a great deal. I don't think we can afford your good offices anymore."

A cloud passed in front of the sun, and the garden seemed suddenly chilly in its shadow.

"This is being blown all out of proportion," the Emperor protested. "The Alorns and the Angaraks have been squabbling over that worthless stone for thousands of years. You've been waiting for the chance to fall on each other, and now you've got an excuse. Well, enjoy yourselves. Tolnedra's not going to get involved as long as I'm her Emperor."

"You're not going to be able to sit to one side in this, Ran Borune," Aunt Pol said.

"Why not? The Orb doesn't concern me one way or the other. Go ahead and destroy each other if you want. Tolnedra will still be here when it's all over."

"I doubt it," Wolf told him. "Your Empire's crawling with Murgos. They could overrun you in a week."

"They're honest merchants—here on honest business."

"Murgos don't have honest business," Aunt Pol told him. "Every Murgo in Tolnedra is here because he was sent by the Grolim High Priest."

"That's an exaggeration," Ran Borune said stubbornly. "The whole world knows that you and your father have an obsessive hatred of all Angaraks, but times have changed."

"Cthol Murgos is still ruled from Rak Cthol," Wolf said, "and Ctuchik is master there. Ctuchik hasn't changed, even if the world has. The merchants from Rak Goska might seem civilized to you, but they all jump when Ctuchik whistles, and Ctuchik's the disciple of Torak."

"Torak's dead."

"Really?" Aunt Pol said. "Have you seen his grave? Have you opened the grave and seen his bones?"

"My Empire's very expensive to run," the Emperor said, "and I need the revenue the Murgos bring me. I've got agents in Rak Goska and all along the South Caravan Route, so I'd know if the Murgos were getting ready for any kind of move against me. I'm just a little suspicious that all this might be the result of some internal contention within the Brotherhood of Sorcerers. You people have your own motives, and I'm not going to let you use my Empire as a pawn in your power struggles."

"And if the Angaraks win?" Aunt Pol said. "How do you plan to deal with Torak?"

"I'm not afraid of Torak."

"Have you ever met him?" Wolf asked.

"Obviously not. Listen, Belgarath, you and your daughter have never been friendly to Tolnedra. You treated us like a defeated enemy after Vo Mimbre. Your information's interesting, and I'll consider it in its proper perspective, but Tolnedran policy is not dominated by Alorn preconceptions. Our economy relies heavily on trade along the South Caravan Route. I'm not going to disrupt my Empire simply because you happen to dislike Murgos."

"You're a fool then," Wolf said bluntly.

"You'd be surprised at how many people think so," the Emperor replied. "Maybe you'll have better luck with my successor. If he's a Vorduvian or a Honeth, you might even be able to bribe him, but Borunes don't take bribes."

"Or advice," Aunt Pol added.

"Only when it suits us, Lady Polgara," Ran Borune said.

"I think we've done everything we can here," Wolf decided.

A bronze door at the back of the garden slammed open, and a tiny girl with flaming hair stormed through, her eyes ablaze. At first Garion thought she was a child, but as she came closer, he realized that she was somewhat older than that. Although she was very small, the short, sleeveless green tunic she wore displayed limbs that were much closer to maturity. He felt a peculiar kind of shock when he saw her—almost, but not quite, like recognition. Her hair was a tumbled mass with long, elaborate curls cascading down over her neck and shoulders, and it was a color that Garion had never seen before, a deep, burnished red that seemed somehow to glow from within. Her skin was a golden color that seemed, as she swept through the shadows of the trees near the gate, to have an almost greenish cast to it. She was in a state verging on sheer rage. "Why am I being kept prisoner here?" she demanded of the Emperor.

"What are you talking about?" Ran Borune asked.

"The legionnaires won't let me leave the palace grounds!"

"Oh," the Emperor said, "that."

"Exactly. *That*."

"They're acting on my orders, Ce'Nedra," the Emperor told her.

"So they said. Tell them to stop it."

"No."

"*No?*" Her tone was incredulous. "*No?*" Her voice climbed several octaves. "What do you mean, no?"

"It's too dangerous for you to be out in the city just now," the Emperor said placatingly.

"Nonsense," she snapped. "I don't intend to sit around in this stuffy palace just because you're afraid of your own shadow. I need some things from the market."

"Send someone."

"I don't *want* to send anyone!" she shouted at him. "I want to go myself."

"Well, you can't," he said flatly. "Spend your time on your studies instead."

"I don't *want* to study," she cried. "Jeebers is a stuffy idiot, and he bores me. I don't want to sit around talking about history or politics or any of the rest of it. I just want an afternoon to myself."

"I'm sorry."

"Please, father," she begged, her tone dropping into a wheedling note. She took hold of one of the folds of his gold mantle and twisted it around one of her tiny fingers. "Please." The look she directed at the Emperor through her lashes would have melted stone.

"Absolutely not," he said, refusing to look at her. "My order stands. You will *not* leave the palace grounds."

"I *hate* you!" she cried. Then she ran from the garden in tears.

"My daughter," the Emperor explained almost apologetically. "You can't imagine what it's like having a child like that."

"Oh, I can imagine, all right," Mister Wolf said, glancing at Aunt Pol.

She looked back at him, her eyes challenging. "Go ahead and say it, father," she told him. "I'm sure you won't be happy until you do."

Wolf shrugged. "Forget it."

Ran Borune looked thoughtfully at the two of them. "It occurs to me that we might be able to negotiate a bit here," he said, his eyes narrowing.

"What did you have in mind?" Wolf asked.

"You have a certain authority among the Alorns," the Emperor suggested.

"Some," Wolf admitted carefully.

"If you were to ask them, I'm sure they'd be willing to

overlook one of the more absurd provisions of the Accords of Vo Mimbre."

"Which one is that?"

"There's really no necessity for Ce'Nedra to journey to Riva, is there? I'm the last emperor of the Borune Dynasty, and when I die, she won't be an Imperial Princess anymore. Under the circumstances, I'd say that the requirement doesn't really apply to her. It's nonsense anyway. The line of the Rivan King became extinct thirteen hundred years ago, so there isn't going to be any bridegroom waiting for her in the Hall of the Rivan King. As you've seen, Tolnedra's a very dangerous place just now. Ce'Nedra's sixteenth birthday's only a year or so off, and the date's well known. If I have to send her to Riva, half the assassins in the Empire are going to be lurking outside the palace gates, waiting for her to come out. I'd rather not take that kind of risk. If you could see your way clear to speak to the Alorns, I might be able to make a few concessions regarding the Murgos—restrictions on their numbers, closed areas, that sort of thing."

"No, Ran Borune," Aunt Pol said flatly. "Ce'Nedra *will* go to Riva. You've failed to understand that the Accords are only a formality. If your daughter's the one destined to become the bride of the Rivan King, no force on earth can prevent her from being in the throne room at Riva on the appointed day. My father's recommendations about the Murgos are only suggestions—for your own good. What you choose to do about the matter is your affair."

"I think we've just about exhausted the possibilities of this conversation," the Emperor stated coldly.

Two important-looking officials came into the garden and spoke briefly to Lord Morin.

"Your Highness," the gray-haired chamberlain said deferentially, "the Minister of Trade wanted to inform you that he's reached an excellent agreement with the trade deputation from Rak Goska. The gentlemen from Cthol Murgos were most accommodating."

"I'm delighted to hear it," Ran Borune said, throwing a meaningful look at Mister Wolf.

"The contingent from Rak Goska would like to pay their respects before they leave," Morin added.

"By all means," the Emperor said. "I'll be delighted to receive them here."

Morin turned and nodded shortly to the two officials near the gate. The officials turned and spoke to someone outside, and the gate swung open.

Five Murgos strode into the garden. Their coarse black robes were hooded, but the hoods were thrown back. The front of their robes were unclasped, and the chain mail shirts they all wore gleamed in the sunlight. The Murgo in front was a bit taller than the others, and his bearing indicated that he was the leader of the deputation. A welter of images and partial memories flooded Garion's mind as he looked at the scar-faced enemy he had known all his life. The strange pull of the silent, hidden linkage between them touched him. It was Asharak.

Something brushed Garion's mind, tentative only—not the powerful force the Murgo had directed at him in the dim hallway in Anheg's palace at Val Alorn. The amulet under his tunic became very cold and yet seemed to burn at the same time.

"Your Imperial Highness," Asharak said, striding forward with a cold smile, "we are honored to be admitted into your august presence." He bowed, his mail shirt clinking.

Barak was holding Hettar's right arm firmly, and Mandorallen moved and took the other.

"I'm overjoyed to see you again, worthy Asharak," the Emperor said. "I'm told that an agreement has been reached."

"Beneficial to both sides, your Highness."

"The best kind of agreement," Ran Borune approved.

"Taur Urgas, King of the Murgos, sends greetings," Asharak said. "His Majesty feels most keenly the desirability of cementing relations between Cthol Murgos and Tolnedra. He hopes that one day he may call your Imperial Highness brother."

"We respect the peaceful intentions and legendary wisdom of Taur Urgas." The Emperor smiled with a certain smugness.

Asharak looked around, his black eyes flat. "Well, Ambar," he said to Silk, "your fortunes seem to have improved since we met last in Mingan's counting room in Darine."

Silk spread his hands in an innocent-looking gesture. "The Gods have been kind—most of them, anyway."

Asharak smiled briefly.

"You know each other?" the Emperor asked, a bit surprised.

"We've met, your Highness," Silk admitted.

"In another kingdom," Asharak added. He looked directly then at Mister Wolf. "Belgarath," he said politely with a brief nod.

"Chamdar," the old man replied.

"You're looking well."

"Thank you."

"It seems that I'm the only stranger here," the Emperor said.

"Chamdar and I have known each other for a very long time," Mister Wolf told him. He glanced at the Murgo with a faintly malicious twinkle in his eyes. "I see that you've managed to recover from your recent indisposition."

Asharak's face flickered with annoyance, and he looked quickly at his shadow on the grass as if for reassurance.

Garion remembered what Wolf had said atop the tor after the attack of the Algroths—something about a shadow returning by an "indirect route." For some reason the information that Asharak the Murgo and Chamdar the Grolim were the same man did not particularly surprise him. Like a complex melody that had been faintly out of tune, the sudden merging of the two seemed right somehow. The knowledge clicked in his mind like a key in a lock.

"Someday you'll have to show me how you did that," Asharak was saying. "I found the experience interesting. My horse had hysterics, however."

"My apologies to your horse."

"Why is it that I feel as if I'm missing about half of this conversation?" Ran Borune asked.

"Forgive us, your Highness," Asharak said. "Ancient Belgarath and I are renewing an old enmity. We've seldom had the opportunity to speak to each other with any degree of civility." He turned and bowed politely to Aunt Pol.

"My Lady Polgara. You're as beautiful as ever." He eyed her with a deliberately suggestive stare.

"You haven't changed much either, Chamdar." Her tone was mild, even bland, but Garion, who knew her so well, recognized immediately the deadly insult she had just delivered to the Grolim.

"Charming," Asharak said with a faint smile.

"This is better than a play," the Emperor cried delightedly. "You people are actually dripping with malice. I wish I'd had the opportunity to see the first act."

"The first act was *very* long, your Highness," Asharak said, "and quite often tedious. As you may have noticed, Belgarath sometimes gets carried away with his own cleverness."

"I'm certain I'll be able to make up for that," Mister Wolf told him with a slight smile. "I promise you that the last act will be extremely short, Chamdar."

"Threats, old man?" Asharak asked. "I thought we'd agreed to be civilized."

"I can't recall when we ever agreed on anything," Wolf said. He turned to the Emperor. "I think we'll leave now, Ran Borune," he said. "With your permission, of course."

"Of course," the Emperor replied. "I'm pleased to have met you—though I still don't believe in you, naturally. My skepticism, however, is theological, not personal."

"I'm glad of that," Wolf said, and quite suddenly he grinned impishly at the Emperor.

Ran Borune laughed.

"I look forward to our next meeting, Belgarath," Asharak said.

"I wouldn't if I were you," Wolf advised him, then turned and led the way out of the Emperor's garden.

Chapter Seventeen

IT WAS MIDAFTERNOON when they emerged from the palace gate. The broad lawns were green in the warm spring sunlight, and the cypress trees stirred in a faint breeze.

"I don't think we want to stay in Tol Honeth too much longer," Wolf said.

"Do we leave now, then?" Mandorallen asked.

"There's something I have to do first," Wolf replied, squinting into the sunlight. "Barak and his cousin will come along with me. The rest of you go on back to Grinneg's house and wait there."

"We'll stop by the central market on our way," Aunt Pol told him. "There are a few things I need."

"This isn't a shopping expedition, Pol."

"The Grolims already know we're here, father," she said, "so there's no point in creeping about like sneak thieves, is there?"

He sighed. "All right, Pol."

"I knew you'd see it my way," she said.

Mister Wolf shook his head helplessly and rode off with Barak and Grinneg. The rest of them rode down the hill from the palace toward the gleaming city below. The streets at the foot of the hill were broad and lined on either side by magnificent houses—each almost a palace in itself.

"The rich and the noble," Silk said. "In Tol Honeth, the closer you live to the palace, the more important you are."

"'Tis oft times thus, Prince Kheldar," Mandorallen observed. "Wealth and position sometimes need the reassurance of proximity to the seat of power. By ostentation and propinquity to the throne, small men are able to avoid facing their own inadequacy."

"I couldn't have said it better myself," Silk said.

The central marketplace of Tol Honeth was a vast square filled with bright-colored booths and stalls where a significant portion of the goods of the world were on display. Aunt Pol dismounted, left her horse with one of the Cherek guards, and moved busily from booth to booth, buying, it appeared, almost everything in sight. Silk's face blanched often at her purchases, since he was paying for them. "Can't you talk to her?" the small man pleaded with Garion. "She's destroying me."

"What makes you think she'd listen to me?" Garion asked.

"You could at least *try*," Silk said desperately.

Three richly mantled men stood near the center of the market, arguing heatedly.

"You're mad, Haldor," one of them, a thin man with a snub nose, said agitatedly. "The Honeths would strip the Empire for their own profit." His face was flushed, and his eyes bulged dangerously.

"Would Kador of the Vorduvians be any better?" the stout man named Haldor demanded. "You're the one who's mad, Radan. If we put Kador on the throne, he'll grind us all under foot. There's such a thing as being *too* imperial."

"How dare you?" Radan almost screamed, his perspiring face growing darker. "Grand Duke Kador is the only possible choice. I'd vote for him even if he hadn't paid me." He flung his arms about wildly as he talked, and his tongue seemed to stumble over his words.

"Kador's a pig," Haldor said flatly, carefully watching Radan as if gauging the impact of his words. "An arrogant, brutal pig with no more right to the throne than a mongrel dog. His great-grandfather bought his way into the House of Vordue, and I'd sooner open a vein than bow to the offspring of a sneak thief from the docks of Tol Vordue."

Radan's eyes almost started from his head at Haldor's calculated insults. He opened his mouth several times as if trying to speak, but his tongue seemed frozen with fury. His face turned purple, and he clawed at the air in front of him. Then his body stiffened and began to arch backward.

Haldor watched him with an almost clinical detachment. With a strangled cry, Radan toppled back onto the cobblestones, his arms and legs threshing violently. His eyes rolled back in his head, and he began to foam at the mouth as his convulsions became more violent. He began to bang his head on the stones, and his twitching fingers clutched at his throat.

"Amazing potency," the third mantled man said to Haldor. "Where did you find it?"

"A friend of mine recently made a voyage to Sthiss Tor," Haldor said, watching Radan's convulsions with interest. "The beautiful part of it is that it's completely harmless unless one gets excited. Radan wouldn't drink the wine until I tasted it first to prove that it was safe."

"You've got the same poison in your own stomach?" the other man asked with astonishment.

"I'm quite safe," Haldor said. "My emotions never get the best of me."

Radan's convulsions had grown weaker. His heels beat at the stones with a rapid pattering sound; then he stiffened, gave a long, gurgling sigh, and died.

"I don't suppose you've got any of the drug left, do you?" Haldor's friend asked thoughtfully. "I'd be willing to pay quite a bit for something like that."

Haldor laughed. "Why don't we go to my house, and we'll talk about it? Over a cup of wine, perhaps?"

The other man threw him a startled glance; then he laughed too, although a bit nervously. The two of them turned and walked away, leaving the dead man sprawled on the stones.

Garion stared in horror at them and then at the black-faced corpse lying so grotesquely twisted in the center of the marketplace. The Tolnedrans near the body seemed to ignore its existence. "Why doesn't somebody do something?" he demanded.

"They're afraid," Silk said. "If they show any concern, they might be mistaken for partisans. Politics here in Tol Honeth are taken very seriously."

"Shouldn't someone notify the authorities?" Durnik suggested, his face pale and his voice shaking.

"I'm sure it's already been taken care of," Silk said. "Let's not stand around staring. I don't think we want to get involved in this sort of thing."

Aunt Pol came back to where they were standing. The two Cherek warriors from Grinneg's house who had been accompanying her were loaded down with bundles and both of them looked a little sheepish about it.

"What are you doing?" she asked Silk.

"We were just watching a bit of Tolnedran politics in action," Silk said, pointing at the dead man in the center of the square.

"Poison?" she asked, noting Radan's contorted limbs.

Silk nodded. "A strange one. It doesn't seem to work unless the victim gets excited."

"Athsat," she said with a grim nod.

"You've heard of it before?" Silk seemed surprised.

She nodded. "It's quite rare, and very expensive. I didn't think the Nyissans would be willing to sell any of it."

"I think we should move away from here," Hettar suggested. "There's a squad of legionnaires coming, and they might want to question any witnesses."

"Good idea," Silk said and led them toward the far side of the marketplace.

Near the row of houses that marked the edge of the square, eight burly men carried a heavily veiled litter. As the litter approached, a slender, jeweled hand reached languidly out from behind the veil and touched one of the porters on the shoulder. The eight men stopped immediately and set the litter down.

"Silk," a woman's voice called from within the litter, "what are you doing back in Tol Honeth?"

"Bethra?" Silk said. "Is that you?"

The veil was drawn back, revealing a lushly endowed woman lounging on crimson satin cushions inside the litter. Her dark hair was elaborately curled with strings of pearls woven into her tresses. Her pink silken gown clung to her body, and golden rings and bracelets clasped her arms and fingers. Her face was breathtakingly beautiful, and her long-lashed eyes were wicked. There was about her a kind of overripeness and an almost overpowering sense of self-indulgent corruption. For some reason Garion felt himself blushing furiously.

"I thought you'd still be running," she said archly to Silk. "The men I sent after you were very professional."

Silk bowed with an ironic little flourish. "They *were* quite good, Bethra," he agreed with a wry grin. "Not quite good enough, but very good, actually. I hope you didn't need them anymore."

"I always wondered why they didn't come back." She laughed. "I should have known, of course. I hope you didn't take it personally."

"Certainly not, Bethra. It's just part of the profession, after all."

"I knew you'd understand," she said. "I had to get rid of you. You were disrupting my entire plan."

Silk grinned wickedly. "I know," he gloated. "And after all you had to go through to set it up—and with the Thull-ish ambassador, no less."

She made a disgusted face.

"Whatever happened to him?" Silk asked.

"He went swimming in the Nedrane."

"I didn't know that Thulls swam all that well."

"They don't—particularly not with large rocks tied to their feet. After you'd destroyed the whole thing, I didn't really need him anymore, and there were some things I didn't want him mentioning in certain quarters."

"You always were prudent, Bethra."

"What are you up to now?" she asked curiously.

Silk shrugged. "A little of this; a little of that."

"The succession?"

"Oh, no." He laughed. "I know better than to get in-volved in that. Which side are you on?"

"Wouldn't you like to know?"

Silk looked around, his eyes narrowing. "I could use some information, Bethra—if you're free to talk about it, of course."

"About what, Silk?"

"The city seems to be awash with Murgos," Silk said. "If you're not presently involved with them, I'd appreciate any-thing you could tell me."

She smiled at him archly. "And what would you be will-ing to pay?" she asked.

"Couldn't we just call it professional courtesy?"

She smiled wickedly at him; then she laughed. "Why

not? I like you, Silk, and I think I'll like you even more if you owe me a favor."

"I'll be your slave," he promised.

"Liar." She thought for a moment. "The Murgos have never really shown all that much interest in trade," she said. "But a few years ago they began arriving in twos and threes; and then late last summer, whole caravans started coming in from Rak Goska."

"You think they want to influence the succession?" Silk asked.

"That would be my guess," she said. "There's a great deal of red gold in Tol Honeth suddenly. My coin chests are full of it."

Silk grinned. "It all spends."

"It does indeed."

"Have they picked any one candidate?"

"Not that I've been able to determine. They seem to be divided into two different factions, and there's quite a bit of antagonism between them."

"That could be a ruse, of course."

"I don't think so. I think the antagonism has to do with the quarrel between Zedar and Ctuchik. Each side wants to get control of the next Emperor. They're spending money like water."

"Do you know the one called Asharak?"

"Ah, *that* one," she replied. "The other Murgos are all afraid of him. At the moment he *seems* to be working for Ctuchik, but I think he's playing some game of his own. He owns the Grand Duke Kador outright, and Kador's closest to the throne right now. That puts Asharak in a very powerful position. That's about all I really know."

"Thank you, Bethra," Silk said respectfully.

"Are you planning to stay in Tol Honeth for long?" she asked.

"Unfortunately no."

"Pity. I was hoping you might be able to come by for a visit. We could talk over old times. I don't have many close friends anymore—or dear enemies, like you."

Silk laughed dryly. "I wonder why," he said. "I don't imagine I could swim much better than the Thullish ambassador did. You're a dangerous woman, Bethra."

"In more ways than one," she admitted, stretching languidly. "But your life's not really in any danger from me, Silk—not anymore."

"It wasn't my life I was worried about." Silk grinned.

"That's another matter, of course," she admitted. "Don't forget that you owe me a favor."

"I hunger for the opportunity to repay my debt," he said impudently.

"You're impossible." She laughed, then gestured to her porters, and they lifted her litter to their shoulders. "Good-bye, Silk," she said.

"Good-bye, Bethra," he replied with a deep bow.

"Absolutely disgusting," Durnik said in a voice strangled with outrage as the porters marched away with the litter. "Why is a woman like that even permitted to stay in the city?"

"Bethra?" Silk asked in surprise. "She's the most brilliant and fascinating woman in Tol Honeth. Men come from all over the world just for an hour or two with her."

"For a price, of course," Durnik said.

"Don't misunderstand her, Durnik," Silk told him. "Her conversation's probably more valuable than—" He coughed slightly with a quick glance at Aunt Pol.

"Really?" Durnik questioned in a voice heavy with sarcasm.

Silk laughed. "Durnik," he said, "I love you like a brother, but you're a terrible prude, do you know that?"

"Leave him alone, Silk," Aunt Pol said firmly. "I like him exactly the way he is."

"I'm only trying to improve him, Lady Polgara," Silk explained innocently.

"Barak's right about you, Prince Kheldar," she said. "You're a very bad man."

"It's all in the line of duty. I sacrifice my more delicate feelings for the sake of my country."

"Of course!"

"Surely you don't imagine that I *enjoy* that sort of thing?"

"Why don't we just let it drop?" she suggested.

Grinneg, Barak, and Mister Wolf returned to Grinneg's house not long after the others had arrived.

"Well?" Aunt Pol asked Wolf as the old man came into the room where they had been waiting.

"He went south," Wolf said.

"South? He didn't turn east toward Cthol Murgos?"

"No," Wolf said. "He's probably trying to avoid a meeting with Ctuchik's people. He'll look for a quiet place to slip across the border. Either that or he's headed for Nyissa. Perhaps he's made some arrangement with Salmissra. We'll have to follow him to find out."

"I met an old friend in the marketplace," Silk said from the chair in which he lounged. "She tells me that Asharak's been involved in the politics of succession. It appears that he's managed to buy the Grand Duke of Vordue. If the Vorduvians get the throne, Asharak's going to have Tolnedra in the palm of his hand."

Mister Wolf scratched thoughtfully at his beard. "We're going to have to do something about him sooner or later. He's beginning to make me just a little tired."

"We could stop over for a day or so," Aunt Pol suggested. "Attend to it once and for all."

"No," Wolf decided. "It's probably best not to do that sort of thing here in the city. The business is likely to be a bit noisy, and Tolnedrans get excited about things they can't understand. I'm sure he'll give us an opportunity later—in some less-populated place."

"Do we leave now, then?" Silk asked.

"Let's wait until early morning," Wolf told him. "We'll probably be followed, but if the streets are empty, it will make things a little more difficult for them."

"I'll talk to my cook, then," Grinneg said. "The least I can do is send you on your way with a good meal to help you face the road. Then, of course, there's still that barrel of ale to be dealt with."

Mister Wolf smiled broadly at that, then caught Aunt Pol's reproving frown. "It would only go flat, Pol," he explained. "Once it's broached, you have to drink it up fairly quickly. It would be a shame to waste it, wouldn't it?"

Chapter Eighteen

THEY LEFT GRINNEG'S HOUSE before dawn the next morning, dressed once more in their traveling clothes. They slipped quietly out a back gate and proceeded through those narrow alleys and back streets Silk always seemed able to find. The sky to the east was beginning to lighten when they reached the massive bronze gate on the south end of the island.

"How long until the gate opens?" Mister Wolf asked one of the legionnaires.

"Not much longer," the legionnaire told him. "Just as soon as we can see the far bank clearly."

Wolf grunted. He had grown quite mellow the evening before and he was obviously troubled by a headache this morning. He dismounted, went to one of the packhorses, and drank from a leather waterskin.

"That isn't going to help, you know," Aunt Pol told him a bit smugly.

He chose not to answer.

"I think it's going to be a lovely day today," she said brightly, looking first at the sky and then at the men around her who slumped in their saddles in attitudes of miserable dejection.

"You're a cruel woman, Polgara," Barak said sadly.

"Did you talk to Grinneg about that ship?" Mister Wolf asked.

"I think so," Barak replied. "I seem to remember saying something about it."

"It's fairly important," Wolf said.

"What's this?" Aunt Pol asked.

"I thought it might not be a bad idea to have a ship waiting off the mouth of the River of the Woods," Wolf said. "If we have to go to Sthiss Tor, it would probably be better to sail there rather than wade through the swamps in northern Nyissa."

"That's a very good idea, actually," she approved. "I'm surprised it occurred to you—considering your condition last night."

"Do you suppose we could talk about something else?" he asked somewhat plaintively.

It grew imperceptibly lighter, and the command to open the gate came from the watchtower on the wall above. The legionnaires slipped the iron bar and swung the ponderous gate open. With Mandorallen at his side, Silk led them out through the thick portal and across the bridge that spanned the dark waters of the Nedrane.

By noon they were eight leagues south of Tol Honeth, and Mister Wolf had somewhat regained his composure, though his eyes still seemed a bit sensitive to the bright spring sunlight, and he winced now and then when a bird sang a bit too near.

"Riders coming up behind," Hettar said.

"How many?" Barak asked.

"Two."

"Ordinary travelers, perhaps," Aunt Pol said.

The two figures on horseback appeared from around a bend behind them and stopped. They spoke together for a moment or two and then came on, their bearing somewhat cautious. They were a peculiar pair. The man wore a green Tolnedran mantle, a garment not really suited for riding. His forehead was quite high, and his hair was carefully combed to conceal his encroaching baldness. He was very skinny, and his ears stuck out from the side of his head like flaps. His companion appeared to be a child dressed in a hooded traveling cloak and with a kerchief across her face to keep out the dust.

"Good day to you," the skinny man greeted them politely as the pair drew alongside.

"Hello," Silk returned.

"Warm for so early in the year, isn't it?" the Tolnedran said.

"We noticed that," Silk agreed.

"I wonder," the skinny man asked, "do you have a bit of water you could spare?"

"Of course," Silk said. He looked at Garion and gestured toward the pack animals. Garion dropped back and unhooked a leather waterskin from one of the packs. The stranger removed the wooden stopper and carefully wiped the mouth of the skin. He offered the bag to his companion. She removed her kerchief and looked at the skin with an expression of perplexity.

"Like this, your—uh—my Lady," the man explained, taking the skin back, raising it in both hands and drinking.

"I see," the girl said.

Garion looked at her more closely. The voice was familiar for some reason, and there was something about her face. She was not a child, though she was very small, and there was a kind of self-indulged petulance about her tiny face. Garion was almost certain he had seen her somewhere before.

The Tolnedran handed the waterskin back to her, and she drank, making a small face at the resinous taste. Her hair was a purplish black, and there were faint dark smears on the collar of her traveling cloak that indicated that the color was not natural.

"Thank you, Jeebers," she said after she had drunk. "And thank you, sir," she said to Silk.

Garion's eyes narrowed as a dreadful suspicion began to grow in his mind.

"Are you going far?" the skinny man asked Silk.

"Quite a ways," Silk answered. "I'm Radek of Boktor, a Drasnian merchant, and I'm bound to the south with Sendarian woolens. This break in the weather destroyed the market in Tol Honeth, so I thought I'd try Tol Rane. It's in the mountains, and it's probably still cold there."

"You're taking the wrong road, then," the stranger said. "The road to Tol Rane lies off to the east."

"I've had trouble on that road," Silk said glibly. "Robbers, you know. I thought it'd be safer to go through Tol Borune."

"What a coincidence," the skinny man told him. "My pupil and I are bound for Tol Borune ourselves."

"Yes," Silk admitted. "Quite a coincidence."

"Perhaps we could ride along together."

Silk looked doubtful.

"I don't see any reason why not," Aunt Pol decided before he could refuse.

"You're most kind, gracious lady," the stranger said. "I am Master Jeebers, Fellow of the Imperial Society, a tutor by profession. Perhaps you've heard of me."

"I can't really say so," Silk told him, "although that's not too remarkable, since we're strangers here in Tolnedra."

Jeebers looked a bit disappointed. "I suppose that's true," he said. "This is my pupil, Lady Sharell. Her father's a grand master merchant, the Baron Reldon. I'm accompanying her to Tol Borune where she's to visit relatives."

Garion knew that was not true. The tutor's name had confirmed his suspicions.

They rode several miles further, with Jeebers babbling animatedly at Silk. He spoke endlessly about his learning and continually prefaced his remarks with references to important people who seemed to rely on his judgment. Although he was tiresome, he appeared to be quite harmless. His pupil rode beside Aunt Pol, saying very little.

"I think it's time we stopped for a bite to eat," Aunt Pol announced. "Would you and your pupil care to join us, Master Jeebers? We have plenty."

"I'm quite overcome by your generosity," the tutor said. "We'd be delighted."

They stopped the horses near a small bridge that crossed a brook and led them into the shade of a thick clump of willows not far from the road. Durnik built a fire, and Aunt Pol began to unload her pots and kettles.

Master Jeebers' pupil sat in her saddle until the tutor quickly stepped over to help her down. She looked at the slightly marshy ground near the brook unenthusiastically. Then she glanced imperiously at Garion. "You—boy," she called. "Fetch me a cup of fresh water."

"The brook's right there," he told her, pointing.

She stared at him in amazement. "But the ground's all muddy," she objected.

"It does seem that way, doesn't it?" he admitted and then quite deliberately turned his back on her and went over to help his Aunt.

"Aunt Pol," he said after several moments of debating with himself.

"Yes, dear?"

"I don't think the Lady Sharell's who she says she is."

"Oh?"

"I'm not completely positive, but I think she's the Princess Ce'Nedra—the one who came into the garden when we were at the palace."

"Yes, dear. I know."

"You know?"

"Of course. Would you hand me the salt, please?"

"Isn't it dangerous to have her with us?"

"Not really," she said. "I think we can manage it."

"Won't she be a lot of bother?"

"An Imperial Princess is supposed to be a lot of bother, dear."

After they had eaten a savory stew which seemed to Garion quite good but which their little guest appeared to find distasteful, Jeebers began to approach a subject which had obviously been on his mind since thy had first met. "Despite the best efforts of the legions, the roads are never entirely safe," the fussy man said. "It's imprudent to travel alone, and the Lady Sharell's been entrusted to my care. Since I'm responsible for her safety, I was wondering if we might travel along with you. We wouldn't be any bother, and I'd be more than happy to pay for whatever food we eat."

Silk glanced quickly at Aunt Pol.

"Of course," she said.

Silk looked surprised.

"There's no reason we can't travel together," she went on. "We're all going to the same place, after all."

Silk shrugged. "Anything you say."

Garion knew the idea was a mistake so serious that it bordered on disaster. Jeebers would not be a good traveling companion, and his pupil showed every sign of quickly becoming intolerable. She was obviously accustomed to extensive personal service, and her demands were probably made without thought. They were still demands, however, and Garion knew immediately who was most likely to be expected to attend to them. He got up and walked around to the far side of the clump of willows.

The fields beyond the trees were pale green in the spring sunshine, and small white clouds drifted lazily across the sky. Garion leaned against a tree and gazed out at the fields without actually seeing them. He would *not* become a servant—no matter who their little guest might be. He wished there were some way he could get that firmly established right at the outset—before things got out of hand.

"Have you lost your senses, Pol?" he heard Mister Wolf say somewhere behind him among the trees. "Ran Borune's probably got every legion in Tolnedra looking for her by now."

"This is my province, Old Wolf," Aunt Pol told him. "Don't interfere. I can manage things so that we won't be bothered by the legions."

"We don't have the time to coddle her," the old man said. "I'm sorry, Pol, but the child's going to be an absolute little monster. You saw the way she acted toward her father."

"It's no great chore to break bad habits," she said, unconcerned.

"Wouldn't it be simpler just to arrange to have her taken back to Tol Honeth?"

"She's already run away once," Aunt Pol answered. "If we send her back, she'll just run away again. I'll feel much more comfortable having her Imperial little Highness where I can put my hands on her when I need her. When the proper time comes, I don't want to have to take the world apart looking for her."

Wolf sighed. "Have it your way, Pol."

"Naturally."

"Just keep the brat away from me," he said. "She sets my teeth on edge. Do any of the others know who she is?"

"Garion does."

"Garion? That's surprising."

"Not really," Aunt Pol said. "He's brighter than he looks."

A new emotion began to grow in Garion's already confused mind. Aunt Pol's obvious interest in Ce'Nedra sent a sharp pang through him. With a certain amount of shame, he realized that he was jealous of the attention the girl was receiving.

In the days that followed, Garion's fears quickly proved to be well-founded. An inadvertant remark about Faldor's farm had revealed quite early to the princess his former status as a scullery-boy, and she used the knowledge heartlessly to browbeat him into a hundred stupid little errands every day. To make it all worse, each time he tried to resist, Aunt Pol would firmly remind him to pay more attention to his manners. Inevitably, he became quite surly about the whole business.

The princess developed a story about the reason for her departure from Tol Honeth as they rode south. The story changed daily, growing more wildly implausible with every passing league. At first she seemed content to be on a simple excursion to visit relatives; then she dropped dark hints about flight from a marriage to an ugly old merchant. Next, there were even darker hints about a plot to capture her and hold her for ransom. Finally, in a crowning effort, she confided to them that the proposed kidnapping was politically motivated—a part of some vast scheme to gain power in Tolnedra.

"She's an awful liar, isn't she?" Garion asked Aunt Pol when they were alone one evening.

"Yes, dear," Aunt Pol agreed. "Lying is an art. A good lie shouldn't be embellished so much. She'll need a lot more practice if she plans to make a career of it."

Finally, about ten days after they had left Tol Honeth, the city of Tol Borune came into sight in the afternoon sun. "It looks like this is where we part company," Silk said to Jeebers with a certain amount of relief.

"Aren't you going into the city?" Jeebers asked.

"I don't think so," Silk answered. "We don't really have any business to take care of there, and the usual explanations and searches just waste time—not to mention the expense of the bribes. We'll go around Tol Borune and pick up the road to Tol Rane on the other side."

"We can ride a bit farther with you then," Ce'Nedra said quickly. "My relatives live on an estate to the south of the city."

Jeebers stared at her in amazement.

Aunt Pol drew in her horse and looked at the small girl with a raised eyebrow. "This seems like as good a place as any for us to have a little talk," she said.

Silk looked quickly at her and then nodded.

"I believe, little lady," Aunt Pol told the girl when they had all dismounted, "that the time has come for you to tell us the truth."

"But I have," Ce'Nedra protested.

"Oh, come now, child," Aunt Pol said. "Those stories of yours have been very entertaining, but you don't actually think anyone believed them, do you? Some of us already know who you are, but I really think we should get it out in the open."

"You know?" Ce'Nedra faltered.

"Of course, dear," Aunt Pol said. "Would you like to tell them, or shall I?"

Ce'Nedra's little shoulders drooped. "Tell them who I am, Master Jeebers," she ordered quietly.

"Do you really think that's wise, your Ladyship?" Jeebers asked nervously.

"They already know anyway," she said. "If they were going to do anything to us, they'd have done it a long time ago. We can trust them."

Jeebers drew in a deep breath and then spoke rather formally. "I have the honor to introduce her Imperial Highness, the Princess Ce'Nedra, daughter to his Imperial Majesty, Ran Borune XXIII, and the jewel of the House of Borune."

Silk whistled, and his eyes widened momentarily. The others showed similar signs of amazement.

"The political situation in Tol Honeth had become far too volatile, too menacing, for her Highness to remain safely in the capital," Jeebers went on. "The Emperor commissioned me to convey his daughter secretly here to Tol Borune where the members of the Borune family can protect her from the plots and machinations of the Vordues, the Honeths, and the Horbites. I'm proud to say that I've managed to execute my commission rather brilliantly—with your help, of course. I'll mention your assistance in my report—a footnote, perhaps, or maybe even an appendix."

Barak pulled at his beard, his eyes thoughtful. "An Imperial Princess travels across half of Tolnedra with only a schoolmaster for protection?" he questioned. "At a time when they're knifing and poisoning each other in the streets?"

"It does seem a trifle risky, doesn't it?" Hettar agreed.

"Did thine Emperor charge thee with this task in person?" Mandorallen asked Jeebers.

"It wasn't necessary," Jeebers said stiffly. "His Highness has a great deal of respect for my judgment and discretion. He knew that I'd be able to devise a safe disguise and a secure mode of travel. The princess assured me of his absolute confidence in me. It all had to be done in utmost secrecy, of course. That's why she came to my chambers in the middle of the night to advise me of his instructions and why we left the palace without telling anyone what we were—" His voice trailed off, and he stared at Ce'Nedra in horror.

"You might as well tell him the truth, dear," Aunt Pol advised the little princess. "I think he's guessed already."

Ce'Nedra's chin lifted arrogantly. "The orders came from me, Jeebers," she told him. "My father had nothing to do with it."

Jeebers went deathly pale and he nearly collapsed.

"What idiocy made you decide to run away from your father's palace?" Barak demanded of the tiny girl. "All Tolnedra's probably looking for you, and we're caught right in the middle."

"Gently," Wolf said to the hulking Cherek. "She may be a princess, but she's still a little girl. Don't frighten her."

"The question's to the point, though," Hettar observed. "If we're caught with an Imperial Princess in our company, we'll all see the inside of a Tolnedran dungeon." He turned to Ce'Nedra. "Do you have an answer, or were you just playing games?"

She drew herself up haughtily. "I'm not accustomed to explaining my actions to servants."

"We're going to have to clear up a few misconceptions before long, I see," Wolf said.

"Just answer the question, dear," Aunt Pol told the girl. "Never mind who asked it."

"My father had imprisoned me in the palace," Ce'Nedra said in a rather offhand way, as if that explained everything. "It was intolerable, so I left. There's another matter, too, but that's a matter of politics. You wouldn't understand."

"You'd probably be surprised at what we'd understand, Ce'Nedra," Mister Wolf told her.

"I'm accustomed to being addressed as my Lady," she said tartly, "or as your Highness."

"And I'm accustomed to being told the truth."

"I thought you were in charge," Ce'Nedra said to Silk.

"Appearances are deceiving," Silk observed blandly. "I'd answer the question."

"It's an old treaty," she said. "I didn't sign it, so I don't see why I should be bound by it. I'm supposed to present myself in the throne room at Riva on my sixteenth birthday."

"We know that," Barak said impatiently. "What's the problem?"

"I'm not going, that's all," Ce'Nedra announced. "I won't go to Riva, and no one can make me go. The queen in the Wood of the Dryads is my kinswoman and she'll give me sanctuary."

Jeebers had partially recovered. "What have you done?" he demanded, aghast. "I undertook this with the clear understanding that I'd be rewarded—even promoted. You've put my head on the block, you little idiot!"

"Jeebers!" she cried, shocked at his words.

"Let's get off the road a ways," Silk suggested. "We've obviously got quite a bit to discuss, and we're likely to be interrupted here on the main highway."

"Probably a good idea," Wolf agreed. "Let's find some quiet place and set up for the night. We'll decide what we're going to do and then we can start out fresh in the morning."

They remounted and rode across the rolling fields toward a line of trees that marked the course of a winding country lane about a mile away.

"How about there?" Durnik suggested, pointing at a broad oak which stood beside the lane, its branches beginning to leaf out in the late afternoon sunlight.

"That should do," Wolf said.

It was pleasant in the dappled shade beneath the spreading limbs of the oak. The lane was lined with low stone walls, mossy and cool. A stile stepped up over one of the walls just there, and a path meandered across the field from it toward a nearby pond, sparkling in the sun.

"We can put the fire down behind one of the walls," Durnik said. "It won't be seen from the main road that way."

"I'll get some wood," Garion volunteered, looking at the dead limbs littering the grass beneath the tree.

They had by now established a sort of routine in the setting up of a night's encampment. The tents were erected, the horses watered and picketed, and the fire was started all within the space of an hour. Then Durnik, who had noticed a few telltale circles on the surface of the pond, heated an iron pin in the fire and carefully hammered it into a hook.

"What's that for?" Garion asked him.

"I thought some fish might be good for supper," the smith said, wiping the hook on the skirt of his leather tunic. He laid it aside then and lifted a second pin out of the fire with a pair of tongs. "Would you like to try your luck too?"

Garion grinned at him.

Barak, who sat nearby combing the snarls out of his beard, looked up rather wistfully. "I don't suppose you'd have time to make another hook, would you?" he asked.

Durnik chuckled. "It only takes a couple minutes."

"We'll need bait," Barak said, getting up quickly. "Where's your spade?"

Not long afterward, the three of them crossed the field to the pond, cut some saplings for poles and settled down to serious fishing.

The fish, it appeared, were ravenous and attacked the worm-baited hooks in schools. Within the space of an hour nearly two dozen respectable-sized trout lay in a gleaming row on the grassy bank of the pond.

Aunt Pol inspected their catch gravely when they returned as the sky turned rosy overhead with the setting of the sun. "Very nice," she told them, "but you forgot to clean them."

"Oh," Barak said. He looked slightly pained. "We thought that—well, what I mean is—as long as *we* caught them—" He left it hanging.

"Go on," she said with a level gaze.

Barak sighed. "I guess we'd better clean them," he regretfully told Durnik and Garion.

"You're probably right," Durnik agreed.

The sky had turned purple with evening, and the stars had begun to come out when they sat down to eat. Aunt Pol had fried the trout to a crisp, golden brown, and even the sulky little princess found nothing to complain about as she ate.

After they had finished, they set aside their plates and took up the problem of Ce'Nedra and her flight from Tol Honeth. Jeebers had sunk into such abject melancholy that he could offer little to the discussion, and Ce'Nedra adamantly announced that even if they were to turn her over to the Borunes in the city, she would run away again. In the end, they reached no conclusion.

"We're in trouble no matter what we do," Silk summed it all up ruefully. "Even if we try to deliver her to her family, there are bound to be some embarrassing questions, and I'm sure she can be counted on to invent a colorful story that will put us in the worst possible light."

"We can talk about it some more in the morning," Aunt Pol said. Her placid tone indicated that she had already made up her mind about something, but she did not elaborate.

Shortly before midnight, Jeebers made his escape. They were all awakened by the thudding of his horse's hooves as the panic-stricken tutor fled at a gallop toward the walls of Tol Borune.

Silk stood in the flickering light of the dying fire, his face angry. "Why didn't you stop him?" he asked Hettar, who had been standing watch.

"I was told not to," the leather-clad Algar said with a glance at Aunt Pol.

"It solves the only real problem we had," Aunt Pol explained. "The schoolmaster would only have been excess baggage."

"You knew he was going to run away?" Silk asked.

"Naturally. I helped him to arrive at the decision. He'll go straight to the Borunes and try to save his own skin by informing them that the princess ran away from the palace on her own and that we have her now."

"You have to stop him then," Ce'Nedra said in a ringing voice. "Go after him! Bring him back!"

"After all the trouble I went to persuading him to leave?" Aunt Pol asked. "Don't be foolish."

"How *dare* you speak to me like that?" Ce'Nedra demanded. "You seem to forget who I am."

"Young lady," Silk said urbanely, "I think you'd be amazed at how little Polgara's concerned about who you are."

"Polgara?" Ce'Nedra faltered. "*The* Polgara? I thought you said that she was your sister."

"I lied," Silk confessed. "It's a vice I have."

"You're not an ordinary merchant," the girl accused him.

"He's Prince Kheldar of Drasnia," Aunt Pol said. "The others have a similar eminence. I'm sure you can see how little your title impresses us. We have our own titles, so we know how empty they are."

"If you're Polgara, then he must be—" The princess turned to stare at Mister Wolf, who had seated himself on the lowest step of the stile to pull on his shoes.

"Yes," Aunt Pol said. "He doesn't really look the part, does he?"

"What are you doing in Tolnedra?" Ce'Nedra asked in a stunned voice. "Are you going to use magic of some kind to control the outcome of the succession?"

"Why should we?" Mister Wolf said, getting to his feet. "Tolnedrans always seem to think that their politics shake the whole world, but the rest of the world's really not all that concerned about who gains the throne in Tol Honeth. We're here on a matter of much greater urgency." He looked off into the darkness in the direction of Tol Borune. "It will take Jeebers a certain amount of time to convince the people in the city that he's not a lunatic," he said, "but it would probably be a good idea if we left the area. I imagine we'd better stay away from the main highway."

"That's no problem," Silk assured him.

"What about me?" Ce'Nedra asked.

"You wanted to go to the Wood of the Dryads," Aunt Pol told her. "We're going in that direction anyway, so you'll stay with us. We'll see what Queen Xantha says when we get you there."

"Am I to consider myself a prisoner then?" the princess asked stiffly.

"You can if it makes you feel better, dear," Aunt Pol said. She looked at the tiny girl critically in the flickering firelight. "I'm going to have to do something about your hair, though. What did you use for dye? It looks awful."

Chapter Nineteen

THEY MOVED RAPIDLY SOUTH for the next few days, traveling frequently at night to avoid the mounted patrols of legionnaires who were beating the countryside in their efforts to locate Ce'Nedra.

"Maybe we should have hung on to Jeebers," Barak muttered sourly after one near-brush with the soldiers. "He's roused every garrison from here to the border. It might have been better to have dropped him off in some isolated place or something."

"That 'or something' has a certain ring of finality to it, old friend," Silk said with a sharp little grin.

Barak shrugged. "It's a solution to a problem."

Silk laughed. "You really should try not to let your knife do all your thinking for you. That's the one quality we find least attractive in our Cherek cousins."

"And we find this compulsion to make clever remarks which seems to overwhelm our Drasnian brothers now and then almost equally unattractive," Barak told him coolly.

"Nicely put," Silk said with mock admiration.

They rode on, watchful, always ready to hide or to run. During those days they relied heavily on Hettar's curious ability. Since the patrols searching for them were inevitably mounted, the tall, hawk-faced Algar swept their surroundings with his mind, searching for horses. The warnings he could thus provide usually gave them sufficient notice of the approach of the patrols.

"What's it like?" Garion asked him one cloudy midmorning as they rode along a seldom-used and weed-grown track to which Silk had led them. "I mean being able to hear a horse's thoughts?"

"I don't think I can describe it exactly," Hettar answered. "I've always been able to do it, so I can't imagine what it's like not doing it. There's a kind of reaching-out in a horse's mind—a sort of inclusiveness. A horse seems to think 'we' instead of 'I.' I suppose it's because in their natural condition they're members of a herd. After they get to know you, they think of you as a herd mate. Sometimes they even forget that you're not a horse." He broke off suddenly. "Belgarath," he announced sharply, "there's another patrol coming—just beyond that hill over there. Twenty or thirty of them."

Mister Wolf looked about quickly. "Have we got time to reach those trees?" He pointed at a thick stand of scrub maple about a half mile ahead.

"If we hurry."

"Then run!" Wolf ordered, and they all kicked their horses into a sudden burst of speed. They reached the trees just as the first few raindrops of the spring shower that had been threatening all morning pattered on the broad leaves. They dismounted and pushed in among the springy saplings, worming their way back out of sight, leading their horses.

The Tolnedran patrol came over the hilltop and swept down into the shallow valley. The captain in charge of the legionnaires pulled in his horse not far from the stand of maples and dispersed his men with a series of sharp commands. They moved out in small groups, scouting the weedy road in both directions and surveying the surrounding countryside from the top of the next rise. The officer and a civilian in a gray riding cloak remained behind, sitting their horses beside the track.

The captain squinted distastefully up into the sprinkling rain. "It's going to be a wet day," he said, dismounting and pulling his crimson cloak tighter around him.

His companion also swung down and turned so that the party hiding among the maples was able to see his face. Garion felt Hettar tense suddenly. The man in the cloak was a Murgo.

"Over here, Captain," the Murgo said, leading his horse into the shelter provided by the outspreading limbs of the saplings at the edge of the stand.

The Tolnedran nodded and followed the man in the riding cloak.

"Have you had a chance to think over my offer?" the Murgo asked.

"I thought it was only speculation," the captain replied. "We don't even know that these foreigners are in this quadrant."

"My information is that they're going south, captain," the Murgo told him. "I think you can be quite certain that they're somewhere in your quadrant."

"There's no guarantee that we'll find them, though," the captain said. "And even if we do, it'd be very difficult to do what you propose."

"Captain," the Murgo explained patiently, "it's for the safety of the princess, after all. If she's returned to Tol Honeth, the Vorduvians are going to kill her. You've read those documents I brought you."

"She'll be safe with the Borunes," the captain said. "The Vorduvians aren't going to come into Southern Tolnedra after her."

"The Borunes are only going to turn her over to her father. You're a Borune yourself. Would *you* defy an Emperor of your own house?"

The captain's face was troubled.

"Her only hope of safety is with the Horbites," the Murgo pressed.

"What guarantees do I have that she'll be safe with them?"

"The best guarantee of all—politics. The Horbites are

doing everything in their power to block the Grank Duke
Kador on his march to the throne. Since he wants the princess dead, the Horbites naturally want to keep her alive.
It's the only way really to insure her safety—and you become a wealthy man in the process." He jingled a heavy
purse suggestively.

The captain still looked doubtful.

"Suppose we double the amount," the Murgo said in a
voice that almost purred.

The captain swallowed hard. "It *is* for her safety, isn't
it?"

"Of course it is."

"It's not as if I were betraying the House of Borune."

"You're a patriot, Captain," the Murgo assured the officer with a cold smile.

Aunt Pol was holding Ce'Nedra's arm quite firmly as
they crouched together among the trees. The tiny girl's face
was outraged, and her eyes were blazing.

Later, after the legionnaires and their Murgo friend had
departed, the princess exploded. "How *dare* they?" she
raged. "And for money!"

"That's Tolnedran politics for you," Silk said as they led
their horses out of the stand of saplings into the drizzly
morning.

"But he's a Borune," she protested, "a member of my
own family."

"A Tolnedran's first loyalty is to his purse," Silk told
her. "I'm surprised you haven't discovered that by now,
your Highness."

A few days later they topped a hill and saw the Wood of
the Dryads spreading like a green smudge on the horizon.
The showers had blown off, and the sun was very bright.

"We'll be safe once we reach the Wood," the princess
told them. "The legions won't follow us there."

"What's to stop them?" Garion asked her.

"The treaty with the Dryads," she said. "Don't you know
anything?"

Garion resented that.

"There's no one about," Hettar reported to Mister Wolf.
"We can go now or wait for dark."

"Let's make a run for it," Wolf said. "I'm getting tired

of dodging patrols." They started down the hill at a gallop toward the forest lying ahead of them.

There seemed to be none of the usual brushy margin which usually marked the transition from fields to woodlands. The trees simply began. When Wolf led them beneath those trees, the change was as abrupt as if they had suddenly gone inside a house. The Wood itself was a forest of incredible antiquity. The great oaks spread so broadly that the sky was almost never visible. The forest floor was mossy and cool, and there was very little undergrowth. It seemed to Garion that they were all quite tiny under the vast trees, and there was a strange, hushed quality about the wood. The air was very still, and there was a hum of insects and, from far overhead, a chorus of birdsong.

"Strange," Durnik said, looking around, "I don't see any sign of woodcutters."

"Woodcutters?" Ce'Nedra gasped. "In here? They wouldn't dare come into this wood."

"The wood is inviolate, Durnik," Mister Wolf explained. "The Borune family has a treaty with the Dryads. No one has touched a tree here for over three thousand years."

"This is a curious place," Mandorallen said, looking around a bit uncomfortably. "Methinks I feel a presence here—a presence not altogether friendly."

"The Wood is alive," Ce'Nedra told him. "It doesn't really like strangers—but don't worry, Mandorallen, you're safe as long as you're with me." She sounded quite smug about it.

"Are you sure the patrols won't follow us?" Durnik asked Mister Wolf. "Jeebers knew we were coming here, after all, and I'm sure he told the Borunes."

"The Borunes won't violate their treaty with the Dryads," Wolf assured him. "Not for any reason."

"I've never known of a treaty a Tolnedran wouldn't step around if it was to his advantage." Silk spoke skeptically.

"This one is a bit different," Wolf said. "The Dryads gave one of their princesses to a young noble of the House of Borune. She became the mother of the Emperor of the First Borune Dynasty. The fortunes of the Borunes are very intimately tied up with the treaty. They're not going to gamble with that—not for any reason."

"What exactly is a Dryad?" Garion asked. The strange sense of a presence, an awareness in the wood, made him want to talk to cover the oppressive, watchful silence.

"A small group," Mister Wolf said. "Quite gentle. I've always rather liked them. They aren't human, of course, but that's not all that important."

"I'm a Dryad," Ce'Nedra said rather proudly.

Garion stared at her.

"Technically she's right," Wolf said. "The Dryad line seems to breed true on the female side of the House of Borune. That's one of the things that keeps the family honest about the treaty—all those wives and mothers who'd pack up and leave if it were ever broken."

"She *looks* human," Garion objected, still staring at the princess.

"The Dryads are so closely related to humans that the differences are hardly significant," Wolf said. "That probably explains why they didn't go mad like the other monsters did when Torak cracked the world."

"Monsters!" Ce'Nedra protested loudly.

"Your pardon, Princess," Wolf apologized. "It's an Ulgo term used to describe the non-humans who supported Gorim at Prolgu when he met with the God UL."

"Do I look like a monster to you?" she demanded, tossing her head angrily.

"A poor choice of words, perhaps," Wolf murmured. "Forgive me."

"Monsters indeed!" Ce'Nedra fumed.

Wolf shrugged. "There's a stream not far ahead, if I remember right. We'll stop there and wait until word of our arrival reaches Queen Xantha. It's not a good idea to go into the territory of the Dryads without the queen's permission. They can get quite nasty if they're provoked."

"I thought you said they were gentle," Durnik said.

"Within reason," Wolf told him. "But it's not a good idea to irritate people who communicate with trees when you're in the middle of a forest. Unpleasant things have a way of happening." He frowned. "That reminds me. You'd better stow your axe away out of sight. Dryads have strong feelings about axes—and fires. They're most unreasonable about fire. We'll have to keep our fires small and only for cooking."

They rode in under a colossal oak beside a sparkling stream purling over mossy rocks, dismounted and set up their dun-colored tents. After they had eaten, Garion wandered around feeling bored. Mister Wolf was napping, and Silk had lured the others into a dice game. Aunt Pol had seated the Princess on a log and was stripping the purple dye from her hair.

"If you don't have anything else to do, Garion," she said, "why don't you go bathe?"

"Bathe?" he asked. "Where?"

"I'm sure you'll find a pool somewhere along the stream," she said, carefully lathering Ce'Nedra's hair.

"You want me to bathe in that water? Aren't you afraid I'll catch cold?"

"You're a healthy boy, dear," she told him, "but a very dirty one. Now go wash."

Garion gave her a dark look and went to one of the packs for clean clothing, soap, and a towel. Then he stamped off upstream, grumbling at every step.

Once he was alone under the trees, he felt even more strongly that peculiar sense of being watched. It was not anything definable. There seemed to be nothing specific about it, but rather it felt as if the oaks themselves were aware of him and were passing information about his movements among themselves with a kind of vegetative communication he could not begin to understand. There seemed to be no menace in it—merely a kind of watchfulness.

Some distance from the tents he found a fairly large pool where the stream dropped in a waterfall from the rocks above. The water in the pool was very clear, and he could see the bright pebbles on the bottom and several large trout that eyed him warily. He tested the water with his hand and shuddered. He considered subterfuge—a quick splashing of water on his body and a bit of soap on the more obvious smudges—but on reflection, he gave up the notion. Aunt Pol would settle for nothing less than a complete bath. He sighed bitterly and began to take off his clothing.

The first shock was awful, but after a few minutes he found that he could bear it. In a short time it even became exhilarating. The waterfall provided a convenient means for rinsing off the soap, and before long he found that he was actually enjoying himself.

"You're making an awful lot of noise," Ce'Nedra said, standing on the bank and appraising him quite calmly.

Garion immediately dove to the bottom of the pool.

Unless one was a fish, however, one could hardly remain underwater indefinitely. After about a minute, he struggled to the surface and popped his head out of the water, gasping and sputtering.

"Whatever are you doing?" Ce'Nedra asked. She was wearing a short white tunic, sleeveless and belted at the waist, and open sandals with laces that crisscrossed her slender ankles and calves and tied just below her knees. She carried a towel in one hand.

"Go away," Garion spluttered.

"Don't be so silly," she said, sitting down on a large stone and beginning to unlace her sandals. Her coppery hair was still damp and tumbled in a heavy mass about her shoulders.

"What are you doing?"

"I want to bathe," she said. "Are you going to be much longer?"

"Go someplace else," Garion cried, starting to shiver, but remaining determinedly crouched over in the water with only his head sticking out.

"This place looks just fine," she said. "How's the water?"

"Cold," he chattered, "but I'm not coming out until you go away."

"Don't be such a ninny," she told him.

He shook his head stubbornly, his face flaming.

She sighed with exasperation. "Oh, very well," she said. "I won't look, but I think you're being very silly. At the baths in Tol Honeth, no one thinks anything at all about such things."

"This isn't Tol Honeth," he told her pointedly.

"I'll turn my back, if that'll make you feel better," she said, getting up and standing with her back to the pool.

Not entirely trusting her, Garion crept from the pool and, still dripping, jerked on his drawers and hose. "All right," he called, "you can have the pool now." He mopped at his streaming face and hair with his towel. "I'm going back to the tents."

"The Lady Polgara says that you're to stay with me," she said, calmly untying the cord about her waist.

"Aunt Pol said *what*?" he demanded, terribly shocked.

"You're supposed to stay with me to protect me," she told him. She took hold of the hem of her tunic, obviously preparing to take it off.

Garion spun about and stared determinedly at the trees. His ears flamed, and his hands trembled uncontrollably.

She laughed a small, silvery laugh, and he could hear splashing as she entered the pool. She squealed from the shock of the cold water, and then there was more splashing.

"Bring me the soap," she commanded.

Without thinking, he bent to pick up the soap and caught one brief glimpse of her standing waist-deep in the water before he shut his eyes tightly. He backed toward the pool, his eyes closed and the hand holding the soap thrust out awkwardly behind him.

She laughed again and took the soap from his hand.

After what seemed an eternity, the princess completed her bath, emerged from the pool, dried herself and put her clothes back on. Garion kept his eyes firmly shut the entire time.

"You Sendars have such curious notions," she said as they sat together in the sun-warmed glade beside the pool. She was combing her deep red hair, her head inclined to one side and the comb pulling down through the thick, damp tangles. "The baths in Tol Honeth are open to all, and athletic contests are always conducted without clothing. Just last summer I myself ran against a dozen other girls in the Imperial Stadium. The spectators were most appreciative."

"I can imagine," Garion said dryly.

"What's that?" she asked, pointing at the amulet resting against his bare chest.

"My grandfather gave it to me last Erastide," Garion answered.

"Let me see." She held out her hand.

He leaned forward.

"Take it off so I can see it," she ordered.

"I'm not supposed to take it off," he told her. "Mister Wolf and Aunt Pol say I'm never supposed to take it off for any reason. I think there's a spell of some kind on it."

"What a strange idea," she remarked as she bent to examine the amulet. "They aren't really sorcerers, are they?"

"Mister Wolf is seven thousand years old," Garion said. "He knew the God Aldur. I've seen him make a tree grow from a small twig in a matter of minutes and set rocks on fire. Aunt Pol cured a blind woman with a single word, and she can turn herself into an owl."

"I don't believe in such things," Ce'Nedra told him. "I'm sure there's another explanation."

Garion shrugged and pulled on his linen shirt and brown tunic. He shook his head and raked his fingers through his still-damp hair.

"You're making an awful mess of it," she observed critically. "Here." She stood up and stepped behind him. "Let me do it." She put the comb to his hair and began pulling it through carefully. "You have nice hair for a man," she said.

"It's just hair," he said indifferently.

She combed in silence for a moment or two, then took his chin in her hand, turned his head and looked at him critically. She touched his hair at the sides a time or two until it was arranged to her satisfaction. "That's better," she decided.

"Thank you." He was a bit confused by the change in her.

She sat down again on the grass, clasped her arms around one knee and gazed at the sparkling pool. "Garion," she said finally.

"Yes?"

"What's it like to grow up as an ordinary person?"

He shrugged. "I've never been anything but an ordinary person," he told her, "so I wouldn't know what to compare it to."

"You know what I mean. Tell me about where you grew up—and what you did and all."

So he told her about Faldor's farm, about the kitchen and Durnik's smithy and Doroon and Rundorig and Zubrette.

"You're in love with Zubrette, aren't you?" She asked it almost accusingly.

"I thought I was, but so much has happened since we left the farm that sometimes I can't even remember what she looks like. I think I could do without being in love anyway. From what I've seen of it, it's pretty painful most of the time."

"You're impossible," she said, and then she smiled at him, her little face framed in the blazing mass of her sun-touched hair.

"Probably," he admitted. "All right, now you tell me what it's like to grow up as a very special person."

"I'm not that special."

"You're an Imperial Princess," he reminded her. "I'd call that pretty special."

"Oh, that," she said, and then giggled. "You know, sometimes since I joined you people, I almost forget that I'm an Imperial Princess."

"Almost," he said with a smile, "but not quite."

"No," she agreed, "not quite." She looked out across the pool again. "Most of the time being a princess is very boring. It's all ceremonies and formalities. You have to stand around most of the time listening to speeches or receiving state visitors. There are guards around all the time, but sometimes I sneak away so I can be by myself. It makes them furious." She giggled again, and then her gaze turned pensive. "Let me tell your fortune," she said, taking his hand.

"Can you tell fortunes?" Garion asked.

"It's only make-believe," she admitted. "My maids and I play at it sometimes. We all promise each other high-born husbands and many children." She turned his hand over and looked at it. The silvery mark on his palm was very plain now that the skin was clean. "Whatever is that?" she asked.

"I don't know."

"It's not a disease, is it?"

"No," he said. "It has always been there. I think it has something to do with my family. Aunt Pol doesn't like to have people see it for some reason, so she tries to keep it hidden."

"How could you hide something like that?"

"She finds things for me to do that keep my hands dirty most of the time."

"How strange," she said. "I have a birthmark too—right over my heart. Would you like to see it?" She took hold of the neck of her tunic.

"I'll take your word for it," Garion told her, blushing furiously.

She laughed a silvery, tinkling little laugh. "You're a strange boy, Garion. You're not at all like the other boys I've met."

"They were Tolnedrans probably," Garion pointed out. "I'm a Sendar—or at least that's the way I was raised—so there are bound to be differences."

"You sound as if you're not sure what you are."

"Silk says I'm not a Sendar," Garion said. "He says he isn't sure exactly what I am, and that's very odd. Silk can recognize anybody for what he is immediately. Your father thought I was a Rivan."

"Since the Lady Polgara's your Aunt and Belgarath's your Grandfather, you're probably a sorcerer," Ce'Nedra observed.

Garion laughed. "Me? That's silly. Besides, the sorcerers aren't a race—not like Chereks or Tolnedrans or Rivans. It's more like a profession, I think—sort of like being a lawyer or a merchant—only there aren't any new ones. The sorcerers are all thousands of years old. Mister Wolf says that maybe people have changed in some way so that they can't become sorcerers anymore."

Ce'Nedra had leaned back and was resting on her elbows, looking up at him. "Garion?"

"Yes?"

"Would you like to kiss me?"

Garion's heart started to pound.

Then Durnik's voice called to them from not far away, and for one flaming instant Garion hated his old friend.

Chapter Twenty

"MISTRESS POL SAYS THAT IT'S TIME for you to come back to the tents," Durnik told them when he reached the glade. There was a faint hint of amusement on his plain, dependable face, and he looked knowingly at the two of them.

Garion blushed and then grew angry with himself for blushing. Ce'Nedra, however, showed no concern at all.

"Have the Dryads come yet?" she asked, getting to her feet and brushing the grass from the back of her tunic.

"Not yet," Durnik answered. "Wolf says that they should find us soon. There seems to be some kind of storm building up to the south, and Mistress Pol thought the two of you ought to come back."

Garion glanced at the sky and saw a layer of inky clouds moving up from the south, staining the bright blue sky as they rolled ponderously northward. He frowned. "I've never seen clouds like that, have you, Durnik?"

Durnik looked up. "Strange," he agreed.

Garion rolled up the two wet towels, and they started back down the stream. The clouds blotted out the sun, and the woods became suddenly very dark. The sense of watchfulness was still there, that wary awareness they had all felt since they had entered the wood, but now there was something else as well. The great trees stirred uneasily, and a million tiny messages seemed to pass among the rustling leaves.

"They're afraid," Ce'Nedra whispered. "Something's frightening them."

"What?" Durnik asked.

"The trees—they're afraid of something. Can't you feel it?"

223

He stared at her in perplexity.

Far above them the birds suddenly fell silent, and a chill breeze began to blow, carrying with it a foul reek of stagnant water and rotting vegetation.

"What's that smell?" Garion asked, looking about nervously.

"Nyissa is south of here," Ce'Nedra said. "It's mostly swamps."

"Is it that close?" Garion asked.

"Not really," she said with a small frown. "It must be sixty leagues or more."

"Would a smell carry that far?"

"It's not likely," Durnik said. "At least it wouldn't be in Sendaria."

"How far is it to the tents?" Ce'Nedra asked.

"About a half-mile," Durnik answered.

"Maybe we should run," she suggested.

Durnik shook his head. "The ground's uneven," he said, "and running in bad light's dangerous. We can walk a bit faster, though."

They hurried on through the gathering gloom. The wind began to blow harder, and the trees trembled and bent with its force. The strange fear that seemed to permeate the wood grew stronger.

"There's something moving over there," Garion whispered urgently and pointed at the dark trees on the other side of the stream.

"I don't see anything," Ce'Nedra said.

"There, just beyond the tree with the large white limb. Is it a Dryad?"

A vague shape slid from one tree to another in the half-light. There was something chillingly wrong with the figure. Ce'Nedra stared at it with revulsion. "It's not a Dryad," she said. "It's something alien."

Durnik picked up a fallen limb and gripped it like a cudgel with both hands. Garion looked quickly around and saw another limb. He too armed himself.

Another figure shambled between two trees, a bit closer this time.

"We'll have to chance it," Durnik said grimly. "Be careful, but run. Get the others. Now go!"

Garion took Ce'Nedra's hand, and they started to run along the streambank, stumbling often. Durnik lagged farther and farther behind, his two-handed club swinging warningly about him.

The figures were now all around them, and Garion felt the first surges of panic.

Then Ce'Nedra screamed. One of the figures had risen from behind a low bush directly in front of them. It was large and ill-shaped, and there was no face on the front of its head. Two eye-holes stared vacantly as it shambled forward with its half-formed hands reaching out for them. The entire figure was a dark gray mud color, and it was covered with rotting, stinking moss that adhered to its oozing body.

Without thinking, Garion thrust Ce'Nedra behind him and leaped to the attack. The first blow of his club struck the creature solidly in the side, and the club merely sank into the body with no visible effect. One of the outstretched hands touched his face, and he recoiled from that slimy touch with revulsion. Desperately he swung again and struck the thing solidly on the forearm. With horror he saw the arm break off at the elbow. The creature paused to pick up the still-moving arm.

Ce'Nedra screamed again, and Garion spun about. Another of the mud-men had come up behind her and had grasped her about the waist with both arms. It was starting to turn, lifting the struggling princess from the ground when Garion swung his club with all his might. The blow was not aimed at head or back, but rather at the ankles.

The mud-man toppled backward with both of its feet broken off. Its grip about Ce'Nedra's waist, however, did not loosen as it fell.

Garion jumped forward, discarding his club and drawing his dagger. The substance of the thing was surprisingly tough. Vines and dead twigs were encased in the clay which gave it its shape. Feverishly, Garion cut away one of the arms and then tried to pull the screaming princess free. The other arm still clung to her. Almost sobbing with the need to hurry, Garion started hacking at the remaining arm.

"Look out!" Ce'Nedra shrieked. "Behind you!"

Garion looked quickly over his shoulder. The first mud-man was reaching for him. He felt a cold grip about his ankle. The arm he had just severed had inched its way across the ground and grasped him.

"Garion!" Barak's voice roared from a short distance off.

"Over here!" Garion shouted. "Hurry!"

There was a crashing in the bushes, and the great, red-bearded Cherek appeared, sword in hand, with Hettar and Mandorallen close behind. With a mighty swing, Barak cut off the head of the first mud-man. It sailed through the air and landed with a sickening thump several yards away. The headless creature turned and groped blindly, trying to put its hands on its attacker. Barak paled visibly and then chopped away both outstretched arms. Still the thing shambled forward.

"The legs," Garion said quickly. He bent and hacked at the clay hand about his ankle.

Barak lopped off the mud-man's legs, and the thing fell. The dismembered pieces crawled toward him.

Other mud-men had appeared, and Hettar and Mandorallen were laying about them with their swords, filling the air with chunks and pieces of living clay.

Barak bent and ripped away the remaining arm which held Ce'Nedra. Then he jerked the girl to her feet and thrust her at Garion. "Get her back to the tents!" he ordered. "Where's Durnik?"

"He stayed behind to hold them off," Garion said.

"We'll go help him," Barak said. "Run!"

Ce'Nedra was hysterical, and Garion had to drag her to the tents.

"What is it?" Aunt Pol demanded.

"Monsters out there in the woods," Garion said, pushing Ce'Nedra at her. "They're made out of mud, and you can't kill them. They've got Durnik." He dove into one of the tents and emerged a second later with his sword in his hand and fire in his brain.

"Garion!" Aunt Pol shouted, trying to disentangle herself from the sobbing princess. "What are you doing?"

"I've got to help Durnik," he said.

"You stay where you are."

"No!" he shouted. "Durnik's my friend." He dashed back toward the fight, brandishing his sword.

"Garion! Come back here!"

He ignored her and ran through the dark woods.

The fray was raging about a hundred yards from the tents. Barak, Hettar and Mandorallen were systematically chopping the slime-covered mud-men into chunks, and Silk darted in and out of the mêlée, his short sword leaving great gaping holes in the thick, moss-covered monsters. Garion plunged into the fight, his ears ringing and a kind of desperate exultation surging through him.

And then Mister Wolf and Aunt Pol were there with Ce'Nedra hovering ashen-faced and trembling behind them. Wolf's eyes blazed, and he seemed to tower over them all as he gathered his will. He thrust one hand forward, palm up. "Fire!" he commanded, and a sizzling bolt of lightning shot upward from his hand into the whirling clouds overhead. The earth trembled with the violence of the shattering thunderclap. Garion reeled at the force of the roaring in his mind.

Aunt Pol raised her hand. "Water!" she said in a powerful voice.

The clouds burst open, and rain fell so heavily that it seemed that the air itself had turned to water.

The mud-men, still mindlessly stumbling forward, began to ooze and dissolve in the thundering downpour. With a kind of sick fascination, Garion watched them disintegrate into sodden lumps of slime and rotten vegetation, surging and heaving as the pounding rain destroyed them.

Barak reached forward with his dripping sword and tentatively poked at the shapeless lump of clay that had been the head of one of their attackers. The lump broke apart, and a coiled snake unwound from its center. It raised itself as if to strike, and Barak chopped it in two.

Other snakes began to appear as the mud which had encased them dissolved in the roaring deluge. "That one," Aunt Pol said, pointing at a dull green reptile struggling to free itself from the clay. "Fetch it for me, Garion."

"Me?" Garion gasped, his flesh crawling.

"I'll do it," Silk said. He picked up up a forked stick and pinned the snake's head down with it. Then he carefully took hold of the wet skin at the back of the serpent's neck and lifted the twisting reptile.

"Bring it here," Aunt Pol ordered, wiping the water from her face.

Silk carried the snake to her and held it out. The forked tongue flickered nervously, and the dead eyes fixed on her.

"What does this mean?" she demanded of the snake.

The serpent hissed at her. Then in a voice that was a sibilant whisper it replied, "That, Polgara, is the affair of my mistress."

Silk's face blanched as the dripping snake spoke, and he tightened his grip.

"I see," Aunt Pol said.

"Abandon this search," the snake hissed. "My mistress will allow you to go no further."

Aunt Pol laughed scornfully. "Allow?" she said. "Your mistress hasn't the power to allow me anything."

"My mistress is the queen of Nyissa," the snake said in its whispering hiss. "Her power there is absolute. The ways of the serpent are not the ways of men, and my mistress is queen of the serpents. You will enter Nyissa at your own peril. We are patient and not afraid. We will await you where you least expect us. Our sting is a small injury, scarce noted, but it is death."

"What's Salmissra's interest in this matter?" Aunt Pol asked.

The serpent's flickering tongue darted at her. "She has not chosen to reveal that to me, and it is not in my nature to be curious. I have delivered my message and already received my reward. Now do with me as you wish."

"Very well," Aunt Pol said. She looked coldly at the snake, her face streaming in the heavy rain.

"Shall I kill it?" Silk asked, his face set and his fingers white-knuckled from the strain of holding the thick-coiling reptile.

"No," she said quietly. "There's no point in destroying so excellent a messenger." She fixed the snake with a flinty look. "Return with these others to Salmissra," she said. "Tell her that if she interferes again, I'll come after her, and the deepest slime-pit in all Nyissa won't hide her from my fury."

"And my reward?" the snake asked.

"You have your life as a reward," she said.

"That's true," the serpent hissed. "I will deliver your message, Polgara."

"Put it down," Aunt Pol told Silk.

The small man bent and lowered his arm to the ground. The snake uncoiled from about his arm, and Silk released it and jumped back. The snake glanced once at him, then slithered away.

"I think that's enough rain, Pol," Wolf said, mopping at his face.

Aunt Pol waved her hand almost negligently, and the rain stopped as if a bucket had emptied itself.

"We have to find Durnik," Barak reminded them.

"He was behind us." Garion pointed back up the now-overflowing stream. His chest felt constricted with a cold fear at what they might find, but he steeled himself and led the way back into the trees.

"The smith is a good companion," Mandorallen said. "I should not care to lose him." There was a strange, subdued quality in the knight's voice, and his face seemed abnormally pale in the dim light. The hand holding his great broadsword, however, was rock-steady. Only his eyes betrayed a kind of doubt Garion had never seen there before.

Water dripped around them as they walked through the sodden woods. "It was about here," Garion said, looking around. "I don't see any sign of him."

"I'm up here." Durnik's voice came from above them. He was a goodly distance up a large oak tree and was peering down. "Are they gone?" He carefully began climbing down the slippery tree trunk. "The rain came just in time," he said, jumping down the last few feet. "I was starting to have a little trouble keeping them out of the tree."

Quickly, without a word, Aunt Pol embraced the good man, and then, as if embarrassed by that sudden gesture, she began to scold him.

Durnik endured her words patiently, and there was a strange expression on his face.

Chapter Twenty-One

GARION'S SLEEP THAT NIGHT WAS TROUBLED. He awoke frequently, shuddering at the remembered touch of the mud-men. But in time the night, as all nights must, came to an end, and the morning dawned clear and bright. He drowsed for a while, rolled in his blankets, until Ce'Nedra came to get him up.

"Garion," she said softly, touching his shoulder, "are you awake?"

He opened his eyes and looked up at her. "Good morning."

"Lady Polgara says that you're supposed to get up," she told him.

Garion yawned, stretched and sat up. He glanced out the tent flap and saw that the sun was shining.

"She's teaching me how to cook," Ce'Nedra said rather proudly.

"That's nice," Garion told her, pushing his hair out of his eyes.

She looked at him for a long moment, her small face serious and her green eyes intent. "Garion."

"Yes?"

"You were very brave yesterday."

He shrugged slightly. "I'll probably get a scolding for it today."

"What for?"

"Aunt Pol and my grandfather don't like it when I try to be brave," he explained. "They think I'm still a child, and they don't want me to get hurt."

"Garion!" Aunt Pol called from the small fire where she was cooking. "I need more firewood."

Garion sighed and rolled out of his blankets. He pulled

230

on his half-boots, belted on his sword and went off into the woods.

It was still damp under the huge oaks from the downpour Aunt Pol had called down the day before, and dry wood was hard to find. He wandered about, pulling limbs out from under fallen trees and from beneath overhanging rocks. The silent trees watched him, but they seemed somehow less unfriendly this morning.

"What are you doing?" a light voice came from above him.

He looked up quickly, his hand going to his sword.

A girl was standing on a broad limb just over his head. She wore a belted tunic and sandals. Her hair was a tawny color, her gray eyes were curious, and her pale skin had that faint greenish hue to it that identified her as a Dryad. In her left hand she held a bow, and her right held an arrow against the taut string. The arrow was pointed directly at Garion.

He carefully took his hand away from his sword. "I'm gathering wood," he said.

"What for?"

"My aunt needs it for the fire," he explained.

"Fire?" The girl's face hardened, and she half-drew her bow.

"A small one," he said quickly, "for cooking."

"Fire isn't permitted here," the girl said sternly.

"You'll have to explain that to Aunt Pol," Garion told her. "I just do what I'm told."

The girl whistled, and another girl came from behind a nearby tree. She also carried a bow. Her hair was almost as red as Ce'Nedra's, and her skin was also touched with the color of leaves.

"It says it's gathering wood," the first girl reported, "for a fire. Do you think I should kill it?"

"Xantha says we're supposed to find out who they are," the red-haired one said thoughtfully. "If it turns out that they don't have any business here, then you can kill it."

"Oh, very well," the tawny-haired girl agreed, with obvious disappointment. "But don't forget that I found this one. When the time comes, I get to kill it."

Garion felt the hair beginning to rise on the back of his neck.

The red-haired one whistled, and a half-dozen other armed Dryads drifted out of the trees. They were all quite small, and their hair was various shades of reds and golds, not unlike the color of autumn leaves. They gathered about Garion, giggling and chattering as they examined him.

"That one is mine," the tawny-haired Dryad said, climbing down from the tree. "I found it, and Xera says that I get to kill it."

"It looks healthy," one of the others observed, "and quite tame. Maybe we should keep it. Is it a male?"

Another one giggled. "Let's check and find out."

"I'm a male," Garion said quickly, blushing in spite of himself.

"It seems a shame to waste it," one remarked. "Maybe we could keep it for a while and then kill it."

"It's mine," the tawny-haired Dryad stated stubbornly, "and if I want to kill it, I will." She took hold of Garion's arm possessively.

"Let's go look at the others," the one called Xera suggested. "They're building fires, and we'll want to stop that."

"*Fires?*" several of the others gasped, and they all glared at Garion accusingly.

"Only a small one," Garion said quickly.

"Bring it along," Xera ordered and started off through the Wood toward the tents. Far overhead the trees murmured to each other.

Aunt Pol was waiting calmly when they reached the clearing where the tents were. She looked at the Dryads clustered around Garion without changing expression. "Welcome, ladies," she said.

The Dyrads began whispering to each other.

"Ce'Nedra!" the one called Xera exclaimed.

"Cousin Xera," Ce'Nedra replied, and the two ran to embrace each other. The other Dryads came out a little farther into the clearing, looking nervously at the fire.

Ce'Nedra spoke quickly with Xera, explaining to her cousin who they were, and Xera motioned for the others to come closer. "It seems that these are friends," she said. "We'll take them to my mother, Queen Xantha."

"Does that mean that I won't get to kill this one?" The tawny-haired Dryad demanded petulantly, pointing a small finger at Garion.

"I'm afraid not," Xera answered.

The tawny one stamped away, pouting.

Garion breathed a sigh of relief.

Then Mister Wolf came out of one of the tents and looked at the cluster of Dryads with a broad smile.

"It's Belgarath!" one of the Dryads squealed and ran to him happily. She threw her arms around his neck, pulled his head down and kissed him soundly. "Did you bring us any sweets?" she demanded.

The old man put on a sober expression and began rummaging through his many pockets. Bits of sweetmeats began to appear just as quickly disappeared as the Dryads gathered about him, snatching them as fast as he took them from his pockets.

"Have you got any new stories for us?" one of the Dryads asked.

"Many stories," Wolf told her, touching one finger to the side of his nose slyly. "But we ought to wait so your sisters can hear them too, shouldn't we?"

"We want one just for ourselves," the Dryad said.

"And what would you give me for this special story?"

"Kisses," the Dryad offered promptly. "Five kisses from each of us."

"I've got a very good story," Wolf bargained. "It's worth more than five. Let's say ten."

"Eight," the little Dryad countered.

"All right," Wolf agreed. "Eight sounds about right."

"I see you've been here before, Old Wolf," Aunt Pol remarked dryly.

"I visit from time to time," he admitted with a bland expression.

"Those sweets aren't good for them, you know," she chided.

"A little bit won't hurt them, Pol," he said, "and they like them very much. A Dryad will do almost anything for sweets."

"You're disgusting," she told him.

The Dryads were all clustered around Mister Wolf, looking almost like a garden of spring flowers—all, that is, except for the tawny one who'd captured Garion. She stood a bit apart, sulking and fingering the point of her arrow. She finally came over to Garion. "You're not thinking about running away, are you?" she asked hopefully.

"No," Garion denied emphatically.

She sighed with disappointment. "I don't suppose you'd consider it, would you—as a special favor to me?"

"I'm sorry," he said.

She sighed again, bitterly this time. "I never get to have any fun," she complained and went to join the others.

Silk emerged from a tent, moving slowly and carefully; and after the Dryads had become accustomed to him, Durnik appeared.

"They're just children, aren't they?" Garion commented to Aunt Pol.

"They seem to be," she said, "but they're much older than they look. A Dryad lives as long as her tree does, and oak trees live for a long time."

"Where are the boy Dryads?" he asked. "All I see are girls."

"There aren't any boy Dryads, dear," she explained, returning to her cooking.

"Then how—? I mean—" He faltered and felt his ears growing hot.

"They catch human males for that," she said. "Travelers and the like."

"Oh." He delicately let the subject drop.

After they had eaten breakfast and carefully quenched their fire with water from the stream, they saddled their horses and started off through the Wood. Mister Wolf walked ahead with the tiny Dryads still gathered around him, laughing and chattering like happy children. The murmuring of the trees about them was no longer unfriendly, and they moved through a kind of welcoming rustle from a million leaves.

It was late afternoon by the time they reached a large clearing in the center of the Wood. Standing alone in the middle of the clearing was an oak so large that Garion could hardly accept the idea that anything so enormous could be alive. Here and there in its mossy trunk were openings almost like caverns, and its lower limbs were as broad as highways and they spread out to shade nearly the entire clearing. There was about the tree a sense of vast age and a patient wisdom. Tentatively Garion felt a faint touch on his mind, almost like the soft brush of a leaf against his face. The touch was unlike anything he had ever felt before, but it also seemed to welcome him.

The tree was literally alive with Dryads, clustering randomly on the limbs like blossoms. Their laughter and girlish chatter filled the air like birdsongs.

"I'll tell my mother you've arrived," the one called Xera said and went toward the tree.

Garion and the others dismounted and stood uncertainly near their horses. From overhead Dryads peered curiously down at them, whispering among themselves and giggling often.

For some reason the frank, mirthful stares of the Dryads made Garion feel very self-conscious. He moved closer to Aunt Pol and noticed that the others were also clustering around her as if unconsciously seeking her protection.

"Where's the princess?" she asked.

"She's just over there, Mistress Pol," Durnik answered, "visiting with that group of Dryads."

"Keep your eye on her," Aunt Pol said. "And where's my vagrant father?"

"Near the tree," Garion replied. "The Dryads seem very fond of him."

"The old fool," Aunt Pol said darkly.

Then, from a hollow in the tree some distance above the first broad limbs, another Dryad appeared. Instead of the short tunic the others wore, this one was garbed in a flowing green gown, and her golden hair was caught in with a circlet of what appeared to be mistletoe. Gracefully she descended to the ground.

Aunt Pol went forward to meet her, and the others trailed behind at a respectful distance.

"Dear Polgara," the Dryad said warmly, "it's been so long."

"We all have our duties, Xantha," Aunt Pol explained.

The two embraced fondly.

"Have you brought us these as gifts?" Queen Xantha asked, looking admiringly at the men standing behind Aunt Pol.

Aunt Pol laughed. "I'm afraid not, Xantha. I'd be happy to give them to you, but I think I may need them later."

"Ah well," the queen said with a mock sigh. "Welcome all," she greeted them. "You'll sup with us, of course."

"We'd be delighted," Aunt Pol said. Then she took the queen's arm. "Can we talk for a moment first, Xantha?" The two moved apart from the others and spoke quietly together as the Dryads carried bundles and sacks down from the hollows in the tree and began to lay a feast on the grass beneath the broad limbs.

The meal which was spread out looked peculiar. The common food of the Dryads seemed to consist entirely of fruits, nuts and mushrooms, all prepared without any cooking. Barak sat down and looked sourly at what was offered. "No meat," he grumbled.

"It heats up your blood anyway," Silk told him.

Barak sipped suspiciously at his cup. "Water," he said with distaste.

"You might find it a novelty to go to bed sober for a change," Aunt Pol observed as she rejoined them.

"I'm sure it's unhealthy," Barak said.

Ce'Nedra seated herself near Queen Xantha. She obviously wanted to talk to her, but since there was no opportunity for privacy, she finally spoke out in front of them all. "I have a favor to ask, your Highness."

"You may ask, child," the queen said, smiling.

"It's only a small thing," Ce'Nedra explained. "I'll need sanctuary for a few years. My father's growing unreasonable in his old age. I'll have to stay away from him until he comes to his senses."

"In what way is Ran Borune growing unreasonable?" Xantha asked.

"He won't let me go out of the palace, and he insists that I go to Riva on my sixteenth birthday," Ce'Nedra said in an outraged tone. "Have you ever heard of such a thing?"

"And why does he want you to go to Riva?"

"Some foolish treaty. No one even remembers the reason for it."

"If it's a treaty, it must be honored, dear," the queen said gently.

"I won't go to Riva," Ce'Nedra announced. "I'll stay here until after my sixteenth birthday's passed, and that'll be the end of it."

"No, dear," the queen said firmly, "you won't."

"*What?*" Ce'Nedra was stunned.

"We have a treaty too," Xantha explained. "Our agreement with the House of Borune is most explicit. Our Wood remains inviolate only for so long as the female descendants of the Princess Xoria stay with the Borunes. It's your duty to remain with your father and to obey him."

"But I'm a Dryad," Ce'Nedra wailed. "I belong here."

"You're also human," the queen said, "and you belong with your father."

"I don't want to go to Riva," Ce'Nedra protested. "It's degrading."

Xantha looked at her sternly. "Don't be a foolish child," she said. "Your duties are clear. You have a duty as a Dryad, as a Borune, and as an Imperial Princess. Your silly little whims are quite beside the point. If you have an obligation to go to Riva, then you must go."

Ce'Nedra appeared shaken by the finality of the queen's tone, and she sulked in silence after that.

Then the queen turned to Mister Wolf. "There are many rumors abroad," she said, "and some of them have even reached us here. I think something momentous is happening out there in the world of the humans, and it may even touch our lives in this Wood. I think I should know what this thing is."

Wolf nodded gravely. "I expect you should," he agreed. "The Orb of Aldur has stolen from the throne in the Hall of the Rivan King by Zedar the Apostate."

Xantha caught her breath. "How?" she demanded.

Wolf spread his hands. "We don't know. Zedar's trying to reach the kingdoms of the Angaraks with the Orb. Once he's there, he'll try to use its power to awaken Torak."

"That must never happen," the Queen said. "What's being done?"

"The Alorns and the Sendars are getting ready for war," Wolf replied. "The Arends have promised aid, and Ran Borune has been advised, though he didn't make any promises. The Borunes can be difficult at times." He glanced at the pouting Ce'Nedra.

"Then it means war?" the queen asked sadly.

"I'm afraid so, Xantha," he said. "I'm pursuing Zedar with these others, and I hope we can catch him and get the Orb back before he can reach Torak with it. If we're successful, I think the Angaraks will attack the West anyway out of desperation. Certain ancient prophecies are getting close to their fulfillment. There are signs everywhere, and even the twisted perceptions of the Grolims can read them."

The Queen sighed. "I've seem some of the signs myself, Belgarath," she said. "I'd hoped I was wrong. What does this Zedar look like?"

"A great deal like me," Wolf told her. "We served the same Master for a very long time, and that puts a certain mark on people."

"Someone like that passed through the upper reaches of our Wood last week and crossed over into Nyissa," Xantha said. "If we'd known, we might have been able to detain him."

"We're closer than I thought, then. Was he alone?"

"No," Xantha reported. "He had two of the servants of Torak with him and a small boy."

Wolf looked startled. "A boy?"

"Yes—about six years old or so."

The old man frowned, and then his eyes opened very wide. "So *that's* how he did it," he exclaimed. "I never thought of that."

"We can show you where he crossed the river into Nyissa," the queen offered. "I should warn you though that it's going to be dangerous for so large a party to go there. Salmissra has eyes everywhere in those swamps."

"I've already made plans for that," Mister Wolf assured her. He turned to Barak. "Are you sure that ship's going to be waiting at the mouth of the River of the Woods?" he asked.

"She'll be there," Barak rumbled. "Her captain's a dependable man."

"Good," Wolf said. "Silk and I'll pick up Zedar's trail then, and the rest of you can follow the river to the sea. Take the ship down the coast and then up the River of the Serpent to Sthiss Tor. We'll meet you there."

"Dost thou think it wise to separate our party in so perilous a place as Nyissa?" Mandorallen asked.

"It's necessary," Wolf said. "The snake people are at home in their jungles, and they don't like outsiders. Silk and I can move swiftly and with greater stealth if we're alone."

"Where do you want us to meet you?" Barak asked.

"There's a Drasnian trade enclave near the wharves in Sthiss Tor," Silk said. "Several of the merchants there are my friends. Just ask for Radek of Boktor. If we can't meet you there, we'll leave word of our whereabouts with the merchants."

"What about me?" Ce'Nedra asked.

"I think you'll have to stay with us," Aunt Pol answered.

"There's no reason for me to go to Nyissa," Ce'Nedra said.

"You'll go because I tell you to go," Aunt Pol told the tiny girl. "I'm not your father, Ce'Nedra. Your pouting doesn't wring my heart, and your fluttering eyelashes don't really impress me."

"I'll run away," Ce'Nedra threatened.

"That would be very foolish," Aunt Pol said coldly. "I'd just have to bring you back again, and you'd find that unpleasant. Affairs in the world just now are much too serious to allow the whims of one spoiled little girl to have very much importance. You'll stay with me, and you *will* stand in the Hall of the Rivan King on your sixteenth birthday—even if I have to take you there in chains. We're all much too busy to pamper you any further."

Ce'Nedra stared at her, and then she suddenly burst into tears.

Chapter Twenty-Two

THE NEXT MORNING before the sun rose and while filmy mist still hovered beneath the limbs of the great oaks, Silk and Mister Wolf made preparations to leave for Nyissa. Garion sat on a log, somberly watching the old man bundle up some food.

"Why so glum?" Wolf asked him.

"I wish we didn't have to separate this way," Garion said.

"It's only for a couple of weeks."

"I know, but I still wish—" Garion shrugged.

"Keep an eye on your Aunt for me while I'm gone," Wolf said, tying up his bundle.

"All right."

"And keep your amulet on. Nyissa's a dangerous place."

"I'll remember," Garion promised. "You'll be careful, won't you, grandfather?"

The old man looked at him gravely, his white beard glistening in the misty light. "I'm always careful, Garion," he said.

"It's getting late, Belgarath," Silk called, leading two horses up to where the two of them were talking.

Wolf nodded. "We'll see you in two weeks in Sthiss Tor," he said to Garion.

Garion embraced the old man quickly and then turned away so that he wouldn't have to watch the two of them leave. He crossed the clearing to where Mandorallen stood pensively looking out into the mist.

"Parting is a melancholy business," the knight said moodily. He sighed.

"It's more than that though, isn't it, Mandorallen?" Garion asked.

"Thou art a perceptive lad."

"What's been troubling you? You've been acting strangely for the last two days."

"I have discovered a strange feeling within myself, Garion, and I like it not."

"Oh? What is it?"

"Fear," Mandorallen said shortly.

"Fear? Of what?"

"The clay men. I know not why, but their very existence struck a chill into my soul."

"They frightened us all, Mandorallen," Garion told him.

"I have never been afraid before," Mandorallen said quietly.

"Never?"

"Not even as a child. The clay men made my very flesh creep, and I wanted most desperately to run away."

"But you didn't," Garion pointed out. "You stayed and fought."

"That time yes," Mandorallen admitted. "But what of next time? Now that fear has found its way into my spirit, who can say when it might return? In some desperate hour when the outcome of our quest hangs in the balance, might not vile fear lay its cold hand upon my heart and unman me? It is that possibility which doth gnaw upon my soul. I am sorely ashamed of my weakness and my fault."

"Ashamed? For being human? You're too hard on yourself, Mandorallen."

"Thou art kind thus to excuse me, lad, but my failing is too grievous for such simple forgiveness. I have striven for perfection and struck, I think, not too far off the mark; but now that perfection, which was the marvel of the world, is flawed. It is a bitter thing to accept." He turned, and Garion was startled to see tears standing in his eyes. "Wilt thou assist me into mine armor?" he asked.

"Of course."

"I feel profoundly the need to be encased in steel. 'Twill perchance strengthen my cowardly heart."

"You're not a coward," Garion insisted.

Mandorallen sighed sadly. "Only time can reveal that."

When it was time to leave, Queen Xantha spoke briefly to them. "I wish you all well," she said. "I'd help you in your search if possible, but a Dryad's bound to her tree by ties which can't be broken. My tree here is very old, and I must care for him." She looked fondly up at the vast oak rising into the morning mist. "We're in bondage to each other, but it's a bondage of love."

Once again Garion felt that same faint touch on his mind that he had experienced the day before when he had first seen the huge tree. There was a sense of farewell in that touch, and what seemed to be a warning.

Queen Xantha exchanged a startled glance with Aunt Pol and then looked at Garion rather closely. "Some of my younger daughters will guide you to the river that marks the southern border of our Wood," she continued. "From there your way to the sea is clear." Her voice showed no sign of any change, but her eyes seemed thoughtful.

"Thank you, Xantha," Aunt Pol said warmly, embracing the Dryad queen. "If you can send word to the Borunes that Ce'Nedra's safe and with me, it might relieve the Emperor's mind somewhat."

"I will, Polgara," Xantha promised.

They mounted then and followed the half-dozen or so Dryads who flitted ahead of them like butterflies, guiding them southward into the forest. For some reason Garion felt profoundly depressed, and he paid little attention to his surroundings as he rode beside Durnik along the winding forest trail.

About midmorning it began to grow darker under the trees, and they rode in silence through the now-somber wood. The warning Garion had seemed to hear in Queen Xantha's clearing echoed somehow in the creak of limbs and the rustling of leaves.

"The weather must be changing," Durnik said, looking up. "I wish I could see the sky."

Garion nodded and tried to shake off the sense of impending danger.

Mandorallen in his armor and Barak in his mail shirt rode at the head of the party, and Hettar in his horsehide jacket with steel plates riveted to it rode at the rear. The ominous sense of foreboding seemed to have reached them all, and they rode warily with their hands near their weapons and their eyes searching for trouble.

Then quite suddenly Tolnedran legionnaires were all around them, rising from the bushes or stepping out from behind trees. They made no attempt to attack, but stood in their brightly polished breastplates with their short spears at the ready.

Barak swore, and Mandorallen reined in his charger sharply. "Stand aside!" he ordered the soldiers, lowering his lance.

"Easy," Barak cautioned.

The Dryads, after one startled look at the soldiers, melted into the gloomy woods.

"What thinkest thou, Lord Barak?" Mandorallen asked blithely. "They cannot be over an hundred. Shall we attack them?"

"One of these days you and I are going to have to have a long talk about a few things," Barak said. He glanced back over his shoulder and saw that Hettar was edging closer, then he sighed. "Well, I suppose we might as well get on with it." He tightened the straps on his shield and loosened his sword in its sheath. "What do you think, Mandorallen? Should we give them a chance to run away?"

"A charitable suggestion, Lord Barak," Mandorallen agreed.

Then, some distance up the trail, a body of horsemen rode out from under the shadowy trees. Their leader was a large man wearing a blue cloak trimmed with silver. His breastplate and helmet were inlaid with gold, and he rode a prancing chestnut stallion whose hooves churned the damp leaves lying on the ground. "Splendid," he said as he rode up. "Absolutely splendid."

Aunt Pol fixed the newcomer with a cold eye. "Don't the legions have anything better to do than to waylay travelers?" she demanded.

"This is my legion, Madam," the man in the blue cloak said arrogantly, "and it does what I tell it to. I see that you have the Princess Ce'Nedra with you."

"Where I go and with whom is my concern, your Grace," Ce'Nedra said loftily. "It's of no concern to the Grand Duke Kador of the House of Vordue."

"Your father is most concerned, Princess," Kador said. "All Tolnedra's searching for you. Who are these people?"

Garion tried with a dark scowl and a shake of his head to warn her, but it was too late.

"The two knights who lead our party are Sir Mandorallen, Baron of Vo Mandor, and Lord Barak, Earl of Trellheim," she announced. "The Algar warrior who guards our rear is Hettar, son of Cho-Hag, Chief of the Clan-Chiefs of Algaria. The lady—"

"I can speak for myself, dear," Aunt Pol said smoothly. "I'm curious to know what brings the Grand Duke of Vordue so far into southern Tolnedra."

"I have interests here, Madam," Kador said.

"Evidently," Aunt Pol replied.

"All the legions of the Empire are searching for the princess, but it's I who have found her."

"I'm amazed to find a Vorduvian so willing to aid in the search for a Borune princess," Aunt Pol observed. "Especially considering the centuries of enmity between your two houses."

"Shall we cease this idle banter?" Kador suggested icily. "My motives are my own affair."

"And unsavory, no doubt," she added.

"I think you forget yourself, Madam," Kador said. "I am, after all, who I am—and more to the point, who I will become."

"And who will you become, your Grace?" she inquired.

"I will be Ran Vordue, Emperor of Tolnedra," Kador announced.

"Oh? And just what's the future Emperor of Tolnedra doing in the Wood of the Dryads?"

"I'm doing what's necessary to protect my interests," Kador said stiffly. "For the moment, it's essential that the Princess Ce'Nedra be in my custody."

"My father may have something to say about that, Duke Kador," Ce'Nedra said, "and about this ambition of yours."

"What Ran Borune says is of no concern to me, your Highness," Kador told her. "Tolnedra needs me, and no Borune trick is going to deny me the Imperial Crown. It's obvious that the old man plans to marry you to a Honeth or a Horbite to raise some spurious claim to the throne. That could complicate matters, but I intend to keep things simple."

"By marrying me yourself?" Ce'Nedra asked scornfully. "You'll never live that long."

"No," Kador said. "I wouldn't be interested in a Dryad wife. Unlike the Borunes, the House of Vordue believes in keeping its line pure and uncontaminated."

"So you're going to hold me prisoner?" Ce'Nedra asked.

"That'd be impossible, I'm afraid," Duke Kador told her. "The Emperor has ears everywhere. It's really a shame you ran away just when you did, your Highness. I'd gone to a great expense to get one of my agents into the Imperial kitchen and to obtain a quantity of a rare Nyissan poison. I'd even taken the trouble to compose a letter of sympathy to your father."

"How considerate of you," Ce'Nedra said, her face turning pale.

"Unfortunately, I'll have to be more direct now," Kador went on. "A sharp knife and a few feet of dirt should end your unfortunate involvement in Tolnedran politics. I'm very sorry, Princess. There's nothing personal in it, you understand, but I have to protect my interests."

"Thy plan, Duke Kador, hath one small flaw," Mandorallen said, carefully leaning his lance against a tree.

"I fail to see it, Baron," Kador said smugly.

"Thine error lay in rashly coming within reach of my sword," Mandorallen told him. "Thy head is forfeit now, and a man with no head has little need of a crown."

Garion knew that a part of Mandorallen's brashness arose from his desperate need to prove to himself that he was no longer afraid.

Kador looked at the knight apprehensively. "You wouldn't do that," he said without much certainty. "You're too badly outnumbered."

"Thou art imprudent to think so," Mandorallen said. "I am the hardiest knight on life and fully armed. Thy soldiers will be as blades of grass before me. Thou art doomed, Kador." And with that he drew his great sword.

"It was bound to happen," Barak said wryly to Hettar and drew his own sword.

"I don't think we'll do that," a new voice announced harshly. A familiar black-robed man rode out from behind a nearby tree on a sable-colored horse. He muttered a few quick words and gestured sharply with his right hand. Garion felt a dark rush and a strange roaring in his mind. Mandorallen's sword spun from his grip.

"My thanks, Asharak," Kador said in a relieved tone. "I hadn't anticipated that."

Mandorallen pulled off his mailed gauntlet and nursed his hand as if he had been struck a heavy blow. Hettar's eyes narrowed, and then went strangely blank. The Murgo's black mount glanced curiously at him once and then looked away almost contemptuously.

"Well, Sha-dar," Asharak gloated with an ugly smirk on his scarred face, "would you like to try that again?"

Hettar's face had a sick look of revulsion on it. "It's not a horse," he said. "It looks like a horse, but it's something else."

"Yes," Asharak agreed. "Quite different, really. You can sink yourself into its mind if you want, but I don't think you'll like what you find there." He swung down from his saddle and walked toward them, his eyes burning. He stopped in front of Aunt Pol and made an ironic bow. "And so we meet again, Polgara."

"You've been busy, Chamdar," she replied.

Kador, in the act of dismounting, seemed startled. "You know this woman, Asharak?"

"His name is Chamdar, Duke Kador," Aunt Pol said, "and he's a Grolim priest. You thought he was only buying your honor, but you'll soon find that he's bought much more than that." She straightened in her saddle, the white lock at her brow suddenly incandescently bright. "You've been an interesting opponent, Chamdar. I'll almost miss you."

"Don't do it, Polgara," the Grolim said quickly. "I've got my hand around the boy's heart. The instant you start to gather your will, he'll die. I know who he is and how much you value him."

Her eyes narrowed. "An easy thing to say, Chamdar."

"Would you like to test it?" he mocked.

"Get down off your horses," Kador ordered sharply, and the legionnaires all took a threatening step forward.

"Do as he says," Aunt Pol ordered quietly.

"It's been a long chase, Polgara," Chamdar said. "Where's Belgarath?"

"Not far," she told him. "Perhaps if you start running now, you can get away before he comes back."

"No, Polgara." He laughed. "I'd know if he were that close." He turned and looked intently at Garion. "You've grown, boy. We haven't had a chance to talk for quite some time, have we?"

Garion stared back at the scarred face of his enemy, alert, but strangely not afraid. The contest between them for which he had been waiting all his life was about to begin, and something deep within his mind told him that he was ready.

Chamdar looked into his eyes, probing. "He doesn't know, does he?" he asked Aunt Pol. And then he laughed. "How like a woman you are, Polgara. You've kept the secret from him simply for the sake of the secret itself. I should have taken him away from you years ago."

"Leave him alone, Chamdar," she ordered.

He ignored that. "What's his real name, Polgara? Have you told him yet?"

"That doesn't concern you," she said flatly.

"But it does, Polgara. I've watched over him almost as carefully as you have." He laughed again. "You've been his mother, but I've been his father. Between us we've raised a fine son—but I still want to know his real name."

She straightened. "I think this has gone far enough, Chamdar," she said coldly. "What are your terms?"

"No terms, Polgara," the Grolim answered. "You and the boy and I are going to the place where Lord Torak awaits the moment of his awakening. My hand will be about the boy's heart the entire time, so you'll be suitably docile. Zedar and Ctuchik are going to destroy each other fighting over the Orb—unless Belgarath finds them first and destroys them himself—but the Orb doesn't really interest me. It's been you and the boy I've been after from the very beginning."

"You weren't really trying to stop us, then?" she asked.

Chamdar laughed. "Stop you? I've been trying to help

you. Ctuchik and Zedar both have underlings here in the West. I've delayed and deceived them at every turn just so you could get through. I knew that sooner or later Belgarath would find it necessary to pursue the Orb alone, and when that happened, I could take you and the boy."

"For what purpose?"

"You still don't see?" he asked. "The first two things Lord Torak sees when he awakens will be his bride and his mortal enemy, kneeling in chains before him. I'll be exalted above all for so royal a gift."

"Let the others go then," she said.

"The others don't concern me," Chamdar said. "I'll leave them with the noble Kador. I don't imagine he'll find it convenient to keep them alive, but that's up to him. I've got what I want."

"You swine!" Aunt Pol raged helplessly. "You filthy swine!"

With a bland smile Chamdar slapped her sharply across the face. "You really must learn to control your tongue, Polgara," he said.

Garion's brain seemed to explode. Dimly he saw Durnik and the others being restrained by the legionnaires, but no soldier seemed to consider him a danger. He started toward his enemy without thinking, reaching for his dagger.

"Not that way!" It was that dry voice in his mind that had always been there, but the voice was no longer passive, disinterested.

"I'll kill him!" Garion said silently in the vaults of his brain.

"Not that way!" the voice warned again. *"They won't let you—not with your knife."*

"How, then?"

"Remember what Belgarath said—the Will and the Word."

"I don't know how. I can't do that."

"You are who you are. I'll show you. Look!" Unbidden and so clearly that it was almost as if he were watching it happen, the image of the God Torak writhing in the fire of Aldur's Orb rose before his eyes. He saw Torak's face melting and his fingers aflame. Then the face shifted and altered until it was the face of the dark watcher whose mind

had been linked with his for as long as he could remember. He felt a terrible force building in him as the image of Chamdar wrapped in seething flame stood before him.

"Now!" the voice commanded him. *"Do it!"*

It required a blow. His rage would be satisfied with nothing less. He leaped at the smirking Grolim so quickly that none of the legionnaires could stop him. He swung his right arm, and at the instant his palm struck Chamdar's scarred left cheek, he felt all the force that had built in him surge out from the silvery mark on his palm. "Burn!" he commanded, willing it to happen.

Taken off guard, Chamdar jerked back. A momentary anger began to appear on his face, and then his eyes widened with an awful realization. For an instant he stared at Garion in absolute horror, and then his face contorted with agony. "No!" he cried out hoarsely, and then his cheek began to smoke and seethe where the mark on Garion's hand had touched it. Wisps of smoke drifted from his black robe as if it had suddenly been laid on a red-hot stove. Then he shrieked and clutched at his face. His fingers burst into flame. He shrieked again and fell writhing to the damp earth.

"Stand still!" It was Aunt Pol's voice this time, sounding sharply inside Garion's head.

Chamdar's entire face was engulfed in flames now, and his shrieks echoed in the dim wood. The legionnaires recoiled from the burning man, and Garion suddenly felt sick. He started to turn away.

"Don't weaken!" Aunt Pol's voice told him. *"Keep your will on him!"*

Garion stood over the blazing Grolim. The wet leaves on the ground smoked and smoldered where Chamdar thrashed and struggled with the fire that was consuming him. Flames were spurting from his chest, and his shrieks grew weaker. With an enormous effort, he struggled to his feet and held out his flaming hands imploringly to Garion. His face was gone, and greasy black smoke rolled off his body, drifting low to the ground. "Master," he croaked, "have mercy!"

Garion's heart wrenched with pity. All the years of the secret closeness between them pulled at him.

"No!" Aunt Pol's stern voice commanded. *"He'll kill you if you release him!"*

"I can't do it," Garion said. *"I'm going to stop it."* As once before, he began to gather his will, feeling it build in him like some vast tide of pity and compassion. He half-reached toward Chamdar, focusing his thought on healing.

"Garion!" Aunt Pol's voice rang. *"It was Chamdar who killed your parents!"*

The thought forming in his mind froze.

"Chamdar killed Geran and Ildera. He burned them alive—just as he's burning now. Avenge them, Garion! Keep the fire on him!"

All the rage and fury he had carried within him since Wolf had told him of the deaths of his parents flamed in his brain. The fire, which a moment before he had almost extinguished, was suddenly not enough. The hand he had begun to reach out in compassion stiffened. In terrible anger he raised it, palm out. A strange sensation tingled in that palm, and then his own hand burst into flames. There was no pain, not even a feeling of heat, as a bright blue fire burst from the mark on his hand and wreathed up through his fingers. The blue fire became brighter—so bright that he could not even look at it.

Even in the extremity of his mortal agony, Chamdar the Grolim recoiled from that blazing hand. With a hoarse, despairing cry he tried to cover his blackened face, staggered back a few steps, and then, like a burning house, he collapsed in upon himself and sank back to earth.

"It is done!" Aunt Pol's voice came again. *"They are avenged!"* And then her voice rang in the vaults of his mind with a soaring exultation. *"Belgarion!"* she sang. *"My Belgarion!"*

Ashen-faced Kador, trembling in every limb, backed in horror from the still-burning heap that had been Chamdar the Grolim. "Sorcery!" he gasped.

"Indeed," Aunt Pol said coolly. "I don't think you're ready for this kind of game yet, Kador."

The frightened legionnaires were also backing away, their eyes bulging at what they had just seen.

"I think the Emperor's going to take this whole affair

rather seriously," Aunt Pol told them. "When he hears that you were going to kill his daughter, he'll probably take it personally."

"It wasn't us," one of the soldiers said quickly. "It was Kador. We were just following orders."

"He *might* accept that as an excuse," she said doubtfully. "If it were me, though, I'd take him some kind of gift to prove my loyalty—something appropriate to the circumstances." She looked significantly at Kador.

Several of the legionnaires took her meaning, drew their swords and moved into position around the Grand Duke.

"What are you doing?" Kador demanded of them.

"I think you've lost more than a throne today, Kador," Aunt Pol said.

"You can't do this," Kador told the legionnaires.

One of the soldiers put the point of his sword against the Grand Duke's throat. "We're loyal to the Emperor, my Lord," he said grimly. "We're placing you under arrest for high treason, and if you give us any trouble, we'll settle for just delivering your head to Tol Honeth—if you take my meaning."

One of the legion officers knelt respectfully before Ce'Nedra. "Your Imperial Highness," he said to her, "how may we serve you?"

The princess, still pale and trembling, drew herself up. "Deliver this traitor to my father," she said in a ringing voice, "and tell him what happened here. Inform him that you have arrested the Grand Duke Kador at my command."

"At once, your Highness," the officer said, springing to his feet. "Chain the prisoner!" he ordered sharply, then turned back to Ce'Nedra. "May we provide you an escort to your destination, your Highness?"

"That won't be necessary, captain," she told him. "Just remove this traitor from my sight."

"As your Highness wishes," the captain said with a deep bow. He gestured sharply, and the soldiers led Kador away.

Garion was staring at the mark on his palm. There was no sign of the fire that had burned there.

Durnik, released now from the grip of the soldiers,

looked at Garion, his eyes wide. "I thought I knew you," he whispered. "Who are you, Garion, and how did you do this?"

"Dear Durnik," Aunt Pol said fondly, touching his arm. "Still willing to believe only what you can see. Garion's the same boy he's always been."

"You mean it was you?" Durnik looked at Chamdar's body and pulled his eyes quickly away.

"Of course," she said. "You know Garion. He's the most ordinary boy in the world."

But Garion knew differently. The Will had been his, and the Word had come from him.

"*Keep still!*" her voice warned inside his head. "*No one must know.*"

"*Why did you call me Belgarion?*" he demanded silently.

"*Because it's your name,*" her voice replied. "*Now try to act natural and don't bother me with questions. We'll talk about it later.*" And then her voice was gone.

The others stood around awkwardly until the legionnaires left with Kador. Then, when the soldiers were out of sight and the need for imperial self-possession was gone, Ce'Nedra began to cry. Aunt Pol took the tiny girl in her arms and began to comfort her.

"I guess we'd better bury this," Barak said, nudging what was left of Chamdar with his foot. "The Dryads might be offended if we went off and left it still smoking."

"I'll fetch my spade," Durnik said.

Garion turned away and brushed past Mandorallen and Hettar. His hands were trembling violently, and he was so exhausted that his legs barely held him.

She had called him Belgarion, and the name had rung in his mind as if he had always known that it was his—as if for all his brief years he had been incomplete until in that instant the name itself had completed him. But Belgarion was a being who with Will and Word and the touch of his hand could turn flesh into living fire.

"*You did it!*" he accused the dry awareness in one corner of his mind.

"*No,*" the voice replied. "*I only showed you how. The Will and the Word and the touch were all yours.*"

Garion knew that it was true. With horror he remembered his enemy's final supplication and the flaming, incandescent hand with which he had spurned that agonized appeal for mercy. The revenge he had wanted so desperately for the past several months was dreadfully complete, but the taste of it was bitter, bitter.

Then his knees buckled, and he sank to the earth and wept like a broken-hearted child.

Part Three

NYISSA

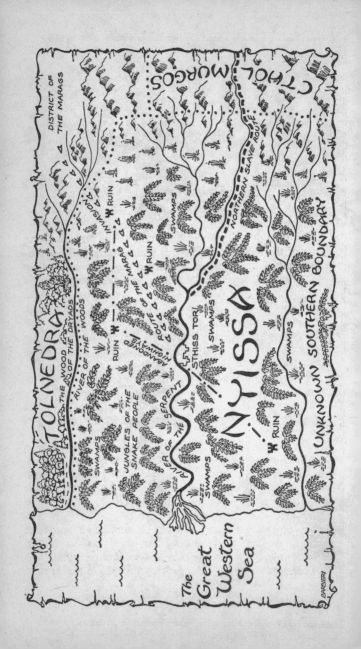

Chapter Twenty-Three

THE EARTH WAS STILL THE SAME. The trees had not changed, nor had the sky. It was still spring, for the seasons had not altered their stately march. But for Garion nothing would ever again be the way that it had been.

They rode down through the Wood of the Dryads to the banks of the River of the Woods which marked the southern boundary of Tolnedra, and from time to time as they rode he caught strange glances from his friends. The looks were speculative, thoughtful, and Durnik—good, solid Durnik—behaved as if he were almost afraid. Only Aunt Pol seemed unchanged, unconcerned. *"Don't worry about it, Belgarion,"* her voice murmured in his mind.

"Don't call me that," he replied with an irritated thought.

"It's your name," the silent voice said. *"You might as well get used to it."*

"Leave me alone."

And then the sense of her presence in his mind was gone.

It took them several days to reach the sea. The weather remained intermittently cloudy, though it did not rain. A stiff onshore breeze was blowing when they rode out onto the wide beach at the mouth of the river. The surf boomed against the sand, and whitecaps flecked the tops of the waves.

Out beyond the surf, a lean, black Cherek war-boat swung at anchor, the air above her alive with screeching gulls. Barak pulled his horse in and shaded his eyes. "She looks familiar," he rumbled, peering intently at the narrow ship.

Hettar shrugged. "They all look the same to me."

"There's all the difference in the world," Barak said, sounding a bit injured. "How would you feel if I said that all horses looked the same?"

"I'd think you were going blind."

Barak grinned at him. "It's exactly the same thing," he said.

"How do we let them know we're here?" Durnik asked.

"They know already," Barak said, "unless they're drunk. Sailors always watch an unfriendly shore very carefully."

"Unfriendly?" Durnik asked.

"Every shore is unfriendly when a Cherek war-boat comes in sight," Barak answered. "It's some kind of superstition, I think."

The ship came about and her anchor was raised. Her oars came out like long, spidery legs, and she seemed to walk through the froth-topped combers toward the mouth of the river. Barak led the way toward the riverbank, then rode along the broad flow until he found a spot deep enough so that the ship could be moored next to the shore.

The fur-clad sailors who threw Barak a mooring line looked familiar, and the first one who leaped across to the riverbank was Greldik, Barak's old friend.

"You're a long ways south," Barak said as if they had only just parted.

Greldik shrugged. "I heard you needed a ship. I wasn't doing anything, so I thought I'd come down and see what you were up to."

"Did you talk to my cousin?"

"Grinneg? No. We made a run down from Kotu to the harbor at Tol Horb for some Drasnian merchants. I ran into Elteg—you remember him—black beard, only one eye?"

Barak nodded.

"He told me that Grinneg was paying him to meet you here. I remembered that you and Elteg didn't get along very well, so I offered to come down instead."

"And he agreed?"

"No," Greldik replied, pulling at his beard. "As a matter of fact, he told me to mind my own business."

"I'm not surprised," Barak said. "Elteg always was greedy, and Grinneg probably offered him a lot of money."

"More than likely." Greldik grinned. "Elteg didn't say how much, though."

"How did you persuade him to change his mind?"

"He had some trouble with his ship," Greldik said with a straight face.

"What kind of trouble?"

"It seems that one night after he and his crew were all drunk, some scoundrel slipped aboard and chopped down his mast."

"What's the world coming to?" Barak asked, shaking his head.

"My thought exactly," Greldik agreed.

"How did he take it?"

"Not very well, I'm afraid," Greldik said sadly. "When we rowed out of the harbor, he sounded as if he was inventing profanities on the spot. You could hear him for quite some distance."

"He should learn to control his temper. That's the kind of behavior that gives Chereks a bad name in the ports of the world."

Greldik nodded soberly and turned to Aunt Pol. "My Lady," he said with a polite bow, "my ship is at your disposal."

"Captain," she asked, acknowledging his bow. "How long will it take you to get us to Sthiss Tor?"

"Depends on the weather," he answered, squinting at the sky. "Probably ten days at the most. We picked up fodder for your horses on the way here, but we'll have to stop for water from time to time."

"We'd better get started then," she said.

"Depends on the weather," he answered, squinting at the ship, but Hettar managed it without too much difficulty. Then they pushed away from the bank, crossed the bar at the mouth of the river and reached the open sea. The crew raised the sails, and they quartered the wind down along the gray-green coastline of Nyissa.

Garion went forward to his customary place in the bow of the ship and sat there, staring bleakly out at the tossing sea. The image of the burning man back in the forest filled his mind.

There was a firm step behind him and a faint, familiar fragrance. "Do you want to talk about it?" Aunt Pol asked.

"What's there to talk about?"

"Many things," she told him.

"You knew I could do that kind of thing, didn't you?"

"I suspected it," she said, sitting down beside him. "There were several hints. One can never be sure, though, until it's used for the first time. I've known any number of people who had the capability and just never used it."

"I wish I never had," Garion said.

"I don't see that you really had much choice. Chamdar was your enemy."

"But did it have to be that way?" he demanded. "Did it have to be fire?"

"The choice was yours," she answered. "If fire bothers you so much, don't do it that way next time."

"There isn't going to be a next time," he stated flatly. "Not ever."

"Belgarion," her voice snapped within his mind, *"stop this foolishness at once. Stop feeling sorry for yourself."*

"Quit that," he said aloud. "Stay out of my mind—and don't call me Belgarion."

"You *are* Belgarion," she insisted. "Like it or not, you will use the power again. Once it's been released, you can never cage it up. You'll get angry or frightened or excited, and you'll use it without even thinking. You can no more choose not to use it than you can choose not to use one of your hands. The important thing now is to teach you how to control it. We can't have you blundering through the world uprooting trees and flattening hills with random thoughts. You must learn to control it and yourself. I didn't raise you to let you become a monster."

"It's too late," he said. "I'm already a monster. Didn't you see what I did back there?"

"All this self-pity is very tedious, Belgarion," her voice told him. *"I don't think we're getting anywhere."* She stood up. "Do try to grow up a little, dear," she said aloud. "It's very hard to instruct someone who's so self-absorbed that he won't listen."

"I'll never do it again," he told her defiantly.

"Oh yes, you will, Belgarion. You'll learn and you'll

*practice and you'll develop the discipline this requires. If
you don't want to do it willingly, then we'll have to do it
the other way. Think about it, dear, and make up your
mind—but don't take too long. It's too important to be put
off.*" She reached out and gently touched his cheek; then
she turned and walked away.

"*She's right, you know,*" the voice in his mind told him.

"*You stay out of this,*" Garion said.

In the days that followed, he avoided Aunt Pol as much
as possible, but he could not avoid her eyes. Wherever he
went on the narrow ship, he knew that she was watching
him, her eyes calm, speculative.

Then, at breakfast on the third day out, she looked at his
face rather closely as if noticing something for the first
time. "Garion," she said, "you're starting to look shaggy.
Why don't you shave?"

Garion blushed furiously and put his fingers to his chin.
There were definitely whiskers there—downy, soft, more
like fuzz than bristles, but whiskers all the same.

"Thou art truly approaching manhood, young Garion,"
Mandorallen assured him rather approvingly.

"The decision doesn't have to be made immediately, Polgara," Barak said, stroking his own luxuriant red beard.
"Let the whiskers grow for a while. If they don't turn out
well, he can always shave them off later."

"I think your neutrality in the matter is suspect, Barak,"
Hettar remarked. "Don't most Chereks wear beards?"

"No razor's ever touched my face," Barak admitted.
"But I just don't think it's the sort of thing to rush into.
It's very hard to stick whiskers back on if you decide later
that you wanted to keep them after all."

"I think they're kind of funny," Ce'Nedra said. Before
Garion could stop her, she reached out two tiny fingers
and tugged the soft down on his chin. He winced and
blushed again.

"They come off," Aunt Pol ordered firmly.

Wordlessly, Durnik went below decks. When he came
back, he carried a basin, a chunk of brown-colored soap, a
towel, and a fragment of mirror. "It isn't really hard, Garion," he said, putting the things on the table in front of the
young man. Then he took a neatly folded razor out of a

case at his belt. "You just have to be careful not to cut yourself, that's all. The whole secret is not to rush."

"Pay close attention when you're near your nose," Hettar advised. "A man looks very strange without a nose."

The shaving proceeded with a great deal of advice, and on the whole it did not turn out too badly. Most of the bleeding stopped after a few minutes, and, aside from the fact that his face felt as if it had been peeled, Garion was quite satisfied with the results.

"Much better," Aunt Pol said.

"He'll catch cold in his face now," Barak predicted.

"Will you stop that?" she told him.

The coast of Nyissa slid by on their left, a blank wall of tangled vegetation, festooned with creepers and long tatters of moss. Occasional eddies in the breeze brought the foul reek of the swamps out to the ship. Garion and Ce'Nedra stood together in the prow of the ship, looking toward the jungle.

"What are those?" Garion asked, pointing at some large things with legs slithering around on a mud bank along a stream that emptied into the sea.

"Crocodiles," Ce'Nedra answered.

"What's a crocodile?"

"A big lizard," she said.

"Are they dangerous?"

"Very dangerous. They eat people. Haven't you ever read about them?"

"I can't read," Garion admitted without thinking.

"What?"

"I can't read," Garion repeated. "Nobody ever taught me how."

"That's ridiculous!"

"It's not my fault," he said defensively.

She looked at him thoughtfully. She had seemed almost half-afraid of him since the meeting with Chamdar, and her insecurity had probably been increased by the fact that, on the whole, she had not treated him very well. Her first assumption that he was only a servant boy had gotten their whole relationship off on the wrong foot, but she was far too proud to admit that initial mistake. Garion could almost hear the little wheels clicking around in her head.

"Would you like to have me teach you how?" she offered. It was probably the closest thing he'd ever get to an apology from her.

"Would it take very long?"

"That depends on how clever you are."

"When do you think we could start?"

She frowned. "I've got a couple of books, but we'll need something to write on."

"I don't know that I need to learn how to write," he said. "Reading ought to be enough for right now."

She laughed. "They're the same thing, you goose."

"I didn't know that," Garion said, flushing slightly. "I thought—" He floundered with the whole idea. "I guess I never really thought about it," he concluded lamely. "What sort of thing do we need to write on?"

"Parchment's the best," she said, "and a charcoal stick to write with—so we can rub it off and write on the parchment again."

"I'll go talk to Durnik," he decided. "He'll be able to think of something."

Durnik suggested sailcloth and a charred stick. Within an hour Garion and Ce'Nedra were sitting in a sheltered spot in the bow of the ship, their heads close together over a square of canvas nailed to a plank. Garion glanced up once and saw Aunt Pol not far away. She was watching the two of them with an indecipherable expression. Then he lowered his eyes again to the strangely compelling symbols on the canvas.

His instruction went on for the next several days. Since his fingers were naturally nimble, he quickly picked up the trick of forming the letters.

"No, no," Ce'Nedra said one afternoon, "you've spelled it wrong—used the wrong letters. You name's Garion, not Belgarion."

He felt a sudden chill and looked down at the canvas square. The name was spelled out quite clearly—"Belgarion."

He looked up quickly. Aunt Pol was standing where she usually stood, her eyes on him as always.

"Stay out of my mind!" He snapped the thought at her.

"Study hard, dear," her voice urged him silently.

"Learning of any kind is useful, and you have a great deal to learn. The sooner you get the habit, the better." Then she smiled, turned and walked away.

The next day, Greldik's ship reached the mouths of the River of the Serpent in central Nyissa, and his men struck the sail and set their oars into the locks along the sides of the ship in preparation for the long pull upriver to Sthiss Tor.

Chapter Twenty-Four

THERE WAS NO AIR. It seemed as if the world had suddenly been turned into a vast, reeking pool of stagnant water. The River of the Serpent had a hundred mouths, each creeping sluggishly through the jellied muck of the delta as if reluctant to join the boisterous waves of the sea. The reeds which grew in that vast swamp reached a height of twenty feet and were as thick as woven fabric. There was a tantalizing sound of a breeze brushing the tops of the reeds, but down among them, all thought or memory of breeze was lost. There was no air. The delta steamed and stank beneath a sun that did not burn so much as boil. Each breath seemed to be half-water. Insects rose in clouds from the reeds and settled in mindless gluttony on every inch of exposed skin, biting, feeding on blood.

They were a day and a half among the reeds before they reached the first trees, low, scarcely more than bushes. The main river channel began to take shape as they moved slowly on into the Nyissan heartland. The sailors sweated and swore at their oars, and the ship moved slowly against the current, almost as if she struggled against a tide of thick oil that clung to her like some loathsome glue.

The trees grew taller, then immense. Great, gnarled roots twisted up out of the ooze along the banks like grotesquely misshapen legs, and trunks vast as castles reached up into the steaming sky. Ropey vines undulated down from the limbs overhead, moving, seeming to writhe with a kind of vegetable will of their own in the breathless air. Shaggy tatters of grayish moss descended in hundred-foot-long streamers from the trees, and the river wound spitefully in great coils that made their journey ten times as long as it needed to be.

"Unpleasant sort of place," Hettar grumbled, dispiritedly looking out over the bow at the weedy surface of the river ahead. He had removed his horsehide jacket and linen undertunic, and his lean torso gleamed with sweat. Like most of them, he was covered with the angry welts of insect bites.

"My very thought," Mandorallen agreed.

One of the sailors shouted and jumped up, kicking at his oar-handle. Something long, slimy, and boneless had crawled unseen up his oar, seeking his flesh with an eyeless voracity.

"Leech," Durnik said with a shudder as the hideous thing dropped with a wet plop back into the stinking river. "I've never seen one so big. It must be a foot long or more."

"Probably not a good place for swimming," Hettar observed.

"I wasn't considering it," Durnik said.

"Good."

Aunt Pol, wearing a light linen dress, came out of the cabin beneath the high stern where Greldik and Barak were taking turns at the tiller. She had been caring for Ce'Nedra, who had drooped and wilted like a flower in the brutal climate of the river.

"Can't you do something?" Garion demanded of her silently.

"About what?"

"All of this." He looked around helplessly.

"What do you want me to do?"

"Drive off the bugs, if nothing else."

"Why don't you do it yourself, Belgarion?"

He set his jaw. *"No!"* It was almost a silent shout.

"It isn't really very hard."

"*No!*"

She shrugged and turned away, leaving him seething with frustration.

It took them three more days to reach Sthiss Tor. The city was embraced in a wide coil of the river and was built of black stone. The houses and buildings were low and for the most part were windowless. In the center of the city a vast pile of a building rose with strangely shaped spires and domes and terraces, oddly alien-looking. Wharves and jetties poked out into the turbid river, and Greldik guided his ship toward one which was much larger than the rest. "We have to stop at customs," he explained.

"Inevitably," Durnik said.

The exchange at customs was brief. Captain Greldik announced that he was delivering the goods of Radek of Boktor to the Drasnian trade enclave. Then he handed a jingling purse to the shaven-headed customs official, and the ship was allowed to proceed without inspection.

"You owe me for that, Barak," Greldik said. "The trip here was out of friendship, but the money's something else again."

"Write it down someplace," Barak told him. "I'll take care of it when I get back to Val Alorn."

"*If* you ever get back to Val Alorn," Greldik said sourly.

"I'm sure you'll remember me in your prayers, then," Barak said. "I know you pray for me all the time anyway, but now you've got a bit more incentive."

"Is every official in the whole world corrupt?" Durnik demanded irritably. "Doesn't anyone do his job the way it's supposed to be done without taking bribes?"

"The world would come to an end if one of them did," Hettar replied. "You and I are too simple and honest for these affairs, Durnik. We're better off leaving this kind of thing to others."

"It's disgusting, that's all."

"That may be true," Hettar agreed, "but I'm just as happy that the customs man didn't look below decks. We might have had some trouble explaining the horses."

The sailors had backed the ship into the river again and rowed toward a series of substantial wharves. They pulled up beside the outer wharf, shipped their oars and looped the hawsers around the tar-blackened pilings of a mooring spot.

"You can't moor here," a sweaty guard told them from the wharf. "This is for Drasnian ships."

"I'll moor anyplace it suits me," Greldik said shortly.

"I'll call out the soldiers," the guard threatened. He took hold of one of their hawsers and pulled out a long knife.

"If you cut that rope, friend, I'll come down there and tear off your ears," Greldik warned.

"Go ahead and tell him," Barak suggested. "It's too hot for fighting."

"My ship's carrying Drasnian goods," Greldik told the guard on the wharf, "belonging to a man named Radek— from Boktor, I think."

"Oh," the guard said, putting away his knife, "why didn't you say so in the first place?"

"Because I didn't like your attitude," Greldik replied bluntly. "Where do I find the man in charge?"

"Droblek? His house is just up that street past the shops. It's the one with the Drasnian emblem on the door."

"I've got to talk with him," Greldik said. "Do I need a pass to go off the wharf? I've heard some strange things about Sthiss Tor."

"You can move around inside the enclave," the guard informed him. "You only need a pass if you want to go into the city."

Greldik grunted and went below. A moment later he came back with several packets of folded parchment. "Do you want to talk to this official?" he asked Aunt Pol. "Or do you want me to take care of it?"

"We'd better come along," she decided. "The girl's asleep. Tell your men not to disturb her."

Greldik nodded and spoke briefly to his first mate. The sailors ran a plank across to the wharf, and Greldik led the way ashore. Thick clouds were rolling in overhead, darkening the sun.

The street which ran down to the wharf was lined on both sides with the shops of Drasnian merchants, and Nyissans moved torpidly from shop to shop, stopping now and then to haggle with the sweating shopkeepers. The Nyissan men all wore loose-fitting robes of a light, iridescent fabric, and their heads were all shaved completely bald. As he walked along behind Aunt Pol, Garion noticed with a certain distaste that the Nyissans wore elaborate makeup on their eyes, and that their lips and cheeks were rouged. Their speech was rasping and sibilant, and they all seemed to affect a lisp.

The heavy clouds had by now completely obscured the sky, and the street seemed suddenly dark. A dozen wretched, near-naked men were repairing a section of cobblestones. Their unkempt hair and shaggy beards indicated that they were not Nyissan, and there were shackles and chains attached to their ankles. A brutal-looking Nyissan stood over them with a whip, and the fresh welts and cuts on their bodies spoke mutely of the freedom with which he used it. One of the miserable slaves accidentally dropped an armload of crudely squared-off stones on his foot and opened his mouth with an animal-like howl of pain. With horror, Garion saw that the slave's tongue had been cut out.

"They reduce men to the level of beasts," Mandorallen growled, his eyes burning with a terrible anger. "Why has this cesspool not been cleansed?"

"It was once," Barak said grimly. "Just after the Nyissans assassinated the Rivan King, the Alorns came down here and killed every Nyissan they could find."

"Their numbers appear undiminished," Mandorallen said, looking around.

Barak shrugged. "It was thirteen hundred years ago. Even a single pair of rats could reestablish their species in that length of time."

Durnik, who was walking beside Garion, gasped suddenly and averted his eyes, blushing furiously.

A Nyissan lady had just stepped from a litter carried by eight slaves. The fabric of her pale green gown was so flimsy that it was nearly transparent and left very little to the imagination. "Don't look at her, Garion," Durnik whispered hoarsely, still blushing. "She's a wicked woman."

"I'd forgotten about that," Aunt Pol said with a thoughtful frown. "Maybe we should have left Durnik and Garion on the ship."

"Why's she dressed like that?" Garion asked, watching the nearly nude woman.

"Undressed, you mean." Durnik's voice was strangled with outrage.

"It's the custom," Aunt Pol explained. "It has to do with the climate. There are some other reasons, of course, but we don't need to go into those just now. All Nyissan women dress that way."

Barak and Greldik were watching the woman also, their broad grins appreciative.

"Never mind," Aunt Pol told them firmly.

Not far away a shaven-headed Nyissan stood leaning against a wall, staring at his hand and giggling senselessly. "I can see right through my fingers," he announced in a hissing lisp. "Right through them."

"Drunk?" Hettar asked.

"Not exactly," Aunt Pol answered. "Nyissans have peculiar amusements—leaves, berries, certain roots. Their perceptions get modified. It's a bit more serious than the common drunkenness one finds among Alorns."

Another Nyissan shambled by, his gait curiously jerky and his expression blank.

"Doth this condition prevail widely?" Mandorallen asked.

"I've never met a Nyissan yet who wasn't at least partially drugged," Aunt Pol said. "It makes them difficult to talk to. Isn't that the house we're looking for?" She pointed at a solid building across the street.

There was an ominous rumble of thunder off to the south as they crossed to the large house. A Drasnian servant in a linen tunic answered their knock, let them into a dimly lighted antechamber, and told them to wait.

"An evil city," Hettar said quietly. "I can't see why any Alorn in his right mind would come here willingly."

"Money," Captain Greldik replied shortly. "The Nyissan trade is very profitable."

"There are more important things than money," Hettar muttered.

An enormously fat man came into the dim room. "More light," he snapped at his servant. "You didn't have to leave them here in the dark."

"You said that the lamps just made it hotter," the servant protested in a surly tone. "I wish you'd make up your mind."

"Never mind what I said; just do as I say."

"The climate's making you incoherent, Droblek," the servant noted acidly. He lit several lamps and left the room muttering to himself.

"Drasnians make the world's worst servants," Droblek grumbled. "Shall we get down to business?" He lowered his vast bulk into a chair. The sweat rolled continually down his face and into the damp collar of his brown silk robe.

"My name's Greldik," the bearded seaman said. "I've just arrived at your wharves with a shipload of goods belonging to the merchant, Radek of Boktor." He presented the folded packets of parchment.

Droblek's eyes narrowed. "I didn't know that Radek was interested in the southern trade. I thought he dealt mostly in Sendaria and Arendia."

Greldik shrugged indifferently. "I didn't ask him. He pays me to carry his goods in my ship, not to ask questions about his business."

Droblek looked at them all, his sweating face expressionless. Then his fingers moved slightly. —*Is everything here what it seems to be?*— The Drasnian secret language made his fat fingers suddenly nimble.

Can we speak openly here?— Aunt Pol's fingers asked him. Her gestures were stately, somehow archaic. There was a kind of formality to her movements that Garion had not seen in the signs made by others.

As openly as anyplace in this pest-hole— Droblek replied, —*You have a strange accent, lady. There's something about it that it seems I should remember*—

—*I learned the language a very long time ago*— she replied. —*You know who Radek of Boktor really is, of course*—

"Naturally," Droblek said aloud. "Everyone knows that. Sometimes he calls himself Ambar of Kotu—when he wants to have dealings that are not, strictly speaking, legitimate."

"Shall we stop fencing with each other, Droblek?" Aunt Pol asked quietly. "I'm quite certain you've received instructions from King Rhodar by now. All this dancing about is tiresome."

Droblek's face darkened. "I'm sorry," he said stiffly. "I'll need a bit more in the way of verification."

"Don't be an idiot, Droblek," Barak rumbled at the fat man. "Use your eyes. You're an Alorn; you know who the lady is."

Droblek looked suddenly at Aunt Pol, his eyes going very wide. "It's not possible," he gasped.

"Would you like to have her prove it to you?" Hettar suggested. The house shook with a sudden crash of thunder.

"No, no," Droblek refused hastily, still staring at Aunt Pol. "It just never occurred to me—I mean, I just never—" He floundered with it.

"Have you heard from Prince Kheldar or my father?" Aunt Pol asked crisply.

"Your father? You mean—? Is *he* involved in this too?"

"Really, Droblek," she said tartly, "don't you *believe* the communications King Rhodar sends you?"

Droblek shook his head like a man trying to clear his mind. "I'm sorry, Lady Polgara," he said. "You surprised me, that's all. It takes a moment to get used to. We didn't think you'd be coming this far south."

"It's obvious then that you haven't received any word from Kheldar or the old man."

"No, my Lady," Droblek said. "Nothing. Are they supposed to be here?"

"So they said. They were either going to meet us here or send word."

"It's very hard to get messages any place in Nyissa," Droblek explained. "The people here aren't very reliable. The prince and your father could be upcountry, and their messenger could very well have gone astray. I sent a message to a place not ten leagues from the city once, and it took six months to arrive. The Nyissan who was carrying it found a certain berry patch along the way. We found him sitting in the middle of the patch, smiling." Droblek made a sour face. "There was moss growing on him," he added.

"Dead?" Durnik asked.

Droblek shrugged. "No, just very happy. He enjoyed the berries very much. I dismissed him at once, but he didn't seem to mind. For all I know, he's still sitting there."

"How extensive is your network here in Sthiss Tor?" Aunt Pol asked.

Droblek spread his pudgy hands modestly. "I manage to pick up a bit of information here and there. I've got a few people in the palace and a minor official at the Tolnedran embassy. The Tolnedrans are very thorough." He grinned impishly. "It's cheaper to let them do all the work and then buy the information after they've gathered it."

"If you can believe what they tell you," Hettar suggested.

"I never take what they say at face value," Droblek said. "The Tolnedran ambassador knows that I've bought his man. He tries to trip me up with false leads now and then."

"Does the ambassador know that you know?" Hettar asked.

"Of course he does." The fat man laughed. "But he doesn't think that I'm aware of the fact that he knows that I know." He laughed again. "It's all terribly complicated, isn't it?"

"Most Drasnian games usually are," Barak observed.

"Does the name Zedar mean anything to you?" Aunt Pol asked.

"I've heard it, naturally," Droblek said.

"Has he been in touch with Salmissra?"

Droblek frowned. "I couldn't say for sure. I haven't heard that he has, but that doesn't mean that he hasn't. Nyissa's a murky sort of place, and Salmissra's palace is the murkiest spot in the whole country. You wouldn't believe some of the things that go on there."

"I'd believe them," Aunt Pol said, "and probably things you haven't even begun to guess." She turned back to the others. "I think we're at a standstill. We can't make any kind of move until we hear from Silk and the Old Wolf."

"Could I offer you my house?" Droblek asked.

"I think we'll stay on board Captain Greldik's ship," she told him. "As you say, Nyissa's a murky place, and I'm sure that the Tolnedran ambassadors bought a few people in *your* establishment."

"Naturally," Droblek agreed. "But I know who they are."

"We'd better not chance it," she told him. "There are several reasons for our avoiding Tolnedrans just now. We'll stay aboard the ship and keep out of sight. Let us know as soon as Prince Kheldar gets in touch with you."

"Of course," Droblek said. "You'll have to wait until the rain lets up, though. Listen to it." There was the thundering sound of a downpour on the roof overhead.

"Will it last long?" Durnik asked.

Droblek shrugged. "An hour or so usually. It rains every afternoon during this season."

"I imagine it helps to cool the air," the smith said.

"Not significantly," the Drasnian told him. "Usually it just makes things worse." He mopped the sweat from his fat face.

"How can you live here?" Durnik asked.

Droblek smiled blandly. "Fat men don't move around all that much. I'm making a great deal of money, and the game I'm playing with the Tolnedran ambassador keeps my mind occupied. It's not all that bad, once you get used to it. It helps if I keep telling myself that."

They sat quietly then, listening to the pounding rain.

Chapter Twenty-Five

FOR THE NEXT SEVERAL DAYS they all remained aboard Greldik's ship, waiting for word from Silk and Mister Wolf. Ce'Nedra recovered from her indisposition and appeared on deck wearing a pale-colored Dryad tunic which seemed to Garion to be only slightly less revealing than the gowns worn by Nyissan women. When he rather stiffly suggested that she ought to put on a few more clothes, however, she merely laughed at him. With a single-mindedness that made him want to grind his teeth, she returned to the task of teaching him to read and write. They sat together in an out-of-the-way spot on deck, pouring over a tedious book on Tolnedran diplomacy. The whole business seemed to Garion to be taking forever, though in fact his mind was very quick, and he was learning surprisingly fast. Ce'Nedra was too thoughtless to compliment him, though she seemed to await his next mistake almost breathlessly, delighting it seemed in each opportunity to ridicule him. Her proximity and her light, spicy perfume distracted him as they sat close beside each other, and he perspired as much from their occasional touch of hand or arm or hip as he did from the climate. Because they were both young, she was intolerant and he was stubborn. The sticky, humid heat made them both short-tempered and irritable, so the lessons erupted into bickering more often than not.

When they arose one morning, a black, square-rigged Nyissan ship rocked in the river current at a nearby wharf. A foul, evil kind of reek carried to them from her on the fitful morning breeze.

"What's that smell?" Garion asked one of the sailors.

"Slaver," the sailor answered grimly, pointing at the Nyissan ship. "You can smell them twenty miles away when you're at sea."

Garion looked at the ugly black ship and shuddered.

Barak and Mandorallen drifted across the deck and joined Garion at the rail. "Looks like a scow," Barak said of the Nyissan ship, his voice heavy with contempt. He was stripped to the waist, and his hairy torso ran with sweat.

"It's a slave ship," Garion told him.

"It smells like an open sewer," Barak complained. "A good fire would improve it tremendously."

"A sorry trade, my Lord Barak," Mandorallen said. "Nyissa hath dealt in human misery for untold centuries."

"Is that a Drasnian wharf?" Barak asked with narrowed eyes.

"No," Garion answered. "The sailors say that everything on that side's Nyissan."

"That's a shame," Barak growled.

A group of mail-shirted men in black cloaks walked out

onto the wharf where the slave ship was moored and stopped near the vessel's stern.

"Oh-oh," Barak said. "Where's Hettar?"

"He's still below," Garion replied. "What's the matter?"

"Keep an eye out for him. Those are Murgos."

The shaven-headed Nyissan sailors pulled open a hatch on their ship and barked a few rough orders down into the hold. Slowly, a line of dispirited-looking men came up. Each man wore an iron collar, and a long chain fastened them together.

Mandorallen stiffened and began to swear.

"What's wrong?" Barak asked.

"Arendishmen!" the knight exclaimed. "I had heard of this, but I did not believe it."

"Heard of what?"

"An ugly rumor hath persisted in Arendia for some years," Mandorallen answered, his face white with rage. "We are told that some of our nobles have upon occasion enriched themselves by selling their serfs to the Nyissans."

"Looks like it's more than a rumor," Barak said.

"There," Mandorallen growled. "See that crest upon the tunic of that one there? It's the crest of Vo Toral. I know the Baron of Vo Toral for a notorious spendthrift, but had not thought him dishonorable. Upon my return to Arendia, I will denounce him publicly."

"What good's that going to do?" Barak asked.

"He will be forced to challenge me," Mandorallen said grimly. "I will prove his villainy upon his body."

Barak shrugged. "Serf or slave—what's the difference?"

"Those men have rights, my Lord," Mandorallen stated. "Their Lord is required to protect them and care for them. The oath of knighthood demands it of us. This vile transaction hath stained the honor of every true Arendish knight. I shall not rest until I have bereft that foul baron of his miserable life."

"Interesting idea," Barak said. "Maybe I'll go with you."

Hettar came up on deck, and Barak moved immediately to his side and began talking quietly to him, holding one of his arms firmly.

"Make them jump around a bit," one of the Murgos ordered harshly. "I want to see how many are lame."

A heavy-shouldered Nyissan uncoiled a long whip and began to flick it deftly at the legs of the chained men. The slaves began to dance feverishly on the wharf beside the slave ship.

"Dog's blood! Mandorallen swore, and his knuckles turned white as he gripped the railing.

"Easy," Garion warned. "Aunt Pol says we're supposed to stay pretty much out of sight."

"It cannot be borne!" Mandorallen cried.

The chain that bound the slaves together was old and pitted with rust. When one slave tripped and fell, a link snapped, and the man found himself suddenly free. With an agility born of desperation, he rolled quickly to his feet, took two quick steps and plunged off the wharf into the murky waters of the river.

"This way, man!" Mandorallen called to the swimming slave.

The burly Nyissan with the whip laughed harshly and pointed at the escaping slave. "Watch," he told the Murgos.

"Stop him, you idiot," one of the Murgos snapped. "I paid good gold for him."

"It's too late." The Nyissan looked on with an ugly grin. "Watch."

The swimming man suddenly shrieked and sank out of sight. When he came up again, his face and arms were covered with the slimy, foot-long leeches that infested the river. Screaming, the struggling man tore at the writhing leeches, ripping out chunks of his own flesh in his efforts to pull them off.

The Murgos began to laugh.

Garion's mind exploded. He gathered himself with an awful concentration, pointed one hand at the wharf just beyond their own ship and said, "Be there!" He felt an enormous surge as if some vast tide were rushing out of him, and he reeled almost senseless against Mandorallen. The sound inside his head was deafening.

The slave, still writhing and covered with the oozing leeches, was suddenly lying on the wharf. A wave of exhaustion swept over Garion; if Mandorallen had not caught him, he would have fallen.

"Where did he go?" Barak demanded, still staring at the turbulent spot on the surface of the river where the slave had been an instant before. "Did he go under?"

Wordlessly and with a shaking hand, Mandorallen pointed at the slave, who lay still weakly struggling on the Drasnian wharf about twenty yards in front of the bow of their ship.

Barak looked at the slave, then back at the river. The big man blinked with surprise.

A small boat with four Nyissans at the oars put out from the other wharf and moved deliberately toward Greldik's ship. A tall Murgo stood in the bow, his scarred face angry.

"You have my property," he shouted across the intervening water. "Return the slave to me at once."

"Why don't you come and claim him, Murgo?" Barak called back. He released Hettar's arm. The Algar moved to the side of the ship, stopping only to pick up a long boat-hook.

"Will I be unmolested?" the Murgo asked a bit doubtfully.

"Why don't you come alongside, and we'll discuss it?" Barak suggested pleasantly.

"You're denying me my rights to my own property," the Murgo complained.

"Not at all," Barak told him. "Of course there might be a fine point of law involved here. This wharf is Drasnian territory, and slavery isn't legal in Drasnia. Since that's the case, the man's not a slave anymore."

"I'll get my men," the Murgo said. "We'll take the slave by force if we have to."

"I think we'd have to look on that as an invasion of Alorn territory," Barak warned with a great show of regret. "In the absence of our Drasnian cousins, we'd almost be compelled to take steps to defend their wharf for them. What do you think, Mandorallen?"

"Thy perceptions are most acute, my Lord," Mandorallen replied. "By common usage, honorable men are morally obliged to defend the territory of kinsmen in their absence."

"There," Barak said to the Murgo. "You see how it is.

My friend here is an Arend, so he's totally neutral in this matter. I think we'd have to accept his interpretation of the affair."

Greldik's sailors had begun to climb the rigging by now, and they clung to the ropes like great, evil-looking apes, fingering their weapons and grinning at the Murgo.

"There is yet another way," the Murgo said ominously.

Garion could feel a force beginning to build, and a faint sound seemed to echo inside his head. He drew himself up, putting his hands on the wooden rail in front of him. He felt a terrible weakness, but he steeled himself and tried to gather his strength.

"That's enough of that," Aunt Pol said crisply, coming up on deck with Durnik and Ce'Nedra behind her.

"We were merely having a little legal discussion," Barak said innocently.

"I know what you were doing," she snapped. Her eyes were angry. She looked coldly across the intervening stretch of river at the Murgo. "You'd better leave," she told him.

"I have something to retrieve first," the man in the boat called back.

"I'd forget about it!"

"We'll see," he said. He straightened and began muttering as if to himself, his hands moving rapidly in a series of intricate gestures. Garion felt something pushing at him almost like a wind, though the air was completely still.

"Be sure you get it right," Aunt Pol advised quietly. "If you forget even the tiniest part of it, it'll explode in your face."

The man in the boat froze, and a faintly worried frown crossed his face. The secret wind that had been pushing at Garion stopped. The man began again, his fingers weaving in the air and his face fixed with concentration.

"You do it like this, Grolim," Aunt Pol said. She moved her hand slightly, and Garion felt a sudden rush as if the wind pushing at him had turned and begum to blow the other way. The Grolim threw his hands up and reeled back, stumbling and falling into the bottom of his boat. As if it had been given a heavy push, the boat surged backward several yards.

The Grolim half-raised, his eyes wide and his face deathly pale.

"Return to your master, dog," Aunt Pol said scathingly. "Tell him to beat you for not learning your lessons properly."

The Grolim spoke quickly to the Nyissans at the oars, and they immediately turned the boat and rowed back toward the slave ship.

"We had a nice little fight brewing there, Polgara," Barak complained. "Why did you have to spoil it?"

"Grow up," she ordered bluntly. Then she turned on Garion, her eyes blazing and the white lock at her brow like a streak of fire. "You idiot! You refuse any kind of instruction, and then you burst out like a raging bull. Have you the slightest conception of what an uproar translocation causes? You've alerted every Grolim in Sthiss Tor to the fact that we're here."

"He was dying," Garion protested, gesturing helplessly at the slave lying on the wharf. "I had to do something."

"He was dead as soon as he hit the water," she said flatly. "Look at him."

The slave had stiffened into an arched posture of mortal agony, his head twisted back and his mouth agape. He was obviously dead. "What happened to him?" Garion asked, feeling suddenly sick.

"The leeches are poisonous. Their bites paralyze their victims so that they can feed on them undisturbed. The bites stopped his heart. You exposed us to the Grolims for the sake of a dead man."

"He wasn't dead when I did it!" Garion shouted at her. "He was screaming for help." He was angrier than he had ever been in his life.

"He was beyond help." Her voice was cold, even brutal.

"What kind of monster are you?" he asked from between clenched teeth. "Don't you have any feelings? You'd have just let him die, wouldn't you?"

"I don't think this is the time or place to discuss it."

"No! This *is* the time—right now, Aunt Pol. You're not even human, did you know that? You left being human behind so long ago that you can't even remember where you lost it. You're four thousand years old. Our whole lives go by while you blink your eyes. We're just an entertainment for you—an hour's diversion. You manipulate us like puppets for your own amusement. Well, I'm tired of being manipulated. You and I are finished!"

It probably went further than he'd intended, but his anger had finally run away with him, and the words seemed to rush out before he could stop them.

She looked at him, her face as pale as if he had suddenly struck her. Then she drew herself up. "You stupid boy," she said in a voice that was all the more terrible because it was so quiet. "Finished? You and I? How can you even begin to understand what I've had to do to bring you to this world? You've been my only care for over a thousand years. I've endured anguish and loss and pain beyond your ability to understand what the words mean—all for you. I've lived in poverty and squalor for hundreds of years at a time—all for you. I gave up a sister I loved more than my life itself—all for you. I've gone through fire and despair worse than fire a dozen times over—all for you. And you think this has all been an entertainment for me?—some idle amusement? You think the kind of care I've devoted to you for a thousand years and more comes cheaply? You and I will *never* be finished, Belgarion. *Never!* We will go on together until the end of days if necessary. We will never be finished. You owe me too much for that!"

There was a dreadful silence. The others, shocked by the intensity of Aunt Pol's words, stood staring first at her and then at Garion.

Without speaking further, she turned and went below decks again.

Garion looked around helplessly, suddenly terribly ashamed and terribly alone.

"I *had* to do it, didn't I?" he asked of no one in particular and not entirely sure exactly what it was that he meant.

They all looked at him, but no one answered his question.

Chapter Twenty-Six

BY MIDAFTERNOON THE CLOUDS had rolled in again, and the thunder began to rumble off in the distance as the rain swept in to drown the steaming city once more. The afternoon thunderstorm seemed to come at the same time each day, and they had even grown accustomed to it. They all moved below deck and sat sweltering as the rain roared down on the deck above them.

Garion sat stiffly, his back planted against a rough-hewn oak rib of the ship and watched Aunt Pol, his face set stubbornly and his eyes unforgiving.

She ignored him and sat talking quietly with Ce'Nedra.

Captain Greldik came through the narrow companionway door, his face and beard streaming water. "The Drasnian—Droblek—is here," he told them. "He says he's got word for you."

"Send him in," Barak said.

Droblek squeezed his vast bulk through the narrow door. He was totally drenched from the rain and stood dripping on the floor. He wiped his face. "It's wet out there," he commented.

"We noticed," Hettar said.

"I've received a message," Droblek told Aunt Pol. "It's from Prince Kheldar."

"Finally," she said.

"He and Belgarath are coming downriver," Droblek reported. "As closely as I can make out, they should be here in a few days—a week at the most. The messenger isn't very coherent."

Aunt Pol looked at him inquiringly.

"Fever," Droblek explained. "The man's a Drasnian, so he's reliable—one of my agents at an upcountry trading post—but he's picked up one of the diseases that infest this stinking swamp. He's a little delirious just now. We hope we can break the fever in a day or so and get some sense out of him. I came as soon as I got the general idea of his message. I thought you'd want to know immediately."

"We appreciate your concern," Aunt Pol said.

"I'd have sent a servant," Droblek explained, "but messages sometimes go astray in Sthiss Tor, and servants sometimes get things twisted around." He grinned suddenly. "That's not the real reason, of course."

Aunt Pol smiled. "Of course not."

"A fat man tends to stay in one place and let others do his walking around for him. From the tone of King Rhodar's message, I gather that this business might be the most important thing happening in the world just now. I wanted to take part in it." He made a wry face. "We all lapse into childishness from time to time, I suppose."

"How serious is the condition of the messenger?" Aunt Pol asked.

Droblek shrugged. "Who can say? Half of these pestilential fevers in Nyissa don't even have names, and we can't really tell one from another. Sometimes people die very quickly from them; sometimes they linger for weeks. Now and then someone even recovers. About all we can do is make them comfortable and wait to see what happens."

"I'll come at once," Aunt Pol said, rising. "Durnik, would you get me the green bag from our packs? I'll need the herbs I have in it."

"It's not always a good idea to expose oneself to some of these fevers, my Lady," Droblek cautioned.

"I won't be in any danger," she said. "I want to question your messenger closely, and the only way I'll be able to get any answers from him is to rid him of his fever."

"Durnik and I'll come along," Barak offered.

She looked at him.

"It doesn't hurt to be on the safe side," the big man said, belting on his sword.

"If you wish." She put on her cloak and turned up the hood. "This may take most of the night," she told Greldik.

"There are Grolims about, so have your sailors stay alert. Put a few of the more sober ones on watch."

"Sober, my Lady?" Greldik asked innocently.

"I've heard the singing coming from the crew's quarters, Captain," she said a bit primly. "Chereks don't sing unless they're drunk. Keep the lid on your ale-barrel tonight. Shall we go, Droblek?"

"At once, my Lady," the fat man assented with a sly look at Greldik.

Garion felt a certain relief after they had gone. The strain of maintaining his rancor in Aunt Pol's presence had begun to wear on him. He found himself in a difficult position. The horror and self-loathing which had gnawed at him since he had unleashed the dreadful fire upon Chamdar in the Wood of the Dryads had grown until he could scarcely bear it. He looked forward to each night with dread, for his dreams were always the same. Over and over again he saw Chamdar, his face burned away, pleading, "Master, have mercy." And over and over again he saw the awful blue flame that had come from his own hand in answer to that agony. The hatred he had carried since Val Alorn had died in that flame. His revenge had been so absolute that there was no possible way he could evade or shift the responsibility for it. His outburst that morning had been directed almost more at himself than at Aunt Pol. He had called her a monster, but it was the monster within himself he hated. The dreadful catalogue of what she had suffered over uncounted years for him and the passion with which she had spoken—evidence of the pain his words had caused her—twisted searingly in his mind. He was ashamed, so ashamed that he could not even bear to look into the faces of his friends. He sat alone and vacant-eyed with Aunt Pol's words thundering over and over in his mind.

The rain slackened on the deck above them as the storm passed. Swirling little eddies of raindrops ran across the muddy surface of the river in the fitful wind. The sky began to clear, and the sun sank into the roiling clouds, staining them an angry red. Garion went up on deck to wrestle alone with his troubled conscience.

Atfer a while he heard a light step behind him. "I suppose you're proud of yourself?" Ce'Nedra asked acidly.

"Leave me alone."

"I don't think so. I think I want to tell you just exactly how we all felt about your little speech this morning."

"I don't want to hear about it."

"That's too bad. I'm going to tell you anyway."

"I won't listen."

"Oh yes, you will." She took him by the arm and turned him around. Her eyes were blazing and her tiny face filled with a huge anger. "What you did was absolutely inexcusable," she said. "Your Aunt raised you from a baby. She's been a mother to you."

"My mother's dead."

"The Lady Polgara's the only mother you ever knew, and what did you give her for thanks? You called her a monster. You accused her of not caring."

"I'm not listening to you," Garion cried. Knowing that it was childish—even infantile—he put his hands over his ears. The Princess Ce'Nedra always seemed to bring out the worst in him.

"Move your hands!" she commanded in a ringing voice. "You're going to hear me even if I have to scream."

Garion, afraid that she meant it, took his hands away.

"She carried you when you were a baby," Ce'Nedra went on, seeming to know exactly where the sorest spot on Garion's wounded conscience lay. "She watched your very first steps. She fed you; she watched over you; she held you when you were afraid or hurt. Does that sound like a monster? She watches you all the time, did you know that? If you even so much as stumble, she almost reaches out to catch you. I've seen her cover you when you're asleep. Does that sound like someone who doesn't care?"

"You're talking about something you don't understand," Garion told her. "Please, just leave me alone."

"Please?" she repeated mockingly. "What a strange time for you to remember your manners. I didn't hear you saying please this morning. I didn't hear a single please. I didn't hear any thank you's either. Do you know what you are, Garion? You're a spoiled child, that's what you are."

That did it! To have this pampered, willful little princess call *him* a spoiled child was more than Garion could bear.

Infuriated, he began to shout at her. Most of what he said was wildly incoherent, but the shouting made him feel better.

They started with accusations, but the argument soon degenerated into name-calling. Ce'Nedra was screeching like a Camaar fishwife, and Garion's voice cracked and warbled between a manly baritone and a boyish tenor. They shook their fingers in each other's faces and shouted. Ce'Nedra stamped her feet, and Garion waved his arms. All in all, it was a splendid little fight. Garion felt much better when it was over. Yelling insults at Ce'Nedra was an innocent diversion compared to some of the deadly things he'd said to Aunt Pol that morning, and it allowed him to vent his confusion and anger harmlessly.

In the end, of course, Ce'Nedra resorted to tears and fled, leaving him feeling more foolish than ashamed. He fumed a bit, muttering a few choice insults he hadn't had the opportunity to deliver, and then he sighed and leaned pensively on the rail to watch night settle in over the dank city.

Though he would not have cared to admit it, even to himself, he was grateful to the princess. Their descent into absurdity had cleared his head. Quite clearly now he saw that he owed Aunt Pol an apology. He had lashed out at her out of his own sense of deep-seated guilt, trying somehow to shift the blame to her. Quite obviously there was no way to evade his own responsibility. Having accepted that, he seemed for some reason to feel better.

It grew darker. The tropical night was heavy, and the smell of rotting vegetation and stagnant water rolled in out of the trackless swamps. A vicious little insect crawled down inside his tunic and began to bite him somewhere between his shoulders where he could not reach.

There was absolutely no warning—no sound or lurch of the ship or any hint of danger. His arms were seized from behind and a wet cloth was pressed firmly over his mouth and nose. He tried to struggle, but the hands holding him were very strong. He tried to twist his head to get his face clear enough to shout for help. The cloth smelled strange—

cloying, sickeningly sweet, thick somehow. He began to feel dizzy, and his struggles grew weaker. He made one last effort before the dizziness overcame him and he sank down into unconsciousness.

Chapter Twenty-Seven

THEY WERE IN A LONG HALLWAY of some sort. Garion could see the flagstone floor quite clearly. Three men were carrying him face down, and his head bobbed and swung on his neck uncomfortably. His mouth was dry, and the thick, sweet smell that had impregnated the cloth they had crushed to his face lingered. He raised his head, trying to look around.

"He's awake," the man holding one of his arms said.

"Finally," one of the others muttered. "You held the cloth to his face too long, Issus."

"I know what I'm doing," the first one said. "Put him down."

"Can you stand?" Issus asked Garion. His shaved head was stubbled, and he had a long scar running from his forehead to his chin directly through the puckered vacancy of an empty eye-socket. His belted robe was stained and spotted.

"Get up," Issus ordered in a hissing kind of voice. He nudged Garion with his foot. Garion struggled to rise. His knees were shaky, and he put his hand on the wall to steady himself. The stones were damp and covered with a kind of mold.

"Bring him," Issus told the others. They took Garion's arms and half-dragged, half-carried him down the damp passageway behind the one-eyed man. When they came out of the corridor, they were in a vaulted area that seemed not so much like a room but rather a large roofed place. Huge pillars, covered with carvings, supported the soaring ceiling, and small oil lamps hung on long chains from above or sat on little stone shelves on the pillars. There was a confused sense of movement as groups of men in varicolored robes drifted from place to place in a kind of langorous stupor.

"You," Issus snapped at a plump young man with dreamy eyes, "tell Sadi, the chief eunuch, that we have the boy."

"Tell him yourself," the young man said in a piping voice. "I don't take orders from your kind, Issus."

Issus slapped the plump young man sharply across the face.

"You hit me!" the plump one wailed, putting his hand to his mouth. "You made my lip bleed—see?" He held out his hand to show the blood.

"If you don't do what I tell you to do, I'll cut your fat throat," Issus told him in a flat, unemotional voice.

"I'm going to tell Sadi what you did."

"Go ahead. And as long as you're there, tell him that we've got the boy the queen wanted."

The plump young man scurried away.

"Eunuchs!" One of the men holding Garion's arm spat.

"They have their uses," the other said with a coarse laugh.

"Bring the boy," Issus ordered. "Sadi doesn't like to be kept waiting."

They pulled Garion across the lighted area.

A group of wretched-looking men with unkempt hair and beards sat chained together on the floor. "Water," one of them croaked. "Please." He stretched out an imploring hand.

Issus stopped and stared at the slave in amazement. "Why does this one still have its tongue?" he demanded of the guard who stood over the slaves.

The guard shrugged. "We haven't had time to attend to that yet."

"Take time," Issus told him. "If one of the priests hear it talk, they'll have you questioned. You wouldn't like that."

"I'm not afraid of the priests," the guard said, but he looked nervously over his shoulder.

"Be afraid," Issus advised him. "And water these animals. They're no good to anybody dead." He started to lead the men holding Garion through a shadowy area between two pillars, then stopped again. "Get out of my way," he said to something lying in the shadows. Grudgingly, the thing began to move. With revulsion Garion realized that it was a large snake.

"Get over there with the others," Issus told the snake. He pointed toward a dimly lighted corner where a large mass seemed to be undulating, moving with a kind of sluggish seething. Faintly Garion could hear the dry hiss of scales rubbing together. The snake which had barred their way flicked a nervous tongue at Issus, then slithered toward the dim corner.

"Someday you're going to get bitten, Issus," one of the men warned. "They don't like being ordered around."

Issus shrugged indifferently and moved on.

"Sadi wants to talk to you," the plump young eunuch said spitefully to Issus as they approached a large polished door. "I told him that you hit me. Maas is with him."

"Good," Issus said. He pushed the door open. "Sadi," he called sharply, "tell your friend I'm coming in. I don't want him making any mistakes."

"He knows you, Issus," a voice on the other side of the door said. "He won't do anything by mistake."

Issus went in and closed the door behind him.

"You can leave now," one of the men holding Garion told the young eunuch.

The plump one sniffed. "I go where Sadi tells me to go."

"And come running when Sadi whistles, too."

"That's between Sadi and me, isn't it?"

"Bring him in," Issus ordered, opening the door again.

The two men pushed Garion into the room. "We'll wait out here," one of them said nervously.

Issus laughed harshly, pushed the door shut with his foot, and pulled Garion to the front of a table where a single oil lamp flickered with a tiny flame that barely held back the darkness. A thin man with dead-looking eyes sat at the table, lightly stroking his hairless head with the long fingers of one hand.

"Can you speak, boy?" he asked Garion. His voice had a strange contralto quality to it, and his silk robe was a solid crimson rather than varicolored.

"Could I have a drink of water?" Garion asked.

"In a minute."

"I'll take my money now, Sadi," Issus said.

"As soon as we're sure this is the right boy," Sadi replied.

"Ask it what its name is," a hissing whisper said from the darkness behind Garion.

"I will, Maas." Sadi looked faintly annoyed at the suggestion. "I've done this before."

"You're taking too long," the whisper said.

"Say your name, boy," Sadi told Garion.

"Doroon," Garion lied quickly. "I'm really very thirsty."

"Do you take me for a fool, Issus?" Sadi asked. "Did you think just any boy would satisfy me?"

"This is the boy you told me to fetch," Issus said. "I can't help it if your information was wrong."

"You say your name is Doroon?" Sadi asked.

"Yes," Garion said. "I'm the cabin-boy on Captain Greldik's ship. Where are we?"

"I'll ask the questions, boy," Sadi said.

"It's lying," the sibilant whisper came from behind Garion.

"I know that, Maas," Sadi replied calmly. "They always do at first."

"We don't have time for all this," the hiss said. "Give it oret. I need the truth immediately."

"Whatever you say, Maas," Sadi agreed. He rose to his feet and disappeared momentarily into the shadows behind the table. Garion heard a clink and then the sound of water pouring. "Remembering that this was your idea, Maas. If *she* becomes angry about it, I don't want to be the one she blames."

"She'll understand, Sadi."

"Here, boy," Sadi offered, coming back into the light and holding out a brown earthenware cup.

"Uh—no, thank you," Garion said. "I guess I'm not really thirsty after all."

"You might as well drink it, boy," Sadi told him. "If you don't, Issus will hold you, and I'll pour it down your throat. It isn't going to hurt you."

"Drink," the hissing voice commanded.

"Better do as they say," Issus advised.

Helplessly Garion took the cup. The water had a strangely bitter taste and seemed to burn his tongue.

"Much better," Sadi said, resuming his seat behind the table. "Now, you say your name is Doroon?"

"Yes."

"Where are you from, Doroon?"

"Sendaria."

"Where exactly in Sendaria?"

"Near Darine on the north coast."

"What are you doing on a Cherek ship?"

"Captain Greldik's a friend of my father," Garion said. For some reason he suddenly wanted to explain further. "My father wanted me to learn about ships. He says that being a sailor's better than being a farmer. Captain Greldik agreed to teach me what I'd need to know to be a sailor. He says I'll be good at it because I didn't even get seasick, and I'm not afraid to climb up the ropes that hold the sails in place, and I'm almost strong enough to pull an oar already, and—"

"What did you say your name was, boy?"

"Garion—I mean—uh—Doroon. Yes, Doroon, and—"

"How old are you, Garion?"

"Fifteen last Erastide. Aunt Pol says that people who are born on Erastide are very lucky, only I haven't noticed that I'm luckier than—"

"And who is Aunt Pol?"

"She's my aunt. We used to live on Faldor's farm, but Mister Wolf came and we—"

"Do people call her something besides Aunt Pol?"

"King Fulrach called her Polgara—that was when Captain Brendig took us all to the palace in Sendar. Then we went to King Anheg's palace in Val Alorn, and—"

"Who's Mister Wolf?"

"My grandfather. They call him Belgarath. I didn't used to believe it, but I guess it has to be true because one time he—"

"And why did you all leave Faldor's farm?"

"I didn't know why at first, but then I found out that it was because Zedar stole the Orb of Aldur off the pommel of the Sword of the Rivan King, and we've got to get it back before Zedar can take it to Torak and wake him up and—"

"This is the boy we want," the hissing voice whispered.

Garion turned around slowly. The room seemed brighter now, as if the tiny flame were putting out more light. In the corner, rearing out of its own coils and with a strangely flattened neck and glowing eyes was a very large snake.

"We can take it to Salmissra now," the snake hissed. It lowered itself to the foor and crawled across to Garion. He felt its cold, dry nose touch his leg, and then, though a hidden part of his mind shrieked, he stood unresisting as the scaly body slowly mounted his leg and coiled upward until the snake's head reared beside his face and its flickering tongue touched his face. "Be very good, boy," the snake hissed in his ear, "very, *very* good." The reptile was heavy, and its coils thick and cold.

"This way, boy," Sadi told Garion, rising to his feet.

"I want my money," Issus demanded.

"Oh," Sadi said almost contemptuously, "that. It's in that pouch there on the table." Then he turned and led Garion from the room.

"Garion." The dry voice that had always been in his mind spoke quietly to him. *"I want you to listen carefully. Don't say anything or let anything show on your face. Just listen to me."*

"W-who are you?" Garion asked silently, struggling with the fog in his brain.

"You know me," the dry voice told him. *"Now listen. They've given you something that makes you do what they want you to do. Don't fight against it. Just relax and don't fight it."*

"But—I said things I shouldn't have. I—"

"That doesn't matter now. Just do as I say. If anything happens and it starts to get dangerous, don't fight. I'll take care of it—but I can't do it if you're struggling. You have to relax so that I can do what has to be done. If you suddenly find yourself doing things or saying things you

don't understand, don't be afraid and don't try to fight. It won't be them; it will be me."

Comforted by this silent reassurance, Garion walked obediently beside Sadi the eunuch while the coils of the snake, Maas, lay heavily about his chest and shoulders and the bluntly pointed reptilian head rested, almost nuzzling, against his cheek.

They entered a large room where the walls were heavily draped and crystal oil lamps hung glittering on silver chains. An enormous stone statue, its upper third lost in the shadows high above, raised its mass titanically at one end of the room, and directly in front of the statue was a low stone platform, carpeted and strewn with cushions. Upon the platform stood a heavy divan that was not quite a chair and not quite a couch.

There was a woman on the divan. Her hair was raven-black, cascading in loose coils down her back and across her shoulders. About her head was an intricately wrought golden crown sparkling with jewels. He gown was white and spun of the filmiest gauze. It did not in any way conceal her body, but rather seemed to be worn only to provide a material to which her jewels and adornments could be attached. Beneath the gauze, her skin was an almost chalky white, and her face was extraordinarily beautiful. Her eyes were pale, even colorless. A large, gold-framed mirror stood on a pedestal at one side of the divan, and the woman lounged at ease, admiring herself in the glass.

To dozen shaven-headed eunuchs in crimson robes knelt in a cluster to one side of the dais, resting on their haunches and gazing at the woman and the statue behind her with worshipful adoration.

Among the cushions at the side of the divan lolled an indolent, pampered-looking young man whose head was not shaved. His hair was elaborately curled, his cheeks were rouged, and his eyes were fantastically made up. He wore only the briefest of loincloths, and his expression was bored and sulky. The woman absently ran the fingers of one hand through his curls as she watched herself in the mirror.

"The queen has visitors," one of the kneeling eunuchs announced in a singsong voice.

"Ah," the others chanted in unison, "visitors."

"Hail, Eternal Salmissra," Sadi the eunuch said, prostrating himself before the dais and the pale-eyed woman.

"What is it, Sadi?" she demanded. Her voice was vibrant and had a strange, dark timbre.

"The boy, my Queen," Sadi announced, his face still pressed to the floor.

"On your knees before the Serpent Queen," the snake hissed in Garion's ear. The coils tightened about Garion's body, and he fell to his knees in their sudden crushing grip.

"Come here, Maas," Salmissra said to the snake.

"The queen summons the beloved serpent," the eunuch intoned.

"Ah."

The reptile uncoiled itself from about Garion's body and undulated up to the foot of the divan, reared half its length above the reclining woman and then lowered itself upon her body, its thick length curving, fitting itself to her. The blunt head reached up to her face, and she kissed it affectionately. The long, forked tongue flickered over her face, and Maas began to whisper sibilantly in her ear. She lay in the embrace of the serpent, listening to its hissing voice and looking at Garion with heavy-lidded eyes.

Then, pushing the reptile aside, the queen rose to her feet and stood over Garion. "Welcome to the land of the snake-people, Belgarion," she said in her purring voice.

The name, which he had heard only from Aunt Pol before, sent a strange shock through Garion, and he tried to shake the fog from his head.

"Not yet," the dry voice in his mind warned him.

Salmissra stepped down from the dais, her body moving with a sinuous grace beneath her transparent gown. She took one of Garion's arms and drew him gently to his feet; then she touched his face lingeringly. Her hand seemed very cold. "A pretty young man," she breathed, almost as if to herself. "So young. So warm." Her look seemed somehow hungry.

A strange confusion seemed to fill Garion's mind. The bitter drink Sadi had given him still lay on his consciousness like a blanket. Beneath it he felt at once afraid and yet strangely attracted to the queen. Her chalky skin and dead eyes were repellent, yet there was a kind of lush invitation about her, an overripe promise of unspeakable delights. Unconsciously he took a step backward.

"Don't be afraid, my Belgarion," she purred at him. "I won't hurt you—not unless you want me to. Your duties here will be very pleasant, and I can teach you things that Polgara hasn't even dreamed of."

"Come away from him, Salmissra," the young man on the dais ordered petulantly. "You know I don't like it when you pay attention to others."

A flicker of annoyance showed in the queen's eyes. She turned and looked rather coldly at the young man. "What you like or don't like doesn't really concern me anymore, Essia," she said.

"What?" Essia cried incredulously. "Do as I say at once!"

"No, Essia," she told him.

"I'll punish you," he threatened.

"No," she said, "you won't. That sort of thing doesn't amuse me anymore, and all your pouting and tantrums have begun to grow boring. Leave now."

"Leave?" Essia's eyes bulged with disbelief.

"You're dismissed, Essia."

"Dismissed? But you can't live without me. You said so yourself."

"We all say things we don't mean sometimes."

The arrogance went out of the young man like water poured from a bucket. He swallowed hard and began to tremble. "When do you want me to come back?" he whined.

"I don't, Essia."

"Never?" he gasped.

"Never," she told him. "Now go, and stop making a scene."

"What's to become of me?" Essia cried. He began to weep, the makeup around his eyes running in grotesque streaks down his face.

"Don't be tiresome, Essia," Salmissra said. "Pick up your belongings and leave—now! I have a new consort." She stepped back up on the dais.

"The queen has chosen a consort," the eunuch intoned.

"Ah," the others chanted. "Hail the consort of Eternal Salmissra, most fortunate of men."

The sobbing young man grabbed up a pink robe and an ornately carved jewel box. He stumbled down from the dais. "*You* did this," he accused Garion. "It's all your fault." Suddenly, out of the folds of the robe draped over his arm, he pulled a small dagger. "I'll fix you," he screamed, raising the dagger to strike.

There was no thought this time, no gathering of will. The surge of force came without warning, pushing Essia away, driving him back. He slashed futilely at the air with his little knife. Then the surge was gone.

Essia lunged forward again, his eyes insane and his dagger raised. The surge came again, stronger this time. The young man was spun away. He fell, and his dagger clattered across the floor.

Salmissra, her eyes ablaze, pointed at the prostrate Essia and snapped her fingers twice. So fast that it seemed almost like an arrow loosed from a bow, a small green snake shot from beneath the divan, its mouth agape and its hiss a kind of snarl. It struck once, hitting Essia high on the leg, then slithered quickly to one side and watched with dead eyes.

Essia gasped and turned white with horror. He tried to rise, but his legs and arms suddenly sprawled out from under him on the polished stones. He gave one strangled cry and then the convulsions began. His heels pattered rapidly on the floor, and his arms flailed wildly. His eyes turned vacant and staring, and a green froth shot like a fountain from his mouth. His body arched back, every muscle writhing beneath his skin, and his head began to pound on the floor. He gave one thrashing, convulsive leap, his entire body bounding up from the floor. When he came down, he was dead.

Salmissra watched him die, her pale eyes expressionless, incurious, with no hint of anger or regret.

"Justice is done," the eunuch announced.

"Swift is the justice of the Queen of the Serpent People," the others replied.

Chapter Twenty-Eight

THERE WERE OTHER THINGS they made him drink—some bitter, some sickeningly sweet—and his mind seemed to sink deeper with each cup he raised to his lips. His eyes began to play strange tricks on him. It seemed somehow that the world had suddenly been drowned and that all of this was taking place under water. The walls wavered and the figures of the kneeling eunuchs seemed to sway and undulate like seaweed in the endless wash and eddy of tide and current. The lamps sparkled like jewels, casting out brilliant colors in slow-falling showers. Garion slumped, all bemused, on the dais near Salmissra's divan, his eyes filled with light and his head washed clean of all thought. There was no sense of time, no desire, no will. He briefly and rather vaguely remembered his friends, but the knowledge that he would never see them again brought only a brief, passing regret, a temporary melancholy that was rather pleasant. He even shed one crystal tear over his loss, but the tear landed on his wrist and sparkled with such an unearthly beauty that he lost himself utterly in contemplating it.

"How did he do it?" the queen's voice said somewhere behind him. Her voice was so beautifully musical that the sound of it pierced Garion's very soul.

"It has power," Maas replied, his serpent voice thrilling Garion's nerves, vibrating them like the strings of a lute. "Its power is untried, undirected, but it is very strong. Beware of this one, beloved Salmissra. It can destroy quite by accident."

"I will control him," she said.

"Perhaps," the snake replied.

"Sorcery requires will," Salmissra pointed out. "I will

take his will away from him. Your blood is cold, Maas, and you've never felt the fire that fills the veins with the taste of oret or athal or kaldiss. Your passions are also cold, and you can't know how much the body can be used to enslave the will. I'll put his mind to sleep and then smother his will with love."

"Love, Salmissra?" the snake asked, sounding faintly amused.

"The term serves as well as any other," she replied. "Call it appetite, if you wish."

"That I can understand," Maas agreed. "But don't underestimate this one—or overestimate your own power. It does not have an ordinary mind. There's something strange about it that I can't quite penetrate."

"We'll see," she said. "Sadi," she called the eunuch.

"Yes, my Queen?"

"Take the boy. Have him bathed and perfumed. He smells of boats and tar and salt water. I don't like such Alorn smells."

"At once, Eternal Salmissra."

Garion was led away to a place where there was warm water. His clothes were taken from him, and he was immersed and soaped and immersed again. Fragrant oils were rubbed into his skin, and a brief loincloth was tied about his waist. Then he was taken quite firmly by the chin and rouge was applied to his cheeks. It was during this process that he realized that the person painting his face was a woman. Slowly, almost incuriously, he let his eyes move around the bath chamber. He realized then that except for Sadi, everyone there was female. It seemed that something about that should bother him—something having to do with appearing naked in the presence of women—but he could not exactly remember what it was.

When the woman had finished painting his face, Sadi the eunuch took his arm and led him again through the dim, endless corridors back to the room where Salmissra half-lay on her divan beneath the statue, admiring herself in the pedestaled mirror beside her.

"Much better," she said, looking Garion up and down with a certain appreciation. "He's much more muscular than I thought. Bring him here."

Sadi led Garion to the side of the queen's divan and gently pressed him down onto the cushions where Essia had lounged.

Salmissra reached out with a lingeringly slow hand and brushed her cold fingertips across his face and chest. Her pale eyes seemed to burn, and her lips parted slightly. Garion's eyes fixed themselves on her pale arm. There was no trace of hair on that white skin.

"Smooth," he said vaguely, struggling to focus on that peculiarity.

"Of course, my Belgarion," she murmured. "Serpents are hairless, and I am the queen of the serpents."

Slowly, puzzled, he raised his eyes to the lustrous black tresses tumbling down across one of her white shoulders.

"Only this," she said, touching the curls with a sensuous kind of vanity.

"How?" he asked.

"It's a secret." She laughed. "Someday perhaps I'll show you. Would you like that?"

"I suppose so."

"Tell me, Belgarion," she said, "do you think I'm beautiful?"

"I think so."

"How old would you say I am?" She spread her arms so that he could see her body through the filmy gauze of her gown.

"I don't know," Garion said. "Older than I am, but not too old."

A brief flicker of annoyance crossed her face. "Guess," she ordered somewhat harshly.

"Thirty perhaps," he decided, confused.

"*Thirty?*" Her voice was stricken. Swiftly she turned to her mirror and examined her face minutely. "You're blind, you idiot!" she snapped, still staring at herself in the glass. "That's not the face of a woman of thirty. Twenty-three—twenty-five at the most."

"Whatever you say," he agreed.

"Twenty-three," she stated firmly. "Not a single day over twenty-three."

"Of course," he said mildly.

"Would you believe that I'm nearly sixty?" she demanded, her eyes suddenly flint-hard.

"No," Garion denied. "I couldn't believe that—not sixty."

"What a charming boy you are, Belgarion," she breathed at him, her glance melting. Her fingers returned to his face, touching, stroking, caressing. Slowly, beneath the pale skin of her naked shoulder and throat, curious patches of color began to appear, a faint mottling of green and purple that seemed to shift and pulsate, growing first quite visible and then fading. Her lips parted again, and her breathing grew faster. The mottling spread down her torso beneath her transparent gown, the colors seeming to writhe beneath her skin.

Maas crept nearer, his dead eyes suddenly coming awake with a strange adoration. The vivid pattern of his own scaly skin so nearly matched the colors that began to emerge upon the body of the Serpent Queen that when he draped a caressing coil across one of her shoulders it became impossible to say exactly where lay the boundary between the snake and the woman.

Had Garion not been in a half-stupor, he would have recoiled from the queen. Her colorless eyes and mottled skin seemed reptilian, and her openly lustful expression spoke of some dreadful hunger. Yet there was a curious attraction about her. Helplessly he felt drawn by her blatant sensuality.

"Come closer, my Belgarion," she ordered softly. "I'm not going to hurt you." Her eyes gloated over her possession of him.

Not far from the dais, Sadi the eunuch cleared his throat. "Divine Queen," he announced, "the emissary of Taur Urgas requests a word with you."

"Of Ctuchik, you mean," Salmissra said, looking faintly annoyed. Then a thought seemed to cross her mind, and she smiled maliciously. The mottling of her skin faded. "Bring the Grolim in," she instructed Sadi.

Sadi bowed and withdrew to return a moment later with a scar-faced man in the garb of a Murgo.

"Give welcome to the emissary of Taur Urgas," the eunuch chanted.

"Welcome," the chorus replied.

"Carefully now," the dry voice in his mind said to Garion. *"That's the one we saw at the harbor."*

Garion looked more carefully at the Murgo and realized that it was true.

"Hail, Eternal Salmissra," the Grolim said perfunctorily, bowing first to the queen and then to the statue behind her. "Taur Urgas, King of Cthol Murgos, sends greetings to the Spirit of Issa and to his handmaiden."

"And are there no greetings from Ctuchik, High Priest of the Grolims?" she asked, her eyes bright.

"Of course," the Grolim said, "but those are customarily given in private."

"Is your errand here on behalf of Taur Urgas or of Ctuchik?" she inquired, turning to examine her reflection in the mirror.

"May we speak in private, your Highness?" the Grolim asked.

"We *are* in private," she said.

"But—" He looked around at the kneeling eunuchs in the room.

"My body servants," she said. "A Nyissan queen is never left alone. You should know that by now."

"And that one? The Grolim pointed at Garion.

"He is also a servant—but of a slightly different kind."

The Grolim shrugged. "Whatever you wish. I salute you in the name of Ctuchik, High Priest of the Grolims and Disciple of Torak."

"The Handmaiden of Issa salutes Ctuchik of Rak Cthol," she responded formally. "What does the Grolim High Priest want of me?"

"The boy, your Highness," the Grolim said bluntly.

"Which boy is that?"

"The boy you stole from Polgara and who now sits at your feet."

She laughed scornfully. "Convey my regrets to Ctuchik," she said, "but that would be impossible."

"It's unwise to deny the wishes of Ctuchik," the Grolim warned.

"It's even more unwise to make demands of Salmissra in her own palace," she said. "What is Ctuchik prepared to offer for this boy?"

"His eternal friendship."

"What need has the Serpent Queen of friends?"

"Gold, then," the Grolim offered with annoyance.

"I know the secret of the red gold of Angarak," she told him. "I don't wish to become a slave to it. Keep your gold, Grolim."

"Might I say that the game you play is very dangerous, your Highness?" the Grolim said coolly. "You've already made Polgara your enemy. Can you afford the enmity of Ctuchik as well?"

"I'm not afraid of Polgara," she answered. "Nor of Ctuchik."

"The queen's bravery is remarkable," he said dryly.

"This is beginning to get tiresome. My terms are very simple. Tell Ctuchik that I have Torak's enemy, and I will keep him—unless—" She paused.

"Unless what, your Highness?"

"If Ctuchik will speak to Torak for me, an agreement might be reached."

"What sort of agreement?"

"I will give the boy to Torak as a wedding gift."

The Grolim blinked.

"If Torak will make me his bride and give me immortality, I will deliver Belgarion up to him."

"All the world knows that the Dragon God of Angarak is bound in slumber," the Grolim objected.

"But he will not sleep forever," Salmissra said flatly. "The priests of Angarak and the sorcerers of Aloria always seem to forget that Eternal Salmissra can read the signs in the heavens as clearly as they. The day of Torak's awakening is at hand. Tell Ctuchik that upon the day that I am wed to Torak, Belgarion will be in his hands. Until that day, the boy is mine."

"I shall deliver your message to Ctuchik," the Grolim said with a stiff, icy bow.

"Leave, then," she told him with an airy wave of her hand.

"So that's it," the voice in Garion's mind said as the Grolim left. *"I should have known, I suppose."*

Maas the serpent suddenly raised his head, his great neck flaring and his eyes burning. "Beware!" he hissed.

"Of the Grolim?" Salmissra laughed. "I have nothing to fear from him."

"Not the Grolim," Maas said. "*That* one." He flickered his tongue at Garion. "Its mind is awake."

"That's impossible," she objected.

"Nevertheless, its mind is awake. It has to do, I think, with that metal thing around its neck."

"Remove the ornament then," she told the snake.

Maas lowered his length to the floor and slid around the divan toward Garion.

"*Remain very still,*" Garion's inner voice told him. "*Don't try to fight.*"

Numbly, Garion watched the blunt head draw closer.

Mass raised his head, his hood flaring. His nervous tongue darted. Slowly he leaned forward. His nose touched the silver amulet hanging about Garion's neck.

There was a bright blue spark as the reptile's head came in contact with the amulet. Garion felt the familiar surge, but tightly controlled now, focused down to a single point. Maas recoiled, and the spark from the amulet leaped out, sizzling through the air, linking the silver disc to the reptile's nose. The snake's eyes began to shrivel and steam poured from his nostrils and his gaping mouth.

Then the spark was gone, and the body of the dead snake writhed and twisted convulsively on the polished stone floor of the chamber.

"*Maas!*" Salmissra shrieked.

The eunuchs scrambled out of the way of the wildly threshing body of the snake.

"My Queen!" a shaved-headed functionary gibbered from the door, "the world is ending!"

"What?" Salmissra tore her eyes from the convulsions of the snake.

"The sun has gone out! Noon is as dark as midnight! The city is gone mad with terror!"

Chapter Twenty-Nine

IN THE TUMULT WHICH FOLLOWED that announcement, Garion sat quietly on the cushions beside Salmissra's throne. The quiet voice in his mind, however, was speaking to him rapidly. *"Stay very still,"* the voice told him. *"Don't say anything, and don't do anything."*

"Get my astronomers here immediately!" Salmissra ordered. "I want to know why I wasn't warned about this eclipse."

"It's not an eclipse, my Queen," the bald functionary wailed, groveling on the polished floor not far from the still-writhing Maas. "The dark came like a great curtain. It was like a moving wall—no wind, no rain, no thunder. It swallowed the sun without a sound." He began to sob brokenly. "We shall never see the sun again."

"Stop that, you idiot," Salmissra snapped. "Get on your feet. Sadi, take this babbling fool out of here and go look at the sky. Then come back to me here. I have to know what's going on."

Sadi shook himself almost like a dog coming out of the water and pulled his fascinated eyes off the dead, fixed grin on the face of Maas. He pulled the blubbering functionary to his feet and led him out of the chamber.

Salmissra turned then on Garion. "How did you do that?" she demanded, pointing at the twitching form of Maas.

"I don't know," he said. His mind was still sunk in fog. Only the quiet corner where the voice lived was alert.

"Take off that amulet," she commanded.

Obediently, Garion reached his hands toward the medallion. Suddenly his hands froze. They would not move. He let them fall. "I can't," he said.

"Take it from him," she ordered one of the eunuchs. The man glanced once at the dead snake, then stared at Garion. He shook his head and backed away in fright.

"Do as I say!" the Snake Queen ordered sharply.

From somewhere in the palace came a hollow, reverberating crash. There was the sound of nails screeching out of heavy wood and the avalanche noise of a wall collapsing. Then, a long way down one of the dim corridors, someone screamed in agony.

The dry consciousness in his mind reached out, probing. *"At last,"* it said with obvious relief.

"What's going on out there?" Salmissra blazed.

"Come with me," the voice in Garion's mind said. *"I need your help."*

Garion put his hands under him and started to push himself up.

"No. This way." A strange image of separation rose in Garion's mind. Unthinking, he willed the separation and felt himself rising and yet not moving. Suddenly he had no sense of his body—no arms or legs—yet he seemed to move. He saw himself—his own body—sitting stupidly on the cushions at Salmissra's feet.

"Hurry," the voice said to him. It was no longer inside his mind but seemed to be somewhere beside him. A dim shape was there, formless but somehow very familiar.

The fog that had clouded Garion's wits was gone, and he felt very alert. "Who are you?" he demanded of the shape beside him.

"There isn't time to explain. Quickly, we have to lead them back before Salmissra has time to do anything."

"Lead who?"

Polgara and Barak."

"Aunt Pol? Where is she?"

"Come," the voice said urgently. Together Garion and the strange presence at his side seemed to waft toward the closed door. They passed through it as if it were no more than insubstantial mist and emerged in the corridor outside.

Then they were flying, soaring down the corridor with no sense of air rushing past or even of movement. A moment later they came out into that vast open hall where

Issus had first brought Garion when they had entered the palace. There they stopped, hovering in the air.

Aunt Pol, her splendid eyes ablaze and a fiery nimbus about her, strode through the hall. Beside her hulked the great shaggy bear Garion had seen before. Barak's face seemed vaguely within that bestial head, but there was no humanity in it. The beast's eyes were afire with raging madness, and its mouth gaped horribly.

Desperate guards tried to push the bear back with long pikes, but the beast swiped the pikes away and fell upon the guards. Its vast embrace crushed them, and its flailing claws ripped them open. The trail behind Aunt Pol and the bear was littered with maimed bodies and quivering chunks of flesh.

The snakes which had lain in the corners were seething across the floor, but as they came into contact with the flaming light which surrounded Aunt Pol, they died even as Maas had died.

Methodically, Aunt Pol was blasting down doors with word and gesture. A thick wall barred her way, and she brushed it into rubble as if it had been made of cobwebs.

Barak raged through the dim hall, roaring insanely, destroying everything in his path. A shrieking eunuch tried desperately to climb one of the pillars. The great beast reared up and hooked his claws into the man's back and pulled him down. The shrieks ended abruptly in a spurt of brains and blood when the massive jaws closed with a sickening crunch on the eunuch's head.

"Polgara!" the presence beside Garion shouted soundlessly. "This way!"

Aunt Pol turned quickly.

"Follow us," the presence said. "Hurry!"

Then Garion and that other part of himself were flying back down the corridor toward Salmissra and the semiconscious body they had recently vacated. Behind them came Aunt Pol and the ravening Barak.

Garion and his strange companion passed again through the heavy, closed door.

Salmissra, her naked body mottled now with rage rather than lust beneath her transparent gown, stood over the vacant-eyed form on the cushions. "Answer me!" she was shouting. "Answer me!"

"When we get back," the shapeless presence said, "let me handle things. We have to buy some time."

And then they were back. Garion felt his body shudder briefly, and he was looking out through his own eyes again. The fog which had benumbed him before came rushing back. "What?" his lips said, though he had not consciously formed the word.

"I said, is this your doing?" Salmissra demanded.

"Is what my doing?" The voice coming from his lips sounded like his, but there was a subtle difference.

"All of it," she said. "The darkness. The attack on my palace."

"I don't think so. How could I? I'm only a boy."

"Don't lie to me, Belgarion," she demanded. "I know who you are. I know what you are. It has to be you. Belgarath himself could not blot out the sun. I warn you, Belgarion, what you have drunk today is death. Even now the poison in your veins is killing you."

"Why did you do that to me?"

"To keep you. You must have more or you will die. You must drink what only I can give you, and you must drink every day of your life. You're mine, Belgarion, *mine!*"

Despairing shrieks came from just outside the door.

The Serpent Queen looked up, startled, then she turned to the huge statue behind her, bowed down in a strange ceremonial way and began to weave her hands through the air in a series of intricate gestures. She started to pronounce an involved formula in a language Garion had never heard before, a language filled with guttural hissings and strange cadences.

The heavy door exploded inward, blasted into splinters, and Aunt Pol stood in the shattered doorway, her white lock ablaze and her eyes dreadful. The great bear at her side roared, his teeth dripping blood and with tatters of flesh still hanging from his claws.

"I've warned you, Salmissra." Aunt Pol spoke in a deadly voice.

"Stop where you are, Polgara," the queen ordered. She did not turn around, and her fingers continued their sinuous weaving in the air. "The boy is dying," she said. "Nothing can save him if you attack me."

Aunt Pol stopped. "What have you done?" she demanded.

"Look at him," Salmissra said. "He has drunk athal and kaldiss. Even now their fire is in his veins. He will need more very soon." Her hands still moved in the air, and her face was fixed in extreme concentration. Her lips began moving again in that guttural hissing.

"Is it true?" Aunt Pol's voice echoed in Garion's mind.

"It seems to be," the dry voice replied. *"They made him drink things, and he seems different now."*

Aunt Pol's eyes widened. *"Who are you?"*

"I've always been here, Polgara. Didn't you know that?"

"Did Garion know?"

"He knows that I'm here. He doesn't know what it means."

"We can talk about that later," she decided. *"Watch very closely. This is what you have to do."* A confused blur of images welled up in Garion's mind. *"Do you understand?"*

"Of course. I'll show him how."

"Can't you do it?"

"No, Polgara," the dry voice said. *"The power is his, not mine. Don't worry. He and I understand each other."*

Garion felt strangely alone as the two voices spoke together in his mind.

"Garion." The dry voice spoke quietly. *"I want you to think about your blood."*

"My blood?"

"We're going to change it for a moment."

"Why?"

"To burn away the poison they gave you. Now concentrate on your blood."

Garion did.

"You want it to be like this." An image of yellow came into Garion's mind. *"Do you understand?"*

"Yes."

"Do it, then. Now."

Garion put his fingertips to his chest and willed his blood to change. He suddenly felt as if he were on fire. His heart began to pound, and a heavy sweat burst out all over his body.

"*A moment longer,*" the voice said.

Garion was dying. His altered blood seared through his veins, and he began to tremble violently. His heart hammered in his chest like a tripping sledge. His eyes went dark, and he began to topple slowly forward.

"*Now!*" the voice demanded sharply. "*Change it back.*"

Then it was over. Garion's heart stuttered and then faltered back to its normal pace. He was exhausted, but the fog in his brain was gone.

"*It's done, Polgara,*" the other Garion said. "*You can do what needs doing now.*"

Aunt Pol had watched anxiously, but now her face became dreadfully stern. She walked across the polished floor toward the dais. "Salmissra," she said, "turn around and look at me."

The queen's hands were raised above her head now, and the hissing words tumbled from her lips, rising finally to a hoarse shout.

Then, far above them in the shadows near the ceiling, the eyes of the huge statue opened and began to glow a deep emerald fire. A polished jewel on Salmissra's crown began also to burn with the same glow.

The statue moved. The sound it made was a kind of ponderous creaking, deafeningly loud. The solid rock from which the huge shape had been hewn bent and flexed as the statue took a step forward and then another.

"Why—did—you—summon—me?" An enormous voice demanded through stiff, stony lips. The voice reverberated hollowly up from the massive chest.

"Defend thy handmaiden, Great Issa," Salmissra cried, turning to look triumphantly at Aunt Pol. "This evil sorceress hath invaded thy domain to slay me. Her wicked power is so great that none may withstand her. I am thy promised bride, and I place myself under thy protection."

"Who is this who defiles my temple?" the statue demanded in a vast roar. "Who dares to raise her hand against my chosen and beloved?" The emerald eyes flashed in dreadful wrath.

Aunt Pol stood alone in the center of the polished floor

with the vast statue looming above her. Her face was un-afraid. "You go too far, Salmissra," she said. "This is forbid-den."

The Serpent Queen laughed scornfully. "Forbidden? What does your forbidding mean to me? Flee now, or face the wrath of Divine Issa. Contend if you will with a God!"

"If I must," Aunt Pol said. She straightened then and spoke a single word. The roaring in Garion's mind at that word was overwhelming. Then, suddenly, she began to grow. Foot by foot she towered up, rising like a tree, ex-panding, growing gigantic before Garion's stunned eyes. Within a moment she faced the great stone God as an equal.

"Polgara?" the God's voice sounded puzzled. "Why have you done this?"

"I come in fulfillment of the Prophecy, Lord Issa," she said. "Thy handmaiden hath betrayed thee and thy broth-ers."

"It cannot be so," Issa said. "She is my chosen one. Her face is the face of my beloved."

"The face is the same," Aunt Pol said, "but this is not the Salmissra beloved of Issa. A hundred Salmissras have served thee in this temple since thy beloved died."

"Died?" the God said incredulously.

"She lies!" Salmissra shrieked. "I am thy beloved, O my Lord. Let not her lies turn thee from me. Kill her."

"The Prophecy approaches its day," Aunt Pol said. "The boy at Salmissra's feet is its fruit. He must be returned to me, or the Prophecy will fail."

"Is the day of the Prophecy come so soon?" the God asked.

"It is not soon, Lord Issa," Aunt Pol said. "It is late. Thy slumber hath encompassed eons."

"Lies! All lies!" Salmissra cried desperately, clinging to the ankle of the huge stone God.

"I must test out the truth of this," the God said slowly. "I have slept long and deeply, and now the world comes upon me unaware."

"Destroy her, O my Lord!" Salmissra demanded. "Her lies are an abomination and a desecration of thy holy pres-ence."

"I will find the truth, Salmissra," Issa said.

Garion felt a brief, enormous touch upon his mind. Something had brushed him—something so vast that his imagination shuddered back from its immensity. Then the touch moved on.

"Ahhh—" The sigh came from the floor. The dead snake Maas stirred. "Ahhh— Let me sleep," it hissed.

"In but a moment," Issa said. "What was your name?"

"I was called Maas," the snake said. "I was counsellor and companion to Eternal Salmissra. Send me back, Lord. I cannot bear to live again."

"Is this my beloved Salmissra?" the God asked.

"Her successor." Maas sighed. "Thy beloved priestess died thousands of years ago. Each new Salmissra is chosen because of her resemblance to thy beloved."

"Ah," Issa said with pain in his huge voice. "And what was this woman's purpose in removing Belgarion from Polgara's care?"

"She sought alliance with Torak," Maas said. "She thought to trade Belgarion to the Accursed One in exchange for the immortality his embrace would bestow upon her."

"His embrace? My priestess would submit to the foul embrace of my mad brother?"

"Willingly, Lord," Maas said. "It is her nature to seek the embrace of any man or God or beast who passes."

A look of repugnance flickered across Issa's stony face. "Has it always been so?" he asked.

"Always, Lord," Maas said. "The potion which maintains her youth and semblance to thy beloved sets her veins afire with lust. That fire remains unquenched until she dies. Let me go, Lord. The pain!"

"Sleep, Maas," Issa granted sorrowfully. "Take my thanks with you down into silent death."

"Ahhh—" Maas sighed and sank down again.

"I too will return to slumber," Issa said. "I must not remain, lest my presence rouse Torak to that war which would unmake the world." The great statue stepped back to the spot where it had stood for thousands of years. The deafening creak and groan of flexing rock again filled the huge chamber. "Deal with this woman as it pleases thee,

Polgara," the stone God said. "Only spare her life out of remembrance of my beloved."

"I will, Lord Issa," Aunt Pol said, bowing to the statue.

"And carry my love to my brother, Aldur," the hollow voice said, fading even as it spoke.

"Sleep, Lord," Aunt Pol said. "May thy slumber wash away thy grief."

"No!" Salmissra wailed, but the green fire had already died in the statue's eyes, and the jewel on her crown flickered and went dark.

"It's time, Salmissra," Aunt Pol, vast and terrible, announced.

"Don't kill me, Polgara," the queen begged, falling to her knees. "Please don't kill me."

"I'm not going to kill you, Salmissra," Aunt Pol told her. "I promised Lord Issa that I would spare your life."

"I didn't make any such promise," Barak said from the doorway. Garion looked sharply at his huge friend, dwarfed now by Aunt Pol's immensity. The bear was gone, and in its place the big Cherek stood, sword in hand.

"No, Barak. I'm going to solve the problem of Salmissra once and for all." Aunt Pol turned back to the groveling queen. "You will live, Salmissra. You'll live for a very long time—eternally, perhaps."

An impossible hope dawned in Salmissra's eyes. Slowly she rose to her feet and looked up at the huge figure rising above her. "Eternally, Polgara?" she asked.

"But I must change you," Aunt Pol said. "The poison you've drunk to keep you young and beautiful is slowly killing you. Even now its traces are beginning to show on your face."

The queen's hands flew to her cheeks, and she turned quickly to look into her mirror.

"You're decaying, Salmissra," Aunt Pol said. "Soon you'll be ugly and old. The lust which fills you will burn itself out, and you'll die. Your blood's too warm; that's the whole problem."

"But how——" Salmissra faltered.

"A little change," Aunt Pol assured her. "Just a small one, and you'll live forever." Garion could feel the force of her will gathering itself. "I will make you eternal, Salmissra." She raised her hand and spoke a single word. The terrible force of that word shook Garion like a leaf in the wind.

At first nothing seemed to happen. Salmissra stood fixed with her pale nakedness gleaming through her gown. Then the strange mottling grew more pronounced, and her thighs pressed tightly together. Her face began to shift, to grow more pointed. Her lips disappeared as her mouth spread, and its corners slid up into a fixed reptilian grin.

Garion watched in horror, unable to take his eyes off the queen. Her gown slid away as her shoulders disappeared and her arms adhered to her sides. Her body began to elongate, and her legs, grown completely together now, began to loop into coils. Her lustrous hair disappeared, and the last vestiges of humanity faded from her face. Her golden crown, however, remained firmly upon her head. Her tongue flickered as she sank down into the mass of her loops and coils. The hood upon her neck spread as she looked with flat, dead eyes at Aunt Pol, who had somehow during the queen's transformation resumed her normal size.

"Ascend your throne, Salmissra," Aunt Pol said.

The queen's head remained immobile, but her coils looped and mounted the cushioned divan, and the sound of coil against coil was a dry, dusty rasp.

Aunt Pol turned to Sadi the eunuch. "Behold the Handmaiden of Issa, the queen of the snake-people, whose dominion shall endure until the end of days, for she *is* immortal now and will reign in Nyissa forever."

Sadi's face was ghastly pale, and his eyes bulged wildly. He swallowed hard and nodded.

"I'll leave you with your queen, then," she told him. "I'd prefer to go peacefully, but one way or another, the boy and I are leaving."

"I'll send word ahead," Sadi agreed quickly. "No one will try to bar your way."

"Wise decision," Barak said dryly.

"All hail the Serpent Queen of Nyissa," one of the crimson-robed eunuchs pronounced in a shaking voice, sinking to his knees before the dais.

"Praise her," the others responded ritualistically, also kneeling.

"Her glory is revealed to us."

"Worship her."

Garion glanced back once as he followed Aunt Pol toward the shattered door. Salmissra lay upon her throne with her mottled coils redundantly piled and her hooded head turned toward the mirror. The golden crown sat atop her head, and her flat, serpent eyes regarded her reflection in the glass. There was no expression on her reptile face, so it was impossible to know what she was thinking.

Chapter Thirty

THE CORRIDORS AND VAULTED HALLS of the palace were empty as Aunt Pol led them from the throne room where the eunuchs knelt, chanting their praises to the Serpent Queen. Sword in hand, Barak stalked grimly through the awful carnage that marked the trail he had left when he had entered. The big man's face was pale, and he frequently averted his eyes from some of the more savagely mutilated corpses that littered their way.

When they emerged, they found the streets of Sthiss Tor darker than night and filled with hysterical crowds wailing in terror. Barak, with a torch he had taken from the palace wall in one hand and his huge sword in the other, led them into the street. Even in their panic the Nyissans made way for him.

"What is this, Polgara?" he growled over his shoulder, waving the torch slightly as if to brush the darkness away. "Is it some kind of sorcery?"

"No," she answered. "It's not sorcery."

Tiny flecks of gray were falling through the torchlight. "Snow?" Barak asked incredulously.

"No," she said. "Ashes."

"What's burning?"

"A mountain," she replied. "Let's get back to the ship as quickly as we can. There's more danger from this crowd than from any of this." She threw her light cloak about Garion's shoulders and pointed down a street where a few torches bobbed here and there. "Let's go that way."

The ash began to fall more heavily. It was almost like dirty gray flour sifting down through the sodden air, and there was a dreadful, sulfurous stink to it.

By the time they reached the wharves, the absolute darkness had begun to pale. The ash continued to drift down, seeping into the cracks between the cobblestones and gathering in little windrows along the edges of the buildings. Though it was growing lighter, the falling ash, like fog, blotted out everything more than ten feet away.

The wharves were total chaos. Crowds of Nyissans, shrieking and wailing were trying to climb into boats to flee from the choking ash that sifted with deadly silence down through the damp air. Mad with terror, many even leaped into the deadly waters of the river.

"We're not going to be able to get through that mob, Polgara," Barak said. "Stay here a moment." He sheathed his sword, jumped up and caught the edge of a low roof. He pulled himself up and stood outlined dimly above them. "Ho, Greldik!" he roared in a huge voice that carried even over the noise of the crowd.

"Barak!" Greldik's voice came back. "Where are you?"

"At the foot of the pier," Barak shouted. "We can't get through the crowd."

"Stay there," Greldik yelled back. "We'll come and get you."

After a few moments there was the tramp of heavy feet on the wharf and the occasional sound of blows. A few cries of pain mingled with the sounds of panic from the crowd. Then Greldik, Mandorallen and a half-dozen burly sailors armed with clubs strode out of the ashfall, clearing a path with brutal efficiency.

"Did you get lost?" Greldik yelled up to Barak.

Barak jumped down from the roof. "We had to stop by the palace," he answered shortly.

"We were growing concerned for thy safety, my Lady," Mandorallen told Aunt Pol, pushing a gibbering Nyissan out of his way. "Good Durnik returned some hours ago."

"We were delayed," she said. "Captain, can you get us on board your ship?"

Greldik gave her an evil grin.

"Let's go then," she urged. "As soon as we get on board, it might be a good idea to anchor out in the river a little way. This ash will settle after a while, but these people are going to be hysterical until it does. Has there been any word from Silk or my father yet?"

"Nothing, my Lady," Greldik said.

"What *is* he doing?" she demanded irritably of no one in particular.

Mandorallen drew his broadsword and marched directly into the face of the crowd, neither slowing nor altering his course. The Nyissans melted out of his path.

The crowd pressing at the edge of the wharf beside Greldik's ship was even thicker, and Durnik, Hettar and the rest of the sailors lined the rail with long boat-hooks, pushing the terror-stricken people away.

"Run out the plank," Greldik shouted as they reached the edge of the wharf.

"Noble captain," a bald Nyissan blubbered, clinging to Greldik's fur vest. "I'll give you a hundred gold pieces if you'll let me aboard your ship."

Disgusted, Greldik pushed him away.

"A thousand gold pieces," the Nyissan promised, clutching Greldik's arm and waving a purse.

"Get this baboon off me," Greldik ordered.

One of the sailors rather casually clubbed the Nyissan into insensibility, then bent and yanked the purse from his grip. He opened the purse and poured the coins out into one hand. "Three pieces of silver," he said with disgust. "All the rest is copper." He turned back and kicked the unconscious man in the stomach.

They crossed to the ship one by one while Barak and Mandorallen held the crowd back with the threat of massive violence.

"Cut the hawsers," Greldik shouted when they were all aboard.

The sailors chopped the thick hawsers loose to a great cry of dismay from the Nyissans crowding the edge of the wharf. The sluggish current pulled the ship slowly away, and wails and despairing moans followed them as they drifted.

"Garion," Aunt Pol said, "why don't you go below and put on some decent clothes? And wash that disgusting rouge off your face. Then come back up here. I want to talk to you."

Garion had forgotten how scantily he was dressed and he flushed slightly and went quickly below deck.

It had grown noticeably lighter when he came back up, dressed again in tunic and hose, but the gray ash still sifted down through the motionless air, making the world around them hazy and coating everything with a heavy layer of fine grit. They had drifted some distance out into the river, and Greldik's sailors had dropped the anchor. The ship swung slowly in the sluggish current.

"Over here, Garion," Aunt Pol called. She was standing near the prow, looking out into the dusty haze. Garion went to her a little hesitantly, the memory of what had happened at the palace still strong in his mind.

"Sit down, dear," she suggested. "There's something I have to talk with you about."

"Yes, ma'am," he said, sitting on the bench there.

"Garion." She turned to look at him. "Did anything happen while you were in Salmissra's palace?"

"What do you mean?"

"You know what I mean," she said rather crisply. "You're not going to embarrass us both by making me ask certain questions, are you?"

"Oh." Garion blushed. "That! No, nothing like that happened." He remembered the lush overripeness of the queen with a certain regret.

"Good. That was the one thing I was afraid of. You can't afford to get involved in any of that sort of thing just yet. It has some peculiar effects on one in your rather special circumstances."

"I'm not sure I understand," he said.

"You have certain abilities," she told him. "And if you start experimenting with that other thing before they're fully matured, the results can sometimes be a bit unpredictable. It's better not to confuse things at this point."

"Maybe it'd be better if something *had* happened, then," Garion blurted. "Maybe it would have fixed it so I couldn't hurt people anymore."

"I doubt it," she said. "Your power's too great to be neutralized so easily. Do you remember what we talked about that day when we left Tolnedra—about instruction?"

"I don't need any instruction," he protested, his tone growing sullen.

"Yes, you do," she said, "and you need it now. Your power is enormous—more power than I've ever seen before, and some of it so complex that I can't even begin to understand it. You *must* begin your instruction before something disastrous happens. You're totally out of control, Garion. If you're really serious about not wanting to hurt people, you should be more than willing to start learning how to keep any accidents from happening."

"I don't *want* to be a sorcerer," he objected. "All I want to do is get rid of it. Can't you help me do that?"

She shook her head. "No. And I wouldn't even if I could. You can't renounce it, my Garion. It's part of you."

"Then I'm going to be a monster?" Garion demanded bitterly. "I'm going to go around burning people alive or turning them into toads or snakes? And maybe after a while I'll get so used to it that it won't even bother me anymore. I'll live forever—like you and grandfather—but I won't be human anymore. Aunt Pol, I think I'd rather be dead."

"Can't you reason with him?" Her voice inside his head spoke directly to that other awareness.

"Not at the moment, Polgara," the dry voice replied. *"He's too busy wallowing in self-pity."*

"He must learn to control the power he has," she said.

"I'll keep him out of mischief," the voice promised. *"I don't think there's much else we can do until Belgarath gets back. He's going through a moral crisis, and we can't really tamper with him until he works out his own solutions to it."*

"I don't like to see him suffering this way."

"You're too tender-hearted, Polgara. He's a sturdy boy, and a bit of suffering won't damage him."

"Will the two of you stop treating me as if I'm not even here?" Garion demanded angrily.

"Mistress Pol," Durnik said, coming across the deck to them, "I think you'd better come quickly. Barak's going to kill himself."

"He's *what?*" she asked.

"It's something about some curse," Durnik explained. "He says he's going to fall on his sword."

"That idiot! Where is he?"

"He's back by the stern," Durnik said. "He's got his sword out, and he won't let anybody near him."

"Come with me." She started toward the stern with Garion and Durnik behind her.

"We have all experienced battle madness, my Lord," Mandorallen was saying, trying to reason with the big Cherek. "It is not a thing of which to be proud, but neither is it a cause for such bleak despair."

Barak did not answer, but stood at the very stern of the ship, his eyes blank with horror and his huge sword weaving in a slow, menacing arc, holding everyone at bay.

Aunt Pol walked through the crowd of sailors and directly up to him.

"Don't try to stop me, Polgara," he warned.

She reached out quite calmly and touched the point of his sword with one finger. "It's a little dull," she said thoughtfully. "Why don't we have Durnik sharpen it? That way it'll slip more smoothly between your ribs when you fall on it."

Barak looked a bit startled.

"Have you made all the necessary arrangements?" she asked.

"What arrangements?"

"For the disposal of your body," she told him. "Really, Barak, I thought you had better manners. A decent man doesn't burden his friends with that kind of chore." She thought a moment. "Burning is customary, I suppose, but the wood here in Nyissa's very soggy. You'd probably smolder for a week or more. I imagine we'll have to settle for just dumping you in the river. The leeches and crayfish should have you stripped to the bone in a day or so."

Barak's expression grew hurt.

"Did you want us to take your sword and shield back to your son?" she asked.

"I don't have a son," he answered sullenly. He was obviously not prepared for her brutal practicality.

"Oh, didn't I tell you? How forgetful of me."

"What are you talking about?"

"Never mind," she said. "It's not important now. Were you just going to fall on your sword, or would you prefer to run up against the mast with the hilt? Either way works rather well." She turned to the sailors. "Would you clear a path so the Earl of Trellheim can get a good run at the mast?"

The sailors stared at her.

"What did you mean about a son?" Barak asked, lowering his sword.

"It would only unsettle your mind, Barak," she answered. "You'd probably make a mess of killing yourself if I told you about it. We'd really rather not have you lying around groaning for weeks on end. That sort of thing is so depressing, you know."

"I want to know what you're talking about!"

"Oh, very well," she said with a great sigh. "Your wife Merel is with child—the result of certain courtesies you exchanged when we visited Val Alorn, I imagine. She looks like a rising moon at the moment, and your lusty brat is making her life miserable with his kicking."

"A son?" Barak said, his eyes suddenly very wide.

"Really, Barak," she protested. "You must learn to pay attention. You'll never make anything of yourself if you keep blundering around with your ears closed like this."

"A son?" he repeated, his sword sliding out of his fingers.

"Now you've dropped it," she chided him. "Pick it up immediately, and let's get on with this. It's very inconsiderate to take all day to kill yourself like this."

"I'm not going to kill myself," he told her indignantly.

"You're not?"

"Of course not," he sputtered, and then he saw the faint

flicker of a smile playing about the corners of her mouth. He hung his head sheepishly.

"You great fool," she said. Then she took hold of his beard with both hands, pulled his head down and kissed his ash-dusted face soundly.

Greldik began to chortle, and Mandorallen stepped forward and caught Barak in a rough embrace. "I rejoice with thee, my friend," he said. "My heart soars for thee."

"Bring up a cask," Greldik told the sailors, pounding on his friend's back. "We'll salute Trellheim's heir with the bright brown ale of timeless Cherek."

"I expect this will get rowdy now," Aunt Pol said quietly to Garion. "Come with me." She led the way back toward the ship's prow.

"Will she ever change back?" Garion asked when they were alone again.

"What?"

"The queen," Garion explained. "Will she ever change back again?"

"In time she won't even want to," Aunt Pol answered. "The shapes we assume begin to dominate our thinking after a while. As the years go by, she'll become more and more a snake and less and less a woman."

Garion shuddered. "It would have been kinder to have killed her."

"I promised Lord Issa that I wouldn't," she said.

"Was that really the God?"

"His spirit," she replied, looking out into the hazy ash-fall. "Salmissra infused the statue with Issa's spirit. For a time at least the statue was the God. It's all very complicated." She seemed a bit preoccupied. "Where *is* he?" She seemed suddenly irritated.

"Who?"

"Father. He should have been here days ago."

They stood together looking out at the muddy river.

Finally she turned from the railing and brushed at the shoulders of her cloak with distaste. The ash puffed from under her fingers in tiny clouds. "I'm going below," she told him, making a face. "It's just too dirty up here."

"I thought you wanted to talk to me," he said.

"I don't think you're ready to listen. It'll wait." She stepped away, then stopped. "Oh, Garion."

"Yes?"

"I wouldn't drink any of that ale the sailors are swilling. After what they made you drink at the palace, it would probably make you sick."

"Oh," he agreed a trifle regretfully. "All right."

"It's up to you, of course," she said, "but I thought you ought to know." Then she turned again and went to the hatch and disappeared down the stairs.

Garion's emotions were turbulent. The entire day had been vastly eventful, and his mind was filled with a welter of confusing images.

"Be quiet," the voice in his mind said.

"What?"

"I'm trying to hear something. Listen."

"Listen to what?"

"There. Can't you hear it?"

Faintly, as if from a very long way off, Garion seemed to hear a muffled thudding.

"What is it?"

The voice did not answer, but the amulet about his neck began to throb in time with the distant thudding.

Behind him he heard a rush of tiny feet.

"Garion!" He turned just in time to be caught in Ce'Nedra's embrace. "I was so worried about you. Where did you go?"

"Some men came on board and grabbed me," he said, trying to untangle himself from her arms. "They took me to the palace."

"How awful!" she said. "Did you meet the queen?"

Garion nodded and then shuddered, remembering the hooded snake lying on the divan looking at itself in the mirror.

"What's wrong?" the girl asked.

"A lot of things happened," he answered. "Some of them weren't very pleasant." Somewhere at the back of his awareness, the thudding continued.

"Do you mean they tortured you?" Ce'Nedra asked, her eyes growing very wide.

"No, nothing like that."

"Well, what happened?" she demanded. "Tell me."

He knew that she would not leave him alone until he did, so he described what had happened as best he could. The throbbing sound seemed to grow louder while he talked, and his right palm began to tingle. He rubbed at it absently.

"How absolutely dreadful," Ce'Nedra said after he had finished. "Weren't you terrified?"

"Not really," he told her, still scratching at his palm. "Most of the time the things they made me drink made my head so foggy I couldn't feel anything."

"Did you really kill Maas?" she asked, "just like that?" She snapped her fingers.

"It wasn't exactly just like that," he tried to explain. "There was a little more to it."

"I *knew* you were a sorcerer," she said. "I told you that you were that day at the pool, remember?"

"I don't want to be," he protested. "I didn't ask to be."

"I didn't ask to be a princess either."

"It's not the same. Being a king or a princess is what one *is*. Being a sorcerer has to do with what one *does*."

"I really don't see that much difference," she objected stubbornly.

"I can make things happen," he told her. "Awful things, usually."

"So?" she said maddeningly. "I can make awful things happen too—or at least I could back in Tol Honeth. One word from me could have sent a servant to the whipping-post—or to the headsman's block. I didn't do it of course, but I could have. Power is power, Garion. The results are the same. You don't have to hurt people if you don't want to."

"It just happens sometimes. It's not that I want to do it." The throbbing had become a nagging thing, almost like a dull headache.

"Then you have to learn to control it."

"Now you sound like Aunt Pol."

"She's trying to help you," the princess said. "She keeps trying to get you to do what you're going to have to do eventually anyway. How many more people are you going to have to burn up before you finally accept what she says?"

"You didn't have to say that." Garion was stung deeply by her words.

"Yes," she told him, "I think I did. You're lucky *I'm* not your aunt. I wouldn't put up with your foolishness the way Lady Polgara does."

"You don't understand," Garion muttered sullenly.

"I understand much better than you think, Garion. You know what your problem is? You don't want to grow up. You want to keep on being a boy forever. You can't, though; nobody can. No matter how much power you have—whether you're an emperor or a sorcerer—you can't stop the years from going by. I realized that a long time ago, but then I'm probably much smarter than you are." Then without any word of explanation, she raised up on her toes and kissed him lightly full on the lips.

Garion blushed and lowered his head in embarrassment.

"Tell me," Ce'Nedra said, toying with the sleeve of his tunic, "was Queen Salmissra as beautiful as they say?"

"She was the most beautiful woman I've ever seen in my life," Garion answered without thinking.

The princess caught her breath sharply. "I *hate* you," she cried from between clenched teeth. Then she turned and ran sobbing in search of Aunt Pol.

Garion stared after her in perplexity. He turned then to stare moodily out at the river and the drifting ash. The tingling in his palm was becoming intolerable, and he scratched at it, digging in with his fingernails.

"You'll just make it sore," the voice in his mind said.

"It itches. I can't stand it."

"Stop being a baby."

"What's causing it?"

"Do you mean to say you really don't know? You've got further to go than I thought. Put your right hand on the amulet."

"Why?"

"Just do it, Garion."

Garion reached inside his tunic and put his burning palm on his medallion. As a key fitting into the lock for which it was made, the contact between his hand and the throbbing amulet seemed somehow enormously right. The tingling became that now-familiar surge, and the throbbing began to echo hollowly in his ears.

"*Not too much,*" the voice warned him. "*You're not trying to dry up the river, you know.*"

"What's happening? What is all this?"

"*Belgarath's trying to find us.*"

"Grandfather? Where?"

"*Be patient.*"

The throbbing seemed to grow louder until Garion's entire body quivered with each thudding beat. He stared out over the rail, trying to see through the haze. The settling ash, so light that it coated the muddy surface of the river, made everything more than twenty paces away indistinct. It was impossible to see the city, and the wails and cries from the hidden streets seemed somehow muffled. Only the slow wash of the current against the hull seemed clear.

Then a long way out on the river, something moved. It was not very large and seemed to be little more than a dark shadow ghosting silently with the current.

The throbbing grew even louder.

The shadow drew closer, and Garion could just begin to make out the shape of a small boat. An oar caught the surface of the water with a small splash. The man at the oars turned to look over his shoulder. It was Silk. His face was covered with gray ash, and tiny rivulets of sweat streaked his cheeks.

Mister Wolf sat in the stern of the little boat, muffled in his cloak and with his hood turned up.

"*Welcome back, Belgarath,*" the dry voice said.

"*Who's that?*" Wolf's voice in Garion's mind sounded startled. "*Is that you, Belgarion?*"

"*Not quite,*" the voice replied. "*Not yet anyway, but we're getting closer.*"

"*I wondered who was making all the noise.*"

"*He overdoes things sometimes. He'll learn eventually.*"

A shout came from one of the sailors clustered around Barak at the stern, and they all turned to watch the small boat drifting toward them.

Aunt Pol came up from below and stepped to the rail. "You're late," she called.

"Something came up," the old man answered across the narrowing gap. He pushed back his hood and shook the floury ash out of his cloak. Then Garion saw that the old man's left arm was bound up in a dirty sling across the front of his body.

"What happened to your arm?" Aunt Pol asked.

"I'd rather not talk about it." There was an ugly scratch running down one of Wolf's cheeks into his short, white beard, and his eyes seemed to glitter with some huge irritation.

The grin on Silk's ash-coated face was malicious as he dipped his oars once, deftly pulling the little boat in beside Greldik's ship with a slight thump.

"I don't imagine you can be persuaded to keep your mouth shut," Wolf said irritably to the small man.

"Would I say anything, mighty sorcerer?" Silk asked mockingly, his ferret eyes wide with feigned innocence.

"Just help me aboard," Wolf told him, his voice testy. His entire bearing was that of a man who had been mortally insulted.

"Whatever you say, ancient Belgarath," Silk said, obviously trying to keep from laughing. He steadied Wolf as the old man awkwardly climbed over the ship's rail.

"Let's get out of here," Mister Wolf curtly told Captain Greldik, who had just joined them.

"Which way, Ancient One?" Greldik asked carefully, clearly not wanting to aggravate the old man further.

Wolf stared hard at him.

"Upstream or down?" Greldik explained mollifyingly.

"Upstream, of course," Wolf snapped.

"How was I supposed to know?" Greldik appealed to Aunt Pol. Then he turned and crossly began barking orders to his sailors.

Aunt Pol's expression was a peculiar mixture of relief and curiosity. "I'm sure your story's going to be absolutely fascinating, father," she said as the sailors began raising the heavy anchors. "I simply can't wait to hear it."

"I can do without the sarcasm, Pol," Wolf told her. "I've had a very bad day. Try not to make it any worse."

That last was finally too much for Silk. The little man, in the act of climbing across the rail, suddenly collapsed in helpless glee. He tumbled forward to the deck, howling with laughter.

Mister Wolf glared at his laughing companion with a profoundly affronted expression as Greldik's sailors ran out their oars and began turning the ship in the sluggish current.

"What happened to your arm, father?" Aunt Pol's gaze was penetrating, and her tone said quite clearly that she did not intend to be put off any longer.

"I broke it," Wolf told her flatly.

"How did you manage that?"

"It was just a stupid accident, Pol. Those things happen sometimes."

"Let me see it."

"In a minute." He scowled at Silk, who was still laughing. "Will you stop that? Go tell the sailors where we're going."

"Where *are* we going, father?" Aunt Pol asked him. "Did you find Zedar's trail?"

"He crossed into Cthol Murgos. Ctuchik was waiting for him."

"And the Orb?"

"Ctuchik's got it now."

"Are we going to be able to cut him off before he gets to Rak Cthol with it?"

"I doubt it. Anyway, we have to go to the Vale first."

"The Vale? Father, you're not making any sense."

"Our Master's summoned us, Pol. He wants us at the Vale, so that's where we're going."

"What about the Orb?"

"Ctuchik's got it, and I know where to find Ctuchik. He isn't going anyplace. For right now, we're going to the Vale."

"All right, father," she concurred placatingly. "Don't excite yourself." She looked at him closely. "Have you been fighting, father?" she asked dangerously.

"No, I haven't been fighting." He sounded disgusted.

"What happened, then?"

"A tree fell on me."

"What?"

"You heard me."

Silk exploded into fresh howls of mirth at the old man's

grudging confession. From the stern of the ship where Greldik and Barak stood at the tiller, the slow beat of the drum began, and the sailors dug in with their oars. The ship slid through the oily water, moving upstream against the current, with Silk's laughter trailing behind in the ash-laden air.

Here ends Book Two of *The Belgariad*.
Book Three, *Magician's Gambit*,
carries the quest on to the Orb through stranger lands and darker magic, while Garion begins to learn the incredible power of the dry voice within his mind.

About the Author

David Eddings was born in Spokane, Washington, in 1931, and was raised in the Puget Sound area north of Seattle. He received a Bachelor of Arts degree from Reed College in Portland, Oregon, in 1954 and a Master of Arts degree from the University of Washington in 1961. He has served in the United States Army, worked as a buyer for the Boeing Company, has been a grocery clerk, and has taught college English. He has lived in many parts of the United States.

His first novel, *High Hunt* (published by Putnam in 1973), was a contemporary adventure story. The field of fantasy has always been of interest to him, however, and he turned to *The Belgariad* in an effort to develop certain technical and philosophical ideas concerning that genre.

Eddings currently resides with his wife, Leigh, in the northwest.